BREAKDOWN

Books by Jonathan Kellerman

NOVELS

ALEX DELAWARE NOVELS

Breakdown (2016)
Motive (2015)
Killer (2014)
Guilt (2013)
Victims (2012)
Mystery (2011)
Deception (2010)
Evidence (2009)
Bones (2008)
Compulsion (2007)
Gone (2006)
Rage (2005)
Therapy (2004)
A Cold Heart (2003)
The Murder Book (2002)
Flesh and Blood (2001)
Dr. Death (2000)
Monster (1999)
Survival of the Fittest (1997)
The Clinic (1997)
The Web (1996)
Self-Defense (1995)

Bad Love (1994)
Devil's Waltz (1993)
Private Eyes (1992)
Time Bomb (1990)
Silent Partner (1989)
Over the Edge (1987)
Blood Test (1986)
When the Bough Breaks (1985)

OTHER NOVELS

The Murderer's Daughter (2015)

The Golem of Paris
(with Jesse Kellerman, 2015)

The Golem of Hollywood
(with Jesse Kellerman, 2014)

True Detectives (2009)

Capital Crimes
(with Faye Kellerman, 2006)

Twisted (2004)

Double Homicide
(with Faye Kellerman, 2004)

The Conspiracy Club (2003)

Billy Straight (1998)

The Butcher's Theater (1988)

GRAPHIC NOVELS
Silent Partner (2012)
The Web (2012)

NONFICTION
With Strings Attached: The Art
and Beauty of Vintage Guitars (2008)
Savage Spawn: Reflections on
Violent Children (1999)
Helping the Fearful Child (1981)
Psychological Aspects of
Childhood Cancer (1980)

FOR CHILDREN
(WRITTEN AND ILLUSTRATED)
Jonathan Kellerman's
ABC of Weird Creatures (1995)
Daddy, Daddy, Can You
Touch the Sky? (1994)

JONATHAN KELLERMAN

BREAKDOWN

AN ALEX DELAWARE NOVEL

BALLANTINE BOOKS

NEW YORK

Doubleday Large Print Home Library Edition

Published in the United States by Ballantine Books, an imprint of Random House, a division of Random House LLC, a Penguin Random House Company, New York.

BALLANTINE and the HOUSE colophon are registered trademarks of Random House LLC.

Printed in the United States of America

ISBN 978-1-62953-859-4

**This Large Print Book carries the
Seal of Approval of N.A.V.H**

For Faye

BREAKDOWN

CHAPTER 1

Noise was everywhere. To avoid it, Tina figured you had to die.

When she and Harry lived in Manhattan, the nerve-scraping clangor of garbage trucks and delivery vans had served as early-morning alarm clocks. Waking up to the din was jarring and souring for Tina but useful for Harry because he slept like a drunk and had to be on the subway by seven.

Here in L.A., nestled in the alleged luxe of upper Bel Air, mornings were quiet. Until they weren't: the house groaning and creaking randomly, scolding reminders that they'd traded New York bedrock for the traitorous sand of earthquake country.

Of **course,** Harry barely noticed. The jolts

to Tina's nervous system made her feel like shedding her skin.

L.A. evenings were "left-coast mellow" for him, **crushingly** still for her. She yearned for the rumble of a late-night bus, the drone of human voices rendered unintelligible at the seventeenth floor, the farting aggression of taxi-horns.

Anything to remind her that other people existed beyond the confines of her personal space. After two months of living on a ridge of soft dirt straddling L.A. the thick, almost slimy stillness was threatening to smother her.

When the creaks and groans weren't freaking her out.

Officially, neighbors existed. The place Harry's firm had leased for them ("midcentury delight," in reality a bland ranch house) was bordered by similar structures. But each was vacant due to traveling owners: a wire service editor currently working in Greece, a merry widow enjoying a round-the-world cruise.

Tina knew those details because the rental agent had informed her how lucky she was to have peace and quiet.

Quiet could only be peaceful if it wasn't polluted by loneliness and unpredictability.

Evenings when Harry worked late proved unnerving.

Even when he was home for dinner, there was bedtime to deal with, the dreaded moment when bedroom lamps were switched off and Harry was snoozing within seconds. Leaving Tina flat on her back, wondering if tonight she'd finally be able to get some rest.

It wasn't only the groans and creaks. There was the matter of the animals.

If she didn't set her white noise machine loud enough, scurries and rustles from the vest-pocket backyard dried her mouth, chilled her skin, and revved up her heart.

If she set the machine whooshing too fiercely, she veered into migraine territory.

Harry, sprawled across the mattress and sawing wood, remained oblivious to her stress. Tina figured he could snore through Armageddon.

Mr. Mellow and High-Strung Babe.

He called her that, good-naturedly. Insisted her overactive nervous system made her hot in bed. Tina had her doubts about that but why argue? She knew she was high-maintenance, it was all a matter of wiring.

More than once, startled awake by what **had** to be a wild beast or a serial killer out in the garden, she'd elbowed the poor guy awake and insisted he check. Drowsy but chuckling, he always complied, finding nothing. One night, especially weary, he said maybe she should try meditation. Or medication. Tina's reaction to that wisdom disabused him of further advice.

Then came **that** night, when even Harry's eyes widened as he heard the chittering. Parting the bedroom drapes, he watched, astonished, as a family of raccoons enjoyed the lap pool.

Mommy, Daddy, and three babies. Diving in gleefully, scampering out to shake off their fur, hurrying back for repeat plunges.

Five of them! Polluting the water with rabies germs and God knew what.

Harry had been fascinated by the spectacle; grinning, he watched. Tina, repelled, had insisted he pound the glass until the intruders fled. Which took a while; the raccoons, cheeky bastards, showed no fear, only sullen resentment.

The following morning Tina phoned Animal Control and received a lecture about human invasion of habitat; apparently raccoons had inalienable rights, too.

So four nights later when she heard sounds from the garden, she gritted her teeth and let Harry sleep through it. But after he left for work, she checked and found trampled vegetation and a pile of grape-sized pellets, a production she Internet-identified as deer scat.

She supposed Bambi foraging out back wasn't terrible...but what if a mountain lion or a coyote had a yen for venison and came back to...OMG, who knew Bel Air meant Wild Kingdom?

From that point on, Tina began using earplugs in addition to the white noise machine and though they caused her to wake up with a sore jaw, she figured she'd finally happened upon an optimal solution.

Wrong, again.

This was a new level of noise, way louder and weirder than the raccoons. An agitated creature? Or worse: angry.

Definitely **something** out there, thrashing. Now moaning. **Now** what sounded like the impact of a paw or a claw on hardscape. An animal tantrum, loud enough to pierce the machine and the plugs. How could Harry sleep through it?

Tina wished she had the courage to have a look herself. Inform him, over breakfast, that she'd made a breakthrough, no need to baby her anymore, she was adapting.

Maybe she'd even start looking for a job soon.

But not tonight, this—horrid symphony—and there it was again, the bumping.

Something injured? Or out to injure? Did coyotes sound like this? She had no idea...she nudged Harry with her little toe. He gulped air, turned over, yanked the covers over his head.

To hell with it, she **would** see for herself.

Bump. Wail. Now a high-pitched cry. Heart racing, chest hurting, but feeling oddly purposeful, Tina bounded out of bed, not even trying to be subtle or quiet because down deep she hoped Harry **would** wake up and come to her rescue.

But he just rolled over again, snored

louder.

Not loud enough to blot out the terrible noise outside.

Scratch scratch scratch. What sounded like slithering. Then a...whimper? Two creatures? A victim and a predator?

Dreading what she'd see, Tina forced herself to fold back the drapes and squint.

No need to focus, there it was, obvious and horrifying, crouched in the left-hand corner of the garden.

Head down, gasping and crying out as it pawed soil, spewing clumps and leaves and dust.

No way it could've spotted Tina but suddenly its head rose and it locked eyes with her.

A glint of madness—a terrible meld of terror and rage.

It screamed.

A duet; Tina was screaming, too.

CHAPTER 2

Psychologists and psychiatrists often rely on voicemail for receiving messages. I use an answering service because if anyone should be offering a live human voice to someone in need, it's a therapist.

On a cloudy morning at ten a.m., I got a call from one of the service operators, a new one named Bradley.

"Dr. Delaware, I've got Doyle Maslow on the line."

"Don't know him."

"Her, sir, and sounds as if **she** knows **you.** She said it's a mental health crisis type of thing."

"Is she the one in crisis?"

"She didn't say, Doctor."

"Put her on."

"Good, sir."

A husky young female voice said, "Dr. Alexander Delaware? This is Kristin Doyle-Maslow, mental health specialist with the Los Angeles County Behavioral and Affective Re-Integration and Services Project."

New one on me but the county sprouts programs like a hydra grows heads.

I said, "I'm not familiar—"

"You wouldn't be. We're funded by a grant from the National Institute of Mental Health, learn about us on our website. LACBAR-I-SP.net. I'm calling about a patient of yours. Zelda Chase."

"She's not my patient."

"Five years ago she was, according to the records, Dr. Delaware."

"Five years ago I evaluated her son—"

"Ovid Chase. There is no record of official termination."

"I consulted at the request of Ms. Chase's psychiatrist, Dr. Louis Sherman—"

"Who is deceased."

"I'm aware of that—"

"Sherman released the file to Ravenswood University Hospital twenty-seven months ago. You are named in that document as therapist of record."

"She was treated at Ravenswood?"

"Not at that time, but all this is irrelevant, Doctor. The important fact is Sherman **did** terminate and you didn't."

Two years and some months ago, Lou had died of cancer, lending cruelty to her wording.

I said, "What exactly would you like me to do?"

"See your patient, Doctor. Who did end up at Ravenswood, a couple of days ago, on a 5150 but has been transferred to us."

Seventy-two-hour involuntary hold.

"What got her committed?"

"She was arrested for trespassing in someone's backyard."

"Where?"

"Bel Air. Why would that matter?"

"Trespassing earned her a 5150?"

"She had an overt psychotic episode and was judged threatening to the safety of others."

Why explain when you can redefine? I said, "Sorry to hear that, but I treat children."

"Dr. Delaware," said Kristin Doyle-Maslow, as if my name were a diagnosis. "The patient has requested you. Would you prefer I tell her you're not the least bit interested in her?"

"Are you a psychotherapist?"

"Pardon?"

I repeated the question. She huffed. "Why is that relevant?"

Because you sure as hell don't have people skills. I said, "What kind of care will Ms. Chase be receiving from your agency?"

"We're not an agency, we're an exploratory program mandated to evaluate and fact-find. That includes the authorization to carry out 5150s because 5150s are evaluative."

"And fact-finding."

"All right, then, Dr. Delaware, I'll tell her you have no desire to—"

"Where are you located?"

"Wilshire near Western. I suggest you come sooner rather than later. She is not a happy camper."

CHAPTER 3

Thumb through a five-year-old trash-magazine and you might come across a photo of Zelda Chase in a sexy outfit, a member of a rarefied species: **Actressa gorgeousa.**

Leggy, shapely, blond, perfectly styled and buffed, camera-ready as she flashed a smile ripe with genetic privilege.

Spend some time with Zelda Chase and all that flecked away like emotional dandruff.

Add a vulnerable child and it got complicated.

I'd done custody consults for years and lots of judges trusted me, but this referral came from Zelda Chase's psychiatrist.

Lou Sherman and I had cross-referred for years—parents sent to him, offspring to me. When he called me one evening in June, I was expecting more of the same. He said, "This is a little different, Alex."

"How so?"

"It's involved. Can we have lunch?"

Lou's office was in Encino but he invited me to Musso & Frank on Hollywood Boulevard, a shopworn ode to Hollywood glamour fighting to assert itself amid the tackiness, dinge, and danger of what used to be Cinema City.

I arrived on time as I always do, found Lou in a corner booth at the north end of the big, mural-lined dining room, well into an example of the best Martini in L.A.

A small man, he'd enlarged himself in customary fashion: sitting up expression-less and ramrod-straight, head fixed in a slight upward tilt. Maybe a souvenir of years spent in the military. Maybe he just got tired of being pushed around on the schoolyard.

His cinnamon-brown face was round and seamed, assembled around a serious nose. His sunbaked skull was crowned by a few remaining wisps of white hair.

New Mexico–born, half Jewish, half Acoma Indian, Lou was the first in his family to go to college. After three stints in the marines, he'd entered Columbia at thirty-five, stayed for medical school, completed a neurology-psychiatry residency at Langley Porter in San Francisco. I interned there and we attended the same seminars, saw each other at social events and traded jokes. Years later, we found ourselves at the venerable med school crosstown where Lou was already tenured and I was a young assistant prof. There, the rapport between us deepened as we came to respect each other's clinical skills.

Lou had always come across imperturbable and quietly confident—what you want in a psychiatrist. But the day he told me about Zelda Chase, he seemed edgy. I ordered a Chivas and waited for him to tell me why.

That was delayed until his second Martini arrived with my scotch, followed by Caesar salads delivered ceremoniously by one of Musso's cranky geriatric waiters.

Finally, crunching a crouton to dust and dabbing his mouth, Lou said, "Five-year-old boy for you, psychotic mother for me. I say you get the better deal."

He seemed to be contemplating a third cocktail but pushed away his glass.

"Making matters worse," he said, "she's an actress. I don't mean because that makes her histrionic, which it probably would if she wasn't well past that psychologically. I mean literally, she's currently working on a TV series and the studio's concerned. So a lot is at stake."

I said, "Psychotic but employable. She keeps it under control?"

"Like I said, Alex, it's complicated. But yeah, so far she has maintained. And who knows, maybe in that business a little looseness is an asset. Zelda Chase. Heard of her?"

I shook my head.

He said, "I figured you weren't much for sitcoms. Hers is called **SubUrban.** Two complete seasons shot with a third planned, meaning halfway to syndication and the potential for big bucks. In the interest of clinical dedication, I endured one episode, here's the gist: Hollywood's notion of comedic family life, meaning a tossed salad of borderlines, narcissists, and undiagnosables living together for no apparent reason. Along with perverse, poorly trained pets and a laugh-track for moral support."

"Sounds like the makings of a classic."

"Shakespeare's writhing in envy." Lou twirled the stem of his glass. "You treat a lot of showbiz people, Alex? Or in your case, their kids?"

"I've had my share."

"Care to generalize?"

I smiled.

He said, "Admirable restraint, young Alexander, but I'll dive right in because I've seen lots of them—have insurance contracts with the studios, the reimbursement's excellent—and the patterns are undeniable. New patient comes in and tells me they write comedy or do stand-up, I can put money on their being profoundly depressed. Sometimes there's a bipolar element, but it's always the depressive side that predominates in clowns. With that, of course, comes the self-medication and the addiction and all the shit that brings. The so-called **dramatic** performers are just that: immature, insecure, look-at-me-Mommy types with blurry identity boundaries. A more mixed bag diagnostically, but if you have to wager, go for Axis 2 issues, I'm talking deeply rooted personality disorders."

That sounded uncharacteristically pat and cruel for Lou and I wondered if he realized it because he frowned and looked into his glass.

"Maybe I've been at it too long, Alex... anyway, Ms. Zelda's a little more interesting. Signs of mood **and** thinking issues. But despite that, she's maintained for forty-plus episodes."

"Something changed to bring her to you."

"Her agent called me," he said. "Don't ask for a name or what the connection is, it's sensitive. The presenting problem is a few nights ago Zelda ended up at the door of an old boyfriend, making a holy ruckus and terrorizing his family. He hadn't seen her in years, is happily married with kids."

"Also an actor?"

"Nope, a cameraman she dated back when she was doing bit parts. You treat any kids of ancillaries—grips, stuntmen, lens guys?"

"I have."

"Solid, working-class types, right? They get a big check, it's three Harleys, not a Mercedes. That's what this fellow is like. I called him and he was a nice guy, no genius but salt of the earth, has himself a nice little spread in Sunland, horses, dogs. Apparently not guard dogs, because in the wee hours, our Ms. Zelda climbed a fence and started pounding on his kitchen door, shrieking for him to stop being a coward, come outside, she knew he still loved her, it was time to reconnect."

"That makes her psychotic?"

"You're thinking I've missed the mark and it's erotomania or some other stalker-type syndrome. And if that's all that happened, you'd be right. Unfortunately she also displayed post-event stereotypic body movements—rocking, blinking—and stretches of elective muteness followed by some of the most intense flights of ideas

I've ever heard. Including the unshakable delusion that said boyfriend had been creeping into her bedroom every night for years to have sex with her, after which he'd brutally rape her anally then pour champagne and propose marriage and the two of them would jet off to Europe. So I have no reservations calling her crazy—oh, yeah, there are command hallucinations as well: When the cops busted her, she told them her mother's voice had ordered her to 'finally make an honest woman out of herself.' A mother she won't identify other than to call her a movie star, which is obviously delusional. After that she tried to bite one of the officers on the hand."

"I see what you mean, Lou."

"Whether all that's schizophrenia or a severe manic phase, I'm still not sure. Could even be both, you know how fuzzy diagnosis can get. Meanwhile, there's pressure on me to come up with the right meds because she's under contract for a third season and they can't write her out without 'messing up the story arcs.' Reason I've called you in, is her son. Who, unbelievably, she's managed to raise alone, daddy unknown. Now, obviously, something needs to be done for the poor kid while I evaluate Mommy and hopefully come up with the right serotonin-boosting cocktail. Another issue is her fitness as a parent. If you could have a look at the boy and make some recommendations—do a bit of social work if placement's called for—I'd be eternally grateful. Compensation's no issue, production company's insurance is paying me portal-to-portal at a **very** generous level and I'll make sure you get the same."

"Okay."

"Just like that," he said. "You've always been an agreeable type, I knew I could count on you. Okay, how about another mood-glossing cocktail?"

Later, walking to the parking lot where his white '61 Jaguar XK150 was protected by cones in the VIP section, he handed the valet a twenty and said, "Thanks again, Alex, we're not talking cure, just management, but maybe we can do some good. I'll call you tomorrow and give you the details, meanwhile here's another tidbit: Her given name's not Zelda, it's Jane. She won't say why she changed it but I'm wondering if she admires F. Scott Fitzgerald's wife. And you know about her."

"She went crazy," I said.

"Oh, yeah."

CHAPTER 4

I had my first look at Zelda Chase two days later in Lou Sherman's cushy, paneled office, sitting next to him in a sensible chair as both of us faced her. Lou and I had decades of experience between us and did our best to come across relaxed and warm. But if she figured us for a tribunal, that wouldn't have been crazy at all.

Not that she'd noticed me; the scant eye contact she'd yielded so far had been reserved for Lou. Fixed on him the way you look at your father when trying to explain a dent in the car.

He said, "Dr. Delaware is a child psychologist—"

"He's going to help me keep Ovid."

"No one's suggesting you shouldn't keep Ovid, Zelda."

"Well," she said. "You know..."

Lou turned to me. I said, "Dr. Sherman has asked me to get to know Ovid so if you need help with him, I can provide it."

Still avoiding me, Zelda Chase said, "Ovid is perfect."

Lou said, "And you, dear? How're you doing?"

"Ovid is perfect."

"I'm sure he is but we need to document that, so Dr. Delaware will be spending time with Ovid and reporting to me."

Zelda Chase studied me for the first time since I'd entered the office. My smile elicited a blink and a tremble. "He seems...you seem okay, Dr. Delaware...thank you, Dr. Lou. I know I messed up with Lowell but he asked for it, don't forget that—anyway, my baby deserves to be taken care of by his mom and he will be, no matter what."

"That's what we're all here to accomplish, Zelda. Meanwhile, of course, you'll stay away from Lowell."

"Oh, yes, that's all past." She sucked in breath. "I'm a good mom, Dr. Lou, you

know that. But maybe I'm also a bad mom."
Hugging herself, she threw up her arms
and let them drop hard. "I don't deserve
the messiah." Crooked smile. "I don't
mean Jesus, don't worry, I'm not that
nuts. I mean my personal savior. He saved
me from loneliness."

I said, "Ovid."

"Ovie saved me by making me a mom."
Her face crumpled. "But maybe not such
a good mom...oh, wow, I screwed up!"

Lou took her hands. "Zelda, this isn't
the time for negative thinking."

"No? Then when is the time? I screwed
up! They're going to take him **from** me!"

She began crying. Lou patted her
shoulder and handed her a tissue. The
same quick-draw sequence I'd performed
so many times.

Zelda Chase's hand faltered around the
gauzy paper and it floated to the carpet.
Lou retrieved it and tossed it in the trash,
handed her a replacement, pressed her
fingers around it, made sure she held on.
Her hand clenched, wadding the tissue
but not releasing as she dabbed her eyes.
Lou selected a third tissue and wiped

away tears she'd missed.

Her free hand took hold of his wrist. Bending low, she rested her head on his forearm. Hair streamed, blocking her face. The sound of her breathing was slow and steady. "Don't let them take him, Dr. Lou."

"Of course not, Zelda." Lou let her remain that way for a moment before easing away. Placed his finger under her chin and gently raised her face so that their eyes met.

Like a plastic doll, she allowed herself to be molded. A stream of fresh drool trailed down her chin. Tissue number four.

Lou said, "Zelda, I want you to concentrate on getting better without having to worry about Ovid. That's why Dr. Delaware's here. He's the premier child psychologist in town. You'll be able to rest assured and take care of yourself and you and Ovid will stay together."

Zelda Chase said, "If you say so, Dr. Lou...you're always right...but I'll worry, anyway, you know me, I worry, I always do." Another wry smile. "Immaculate conception has its own challenges, right, Dr. Lou?"

He stared at her.

Zelda Chase laughed. "Just **kid**-ding,

guys. I'm not **crazy** or anything!"

Lou's smile was tight. "Zelda, I'm glad you're able to joke but it's important that you take this seriously—"

"Oh, you...so **see**-rious." Wink. Tongue flick. Bosom-heaving sigh. Hair flip.

Lou didn't respond.

Zelda Chase laughed. "Fine, I get it, be normal." Then she cried some more, accepted tissue number five with a steady hand and wiped enthusiastically. But frowned as she inspected the paper. "I put crud on it."

Lou and I peered. Nothing visible.

"Crud," she repeated. "You can't see it but it's there, toxic waste, I'm probably leaking poison from that fucked-up hospital food—Dr. Lou, I was so, so, so sick-feeling in there. Like you fly twelve red-eyes in a row and then you have to recite your lines. So thank you **so** much for rescuing me."

She turned to me. "He's the best—hey, but **you're** a cutie. If Ovie was a girl, he'd probably develop a big-time crush on you."

Lou said, "Zelda—"

"I understand, I understand," she said, still studying me. "I'm messed up in the bean but I'm a good person and you're trying to help me and I love you for it, Dr. Lou, but what I'm trying to tell Dr.... what's his name?"

"Delaware, Zelda. Like the state."

"Like the state," she parroted, nailing Lou's inflection perfectly. "My state's the state of confusion...what I'm trying to **state** to you, Dr. **Delaware,** really **express,** really get **across,** what you need to **know,** is that no matter what **I** am, Ovid is normal in the bean, he's a totally normal boy. Okay?"

I said, "Got it."

"Even if you're just saying that and don't mean it, you will mean it after you meet Ovie and you say, wow, what a great boy, totally together and well balanced and so happy, too, so she must've done a good job, she should definitely have him, they can't take him away, he's hers, no one else gets to keep him—here's an example for my psychology files of the way a mom should be—I'm being you, now, Dr. Delaware."

She mimed turning pages. "Even when patient Zelda went out to just have a discussion with Lowell, because they had a thing and she got blamed for it, she deserves compassion and understanding because look, even **then** she made sure Ovie was taken care of on all levels, he had a total babysitter the total time and he was sleeping, anyway, when she went out. **That's** why she went out real **late,** not to wake him, to be a good mom. That's why she had to do it when Ovie was sleeping. So there was no abandonment or negligence, Dr....State of Delaware—and you know that, too, Dr. Lou, because you're a wise man, maybe a magi—magus—whatever, you get me, I'm not stupid or neglectful. Delightfully odd, yes. Quirky, yes. But not stupid and neglectful and anyone else is going to be worse for my baby, okay? I ask that to both of you." Raising her voice: "**Okay? Am I making myself clear** on a medical level?"

Lou inhaled. "We'll do everything we can for you, Zelda."

"I need more than that, I need promises."

He took hold of both her hands again. She grunted and tried to twist away but he held fast. "Listen to me, Zelda: You can help yourself by focusing. Got it?"

Hesitation. Slow nod.

"Focus on the here and now, Zelda. Nothing else."

She bit her lip. Turned away. Lou placed a finger below her chin, gently rotated her to force eye contact.

Risky gesture, I thought, given her instability. But maybe he knew something I didn't because the face she showed him was lamb-like. Then: serene.

"All right, Dr. Lou, you're wise beyond the ages, you always are, a real father figure. I just needed to know everything will be good. Corinna feels that way, when I'm on the set being Corinna I feel that way. She needs the world to be right."

Her shoulders heaved. "I need to know there'll be a happy ending."

"God willing," said Lou.

I'd never known him to be a religious man.

Both of us walked her to the parking lot at the rear of Lou's small building on Ventura near Balboa. Courteous gesture but the real reason was we both wanted to observe her.

Her gait began unsteady but improved with each step as she headed for a black Lincoln Town Car, courtesy of **SubUrban**'s producers, idling in a handicapped space. The uniformed driver jumped out, helped her into the backseat, got back behind the wheel, and rolled toward the driveway. A rear window lowered and Zelda Chase blew us a kiss.

When the limo was out of view, Lou sighed. "And that is the designated patient, Alex."

I said, "How long have you been treating her?"

"Got the call from the agent, went to get the 5150 terminated, spent maybe half an hour with her trying to take a coherent history."

"She made it sound as if you two go back."

"And notice my imperturbable psychiatric wisdom not debating her."

We headed back inside. He said, "Now you understand what I'm dealing with, young Alex. She can come across okay for short periods but nothing really works the way it should, cognitively or affectively. She denies knowing her father and there hasn't been any male in her life for years. So I'm figuring the same kind of pseudo-attachment that led to her freaking out on the ex might be redirected to me. Difference is, I'm ready for it." He grinned. "And professionally trained."

I said, "A magus, to boot. Ergo her glomming onto you."

"Glomming. I like that. We should teach it to the residents, patient exhibits inappropriate glomming. And notice how she did the seductive thing with you, Mr., ahem, Cutie."

"That's **Dr.** Cutie to you."

He squinted. "Yeah, you ain't ugly. So maybe there's some reality testing going on, huh?"

He pulled a bottle of single malt out of a desk drawer, along with two glasses. "Care to join me for some heart-healthy vasodilation?"

"No, thanks."

"Too early in the day? Under normal circumstances, same for me. But being in the presence of all that thespian drama has parched me."

He poured and sipped. "Any diagnostic guesses?"

I shook my head.

"What about prognosis?"

"She's managed to work steadily for two years in a high-pressure business and the boy's important to her. If she stays well groomed and keeps her thoughts to herself, I can see her getting by."

"Exactly," said Lou. "They give her lines, she'll perform. You hear how she got my vocal inflections? It's a gift, no question. But get her off script and keep her talking long enough and it gets curiouser and curiouser. So maybe my treatment plan will minimize chatter and I'll concentrate on chemistry."

I said, "The nature of her job probably also helps. A certain amount of 'individualism' is expected."

"Translate: nuttiness. Speaking of which, I suggest you watch her show long enough to observe her doing her thing. Her character—Corinna—is a ditzy airhead blabbermouth and the writers stick all sorts of non sequiturs and other vocabulary mishaps into her mouth. I wonder if they conceived all that before she was cast or if they built it around her."

He finished his scotch. "My goal right now is to rank her deficits. If her primary deal's schizo, I'll try Haldol. If it's mood, I'll lithium her until the mania fades, or at least as close as I can get."

"You're figuring she'll fight a therapeutic dose?"

"To lithium, I am. You know how it is, a lot of manics end up hating the stuff, numbs them up, life turns gray and boring. And this is a possible manic who gets to act hyper and goofy for a living. In a bizarre way, she'd have logic on her side."

He bumped his glass on the desktop. "I can just see it: She turns sane but can't pull off Corinna anymore and I've got the agent, producers, and network suits surrounding my house with torches and pitchforks. Or she noncomplies well before that and implodes and I stop getting referrals from the industry. That's why I appreciate your seeing the boy, Alex. Something I don't have to deal with. Even if I had kiddie-skills I wouldn't have time."

I said, "So are we looking at alternative placement for the boy or is the emphasis on helping her take care of him?"

"Do your thing, then tell me."

Consulting a thin chart atop his desk, he said, "One thing in our favor: The show's on hiatus for a couple of weeks, though they will be reading potential scripts. Meaning Zelda will be occupied full-time but under less pressure and living away from the kid until I titrate her dose."

"She knows that?"

"She does and she knows she needs to comply or everything falls apart. The deal is I get her evened out and once you give the okay, it's home sweet home."

"Where's she staying?"

"Where else? Bungalow at the Beverly Hills Hotel under a fake name, babysat by a nurse practitioner I respect. Two grand a night but the network's paying because they want her situation kept under wraps so as not to jeopardize the show's third season."

"The boy's at home?"

"With a production assistant from the show..." He opened the chart. "Karen

Gallardo. Here, this is your copy. My preliminary notes, the address, Gallardo's cell. Everything you need to get started but batteries not included."

I laughed and took the chart and he walked me to the door, refilled glass in hand. Maybe he always drank this much, or maybe something about this case had gotten to him.

"Again, thanks, Alex."

"Happy to help," I said. "It actually sounds interesting."

"Does it?" He clicked his tongue twice. "Like that Chinese curse? May you live in interesting times?"

CHAPTER 5

During the time I'd spent in Lou's office, San Fernando Valley dust had coated my old Seville. I headed east on Ventura Boulevard, hoping for a breeze to blow it away but got none. At an Italian place just past Sepulveda, I ate some pasta, drank some iced tea, and read Lou's notes.

Like me, he kept his charting spare and there was little to learn beyond what he'd told me other than the bare details of Zelda Chase's arrest. Charges dropped when the complainants, unnamed, agreed not to press, provided the offender received "counseling."

From the justice system's perspective, a happy ending. But "counseling" is meaningless, vulgarized by talk-show hucksters and encompassing everything from intense psychiatric treatment to the murmurings of nonlicensed "life coaches."

What "counseling" meant in this case was the system was happy to shift responsibility for Zelda Chase's disruptive behavior to Lou Sherman, M.D.

Lou had taken the job but he was smart enough and experienced enough to know a panacea was unlikely. Because psychosis, even clearly diagnosed, is a challenge to treat due to the fact that no one really understands what it is. Or why anti-psychotic drugs work, beyond a hazy notion of manipulating neurotransmitters—brain chemicals like serotonin and dopamine that keep the mental highway buzzing along smoothly.

Compounding the puzzle, many seriously disturbed people don't fit into diagnostic cubbyholes as neatly as big pharma and their science-writer flunkies would have you believe.

If the brain's Mount Everest, the plane hasn't even landed in Nepal.

So good luck to Lou...meanwhile, there was a five-year-old child to meet.

I worked on my fusilli and downed a glass and a half of iced tea before phoning Karen Gallardo. No answer, no voicemail. Finishing my meal, I got back in the Seville, took Van Nuys to the merger with Beverly Glen, climbed up to Mulholland, and began the quick drop to my house in the foothills on the Glen's western edge.

I was home by three, found the house sunlit and silent. Robin had left a note on my desk, plying her calligraphic artist's hand on a scrap of my stationery.

"Darling, out with Julie for lunch, back by 2:30 or so. B's with me."

Julie was Juliette Charmley, a high school friend, attending a dental hygienist seminar near LAX, and B was Blanche, our little blond French bulldog. That meant an animal-friendly lunch spot, my guess a café on Old Topanga overlooking a sparkling creek. The last time Robin and I had been there, a mama coyote had been teaching two pups how to swim and the smaller sib had flashed us a death-stare.

Blanche is a mellow little thing, at first glance more monkey than wolf. But she's still a dog and she's grown territorial about critters in our garden and her presence could prove interesting if the coyotes showed up again.

If I was right, Robin had risked an eventful lunch. Interesting.

I cleared some mail, checked for messages, gave Karen Gallardo another try. Ten rings with no voicemail and I was about to click off when a young voice came on, breathless.

"Chase residence."

"Ms. Gallardo?"

"Who's this?"

I explained

She said, "Okay, yeah, they warned me you'd be calling."

"Warned?"

"Sorry. I meant I was expecting you. Sir."

"I promise I won't bite," I said.

"Pardon—oh, sure. So you're going to want an appointment with Ovie? He's in preschool until three-thirty, I'll be picking him up soon, he can be pretty tired when he gets home."

"How about tomorrow, say four p.m.?"

"Sure. But he could get more tired if it's a long drive to your office. Where are you?"

"Let's do it at four-thirty, to give Ovid a chance to unwind. And I'll come to you."

"You'll analyze him here?" she said.

"That seems like the easiest way."

"Um...okay, sure. What do I tell Ovie?"

"Today, don't tell him anything. Tomorrow, after he gets home—does he usually have a snack?"

"Healthy snack," said Karen Gallardo. "Organic crunch bar and grapes if he wants them, sometimes orange slices."

"Give him his snack first, let him settle down, then tell him a doctor who doesn't give shots and is a friend of his mother will be dropping by to talk to him. I'll take it from there."

"What if he gets upset?"

"Is he a high-strung boy?"

"No, not really."

"If you're relaxed, he should be fine."

"All right..."

"How's he doing without his mom?"

"Actually," said Karen Gallardo, "he seems okay. Today he did say he was a little worried about her, but he didn't cry or anything and I told him she'd be all better soon. Was that wrong? I mean saying that?

This really isn't my thing, I studied film, not psychology."

"Sounds like you're doing fine, Karen."

"I hope...do I need to be here when you analyze him?"

"In the house, yes. In the room, no."

"What room do you want to use?"

"How about we figure that out when I get there?"

"So I don't need to set up anything."

"Nothing, Karen. Just be there with Ovid."

"Do you need directions?"

I'd already mapped it: Hollywood Hills, above Sunset, east of Laurel Canyon. "Got it, Karen. See you tomorrow at four-thirty."

"He's a nice boy—any idea when Zelda will be coming home? Ovie did ask about that."

"Not sure yet, I'll do my best to explain things to him."

"Okay...will you be needing a room with a couch?"

"No, Karen."

"And your name again, sir?"

I was in my office, thinking about what approach to take with Ovid Chase, when I heard the front door open and the voice I love proclaim, "We're here!"

I walked to the living room where Robin, small and sleek and curvy in black jeans and charcoal T-shirt, waved and came over and kissed me. Blanche waited patiently, panting, front paws on my shins. Behind both of them, Julie Charmley, a tall freckled redhead, stood motionless and silent.

Every time I'd seen Julie, she'd been diffident, but this seemed beyond that. Distracted. Not wanting to be here.

"Good to see you, Julie."

"Likewise. Guess I'd better be going."

Robin walked her out and when she returned we went out to the garden and sat on the teak bench facing the koi pond. Within seconds, Blanche was enjoying the slumber of the just.

Robin said, "They're getting divorced. Five kids and Bryce wants full custody."

"What happened?"

"She cheated, he found out. Will that make a difference?"

Julie's husband was a periodontist I'd always found icy and remote. Neither of them would win Parent of the Year but both seemed competent.

I said, "Depends on who's judging. Long affair or one-night stand?"

"Two years long, another dentist in Bryce's practice. Even if Bryce was the forgiving type, Julie doesn't think she deserves forgiveness. I tried to buck her up but it just got her more upset so I kept my mouth shut."

"Fun lunch," I said. "Café Solar?"

"How'd you know?"

"Animal tolerance. Any coyotes show up?"

"I wish," she said. "Anything to distract. That's why I took Blanche, when Julie came in looking the way she did, I figured I needed someone who knows how to smile. What do psychologists call that?"

"Being smart."

The following afternoon I pulled up to the house rented by Zelda Chase, a dirt-brown stucco box perched half a mile above the Chateau Marmont.

The hotel's known to cater to celebrity excess. In return, it gets away with aesthetic touches like selected rooms carpeted in

AstroTurf. Or maybe that's just practicality: When the man/woman of the hour is reacting to last night's partying, pull out a garden hose.

From the Marmont bar to Zelda's front door was a brief stroll and I wondered if Zelda had taken advantage. The door in question was a plywood slab in need of refinishing. No lawn out front, just cracked cement. Address numerals hung askew. A VW Bug took up the narrow driveway.

Not the kind of digs that gets readers of **People** and **Us** fantasizing, but that's the thing about Hollywood: It doesn't really exist. Sure, A-list stars smart enough to bank their earnings can live like potentates until they die, but most of the pretty faces who "make it" enjoy careers as brief as a mayfly's ecstasy.

The brown box was what Zelda Chase had achieved at her apex. What would happen to a seriously troubled woman when her agent stopped taking her calls?

How would her son fare?

Lou Sherman had said Ovid was five years old but the DOB in his chart put him a month from six. Would a birthday party with Mom be in the cards?

The child who answered my knock looked barely five, until you saw the clarity in his eyes. In one hand was a glass of milk.

He said, "You're the doctor who doesn't give shots." Nasal voice, clear enunciation. Close your eyes and you'd guess seven or eight.

My mind camera-clicked details.

Small for his age, thin, short legs, low center of gravity. Long, dark hair draping most of his forehead and fringing skinny shoulders. Possible Latino cast to his features.

He wore a black T-shirt with the logo of a band I'd never heard of, olive-drab cargo pants, high-top Keds loosely laced. Owlish, black-framed eyeglasses were moored to his head by an orange elastic band. The eyes behind the lenses were darker than Zelda's, almost black, wide with curiosity.

I said, "You're Ovid."

He laughed. "I'm Ovid." Aping my words and my inflection with the same uncanny accuracy his mother had displayed. What else had he picked up from her?

"Alex Delaware." I extended my hand.

Fine-boned fingers grabbed it, squeezed once, let go. Five-year-old version of a corporate power shake.

He said, "No shots, really?"

"Really."

"Cooool." His posture was relaxed but he made no move to let me in.

"Anyway, Ovid—"

"I said what kind of doctor and she said psych—lotrist?"

"Psychologist."

He mouthed the word but didn't speak it. "She said she didn't know what that means."

"She being..."

"Karen. She works with my mom. Do you know my mom?"

"I just met her."

"Where?"

"At her doctor's office."

"She was in the hospital. She'll get better."

I said, "Can I come in?"

He moved aside. "She's having a sad time. Not from me. Her own sad."

That's the kind of thing kids are taught by sensitive adults. This kid sounded as if he meant it.

I was about to respond when shouting

from the rear of the house raised my head.

"Omigod—Ovie, you can't answer the door, I told you not to answer!"

"He's the psy-kol-gist, Karen."

The woman who skidded to a halt behind him was late twenties to early thirties, heavyset with a full pallid face that would've gotten her cast as an Irish scullery maid in one of those period PBS shows. The rest of her was twenty-first century: barely enough flat-black hair to pull back in a bristly pony, seven pierces in two ears, a tiny rhinestone above one nostril, the requisite tattoos.

"I was in the bathroom," she gasped. "I told him just wait until I get out—Ovie!"

The boy shrugged.

I said, "Karen, Alex Delaware."

Ovid said, "**Doctor** Alex Delaware."

Karen Gallardo said, "I promise, sir. He's never done this before—Ovid, when I'm in charge, I need you to listen to me."

The boy chugged milk, got some on his chin, wiped it with a bare arm.

"Now you need a napkin."

Ovid used his arm again. "I don't. He's here to talk to me."

Karen Gallardo looked at me. I nodded and she left and Ovid said, "Over here."

He led me past a tiny entry hall into a living room that elevated the house from dump to dump with a view. Of sorts.

In places like Tuscany and Santa Fe, where architectural restraint is linked to good judgment born of tradition, houses blend smoothly into hillsides. In L.A., it's all about asserting your individuality. The panorama outside Zelda Chase's floor-to-ceiling western window was a haze-capped jumble of swimming pools, drought-challenged gardens, and way too much structure on far too little soil.

Still, the eyeful probably trebled the rent, despite cheap brown carpeting, goose-bump ceilings, and by-the-month furniture.

Neat and clean, though, with the sparse furnishings arranged as cleverly as possible and vacuum tracks striping the carpet. A bowl of apples and pears sat at the center of a small dining table, the fruit freshly washed, condensation bubbles freckling the skin.

The handiwork of a maid? Or perhaps

Karen Gallardo had been ordered by the studio to make a good impression.

If so, Ovid Chase answering the door during her bathroom break had blown that, if I was inclined to condemnation. So far I wasn't, just wanted to learn as much as I could about the boy.

He said, "I did this," and settled on the floor behind an elaborate construction of multicolored translucent tiles. What looked to be a postmodern version of a medieval compound, with a multi-spired castle, smaller outbuildings, proportional door-ways and windows, and a horizontal stretch of tiles extending from the front that was probably intended as a bridge over an unseen moat.

The project took up the bulk of the room's central space. Child-oriented environment? If so, this child had made good use of it.

"Nice," I said.

Without comment, he reached for a box of unused tiles, grabbed a handful, and began adding and subtracting, pausing only to regard his work.

I said, "This really is impressive, Ovid."

"Magna-tiles," he said. "It's easy-peasy,

you just stick them and unstick them."
Plucking off a pointed roof, he demonstrated,
transforming a double-spired area to
something that resembled a Gothic arch.

"Easy for you," I said.

Another shrug as he fought not to smile,
finally allowed himself the merest upturn
of lips.

"You spend a lot of time building, Ovid?"

"It's all I like," he said. "Except for food."
Laughter, sudden and burp-like, as if inner
heat needed to be released. Then he
clipped it off and turned serious.

A restrained boy...As I watched him
create, I took in more details: spotless
clothing, clean nails. Even the loose laces
of his high-tops had been knotted carefully.
Identically.

Maybe Karen Gallardo had sorted him
out carefully for the last couple of days, but
my gut told me he was used to taking care
of himself. Had an instinct for it.

He began humming as he worked, nothing
hurried, everything thought out.

Mentally disorganized mom, buttoned-
down kid?

I said, "What kind of food do you like?"

"Tacos, burritos, pho."

"Mexican and Vietnamese, huh?"

He looked up. "Pardon?"

"Pho's a soup from Vietnam."

"I don't know where it's from. We get takeout. It's my favorite."

"Pho?"

"Takeout. It's like…it's here and you get to eat it." A tongue tip materialized between the lips as he reached for more tiles.

"Barn," he muttered. "For the animals." Frowning. "Pretend there's animals."

I said, "What kind?"

He looked up, frowned. "What do you like?"

"I like dogs."

"Uh-uh. Dogs don't live in barns."

"Good point," I said. "How about horses?"

"Maybe a camel," he said. "They spit and they're mean." Slowly spreading smile. "If they spit, they need to be kept in a barn."

For the next half hour, I sat and he built. Terrific attention span, increasing need for order and detail. And complexity.

He removed all the unused tiles from the box and created three piles, organized by shape. When he'd used them up, he said,

"Should I knock it down or just stop?"

"Up to you, Ovid."

"That's what she says."

"Karen?"

"Mom. She lets me do what I want as long as I listen to her."

"Listen about what?"

He began ticking small fingers. "Brush the teeth, use mouthwash, take a bath, go to school, and don't make problems."

"You like school?"

"It's okay. Mostly I know everything."

"Ready to move on to first grade."

"I guess."

"Not sure about first grade?"

"I could also know everything there."

"You find school boring."

"It's okay—when's Mom coming home?"

"I don't know yet, Ovid."

"You will?"

"I'll make sure her doctor tells me as soon as she's ready and I'll tell you."

"What's his name?"

"Dr. Sherman."

"Does he give shots?"

I said, "Not usually."

"But sometimes?"

"Rarely. I don't think your mom's going to be getting shots."

"Then what?"

"Pills, maybe."

"To make her happy."

"To make her feel better, in general."

"She takes good care of me."

"I know."

"How?"

"When I met her I could tell she loves you and cares about you."

Turning back toward his construction, he sliced at a roof, demolished a tower. Swiped again and razed the heart of the castle.

"Now," he said, "I have to start again."

On each of the five days Zelda Chase lived at the Beverly Hills Hotel, I spent time with her son.

On the fourth day, Ovid looked weary. It took an hour and a half of Magna-tile work for him to say that he missed his mother and was "really, really ready for her to come back." I went outside and phoned Lou Sherman and told him that was okay with me if Zelda was capable.

He said, "Matter of fact, I was thinking tomorrow, possibly the next day, good results from Haldol. I still don't have a firm diagnosis but a moderate dose smooths her out. Do you have time to discuss discharge planning—even tomorrow, for dinner, maybe nine, maybe the Valley if you can make it over? My wife's out, one of her meetings, the studio's still picking up the tab so I'll find us somewhere expensive."

"Sounds good, Lou. So I can tell Ovid she's coming home in a day or two?"

"Unless something changes radically— yeah, sure, tell him, anything happens I'll ease up the dose or find something else. No sense keeping her away from him if you think it's okay, she's clearly over the moon about the kid. How's he coping?"

"Optimally," I said. "Smart, well-put-together boy, good internal resources."

"Well, that's reassuring. What kind of resources?"

"Artistic, not a lot of anxiety, good attention span—I'll fill you in if dinner costs enough."

He laughed. "Resources. He'll need them."

The fifth day, I told Ovid the good news.

He said, "Okay," and continued building.

Then he smiled and began working faster. A few minutes later, he stood and circled his newest masterpiece—something Frank Gehry might've designed in grad school.

Rolling toward me, he shook my hand. "Congratulations."

"For what?"

"You were here when I did my best building."

The arrangement was finalized over dinner at the Bistro Garden. I'd be available as needed and Lou would continue to treat Zelda, monitoring her anti-psychotic medication, eventually trying to ease in some psychotherapy.

"Maybe talking will add something; frankly, I've learned nothing about her, Alex. Not even her basic family structure—she won't talk about it other than to say her mother went missing and is probably dead. Then she clams up or changes the subject. Is it relevant? Who knows? The main thing is she doesn't go bonkers and blow everything."

The plans for Ovid's caretaking were clear, as well: Karen Gallardo, always frazzled when I saw her, would return to her production job and through an agency I recommended, Lou would arrange a babysitter with childcare experience to be at the house when Zelda was at work.

I suggested a night-shifter sleeping in, if there was money to pay for it.

"In case she goes trespassing again? Makes sense, I'll make sure there's money for it. Plenty of incentive, season three will start taping soon. You ever catch the show?"

"Not yet."

"Smart, you're better off listening to Bach or the Doors or whoever. And here's your check."

He handed me an envelope. "Take a look, make sure it's okay."

Twice what I'd expected. I said, "It's more than okay, Lou."

"Well, keep that to yourself, Dalai Lama, the studio thinks they're getting a bargain.

Besides, you earned it. We both did. And I'll make sure to get in touch, like you said."

What I'd said was I'd be available if the situation changed but that right now Ovid didn't need treatment because he was bright, creative, and adaptable. His preschool teacher termed him "Sharp as a tack, kind of brilliant, really, especially with building stuff. He tends to play by himself but I see that in artistic kids."

Most important, near the end of the fifth session, hours before his mother's return, I'd asked him if he wanted me to come back and he'd shuffled tiles and tilted his body away from me and said, "You didn't give me any shots and you let me do what I want."

"That was the deal."

"Now I believe you." He looked down. "Please let me build. I'm okay."

As gracious a dismissal as any I'd received.

I said, "It's a deal, Ovid. But if you do ever need me, Ovid, I can be here."

"Nah, I won't," he said. "Maybe you can come for Mom. If she needs you."

"You think she might?"

Shrug. "She sometimes needs people."

Starting work on a tower, higher than any he'd ever built, he said, "People are okay but I don't **need** them."

Lou never called me again. Not about Ovid or Zelda or any other patient and I wondered if something about the case had altered our relationship. Or maybe he simply hadn't needed a child psychologist. Or had retired.

A few weeks later, still curious about Zelda's condition, I googled her, learned **SubUrban** had been canceled early in its third season. The cast had been quoted, some of them lapsing into profanity.

Zelda's comment: "It happened."

I kept searching and found no sign she'd ever gotten another acting job, but no evidence she'd fallen apart.

Off the radar: a performer's nightmare. How could someone as fragile as Zelda cope?

I imagined all sorts of worst-case scenarios, worked hard at sweeping them from my head. She was Lou's patient, not mine, hopefully his treatment had evened her out.

In the best of worlds, he'd managed to do some psychotherapy and had built her up sufficiently to cope with disappointment.

If there had been a problem with Ovid, he'd have called. Put it to rest.

Shortly after that, the Charmleys went to family court and began tearing each other apart. Julie and Bryce each called me asking me to be their custody witness. I refused as tactfully as I could. The result was cold silence from both of them and Robin never heard from Julie again and that necessitated a bit of discussion in our house.

The joys of inhuman relations.

Two and a half years after evaluating Ovid Chase, I was skimming the med school faculty newsletter and saw Lou Sherman's obituary. Seventy-three years old, long illness—which could explain the end of our professional relationship—a widow named Maureen, no kids, no funeral, donations to the cancer society in lieu of flowers.

I phoned his home number to offer condolences, hoping a woman I'd never met wouldn't find that intrusive.

Out of service. I took that as an omen and tried to forget about Lou, though I did think about Ovid from time to time.

Smart, little buttoned-down boy, a self-made expert in constructing his own world. Maybe because his mother had been on the verge of falling apart.

Or that was psychobabble bullshit and the kid just liked playing with Magna-tiles.

Eventually, he slipped from my memory, five years of no news being good news.

Now all that had changed.

CHAPTER 6

The building that housed LACBAR-I-SP resembled what it had once been: a discount furniture outlet in a homely section of mid-city.

The front was mostly windows painted chalky white. All that glass seemed unwise if you were dealing with seriously mentally ill people in a sketchy neighborhood. A sign warned the place was on twenty-four-hour video surveillance despite the obvious lack of a camera. A locked but flimsy door with a call button sent a ludicrous mixed message.

I got buzzed in without announcing who I was, stepped into an empty waiting area backed by another window. No paint on this glass, just dust clouding the image of an elderly woman pecking a desktop keyboard. To her left was a white door marked **No Admittance.** She was aware of me but kept working.

I tapped the glass and she slid open the partition.

"Dr. Delaware to see Zelda Chase."

Closing the glass, she got on the phone, returned to her keyboard.

I stood around for a while before a skinny, white-coated young woman entered the booth and conferred with the receptionist.

The new arrival sported a basic-training brass-colored buzz cut tipped black. The coat was too large, parachute-billowing over a T-shirt and jeans. I'd never met her but I recognized her and knew plenty about her because she liked attention and had sprayed personal data all over cyberspace.

Kristin Doyle-Maslow was twenty-five years old, the possessor of a B.A. in urban studies from Vassar, the only child of a father who practiced gestalt therapy in Newton, Massachusetts, and a mother who lived in Brookline and taught bio-psychiatry at Tufts. She favored "farm to table" cocktails. The list of her favorite bands broke new ground in obscurity. She liked Ethiopian food, especially "the **teff** and the pumpkin," and believed public policy was a "contact sport."

For the past two years she'd worked as an intern at HUD in Washington, "conceiving and authoring position papers on community outreach." No training in psychology or any other mental health field.

As she continued to talk to the typist, she turned and studied me. Young, but afflicted with the kind of severe, pinched face that gets old quickly. Steel-rimmed glasses of a style favored by corporate executives in the fifties didn't help.

She checked a few papers on the typist's desk, finally emerged through the white door.

The T-shirt under her coat was green and read—what else—

LACBAR
Serving the Community With Style

An oversized green plastic badge pinned to the coat's breast pocket informed the world who she was, but she announced,

"Kristin Doyle-Maslow," in a voice that could intimidate a trombone.

I said, "Nice to meet you. How's she doing?"

"By 'she' I assume you mean Ms. Chase."

Stifling a flood of retorts, including references to Amelia Earhart and Marilyn Monroe, I said, "I do."

"There've been no obvious problems." She made a show of producing a ring of keys and unlocking the white door. Breezing through, she left me to catch the swinging panel.

I followed her into a drafty, unoccupied, white space partitioned into cubicles but devoid of furniture or office equipment. The sting of fresh paint was overwhelming. At the rear was another white door marked **No Unauthorized Entry.**

I said, "Your project has just started?"

"We're in the development phase."

"But you're equipped to handle inpatients."

She stopped, adjusted her glasses. "At this point in time, we have one patient. Yours." Her forward march resumed.

I said, "Hold on." Trying to keep my voice even but the vibes set off by those stifled retorts seeped in and raised the volume and hardened my tone.

Kristin Doyle-Maslow's shoulders jumped but she kept walking.

I said, "I need you to explain what's going on. Now."

She stopped and half turned. "You're the psychologist. Isn't explaining your job?"

"What's yours?"

"I'm executive director of LACBAR—"

"Meaning?"

"I conceptualize and organize." Her jaw jutted but her voice had lost conviction and the pale eyes behind her glasses shifted uneasily.

"Okay, now please explain how a 5150 patient ends up here when there's nothing else going on."

"I don't see why that's relevant. She's in distress, she asked for you, I liaisoned."

"With who?"

"I told you. Ravenswood University Hospital. Networking with local caregivers is one of our primary mandates."

"The U. punted to you."

"We were considered ideal for the situation."

I looked around at a thousand square feet of nothing. "I'm here because I evaluated Zelda Chase's son five years ago and his welfare concerns me. Where is Ovid now?"

"No idea. The only reference to him is his name in Sherman's transfer document."

"What did he say about the boy?"

"Just that he existed. Now can we get going—"

"I'd like a copy."

"It's mostly dates—onset of providership, termination. **You** have never terminated."

Making that sound like a felony.

I said, "I'd still like a copy."

"I don't have one. Everything's e-filed at headquarters."

"Where's that?"

"Boston."

"Should be easy enough to get."

"Fine," she said. "But there's nothing in there."

"What about your copy of Ravenswood's chart?"

"No need for us to get that, she wasn't treated there, just inputted. And further-more, I don't see how any of this—"

"Since Ms. Chase got here, she hasn't mentioned Ovid at all?"

"She hasn't talked at all."

"You said she asked for me."

"At Ravenswood," she said. "How else would I know? Now can we proceed?"

"Once I'm oriented. I still don't get why she was sent here when you're a shell operation."

"We are not a shell, we are fully operational."

"Doesn't look fully to me."

"We are **totally** prequalified and authorized by the federal government and cooperating local governments to offer comprehensive mental health services and we'd be meeting our goals if getting things done in this city wasn't the way it is."

Pale eyes fluttered. So did pale hands.

Welcome to L.A.

I said, "Bureaucracy, huh?"

Without a trace of irony, she said, "It's the worst."

"I sympathize, Kristin. Wikipedia says you're into the second year of a three-year grant, meaning you're feeling pressure about your next NIMH site visit. Your mandate **is** primarily outpatient but for that you need to develop a 'network of community referrals,' and so far that hasn't happened because it's as if the city wants to make your life miserable. But don't feel picked on, anyone trying to start a business in L.A. deals with it."

"We are **not** a business, we are—"

"Same difference, Kristin. Let me guess: You leased this property only to encounter the building department, the zoning department, a whole list of ad hoc community boards and committees, the assessor, the health department—I'll bet you're getting **lots** of input from the health department. Because at some point you'll need to feed staff and patients so they classified you as a restaurant and are making you jump through all kinds of hoops. How're you handling nutrition in the meantime? Takeout?"

"High-quality takeout." Her foot tapped. "What-**ever.** Now, can—"

"Because of the delays, you're limited to 'short-term crisis admissions' and the best way to accomplish that is to take in 5150s because they're not lucrative, meaning that local practitioners who you'll need as referral sources don't feel threatened."

And with all the competition for NIMH money, if you don't come through by the time the feds send in their savants to review you, you'll lose the high-titled job you snagged because of your mother's contacts with the congressman who got you the HUD position.

Kristin Doyle-Maslow said, "If you're refusing to provide service, let's terminate this, here and now."

"I'll provide, let's go."

Looking at me doubtfully, she resumed walking. When she reached the second door, I said, "What's the name of the doctor who transferred her to you?"

"Nehru."

I looked at her.

She said, **"What?"**

No room for world history in urban studies?

I said, "Thanks for the info, Kristin."

The restricted area was wide but shallow and quartered into a nursing station and

Inpatient Rooms A, B, and C, each bolted shut and equipped with miniature flaps over peep-spaces. I listened for sound, trying to figure out which room housed Zelda.

Silence.

The station was more homey than clinical: wooden desk in place of a counter, a couple of upholstered chairs, end tables, and a black leather couch that still bore plastic wrapping around its stubby legs. A white metal cabinet with a red cross in the center took up the right-hand wall. To the left, a man in a white uniform sat behind the empty desk reading a paperback. He gave a small wave that I returned, though Kristin Doyle-Maslow didn't.

She said, "He's **finally** here. Her doctor."

The nurse got up and walked toward us. Thirty-five or so, balding, lightly mustachioed, nondescript. His badge was half the size of Doyle-Maslow's but gave out real information.

Kevin Bracht, RN.

We traded names and handclasps.

Bracht said, "Happy to see you, Doc. She's sleeping, that's all she's been basically doing." Eyeing Door A.

Kristin Doyle-Maslow made her exit while talking. "In terms of billing, talk to Yvette out front. Your patient's due to be released tomorrow morning, remittance should arrive within sixty days. If you need to extend the 5150, it can't be here."

"Why not?"

"That's our mandate."

"And she's already been here for two out of three days."

"One and a half days, it's a forty-eight-hour hold, not a seventy-two."

"That's different."

"Overall, she'll be held for seventy-two but part of that was allotted to Ravens-wood, which is fine, we're only authorized to do two-day holds in line with our position statement emphasizing transitioning to comprehensive outpatient services."

Which you're not set up to carry out. Thank you, Joseph Heller.

Kevin Bracht's eyebrows arched.

I said, "No prob, Kristin. Mr. Bracht and I will now liaise."

The sound of the door slamming bisected the sentence. Bracht laughed and said,

"Just Kevin's okay. So now you've had the privilege of meeting The Hyphen."

"Must be fun working for her."

"Almost as fun as a sharp stick in the eye. Soon as Ms. Chase is discharged, I'm out of here."

"Quitting so soon?"

"Not quitting, never hired. It's a temp deal, the agency didn't exactly explain things accurately."

"You're a freelance?"

"I'm a guy who needs to moonlight, Dr. Delaware. Three days a week I work at an applied behavioral analysis home for autistic adults. The wife and I just bought a house, so I do extra hustle. Mostly that's taking care of old folks who need watching for a weekend when their regular caregiver's away. Also some terminals at home and some hospice care."

"Tough stuff but better than this," I said.

"Death I can deal with, Doc. It's normal, it's expected. This, on the other hand, is a weird setup. The Hyphen has no clue about psychiatry or anything else for that matter. Once I realized I'd be stuck here by myself the thought of some crisis coming up began scaring the hell out of me. I mean I'm authorized to call the referring physician but what's that worth? Stuff happens fast, no way am I going to bear responsibility if God forbid there's a situation."

He pointed to Door A again. "No problems so far, knock wood, but I still find myself checking all the time to make sure she doesn't hurt herself. She's wearing the clothes she came in with but I took these and put them away because there's nails in the heel."

From a desk drawer he removed a pair of flat shoes, once black, now gray. "I'll grant you one thing: The room's pretty well designed for psych patients. Can't spot any easy way to get into trouble. But still…"

"Thanks for trying to keep her safe."

His smile returned. "You and I would say 'safe,' The Hyphen would probably say it's optimal injury resistance. Anyway, so far, Ms. Chase has been easy."

"Any symptoms I should know about?"

"Not unless you count nonstop sleep. Which happens with acutes, right? They put out all that energy then they need to hibernate. She **was** kind of agitated when the ambulance brought her in—fighting the restraints, grinding her teeth, so I was expecting the worst. But I talked softly to her and she calmed down and soon she was out like a light. It was like she just needed to hear a human voice."

"What time did she arrive?"

"Around eight yesterday morning. The agency calls me at six, my wife, she's also an RN, is leaving for her shift at Kaiser, it's my turn to get our boy off to preschool and the agency's like 'Right now, Kevin.' And I'm like you've **got** to be kidding. Then they told me what I'd be getting paid and I said, 'Son, you're off to preschool early.'"

"Generous compensation."

"Three times the usual, plus a great food allowance. But I'm starting to feel like I'm the one who got committed. I mean, look at this—talk about solitary confinement. I'm glad you're here to take charge."

"That food allowance is for takeout?"

"You see a stove or even a microwave? The neighborhood's pretty ethnic and The Hyphen has charge accounts everywhere, so that's cool. I had Moroccan for lunch,

Korean for dinner, fresh rolls from a bakery this morning. I ordered extra for Ms. Chase but she's stayed asleep and I ended up tossing it because there's no fridge, who needs food poisoning? She changes her mind, I'll get her fresh. I did manage to get some water into her—dribbled it slowly through her lips. It took a while, you know how flaccid they can get, I had to make sure nothing ended up in her trachea."

"She drank without resistance?"

"She moaned a little at first but I kept telling her she was okay and, again, it seemed to help. I figured hydrating her was the right thing to do."

"Good call."

He seemed relieved. "I mean at some point I have to make decisions and if she got dehydrated, the only alternative would be to I.V. her and who wants to do that? Plus, do you see an I.V. setup anywhere? On order, claims The Hyphen. Same for syringes, tubing, the fridge, everything else that would make this place real."

I pointed to the red-crossed cabinet. "What's in there?"

Kevin Bracht walked over and tapped

the metal door. It swung open. Other than a box of bandages and a packet of rubber gloves, empty.

I said, "No meds in stock?"

"Not even aspirin. Everything needs to be 'patient-specific,' meaning an M.D. needs to order even OTC stuff. Fortunately, she came in medicated, EMTs gave me her pills, they're in my desk."

He walked to the opposite end, retrieved a vial.

Ativan, 3mg, twice daily.

Bracht said, "EMTs said the doc at Ravenswood suggesting kicking it up to three times if she gets agitated but I haven't been comfortable with a secondhand verbal order."

"That could add up to a large dose," I said. "Even twice a day is serious. Five years ago she didn't have much body weight. She any heavier now?"

"Nope, real skinny. Maybe that's why she's still out of it. So you want that off the table?"

"I'm the wrong kind of doctor to ask."

I showed him my card.

He said, "Psycholo— **child** psychologist?

The Hyphen knows that?"

"She sure does."

"No offense, Doc, but why?"

"She needs to build up brownie points for the government by documenting treatment, got me here by claiming Ms. Chase asked for me. You hear anything like that?"

"Haven't heard a syllable out of her. How'd she find you?"

"I evaluated Zelda's son five years ago. He's eleven years old and his mother's locked up and The Hyphen claims there was no mention of him in the chart other than his name. That's what motivated me to show up."

"This is messed up."

"Did the EMTs give you any sort of history when they brought her in?"

"Nope, just the meds." He walked over to Door A, unlatched the wooden flap, peeked through a mesh window, crossed his fingers.

"Still sleeping."

I went over and had a look for myself. The opening was small, affording an attenuated view, but wide enough to reveal a blanket-covered form on what looked like a conventional bed. Buttercup-yellow walls, natural light streaming from a high, stationary window.

Kevin Bracht said, "What now, Doc?"

"I'm going in."

CHAPTER 7

Kevin Bracht unlocked the room and handed me the key. I shut the door quietly but failed to squelch the penitentiary clang that said serious hardware was in play.

The form on the bed faced the wall, obscured by the blanket but for errant strands of hair.

I said, "Zelda?"

No response. I tried again, a bit louder. Lifted the hair. Greasy, bristly. Her neck skin was warm and gave off a vinegar smell. I found a pulse. Slow, steady.

Stepping away, I examined the cell.

A chair was positioned at the side of the bed. Soft brown vinyl for the cushions, hard brown plastic for the frame. Low-watt LEDs on the ceiling provided soft light. The sun augmented, filtering through a high window. The view through the glass was sooty sky peppered with listless blue, creating the kind of blurry abstraction you see at amateur art fairs.

I walked around. The floor was plastic pretending to be oak parquet. The walls were covered in sheets of washable, pebbly stuff you find only in institutions. On the positive side, the hue was a cheerful buttercup yellow and the matching blanket appeared fluffy.

The bed was the big surprise: generous pillow-top mattress atop a box spring.

Bolted to the floor.

In the left-hand corner were a lidless toilet and a sink the size of a salad bowl, both stainless steel with rounded edges. Not a sharp surface anywhere but that didn't matter. Given the right circumstances, the roll of toilet paper near the commode or the toothbrush on the sink could be used to self-destroy.

My eyes rose to a framed print high above the sink, unreachable unless you were a basketball center. Poorly painted landscape.

After meeting Kristin Doyle-Maslow, I

was thankful it wasn't Munch's **The Scream.**

By hospital standards, a decent place but anywhere you can't leave is prison and a day and a half after its debut, this place had acquired the reek of confinement.

I bent to take a closer look at the inaugural patient. The strands of hair were dishwater laced with gray. Thirty-five years old; I could only imagine what life had been like since she lost her job.

Where had she lived? How had she gotten by? Why had she repeated the trespassing that got her busted in Sunland? Had the Bel Air backyard belonged to another ex-lover? Or a man she imagined as such?

Where was her son?

I sat down on the brown chair, tried to shift it closer to the bed. No movement. Another bolt-job.

Zelda continued to sleep and I thought about what it would be like to get stuck in here.

My chest tightened and I felt my pulse begin to race. An issue I'd thought I dealt with years ago.

You could call it claustrophobia. I think of

it as a nasty little childhood memento.

All those hours spent hiding in crawl spaces and sheds, crouched behind shrubbery, or squeezing between rocks, trying to escape my father's unpredictable drunken rages.

I'll never enjoy small spaces but I really thought I'd gotten past notable anxiety. Even Robin doesn't know. No reason for her to know.

But here it was again. Nothing serious, I could handle it. Just as I did years ago, practicing my own preaching, drawing upon all those nifty cognitive behavioral techniques.

Mostly, though, I choose to avoid anything close to confinement, maybe because I don't want to let go of the memories, fearing freedom will soften me when the next big threat rolls around.

I've constructed a world for myself that allows lots of elbow room, living in a spacious, sparely furnished house with a view of miles of canyon and an occasional snip of ocean on clear days. My work— short-term custody and injury work for the court, consults on murders with my best friend, a veteran detective—allows me to come and go as I please.

I run for exercise, choosing times when I'm unlikely to encounter company.

I spend a lot of time by myself and when the dreams arrive unbeckoned and I really need to step out of myself, there's always the grand distraction of helping others.

Now here, in this absurd, surreal place, the person I'd come to help remained drugged up and inert and I craved escape.

Deep breath. Focus.

After a bit of that, I scooted to the edge of the chair and touched Zelda's cheek. Coarse with some kind of rash.

Not a stir. I patted her again, more firmly. My third attempt caused her to frown.

I said, "Zelda?"

She murmured but kept her eyes closed. Then she sat up, shook her shoulders, and looked around. The blanket rolled free, revealing what I first thought was an institutional yellow top but turned out to be a cheap Tijuana blouse with ragged black stitching along the seams.

"Zelda?"

She lay back down, rolled away from me,

returned to sleep.

I sat there and did more deep-breathing, closed my own eyes and tried to summon up a pleasant scene.

What I ended up thinking about was a small boy building castles with tiles and that brought on the what-ifs.

A woman's voice shook me alert.

"You."

Not an accusation, just a pronoun uttered without inflection.

As if the word existed in a vacuum.

Zelda Chase had sat up again, blanket gathered at her waist. This time her eyes were wide open and aimed at me.

"You," she repeated.

"Do you know who I am, Zelda?"

Confusion.

I said, "Dr. Delaware."

Her lips screwed up like a pig's tail. She scratched her chin, then her cheek, then her forehead. Burped loudly and did it again and rotated her head and flittered her fingers.

Five years had wreaked decades of damage, the once-oval face a lopsided hatchet collapsed at cheek and jaw. A caved-in mouth said most of her teeth were gone. Her complexion was livid— street sunburn—her lips shrunken and blistered and parched. Deep furrows ran vertically from her nostrils to her chin. Her eyes were pink where they should've been white. Thirty-five years old, but I'd have guessed fifty-five, minimum.

"Zelda—"

She drew her hands up defensively but without confidence, like an outclassed boxer.

I sat back as far as I could in the immovable chair. "Alex Delaware. We met a few years ago."

Nothing.

"I was told you asked for me."

The hands dropped a bit. The near-stuporous confusion behind them might've been mental illness but I bet the real cause was Kristin Doyle-Maslow's manipulation. Zelda had no conscious need to see me; The Hyphen's project required an inaugural documented patient and I was the sucker who'd responded to a guilt trip.

I tried anyway. "We met five years ago, Zelda. When you were seeing Dr. Sherman."

Blank stare.

"He was your psychiatrist, Zelda."

A single blink.

"I'm a child psychologist, Zelda. I spent some time with Ovid."

Blink blink blink.

"I got to know Ovid while you saw Dr. Sherman. While you lived in the Beverly Hills Hotel."

Blank as the wall behind her.

I continued, prattling like a serious obsessive. "Dr. Sherman and I arranged babysitting for Ovid so you could return to work. Actually, I did. From the HGK agency?"

Now a hapless smile, the kind you see with aphasia patients who know something's wrong but aren't sure what it is.

"Do you know where you are, Zelda?"

Brow-knitting consternation. I repeated the question, expecting very little.

She said, "Here."

"Where's here, Zelda?"

"This..."

"Do you know what this is?"

She squinted. Laced her hands together and dropped them into her lap.

Maybe the lack of acuity was a good thing, what the hell would I tell her? You're a federally funded lab rat?

Where was the boy?

I said, "Yesterday, you were in a hospital, Zelda. You were moved here but just for a couple of days."

No reaction.

"Do you know what day it is, Zelda?"

"Now."

My next question was routine and idiotic. "How about a day of the week?"

I might've been speaking Albanian.

"Do you remember what got you to the hospital, Zelda?"

Her hands pulled apart and shot up, blocking her face. Twin fists made small tight arcs.

"Zelda, I'm sorry if these questions—"

"Disappeared," she said, suddenly loud and harsh.

"Who disappeared, Zelda?"

"Mommy."

"Your mother—"

"No no," she said, punching air. "Nonononononononono."

All those syllables but any budding anger

was gone—more like a weary mantra. She slumped, pressed her hands to her temples.

I said, "Mommy—"

"Gone."

"When?"

Nothing.

"You were looking for your mommy."

She snuffled.

"You didn't find her."

She regarded me as if I were the crazy one. "I find her, they don't put me here."

"Of course—so you were looking for Mommy when—"

Growling in frustration, she slammed back down, drew the blanket over her head.

"Zelda—"

The blanket heaved. I waited.

This time her sleep was punctuated by aggressive, raspy snoring.

For the next half hour I waited, passing time and suppressing my tension by conjuring pleasant imagery. Intruded upon far too often by bad thoughts.

Eleven years old.

When Zelda's breathing slowed further and she showed no sign of waking, I used the key and let myself out.

Kevin Bracht looked up from his book. "Anything?"

I shook my head.

"So what now, Doc?"

I gave him my card. "I'll be by tomorrow before she's discharged. Let me know if there's any sort of problem."

He walked me to the door. "What'll happen to her?"

"I'll try to get her somewhere safe."

"But only if she agrees. What a system."

I knew what he meant. The rule for involuntary commitment was clear: If a patient displayed imminent danger to others or self, I'd be obligated to file. If not, total freedom, no exceptions. That started me wondering what Zelda had done to qualify in the first place. I asked Bracht if he had any idea.

"Nope, they just brought her in and said she'd been arrested."

"I didn't see any abrasions or signs of a struggle."

"Me, neither. Except for that initial period when they restrained her, she's been exactly what you just saw. Should I try to push more meds? Off the record."

"No, just keep an eye on her."

"You bet, Doc. I could also look out for a reason to recommit her."

I shook my head. "If it's real, you'll know."

"True."

When I reached the door, he said, "I hope I wasn't out of line. About another hold. I was just thinking of her safety. I mean, what's someone like her going to do out there?"

"That's how I took it, Kevin. I'm glad you're here."

"Thanks, Doc." He laughed. "Wish I was."

I stepped back into the maze of cubicles. Kristin Doyle-Maslow was at a nearby station, working an iPad. She didn't seem to notice as I approached but when I was a foot away she startled and clicked off.

Not before I had a look at her screen.

Watching a movie. Something with shields and lances and lots of blood.

I kept going.

She said, "What's the status?"

I said, "Quo."

"Huh? Oh, ha ha. So when are you coming back?"

"When will she be discharged?"

Back to the iPad; she touched a screen. "Three p.m. tomorrow."

"I'll be here before then."

"What if there's an event?"

"An event?"

"A problem."

Why not just say that? "Your nurse has my number. Do you have any post-discharge plans?"

"Isn't that your job?"

I walked past her.

"That's it?" she called out.

"What more could there be?" I said.

"If you know of other patients who'd fit well with our program, you should tell them."

I sat in the Seville, phoned the U.'s medical center, and asked for Dr. Nehru. The operator said, "We have three. Which one?"

"Psychiatry."

"Hold, please." Gypsy guitar music came on. "That's Dr. Mohan Nehru. Would you like the number?"

I got Psychiatry Department voicemail, returned to the main exchange, and asked a new operator to page Nehru.

"If you're a patient, there's a message line—"

"I'm a colleague. Dr. Alex Delaware. It's about a mutual patient."

"Hold, please...yes, you're on our list... Alexander...oh, you're crosstown but... okay, looks like you've still got privileges here, one moment."

Two **nuevo flamenco** instrumentals later: "He's listed as here today but he's not answering his page."

"What specific service is he on?"

"We don't have that level of information."

The drive to Westwood was on my way home. I turned onto campus at the main southern entrance and made a left at the medical office complex. The health center spans both sides of the street. Bustling, today, like the mini-city it was.

Ravenswood Psychiatric Hospital was one of the newest, prettiest buildings in the complex, a six-story art-piece in limestone and copper endowed by and named after an industrialist whose child died from complications of anorexia. I parked using my faculty permit, clipped on my Western Peds badge, took the elevator to the fifth floor, and pushed the red button on the locked door of Adult Inpatient Psychiatric Services.

The med center has nearly a thousand beds, eighty of which are allotted to Ravenswood. Of those, twenty are pediatric, ten are for Alzheimer's patients who agree to be researched in return for hope, and thirty-five are devoted to the U.'s rehab program for adolescent eating disorders, a service that brings in huge money.

That leaves fifteen beds for general psychiatric care, divided into an eight-bed voluntary ward for patients not much different from the rehabbers next door, and seven beds for 5150 commitments.

No surprise that Zelda had arrived when the place was full. LACBAR didn't amount to much but if it hadn't existed, she'd probably have been sent crosstown to a county-run human zoo with its own issues.

So maybe things had worked out for the best.

If I could do **my** best to find her somewhere to live tomorrow.

Get her settled and more coherent and
willing to tell me where her son was.

Five years ago, she'd been a troubled but
devoted mother. Shortly after that she'd
lost her career and gone who-knew-where.
One positive: Lou Sherman had stuck
with her, maybe even after she'd lost her
insurance. Not transferring her until he
knew he was seriously ill.

But he hadn't called me…

No one had shown up at the locked door
so I pressed again. Several moments
passed before a young nurse studied me
through Lexan panels and buzzed herself
out.

"Can I help you?"

"I'm looking for Dr. Nehru."

She scanned my badge. "Mike's in the
cafeteria, Doctor."

"Thanks. Were you on last night?"

"I wasn't. Why?"

"I just saw a patient who arrived here as
a 5150 and got sent to a place over in mid-
city. Dr. Nehru authorized it and I'm trying
to get hold of the chart, see if he can offer

any clinical advice."

"There's a hospital in mid-city?"

"Not exactly," I said. "It's a community mental health center with a limited inpatient facility."

"Oh. Well, Mike's eating lunch."

The cafeteria was crowded with hordes of white-coated and scrub-suited people hoping for nutrition. Plenty of Indian males, at least two dozen.

Step one: Concentrate on doctors.

Step two: Focus on younger men, given Mohan "Mike" Nehru's status as a resident.

That left five possibilities. I got myself a cup of coffee and began walking by each of them, trying not to be obtrusive as I read their badges.

M. M. Nehru, M.D., was my second target, a smooth-faced, clean-shaven man around thirty, sitting by himself, eating a huge burrito and sipping from a can of Coke as he played with his phone.

I settled across from him. He took a while to realize I was there. Just like Doyle-Maslow with her movie. Cyber-play does that, everyone on digital delay.

Finally, he looked up and I told him why I was there. He scanned my badge. "Sure, I remember her. The one we referred out. How's she doing?"

"She's mostly sleeping. Do you have time to chat?"

"Sure." He pushed his burrito away.

"Don't let me interrupt your meal."

"I'm finished and it's pretty much crap, anyway. So you're with that administrator—Kirsten, whoever? The one with the big-time NIMH funds?"

"Not exactly." I explained my original connection to Zelda Chase via Lou Sherman, how I'd ended up at LACBAR.

He said, "So she worked on you, too. I knew Dr. Sherman, had him in med school, good teacher. When I saw his name in the chart I said, 'Too bad he's not around anymore.' He died, right?"

"Two years ago."

"Yeah. I think I heard that."

"Any way for me to see his notes?"

"We can go upstairs and get a copy but don't expect too much. Basically, he transferred her with no treatment notes except for the meds regimen he had her on."

"What's that?"

"He started her on Haldol, upped the dosage a couple of times, then switched after a year to Ativan, so that's what I went with. I gave her a serious dose before sending her off, figuring she'd probably habituated and would need it to stay calm during transport."

He looked at me. "That work out okay?"

"No problems on the trip and she's sleeping peacefully."

"Okay, good, so what's your plan?"

"Don't have one," I said. "She'll be discharged tomorrow and so far she's done nothing to justify another 5150."

"So she gets kicked to the curb. Same old story."

"Why was she committed in the first place?"

"Good question," said Mike Nehru. "It's not like she was waving a gun at anyone. What the cops said is she created a disturbance in someone's backyard and when they came to get her she freaked out and the cops felt threatened, quote unquote—pretty wimpy, no? Like one of those spoiled-ass college students, everything's a trigger. They said they wouldn't press criminal charges if we cooled her off so I figured I was doing her a favor and we did have a bed, which isn't always the case."

He drank soda. "What's the place like where she is now?"

I described LACBAR.

Mike Mohan said, "What a bullshit artist. She made it sound as if they were well established."

"She's self-serving but the room isn't bad for what it is and there's a full-time nurse assigned to her who knows what he's doing."

"So it worked out," said Nehru. "But if she asks me again I'll tell her where to shove it."

"Nothing like an anatomy lesson."

He grinned. Turned serious. "So after three p.m. tomorrow, she's gone and unprotected. Wish I could say I'm surprised. I'm in my last year, thinking of getting an MBA or an MPH and working as a consultant, maybe doing some public policy work."

I said, "Better the hammer than the nail?"

"Better something that actually has efficacy." He tried another bite of burrito, grimaced and pushed it farther away. A couple of other residents passed by, bleary-eyed; Nehru's eyes were getting there. "I didn't become a physician to be a jailer but let's face it, some people need protection from themselves. The night Ms. Chase came in was hectic, patients I'd already admitted were acting out, and then what's-her-name comes to me and says she's got a solution and shows me all these letters from NIMH. The facilities really are okay?"

"For a couple of days under proper supervision."

"One patient in a skeleton facility. Weird," said Mike Nehru. "So should we go get that chart?"

As he searched his office computer, I said, "When Dr. Sherman began seeing Zelda, he wasn't clear about her diagnosis. Did his notes clarify that?"

"Nope, but given the meds I figured he was concentrating on anxiety rather than bipolar…okay, here it is, let me print."

A single sheet slid out of his printer. Zelda's name, no phone number, just an address long outdated, plus the fact that she had an eight-year-old child once evaluated by me. The final sentence a legalistic-sounding statement that he could no longer assume medical responsibility for the patient and hoped she'd follow through on his advice to enter treatment with someone at the U. Including resumption of her medication. Haldol replaced by Ativan.

Resumption meant she'd stopped, probably against his advice. His mention of the first drug made me wonder if he thought she might need it again.

Sometimes Haldol's the drug of choice when extreme confusion looms.

No sign she'd ever followed through on his advice. The only reason she'd ended up at the U. was proximity to Bel Air.

Mike Nehru said, "That address, Sunset Boulevard, Beverly Hills. Those houses are huge and she sure doesn't look like she's got dough."

I said, "The Beverly Hills Hotel. She was

living in a bungalow there."

"You're kidding. So once upon a time she **was** rich. Amazing, I thought it was a misprint because she came across homeless."

"She probably is now. How was she identified?"

"The cops I.D.'d her by her fingerprints and gave us her name. Once we had it, we looked through our records and found the report."

"Her son's mentioned. Did she say anything about him?"

"Nope, she just screamed at being restrained. Like they all do. Then I got the Ativan in her and she quieted down. But some of the others didn't. It was some night."

CHAPTER 8

Back home, I beelined for my office, found my notes on Ovid, got the name of his preschool and his teacher—Jeanette Robaire—and called.

She still worked there and I was lucky to catch her on break. She had no idea who I was but her voice took on warmth when I said I'd been Ovid Chase's psychologist.

"Ovid. Sure I remember him—the bright ones stay with you. Why would you call me now?"

"I'm looking for him." I gave her the basics, describing Zelda as having emotional problems I couldn't go into.

She said, "Problems. I guess that doesn't shock me, Dr. Delaware. She only came to the school a few times but when I saw her I got the feeling she was trying to be...okay. But it didn't quite work—if that makes sense?"

"Working too hard at it."

"And ending up nervous. As if she wasn't quite sure she'd pulled it off. Someone said she was an actress."

"She was."

"Well, her performance with me wasn't convincing. Not that there was anything threatening about her, just the opposite. Fragile. A beautiful fragile woman. Are you saying they took Ovid away from her? If that's the case, why would you be looking for him?"

"I don't know what happened to him other than he's not with Zelda. And she's in no condition to tell me."

"Oh," said Jeanette Robaire. "That sounds like more than just emotional problems."

"Shortly after I saw Ovid, Zelda lost her job. Did she keep him in your school for the rest of the year?"

"I'm pretty sure she did. But I can't tell you what happened when he left us and

went to first grade. That's the thing with my
job. You lose contact."

"Do you feed to any specific schools?"

"Not really. We get kids from all over
and they spread out. Private and public. If
they have younger sibs who enroll with us,
we sometimes get progress reports from
parents. Zelda's problems, are you worried
they could've led to abuse?"

"There's no sign of that."

"No sign," said Jeanette Robaire. "I wish
you just would've said, 'No way.'"

Next try: HGK Babysitting and Child Care.
No phone listing, nothing on the Internet.
That was L.A.: no shelf life.

Phoning scores of schools and lying was
an unpleasant prospect with no likelihood
of paying off. Time to turn to a higher power.

Milo was away from his desk at West L.A.
substation. I reached him at his cell.

"Hey, Alex."

"I need your help."

"That's a switch. What about?"

"Can we get together?"

"That level of help, huh? I'm free in a

couple of hours. My office okay?"

"Perfect."

No questions asked.

Friend in need.

Milo's situation at LAPD is one of those blips that slides off the screen to everyone's benefit.

Years ago, he'd cut a deal with a police chief nearing retirement, a smooth, political man with plastic ethics. The barter was simple: Milo's discretion in exchange for promotion to lieutenant. The rank usually means desk work. Milo got the higher salary and pension allotment and a mandate to keep working murders.

A new chief, autocratic and reflexively hostile, tolerated the arrangement as long as Milo's solve rate remained nearly perfect.

Different situation from anyone else's, but it's always been different for my friend.

Back in his rookie days, homosexual officers were "nonexistent" in the department and Milo's colleagues were busting heads at gay bars. Self-preservation mandated keeping your private life private and he buttoned himself up in psychosocial exile.

When social norms budged a bit, he kept up the low profile but stopped pretending and soon enough everyone knew. That period was the toughest—the sneers and stares and avoidance, the occasional overt ugliness.

Nowadays, the department has rules against discrimination of any sort and gay officers are on the job. Milo still keeps to himself and I believe it would be that way if he were straight.

Part of the deal with the corrupt chief was getting "creative" work space. The other detectives at West L.A. work out of a big room with lockers and coffee machines, a clamorous environment that bustles with work ethic and frustration and gallows humor.

Milo operates from a windowless former supply closet, a cramped domain behind an unmarked door, set at the end of a utility corridor near interview rooms where people sweat and deny and confess.

Meager square footage for a man who takes up plenty. He's six two or three, depending on posture, with a gourmand gut and the bulk of a lineman gone sedentary.

Stretch too exuberantly and his knuckles brush the walls.

I'd go nuts working there. He loves it.

When I arrived, his door was wide open and he was at his computer, hunting-and-pecking like a studious rhino. Stacks of paper covered his desk, continued onto the floor and the spare chair. Without turning, he swiped at the chair, snowed the linoleum with paper.

I sat down. "New case?"

His fingers stopped moving. "Nah, professional development seminar. Aka knee-deep in cow-slop." He resumed typing. Paused again. "Since eight a.m., I've been at a management seminar for department honchos, of which I am apparently one."

"Congratulations."

"Oh, yeah, I'm touched. And I blame the effect **your** colleagues have had on society."

"Pyschobabble?"

"Hours of interpersonal whoopy doo and sensitivity blah blah blah. They even sent a social worker to tell us we were good human beings despite our aggressive tendencies. When she broke us up into small groups, I split. But I still have to finish this—open-screen test—to prove I was there." He frowned. "Would you say empathy's always necessary for effective management?"

I said, "Hmm."

"No hmming or I'll make you do it."

"If there's no 'it depends' option, I'd go with 'true.'"

He jabbed a key. "Next: Is diversity enriching and facilitative due to cultural changes that have impacted law enforcement in the twenty-first century? Or has it always been advantageous for a well-functioning organization?"

"On that one, I won't budge from 'maybe.'"

He laughed, hunched lower, began pounding the keys progressively harder. Soon he was causing the board to jump and rattle and there was nothing for me to do but sit there and wait him out.

He looked as he usually does, black hair slicked but rebellious, white sideburns shaggy and mal-trimmed ("let's hear it for skunk stripes"), the left side a quarter inch longer than the right.

Sadistic fluorescent bulbs called out every crease, pucker, and pock littering the steppes of his heavy face. Today's fashion statement was a short-sleeved once-white shirt, a blue-and-orange tie that had never known a silkworm, defeated khaki cargo pants, and the usual desert boots, this pair the same muddled gray as the clouds outside the window of Zelda Chase's cell.

They're fashionable now. I didn't have the heart to tell him.

A shiny olive sport coat lay crumpled on the floor. I folded it over my lap and sat there. If either of us exhaled hard, we'd collide.

Clearing the screen, he popped a wheelie with his desk chair, swiveled hard and faced me. Spotting the folded jacket, he said, "Personal valet, I dig it. You also do windows?"

"Help me out and I might."

Oddly bright green eyes studied me as if we'd just met. When he does that, it's unsettling, but I've gotten used to it.

He said, "Tell me about it."

He listened without interruption, said,

"An actress? Never heard of her...okay, this shouldn't be too hard."

Returning to the keyboard, he pulled up a database off-limits to anyone but law enforcement and twelve-year-old hackers. As he typed, he hummed.

The Police's "Every Breath You Take." A joke on multiple levels.

Small print began filling the screen. "Here we go, your gal has a criminal history... such as it is. First offense is that 415 plus trespassing five years ago in Sunland... dismissed. After that it looks like she stayed out of trouble until a couple of years ago when she got nailed for public intoxication in Central Division—Broadway near Fifth...dismissed."

I said, "I thought vagrancy laws weren't enforced."

"You know how it is, Alex. There are no real rules, just back-scratching. My guess is some landlord or developer who contributes to campaigns bitched about transients and the department used a public health or a narcotics angle to conduct a temporary cleanup...whatever it was, it didn't lead to any jail time for

Ms. Chase and after that she stays out of trouble until...fifteen months ago, when she earned herself a second drunk and disorderly, also in Central, Olive Street near Fourth. That's not far from Skid Row."

"So she was probably living downtown."

"That would be my bet...nothing else until a few days ago in Bel Air...dismissed."

He turned to me. "Not exactly a felonious mastermind. And she may have switched her domicile to the streets of the Westside because I can't see her hiking from Central to Poobahland just to invade someone's backyard. Maybe she went natural—living up in the foothills."

I said, "The first Central bust was a few months after her psychiatrist died. If no one replaced him, she could've slid down fast."

"Makes sense. But from a police perspective she hasn't done bad for a crazy woman. I've seen people in her situation rack up dozens of arrests."

"Any addresses on the arrest forms?"

He scrolled back. "For the first one in Sunland, she's on Corte Madera in the Hollywood Hills. For the second, she's on Sunset."

"Beverly Hills?"

"Why the hell would she be in B.H.?"

"Her psychiatrist got the studio to pay for a cottage at the Beverly Hills Hotel. Maybe she lied and said she was still there."

"No, no, this address is East Hollywood... maybe Echo Park."

He logged onto a map-site, fingered a spot. "Officially Hollywood, but right on the border. Let's see what DMV has to say."

No active driver's license or registered vehicles, no state I.D. card issued in lieu of a license.

"Yeah, most likely a street person. No mention of any kid in her paperwork, she probably lost custody. Any father of record?"

"She never let on."

"Okay, let's switch gears and try to find this young'un and put your mind at ease so you can help me with the rest of this touchy-feely bullshit."

He checked several social service websites including Social Security, followed up with calls just to make sure. No record of Zelda or Ovid Chase in the system.

He sighed. "Let's try the bad stuff."

I steeled myself as he logged onto the coroner's site.

Nothing. Thank God.

Same for the L.A. missing child database and those of Orange County, San Diego, San Bernardino, Ventura, Santa Barbara.

Next, he tried the roster of offenders housed by the California Youth Authority. "At least he doesn't seem to be a bad boy. Let's go national."

Plenty of missing eleven-year-old boys all over the country, a sea of prepubescent faces, many age-progressed because they'd been gone for a long time.

The agony of so many families.

No one who could be Ovid Chase.

Milo rolled his chair and faced me. Not a wheelie, just the slow scrape of hard rubber on linoleum. "You probably thought of this already but mental illness can be genetic, right? So what about psych hospitals, a pediatric ward?"

"Sure," I said, dispirited.

"Sorry," he said. "For that, better you call than me."

He found me an empty interview room and

I phoned Ravenswood's pediatric service and used my title. Negative. Same result at County and every other public hospital maintaining an inpatient pediatric psych ward.

When I returned to his office and told Milo, he said, "May I suggest that at this point no news is good news? Like maybe he's living with a picture-perfect adoptive family."

I said, "In a perfect world...The only other place I can think of would be a private psych ward but no way to gain access to their records."

"Private costs a fortune, Alex. I don't see the kid of a homeless woman affording that. Unless he's in a place that takes government money, but if that was the case his name woulda showed up on some social service list. Same for public school, because they'd register him for assistance. And forget fancy boarding schools, right?"

"Right."

"So what next?"

I had no answer.

He said, "When you saw her today she wouldn't talk to you at all about the kid, huh?"

"I mentioned him but didn't push it. I'm not sure she's **able** to talk much. The only thing she got out was something about her mother disappearing. And that got her agitated, so I backed off."

"Was that crazy stuff or do you think you touched a nerve?"

"I have no idea."

"Mommy disappearing—hey, seeing as she was an actress, what about one of those where-are-they-now sites?"

"Tried it," I said. "**SubUrban** lasted two and a half seasons, episodes are listed and she's on the cast, but there are no bios."

"Maybe none of them ever worked again."

"That gives me an idea, Big Guy. I'll try to find her cast-mates. Thanks." I got up. "Can I also have that Echo Park address?"

"Better yet, I'll come with you."

"You've got time?"

"Anything's better than this." Logging off the test, he shrugged into his jacket.

I said, "The great escape."

"It's called executive prioritizing, amigo. They teach it to you at seminars."

CHAPTER 9

The drive to Echo Park took forty-five minutes, during which I called a few private psych hospitals and rehab outfits in the faint hope someone would bend rules. No luck but doing something was better than wallowing in pessimism as Milo cursed his way through traffic.

The East Hollywood address LAPD had for Zelda matched three stories of flaking stucco zigzagged by hundred-year-old fire escapes. One of the few residential throwbacks in an area steadily ceding to strip malls, mail drops, and Central American restaurants.

No signs marking the place but I didn't need my doctorate to know what it was. Defeated men idled on the sidewalk. Lots of empty eyes and slack mouths. As Milo's unmarked pulled up, a shudder coursed through the group. By the time we got out of the car, everyone had returned inside.

Three security locks on the open door. A poster prohibited entry after nine p.m. The lobby was skimpy, painted bright aqua, with a whiteboard on an easel listing rules and regulations for residents of **BrightMornings: A Place of Rebirth.** A plaque on the wall listed sources of funding: a dozen churches and synagogues.

No residents in sight but footsteps thumped on an upper floor. Ornate carving on a battered wooden reception counter said the place had probably once been a hotel, maybe a decent one. I'd prepared myself for another stonewall but the face behind the counter was familiar.

Maybe this would be different.

Tiny young woman in her twenties, filing cards. A lovely Botticelli face was graced by enormous hazel eyes and a mass of dark ringlets. Her fingers were slender and child-sized. Her focus was intense.

Graduate student at the school where I had a faculty position. She'd been in the audience when I'd lectured on pediatric psych a couple of years ago, had asked bright questions. Industrious note-taker, Judith...something.

Our approach drew her away from the cards. Something to do with meal schedules.

"Dr. Delaware?" Her name tag filled in the blank. **J. Meers.**

"Hi, Judith. Is this your clinical placement?"

"No, just a part-time job to augment my funding. I had to stop T.A.'ing in order to concentrate on my dissertation."

"How's that going?"

"It's going." She shrugged. Glanced at Milo.

"This is Lieutenant Sturgis from LAPD. Milo, Judith Meers."

"Hi, Lieutenant. Is one of our guys in trouble?"

I said, "No. We're trying to find a woman named Zelda Chase who listed this as her address."

"That must've been a while back, Dr. Delaware. The program separated the sexes around a year and a half ago and the women are housed in Santa Monica."

Milo said, "Putting distance between males and females."

Judith Meers said, "This is before my time but from what I can gather unisex did cause understandable problems."

"Do you keep records from before the move?"

"I'm afraid not, Lieutenant. Everything pertaining to the women went with them."

As she wrote out the address and number of the Santa Monica shelter, a man came down the stairs, gripping the banister, teetering, nearly tumbling.

Emaciated, with haunted eyes that looked nowhere. Flaccid lips moved but produced no sound. He could've been forty or a hundred.

He passed by without noting us, trudged through the doorway, and shuffled eastward.

Judith Meers handed me the information and sighed. "At least their basic needs are taken care of."

I said, "What kinds of patients qualify?"

"We're not allowed to offer treatment so they're residents, not patients. Everyone's classified as seriously mentally ill—not a

DSM diagnosis, just an informal judgment. That's part of what I do but it's not at all technical."

Milo said, "You know it when you see it."

"Basically," said Judith Meers. "The goal is to provide a warm, hopefully safe place for nonviolent psychotics and a well-equipped kitchen to serve their nutritional needs."

I said, "Do any of them get treatment elsewhere?"

"Ideally, they obtain their meds and their therapy at various outpatient clinics. When we have drivers available, we take them, but some of the facilities are within walking distance."

"Compliance isn't an issue?"

"It's a huge issue, Dr. Delaware. We try to guide but are careful to avoid power struggles. That's our funding mandate."

"You're privately funded."

"Totally," she said. "The religious institutions have been fantastic. Without them there'd be nothing. There used to be some federal money but it dried up. Tight times, from what I've been told."

Less for this, more for Kristin

Doyle-Maslow.

Milo said, "The nonviolent part, that work out?"

"Pretty much."

"Pretty much?"

Judith Meers said, "I've never had a problem personally, Lieutenant. The guys are pre-screened for lack of aggression and a lot of them actually look out for me. Or think they're being protective."

"Hmm," he said.

"For the most part they're gentle, Lieutenant. It's a part-time job and I'm not here after dark, my husband picks me up at five. His job's in Hollywood, so it works out well."

Milo said, "Tell me he's a bouncer and bigger than me."

She laughed. "Almost as good, he's a litigator for Capitol Records. And yes, he's a substantial man."

I wished her well and we headed for the door.

She said, "Your question about violence. Did the woman you're looking for do something criminal?"

I said, "No. It's her son we're really after.

She was found alone, having a major psychotic break. He's eleven years old and so far we haven't been able to trace him."

"That age, living on the streets?" She frowned. "I'll ask around, maybe some of the guys remember. But as you might imagine, most of them are pretty out of touch and she hasn't lived here for a while."

"Anything you can do would be appreciated, Judith."

"Eleven years old. She refuses to say where he is?"

"She may not be sufficiently in touch to actually know."

"Darn," she said. "But it's what we sign up for, right, Dr. Delaware?"

We drove to Santa Monica. BrightMornings–Westside was a former motel on Pico, a U-shaped collection of white units with blue doors, set behind a sun-seared asphalt lot. Once-white parking lines from the motel days were worn to gray stubble. The neighbors were a discount tire dealer and a plumbing supplies outfit.

No open-door policy here; a slatted electric gate blocked entry. Milo rang in and identified himself. The door to the central unit opened and a woman peered out then reclosed it. It took a while for the gate to begin sliding.

He said, "She probably verified my I.D. Whole different vibe here."

By the time we'd exited the unmarked, the same woman was walking toward us. Fifties, broad-shouldered, with clipped beige hair and a military gait.

She said, "Sherry Andover." Two graduate degrees on her badge: MSW and MPH.

Milo said, "Nice to meet you, ma'am. This is Dr. Delaware, he's a psychologist."

"I know. Judith at Hollywood said you'd be dropping by to talk about Zelda Chase. What'd she do, end up in someone's backyard again?"

I said, "She lived here?"

"For maybe a month, right after we opened, thirteen months ago."

"Backyards were her thing?" said Milo.

"She wandered away, I'd say three, four times. Never went far, mostly we'd find her behind one of the apartment buildings south of Pico, and she didn't cause problems other than digging up some plants that could be tucked back in. In fact, she was kind of neat about it. Putting stuff in a row then she'd go to sleep and someone would find her in the morning and call the cops. Santa Monica PD knows us so they drove her back."

A blue door to the right opened and two women stepped out. One was painfully obese and walked with two canes. The other appeared barely in her twenties and limped. Sherry Andover waved at them. They returned to their room.

"Where's Zelda now, guys?"

I said, "On a 5150 hold until tomorrow."

"Locked up? She's gotten dangerous?"

"She shifted her trespassing to Bel Air."

Sherry Andover said, "Aha, invading the high-line, yeah the system would respond differently to that. So she's **not** violent."

"Not that I've seen. She'll be released tomorrow."

"And you want to bring her here."

Now that you mention it.

I said, "If you can accommodate her."

"A couple of beds just opened," she said. "For the wrong reasons. Yesterday, one of our gals had a fatal encounter with a car. Another left a week ago and ended up stabbed to death in Long Beach. Long domestic history with an abusive boyfriend. So what does she do? Heads straight for the alley where he hangs out."

I said, "How'd they get out with the gate in place?"

"By using that button right there." She pointed to a black dot on the right-hand post. "We're not a locked facility, Doctor. Everyone's free to come and go as they please, the gate's locked only on the outside, to keep problems away from **them.**"

"No need for that at the men's shelter."

"If I was in charge there'd be the same setup there, but with tight funds, the board prioritized. All severely mentally ill people are vulnerable but being female is an additional factor."

Milo said, "So the women leave when they feel like it but have to call in when they return."

"We hope it's a disincentive for wandering away, but it's not as if we're dealing with a rational population."

"Rowing upstream," said Milo. "I can relate."

"Bet you can." She turned to me. "Bet you **both** can. Anyway, sure, we'll take Zelda if she wants to be here and she really is no danger to herself and others. The only caveat being, if those beds book up before tomorrow, she's out of luck."

I said, "If that happens, any suggestions where should I take her?"

"Take her? You're transporting her, personally?"

"Seems the simplest way."

"She's been your patient for a while?"

"She was never my patient. I consulted to her psychiatrist."

"Where's he in all this?"

"Deceased."

"Oh. Okay, I'll make sure there's room for her. If you're confident she won't act out aggressively."

"I can't guarantee anything but nothing indicates she's at risk."

"Appreciate the honesty, Doctor. Let's give it the old-school try."

I said, "So she was here a month."

"Give or take, we don't collect clinical or

personal data."

"Why'd she leave?"

"No idea. One day she was just gone. Like so many of them."

"Any alcohol or drug issues?"

"Not that I saw, Doctor. Why? Is she currently addicted?"

I shook my head. "Any issues at all, besides trespassing?"

"Nope. Is she currently being medicated for her illness? There's a community mental health clinic a few blocks away and if she's willing I can hook her up there."

"The resident who committed her gave her a strong dose of Ativan and prescribed a week's worth. Right now she's pretty drowsy. I don't know how she'll feel once it wears off."

"Same old story," said Sherry Andover. "All right, welcome back, Zelda. Nice meeting you guys. Just push that button and let yourselves out."

I said, "One more thing: I got involved with her because I'm a child psychologist and her psychiatrist asked me to evaluate her son. Would you have any idea where he is?"

Sherry Andover frowned. "She has a son? No indication of that when she was here but we don't take kids so maybe he got placed somewhere."

"If he did, I can't find him."

"And you're concerned about that because..."

"I'd like to know he's okay."

"I don't want to be Ms. Obvious but have you tried social services?"

I rattled off the agencies we'd called.

She said, "Can't add to those." She blew out air. "I need you to be brutally honest: You're not thinking she hurt him, are you? 'Cause that brings us right back to the violence thing and a red flag the size of Alaska."

I said, "Five years ago she was a caring, loving mother and she's never acted out violently with anyone. She's been living on the streets so you're probably right about placement. I'd just like to confirm it."

"Five years ago she was crazy but a good mom."

"She managed to work a full-time job and make sure the boy was well cared for. Then she lost the job and we haven't been able to trace her movements other than her stay at your other facility and here."

"She won't talk about the boy?"

"She's still pretty much out of it. The only thing she did mention was her mother disappearing. Did that come up here?"

"Never that I heard but she might've told one of the other girls. They have all kinds of stories, our residents. Which isn't to say none are true—hey, maybe that's why she invades other people's territory, trying to make it back home symbolically or something? How's that for pop psychology? Think I can get my own talk show?"

I smiled.

"I shouldn't joke but it helps," she said. "I'm just the fool who took this job because my teaching position at Northridge was X'd out."

Milo said, "Hardly."

"Pardon?"

"You don't seem like a fool to me, ma'am. What'd you teach?"

"Public administration. I'm an organizer, never done a minute of therapy. Not officially, anyway."

He said, "But you still get to go home

every night knowing you did something important."

Sherry Andover stared at him then she blushed. "That's got to be the sweetest thing anyone's said to me since my husband proposed—and I won't tell you how **that** worked out. You single?"

Milo smiled and shook his head.

She said, "Okay, I'll take important. And now good manners means I have to say the same applies to you. Which it does. To both of you." She laughed harder. "Look at us, a bunch of saints."

As we drove away, Milo said, "Why'd you ask her about booze and dope?"

"Zelda got busted for drunk and disorderly twice, and I'm wondering if she'll head for some dive bar if she grows restless."

"Or to someone's backyard."

"That, too."

"I wouldn't overthink it, Alex. Like I told you, enforcement's political and people like her don't get put through Breathalyzers, they just get hauled in. The arresting officers were looking for a charge to pin on her so they called her drunk."

"So I shouldn't pub-hop?"

He laughed. "That's a separate issue. What next, fellow important person?"

CHAPTER 10

Back at the station, we agreed there was little left to do.

Milo would check with Central Division to see if anyone remembered Zelda and Ovid and I'd go "the glam route," trying to reach someone associated with **SubUrban.**

After that, it would be time to back away. He was telling the truth. I, not so much.

Moments after he dropped me off I was compiling a list of California boarding schools that accepted pre-adolescents. Workable list: thirty-nine institutions, with student bodies ranging from the intellectually gifted to kids with special needs—mostly defined as learning disabilities and/or weight problems. The latter I eliminated, which cut the roster by fifteen.

Nearly every school was situated where land was plentiful and scenic. When tuition rates were posted, they were at Ivy League levels. Maybe Zelda had managed to create an educational fund before her breakdown, even hired a trustee to guard Ovid's welfare.

Or...

I got to work, spinning the same story to receptionist after receptionist: I was Ovid Chase's uncle, his mother had just been hospitalized for an acute ailment ("Ovid knows the details") and needed to talk to her son. Reactions were invariably sympathetic but when records were checked and Ovid's name didn't show up, confusion gave way to suspicion and I hung up, thankful my home number was blocked.

Two-plus hours of utter failure. I called Kevin Bracht and asked how Zelda was doing.

"No change, Doc, would've called you if there was. I could go in and try to talk to her but I figure let sleeping patients lie."

"Agreed. I'll be by tomorrow to take her to a placement I found. Anything else I should know, Kevin?"

"Just that it's extremely weird being here at night. The Hyphen and her secretary leave at four and the building's locked up tight. I have a key but I'm starting to feel I'm the 5150. So please, Doc. Rescue me."

"Will do," I said. "Try to have a good dinner."

"You bet," said Bracht. "Found a few fancy places on the take-out list. I'm looking forward to steak and lobster, courtesy of the federal government."

"Bon appétit."

"Might as well be **bon** something."

Partial episodes of **SubUrban** were all over the Internet. I was about to view one when Robin came into my office and ruffled my hair.

"Can I distract you long enough for dinner?"

I glanced at my desk clock. Just after eight p.m. "Where we going?"

"Thirty feet away. I barbecued some chicken."

"Oh. Great, thanks—I'd have been happy to help."

She smiled. "I looked in on you an hour

ago and saw a man possessed."

I hadn't seen or heard her. "More like dispossessed."

"Of what?"

"Progress."

That sounded like Milo but Robin was kind enough not to point it out. I got up and drew her to me and kissed her. When we broke, she was breathless and laughing. "Nice to be appreciated, but maybe you should wait to taste the chicken."

The meal was great, my token contribution clearing and loading the dishwasher, then mixing us a couple of Sidecars. "Let's drink out by the pond, handsome. It's a nice night."

Still trying to settle me down.

She'd probably suggest a bath before bedtime. The only person who ever cared much about me. I kept her drink light, tossed extra brandy into mine.

We settled by the water's edge, sipped and watched the fish create gentle eddies.

I reached for Robin's hand, said the right things, made the right facial expressions.

When we returned to the house, she said,

"I haven't bathed yet."

The next morning at eight I caught Milo at home and asked him to get the details of Zelda's Bel Air arrest.

"Why?"

"Sherry Andover's questions about violence stuck with me. I'd like to be on solid ground."

An hour later, he got back to me. "The female resident heard noise in the back-yard and went out and found Zelda crouched in a corner. Zelda stood up and began waving her hands and screaming 'horribly.' That woke the male up and he overpowered Zelda, who tried to fight him off while his girlfriend dialed 911. Does that change anything?"

"It could be worse," I said, "but compared with her previous arrests, it's a step in the wrong direction."

"Speaking of previous, no one at Central remembers her and there's no record of her ever having a kid with her. But I was half wrong about no alcohol testing. They took blood from her the second time and she popped a .21."

"Serious intoxication."

"Yeah and there's more. She was also positive for heroin and meth. No needle marks, so she sniffed. That's a nasty combination, couldn't have done much for her mental status."

"I'll call Andover and tell her. If she turns Zelda down, I'll come up with something else."

"You're really carrying this woman, Alex. Is it something about her or just the kid?"

"Mostly the kid," I said. "But maybe she's also gotten to me—the plunge from what she was to who she is now. She was gorgeous, now she looks like a crone."

"The street can do that to you."

I said, "I need to disengage, huh?"

"Maybe if you do find out the kid's okay, it wouldn't be a bad idea."

"That doesn't look likely." I told him about striking out at boarding schools.

He said, "I figured you'd do something like that and I probably shouldn't say anything, but that's just the Golden State, there're are forty-nine others. And what about them **furrin** countries—isn't Switzerland full of fancy **écoles**? England, too, all those oldy-moldy piles of brick where they cane your bottom for kicks and turn you into a masochistic earl or whatever."

I laughed. "I know, the whole idea's ridiculous. The kid would need a trust fund."

"You're **saying** ridiculous but you're **thinking** maybe before Zelda went completely nuts she set the kid up financially. One can always dream."

"I shouldn't pursue it."

"My opinion's gonna make a difference? Good luck."

SubUrban's Wikipedia listing described the show as "a vehicle for lowbrow, often vulgar, infrequently on-spot humor." Mediocre ratings during the first season hadn't prevented renewal because the network was searching for "edgy comedy aimed at attracting a younger audience." Viewership increased a bit at the beginning of the second season but began to taper at the end. Cancellation came with no warning from the network.

The setting was an apartment building in a nameless midwestern city that served as the hub of a dysfunctional social grouping:

a grumpy widower named Horace and his two children, a fifteen-year-old would-be lothario named (get it!!) Horner and an intellectually precocious, nunnish seventeen-year-old named (this you have to get!!!!) Virginia. The house pets Lou Sherman had cited were an inert, flatulent basset hound who supplied voiceover wisdom and a goldfish in a bowl who enjoyed faking death. Additional charm was supplied by neighbors: a Nigerian couple named Marvis and Bulski who dressed formally and believed themselves above it all, and a caricature-gay fireman named Chad-Michael-Anthony whose sleep patterns had been permanently destroyed by middle-of-the-night alarms. He'd installed a flagpole in his house in order to "practice my leg lock."

Chad-M-A's platonic roommate was the mandatory bombshell, Corinna, played by Zelda Chase clad in costumes that skewed toward lingerie. She'd projected the same triad of traits in every episode: glazed-eye intensity, serpentine body movements, monosyllabic utterances. All of which made her character the show's most frequent object of ridicule.

She also got to work the flagpole.

I watched a scene featuring a lot of her, found it pathetic and creepy, searched for another, had the same reaction, and logged off. Copying down the cast list, I added the production company, H-S Partners, and the assistant who'd babysat Ovid, Karen Gallardo.

Nothing further on the actors but H-S had gone on to create a more successful series involving the wacky world of pest extermination called **Spray Me.**

One carryover from **SubUrban:** the goldfish.

Joel Hyson and Greer Strickland ran the company, currently headquartered in Culver City near the Sony lot. Proceeding alphabetically, I phoned and asked to speak to Hyson. An adenoidal receptionist who sounded around fourteen said, "In a meeting."

"No prob, I'll talk to Greer?"

"About what?"

"Zelda Chase."

"Who?"

"She was on the cast of **SubUrban.**"

"She's not on **Spray**."

"I know that. I'm one of her doctors and I'm doing some follow-up."

"Give me that name again, I'll leave a message."

Locating anyone else's address bottomed out, with only Stevenson Beal, the actor who'd played Chad-Michael-Anthony, listed on a business directory because he had a new gig: real estate agent in Encino.

His voicemail insisted he was **really** interested in what **anyone** had to say. Emmy-caliber performance, but no place for him in the industry.

No justice in the world.

Expanding my boarding school search to five other states, I kept offering my bogus story with no success, saved the best for last and phoned Sherry Andover and told her about Zelda's Bel Air arrest.

She said, "Sounds more aggressive than before…any actual physical contact?"

"None listed in the police report."

"All right, I'll give her the benefit. But I'll be watchful, thanks, Doctor."

"Appreciate it, Sherry."

"If I tightened my criteria too much, I'd be empty and collecting unemployment."

I took a longer-than-usual run, showered, dressed, and drove to LACBAR. This time, Yvette the receptionist managed a nod.

I said, "The boss back there?"

She rolled her eyes. "Boss. That'll be the day." She buzzed me in.

On the far side of the cubicle area, Kristin Doyle-Maslow perched atop a desk and held court for a group of six people. She saw me and waved expansively. To see it, you'd think we socialized regularly. I pretended not to notice and kept walking. She shouted, "Doctor!" loud enough to preclude my faking deafness.

I stopped. She crooked a finger at me. **Come here, Junior.**

I stared as if she were a sideshow curiosity. That creased her face and caused her to hop off the desk and come charging toward me.

When we were inches apart, she forced words out in a labored stage whisper, a sausage machine extruding links. "These. Are. County health managers. Gatekeepers.

We need them. To get with the program. So we can mobilize outpatient services."

"We."

"The treatment community. Come over and meet them, you don't have to say anything, just don't diss me."

I looked at her.

"Please," she growled, destroying any etiquette value the word might have. "How can we help patients if we can't net them?"

"I'm in no position to endorse—"

"Don't endorse **shit,** just come **over,** I'll do the **talking.**"

Six people were staring at me. I followed her over, smiled and stood by as she spieled about community needs, the advantages of outpatient care in the exciting new environment wrought by a meld of treatment advances, government funding, and private citizens combining to "combat mental illness as we all liaise and partner with localities in order to tailor caregiving to diverse, area-specific needs."

Then she smiled at me and I knew she'd break her word. "This is Dr. Delaware, one of our local practitioners. He opted to partner with us in the brief treatment of a seriously ill street person who'd slipped through the cracks and is finally obtaining the care she needs. Because he gets what we're about. In fact, he's here now to see to her overall psychosocial needs and I hope we'll be able to collaborate in the future on optimizing her multimodal care. Any questions for the doctor?"

A woman said, "What type of patient?"

I said, "Can't discuss that."

A man said, "What about ethnicity? Are you truly diverse?"

Kristin Doyle-Maslow said, "She's a seriously ill patient and yes, we are."

"Is she of color?"

I said, "Can't discuss that."

Another man said, "Are you doing something other than pushing meds? Is she being treated with cultural sensitivity?"

Kristin Doyle-Maslow said, "Absolutely. This particular patient—"

"Can't be discussed," I said.

A woman, now glaring at The Hyphen, said, "I appreciate your honoring confidentiality, Doctor."

I said, "Glad you understand," and walked away, feeling sullied.

Thank you, ladies and germs. Now I'll balance a ball on my nose while barking "The Star-Spangled Banner."

As I reached the door, I heard Kristin-Doyle Maslow say, "all about quality care. The absolute best specialists this city has to offer."

Kevin Bracht answered my bell-push wearing the same clothes as last night and looking eroded. Zelda's shoes were atop his desk. I took them.

"How's the dog-and-pony show out there, Doc?"

"Rapidly producing piles of waste."

He cracked up. "Along those lines, I thought of something else that's messed up about this place. Patients get a toilet in their rooms but nurses don't. I was lucky, there are those two unused cells, but if they were full up, I'd need to leave the unit to do my business. That tells me there's no serious intention to ever use this place for inpatient, whole thing's a joke, the sooner you get her out the better we'll all be."

"You bet, Kevin. Let's see how she's doing."

CHAPTER 11

Zelda was still in bed, on her back, bedcovers heaped along the wall. Her hair was gray wire, her eyes half closed and hazy.

I stopped a couple of feet away. "Hi."

Nothing for a moment. Then a smile, gradual, minimal, ambiguous.

I edged closer. "Zelda, I'm taking you out of here."

She blinked rapidly. Her eyes seemed to be acquiring focus. Then, suddenly, the spark was gone, replaced by stupor.

"We need to leave, Zelda."

Her head rotated toward me. Her lips formed silent words I couldn't decipher.

"What's that, Zelda?

She worked at forming the word. "Can-dy."

"You'd like candy."

"Hmm hmm." Childish pout.

"Sure, we can find some candy. First, let's get you out of here."

She rolled away from me.

I said, "I'm taking you to a place you've been before. BrightMornings."

No recognition.

"In Santa Monica, the woman in charge remembers—"

"Mounds," she said. "Coconut."

She'd used heroin and junkies crave sugar. But during this lockup, no withdrawal symptoms had surfaced. Ativan could be partly responsible for that but it couldn't have masked a serious addiction.

Was craving candy a sense memory?

Or she just liked the damn stuff.

She pressed her arms to her sides, stared at the ceiling. The window above her was a pleasant blue rectangle. Pretty day in L.A. I doubted she'd noticed.

"It's time for you to leave, Zelda."

She remained inert and mute. But when I began to repeat myself, she raised herself to her elbows, sat up and straightened her spine and positioned herself with the grace of a dancer. Swinging her feet over the bed, she rose to her feet. Moving in stages, each segment slow and deliberate.

Reverse origami, a woman unfolding sequentially.

Without a word, she walked past me toward the door, barefoot.

I got in front of her and held out her shoes. She began to take them but let go and they dropped to the floor. Before I could pick them up, she'd stepped into them with surprising agility and resumed her trudge.

We stepped into the outer room. Kevin Bracht called out, "Good luck, Zelda."

She continued past him, unresponsive. He began clearing his desk.

Zelda trudged steadily. I kept my steps small, the way you do with a baby learning to walk.

The cubicle area was empty. No opportunity for a "teachable moment."

Here's one of our inpatients. We ensure that their needs are met in a clinically responsible manner...

Not that this patient would've been much of an endorsement, plodding empty-eyed, totally unmindful of her surroundings.

When curiosity goes, a lot else has already vanished.

The rush of noise on Wilshire jarred me but did nothing to Zelda. I guided her toward the Seville and when I seated her in the front, she bent like modeling clay. As I belted her in, she remained still.

Once she was secure, I waited to see if she'd grow anxious but she didn't and I got behind the wheel and eased into westbound traffic.

When I drive, I listen to music, switching between an MP3, old-school CDs, even Paleolithic cassettes courtesy the tape deck the car came with in 1979. My preferences fluctuate but I can't tell you what criteria I use. Sometimes I put the MP3 on random shuffle and serve up a bouillabaisse of Sonny Rollins, Bach, Miles Davis, Santo and Johnny, Vaughan Williams, Patsy Cline, Satie, Gershwin, you name it. Along with sprinkles of street-corner doo-wop and any breed of great guitar music.

No telling how Zelda would react to music

but I chanced it, choosing something melodic and soothing: re-press of an old French recording of Ida Presti, possibly the greatest guitarist who ever lived, and her husband Alexandre Lagoya, pairing on Debussy's "Clair de Lune."

It's a few minutes of gorgeous that rarely fails to settle me. I felt my blood vessels expand, heard my heartbeat slow.

Zelda remained unmoving and unmoved. Existing somewhere else.

Soon, she began to slump, ceding control to the seat belt, head bobbing like a dashboard toy. When I rolled over a rough patch of asphalt, her body flopped passively. Had Mike Nehru's generous feeding of Ativan suppressed her that efficiently? Or was this typical behavior when she wasn't sneaking into other people's backyards and scaring the hell out of them?

That kind of extreme fluctuation would fit a variant of bipolar disorder, but it didn't rule out schizophrenia. Or a combination of the two, as Lou had suggested.

Or some undiagnosed affliction no

psychiatrist could classify beyond the ravages of a brain gone haywire.

Whatever the details, no way could she care for a child. Had she been sane enough to realize that and relinquished custody?

Or...

The music ended. Not an eyeblink from Zelda.

I said, "So you like Mounds."

She said, "Mother."

"What about Mother?"

She yawned and closed her eyes. By the time I reached La Cienega, her mouth had gated open and she was snoring. By Doheny Drive, the shuffle beneath her eyelids was unmistakable. REM sleep. The dream phase.

What does a madwoman dream about?

In this woman's case, something pleasant. She smiled all the way to Santa Monica.

CHAPTER 12

As I pulled up to BrightMornings, Zelda woke up, saw the sunlit sky, and said, "Good night."

Sherry Andover was ready for us, clicking the gate open and telling me where to park. Zelda remained pliable as I drew her out.

"Hi, there, Ms. Chase. Welcome back."

Without a word, Zelda trudged toward the building. Andover sprinted ahead and unlocked the door to Room Six.

The space was no larger than the cell Zelda had just left and was painted an eerily similar yellow. Two windows, both safety-grilled. Clean bathroom equipped with the basics of hygiene, nightstand, closet, one nature print on the wall—grouse in the heather. A change of clothes was folded neatly on the bed pillow. Other garments, including a pair of new sneakers, were visible in the open closet.

The outer surface of the door could be key-locked but no way to secure it from the inside. No guarantee of privacy but freedom easily obtainable.

Zelda lay down on the bed and closed her eyes. Within seconds, her eyelids were ruffling again.

Sherry Andover said, "Glad to see you settle in easily, Ms. C.," and we left.

On the way back to the Seville, I told her about Zelda's request for candy.

She said, "You're thinking junkie-jones?"

I said, "She's had two days with no withdrawal symptoms. I suppose some of that could be the Ativan, but I doubt it could mask everything."

"That's been our experience, too. It calms them down but if they've got a serious habit they're still throwing up and feeling miserable. I'll keep an eye out."

As I got back in the car, she said, "In terms of the candy, we try to keep the food reasonably healthy so the only sweets on hand are a big bag of those little Hershey's Bars some nice person donated to us last Halloween and they're probably stale. I'll try to pick up some Mounds on my way home or tomorrow morning. Why not keep the populace happy?"

"Beyond the call, Sherry."

"Look who's talking." She smiled. "I like coconut, probably steal a few. If she works out I'll get her a roomie but I figured start as if she's a newbie, even though she's been here before. From what I just saw, she's not big in the memory department."

Amnesia could be another effect of the benzodiazepine in her blood. Of psychosis, as well. I said so.

"I don't get into the pharm stuff," she said. "I contacted the outpatient clinic, might be able to get a volunteer to take her the first couple of times. After that, she's on her own."

I thanked her again and started up the engine.

She said, "Candy and Mommy. Guess they're the same to a baby...that's kind of what people like her become, no? She mentions the kid, I'll let you know. Ovid, huh? Naming him after a love poet. That took some imagination."

"Once upon a time," I said, "she was able to imagine."

I spent the rest of the afternoon calling private schools, finally lost my ability to bullshit convincingly, walked to the kitchen and poured coffee. Caffeine was the last thing I needed and I ended up jumpy and wondering how to bleed it off. Then I remembered what Lou had told me about Zelda's name change and began a new search.

No shortage of Jane Chases but none that matched Zelda. Then I realized I had no idea if she'd altered her family name, too, and put the issue aside.

Time to resume being a useful member of society. I scrounged up the fixings for a passable one-dish dinner: lamb shoulder, vegetables, Israeli couscous, everything sprinkled liberally with cumin and cardamom and chili powder. By the time Robin and Blanche came in from the studio, the pot was sizzling and the table was set.

Robin said, "You read my mind, just like

they taught you in school. I've got sawdust all over, let me wash up. You're a very nice man."

No calls that night from Sherry Andover or Milo. From anyone except sociopaths trying to sell me term insurance, home security, and lawn care. I chose to interpret that as encouraging.

By eleven the following morning I'd taken on a new custody case in Superior Court, an evaluation on hold until the two children in question returned from Hong Kong. Meanwhile, the judge would email me background info, with my billable hours commencing upon receipt.

Just as I printed the file, my service put through a call from BrightMornings.

"Dr. Delaware? This is Carlos, I volunteer for Sherry at the shelter. Have you recently seen your patient, Zelda Chase? She left and hasn't returned."

"When?"

"Our gate camera has her pushing the button this morning at five-eighteen. Clients are free to come and go but Sherry decided to drive around looking for her because apparently Zelda has a history of wandering and trespassing and she figured she'd know where to find her. But she didn't locate her and then she had to leave for meetings and she doesn't talk on the phone while driving, so she asked me to call you."

"Could I have Sherry's mobile number, anyway?"

"She really won't answer, Doctor. A fender-bender and three tickets."

"I'll leave a message."

"Suit yourself, Doctor."

I instructed my service to put Andover through immediately. An hour and twenty minutes later, they did just that.

She said, "Not a rousing success. No warning signs, she was starting to look a little more alert, took the initiative to shower, changed into fresh clothes. Grooming's always a good sign but I guess not in this case."

"Carlos said your camera picked her up leaving. What was her emotional state?"

"Can't say, the images we get are distant and blurry, sometimes you can't even identify who it is. I recognized her because of the clothes, I put them in the closet myself. That's when I went to check her room. She even made up the bed."

"Which way did she head?"

"The lens angle doesn't capture that, just that they've triggered the gate and split."

"Thanks for taking the time to search for her."

"I figured if she was a creature of habit, finding her would be easy. Tough luck, but who knows? She wandered out, she could wander in. Wish it would've turned out smoother but at least I got her a Mounds bar. Left it right on her nightstand and she took it with her."

I phoned Milo and told him.

He said, "That didn't last long."

"I don't suppose Central Division could be asked to keep an eye out for her."

"I could get them to say they will but it won't mean much. She have any money for bus-fare?"

"No."

"You think she'd walk all the way from Santa Monica to downtown?"

"Psychotics can cover long distances and she was busted twice downtown."

"Let's say they do find her wandering around Skid Row. Then what?"

"I don't know."

"Love your honesty," he said. "Okay, I'll put in a call but maybe she's got homing instincts and you should start somewhere else. Like the last place she invaded—that house in Bel Air? Not a hop-skip from Santa Monica but a helluva lot closer than Central."

"Good point," I said. "What's the address?"

"Not kosher, amigo. Let's keep the investigatory process procedurally appropriate."

"Meaning?"

"Meaning see you in forty, and I'll drive. You're rescuing me from a shit-pile of paperwork."

CHAPTER 13

There's Bel Air, then there's Bel Air.

The verdant, gently sloping streets a couple of miles below my house contain some of the grandest estates in the world. That's the Bel Air populated by celebrities, heirs, and amassers of fortunes. The Bel Air where open-air buses crammed with squinting tourists snail up and down leafy lanes as smooth liars clutching hand mikes ladle out a broth of vicious gossip and unhappy endings.

You may not be able to live here, folks, but you'll love hearing about all those rich bastards humiliated.

Above all that is a Bel Air that crawls along Mulholland Drive and transitions to the San Fernando Valley, an area exploited during the seventies and eighties by developers eager to cash in on the zip code.

Upper Bel Air costs a fortune but much of it looks like a suburban tract.

No tour buses in sight as Milo hooked west of Mulholland and we were met with the choice of two ungated developments.

To the left, **Bel Aurora,** to the right, **La Belle Aire.**

He checked the address in his pad, swung right, continued for half a mile. Both of us looking for an empty-eyed woman wearing brand-new sneakers.

We'd passed similar neighborhoods along the way, stingily treed streets filled with ranch houses and white boxes set on narrow lots. The lack of shade could be painful: Pivot the wrong way and your eyeballs bleached instantly. Portable basketball hoops in driveways promised youthful exuberance but no kids were in sight.

No one at all; post-nuclear silence is the badge of a fine L.A. neighborhood.

The property Zelda had invaded was on Bel Azura Drive, one of the ranches, positioned on the south side of the street where the views were less dramatic. An older gray BMW sedan sat next to an oil stain. Drapes drawn.

We drove on, reached a cul-de-sac a few blocks up, and returned for a second look.

Milo said, "That bolt in the gate is new. Without it, not much security, I can see why she'd choose it."

He drove away.

We started by guessing the route Zelda might've taken from BrightMornings to Bel Air: Pico to Lincoln, Lincoln north to Wilshire, Wilshire east to the same campus entrance that had led me to Ravenswood Hospital, then, rather than continuing through the U.'s sprawl, a turn on Hilgard and north to Sunset.

After that, it was anyone's guess.

The first few miles of the journey gave Milo the opportunity to query homeless people, roach-coach proprietors, gas station attendants, Santa Monica PD cop-teams. Anyone in a position to notice comings and goings. No success. The beach city teemed with homeless; even a woman as disabled as Zelda would blend in.

He'd come equipped with a wad of cash to loosen civilian tongues—what he calls "my data retrieval trust fund." For as long as I've known him, he's been dipping into his own pocket, not bothering to put in for reimbursement because "that would be like begging my old man for the keys to the car when he was ornery, which was always."

He repeated the line this morning.

I said, "Fine, but let me pay."

"And lose my status as a venture capitalist? I'd rather walk on glass."

Moot point, anyway. Nothing to pay for; no one had seen Zelda.

Back at the station, he said, "What now?"

"Time to move on."

"Glad to hear you say that. Your IQ is better spent on real stuff. Like helping me."

"With what?"

"Nothing at the moment but I prefer my consultants undistracted."

I said, "Sure. But if you could ask Central…"

"Already done. Now go home and take your OCD meds."

"I was thinking Chivas."

"Whatever works."

Two days passed before he phoned at ten-twenty p.m. Robin had gone to bed. The kids from the new custody case might be flying in next week from Hong Kong and I was reviewing their pediatric and school records.

"She's been found, Alex."

"Great—"

"**Not** great. God, I **hate** doing this with anyone, let alone you."

I felt the blood rush from my head. "How?"

"Don't have details, I just got to the scene."

"Where's that?"

"Like it matters? You'll wanna come wherever it is."

"That okay?"

"Okay?" he said. "Far from it. But I'm gonna say no?"

CHAPTER 14

St. Denis Lane was an afterthought at the western edge of Bellagio Road, a night-blackened strip curving past fifteen-foot hedges, keep-out walls, and monumental gateposts. No streetlamps to compete with the stars. Tonight the stars were stingy.

Anyone walking would be unnoticed if they wanted to be.

The oldest, grandest section of Bel Air.

The Bel Air, quiet as a mortuary.

Blue flashers advertised the scene. The cop in the cruiser blocking the road had been told about me and waved me to a parking spot. I continued on foot past two other squad cars and a white coroner's van. Twin gates bolted to fieldstone columns were splayed open. I stepped through and began climbing a crushed-gravel drive.

The punch line at the end of a five-hundred-foot walk was a huge, two-story Spanish Colonial house perched atop a couple of acres of lawn. The uniform stationed at the front door hadn't been told about me and I waited as he radioed Milo. Whatever Milo said earned me a personal escort along the northern side of the house.

The property in back terminated in a dark cloud of forest, its dimensions impossible to gauge. Low-voltage lighting touched upon scalpel-cut hedges, billowing flower gardens, and decades-old citrus trees. The land was terraced gently into three levels, creating surprise as one descended. One tier down was marble statuary, a swimming pool archaic enough to feature a diving board, hexagons of barbered grass set in weathered brick. Level two was announced by a menagerie of topiary animals.

All the action was situated near a prancing topiary horse, the light here harsh from the glare of portable lamps arranged under a staked and taped canvas canopy. Gloria, a coroner's investigator I knew from other death scenes, stood by making notes as jumpsuited techs crouched and worked. Milo was off to the side, pad and pencil out, talking to a white-haired woman.

He saw me but didn't interrupt his interview.

I kept going, closing in on the last thing I wanted to see.

Zelda Chase lay on her back, arms bent unnaturally, mouth gaping, face compressed in terror and pain. She wore a sweatshirt and jeans I recognized from the closet at the shelter. A breeze blew and flowers sweetened the night but the air around the body reeked.

Splotches of green and brown and yellow and rust spread beneath her, some of the clots dotted with whitish clumps I took to be maggots. Then I bent and took a better look and saw that the white granules weren't larvae, they were shreds of undigested food.

Coconut.

The Mounds bar Sherry had given to her.

Blowfies can arrive at a corpse within hours. No insect invasion implied recent death. Meaning Zelda hadn't eaten the candy right away. Despite her mental state, she'd been able to delay gratification.

I walked over to Milo. He gave a small head shake and said, "Doctor." The formality was a signal: I needed to act official and objective.

"Lieutenant."

The woman with him was around seventy, tall and thin with ramrod posture and well-molded features. Up close, the white hair was actually ash blond, just above shoulder-length, cold-waved in the style of another era. She wore a dark-green silk blouse, black slacks, lighter-green flats. Eleven p.m., with a corpse in her garden, she was dressed for casual hosting.

But her expression said this was no party. "Doctor? The coroner?"

Instead of contradicting her, Milo said, "Dr. Delaware, this is Mrs. DePauw, she owns this lovely home and had the misfortune of discovering the body. We were just beginning to talk about it."

I extended my hand, received a cursory press of manicured fingertips. "Enid DePauw, Doctor. This is **quite** an experience."

"Again, so sorry, ma'am," said Milo. "It had to be a terrible shock."

Enid DePauw glanced at the body and winced. "That poor thing is the one to be pitied. And in answer to your question, Lieutenant, I have no idea how she got in. As you can see, I'm walled and gated."

"With all due respect, ma'am, those walls are scalable and I didn't notice any surveillance cameras."

"There are none, Lieutenant. It didn't seem necessary, all these years, we've never had a problem. I do have an alarm for the house and with the exception of a gardener's boy pilfering tools, everything's been peaceful. And that was twenty or so years ago."

"I'm glad, ma'am, but in the future you might want to install cameras, the new ones are inexpensive and they're easy to install."

"I used to have a dog," said Enid DePauw. "Teacup poodle, not much use as a sentry, but he didn't like strangers. The alarm is first-rate, goes directly to the police. I'd hate to deface the gardens or the house with technology and whatnot. So cold and my garden's landmark-quality. Several interesting people have resided here, including Jean Harlow."

"I understand, ma'am. Now if you could tell me exactly what happened."

Enid DePauw bit her lip. "All right…I'd been away at my condo in Palm Springs, returned tonight just after dark with my housekeeper. As I often do when we return from the desert, I gave the girl the night off. Compensation for having to stay late for the drive back."

"So you were here alone when you found the body."

"I was. I usually am, Lieutenant."

Milo looked back at the house.

"I know," said Enid DePauw. "It's far too much for me now that my husband is gone. But I've never had any problems. And the same appeared to be true tonight. The alarm was still set when I walked into the house, nothing at all amiss. I did the usual things. Going through the mail, taking a bath—desert grit can be adhesive. What next…hmm…oh, yes, I fixed myself a nightcap and relaxed in the library. My husband's favorite room. The funny thing is when he was alive, I never spent much time in there, but now...life turns out funny, no?"

A glimpse at the corpse caused rouged lips to quiver. "Poor thing. Is she one of those homeless people? She doesn't have a purse. Though I didn't see any shopping carts like they usually have. Is it out on the road?"

"No, ma'am. What happened next?"

"Sorry, I'm prattling. What happened...I finished my cocktail and thought I'd watch a bit of TV after taking a little stroll in the garden. I find garden strolls relaxing. If you're going to ask me what time it was, I don't know precisely, but I can tell you that immediately after...finding her, I hurried back into the house and dialed 911, so that should inform you."

"Your call came in shortly after ten, ma'am."

"There you go." Another sidelong peek. "Very few teeth in her mouth. She looks as if she's led a hard life. What do you think happened to her?"

"We don't know yet, Mrs. DePauw."

"Those types can hurt themselves, no? But I didn't see any wounds. Then again, I didn't spend much time looking, just hurried inside and reset the alarm and called you people."

A hand settled on her left breast. Floated away, fingers bending and straightening rapidly, as if attacking a piano étude. A noise brought our attention to the body. A tech scraping brick. Another stood nearby entering data on a handheld.

Enid DePauw said, "To end up this way, she'd need to be...out of sorts? Mentally, I mean."

Milo looked at me.

I said, "That's a reasonable assumption."

"Terrible when that happens," said Enid DePauw. "People like that should be cared for, not left to wander the streets."

I said, "Have you noticed other homeless people in the neighborhood?"

"Just one, a man, a black man, pushing one of those supermarket carts piled high with who-knows-what. I notified Bel Air Patrol but by the time they got here, he was gone."

Milo said, "How long ago did that happen,

Mrs. DePauw?"

"Three years? Four? I can't be sure. That experience **was** unsettling. As I drove by, he gave me a look. Which is why I called the patrol. But I haven't seen him since. It really is quite wonderful here."

She frowned. "How long do you people need to be here?"

"We'll be as quick as possible, ma'am, but it could take a while."

"Then I suppose I should go inside and let you go about your business."

"Thank you, ma'am."

She swiveled away, took another look at the body. "Life can be so unfair."

Ascending to the top tier, she reached a bank of French doors that served as the house's rear wall, paused to survey the scene, waved at us, and went inside.

Milo said, "Sorry it came to this, Alex."

I said, "**Do** you have any idea about cause of death?"

"No bullet holes or lacerations, no bump on the head from a fall or a blow, no obvious strangulation. At this point, the working assumption is natural causes. Whatever that means for someone like Zelda."

"She used heroin. Could be an overdose."

"Or her heart just gave out due to bad living."

"The look on her face," I said. "She didn't die peacefully."

"Gloria said the same thing, she's wondering about a seizure." He placed a big hand on my shoulder. "There's no reason for you to stick around."

"Looks to me as if she hasn't been dead long."

"Gloria's guess is within six hours but we'll wait until the pathologist weighs in. Coulda been even uglier for ol' Enid if she got home earlier. She's come out for her stroll, Martini in hand, witnesses it actually happening and has a stroke or something and we've got two bodies. Imagine trying to make sense of that scene."

Gloria began packing up. Milo and I walked over to her.

"Anything new, G?"

"A few specks of what looks like vomitus over there." Pointing to a small staked area a few feet behind the body, just below the steps from the top tier. "Like she was walking and started to get sick and just collapsed."

The tech with the handheld jogged over. "If you don't need the body, Lieutenant, I'm ready to authorize transport."

"Go ahead."

Gloria said, "Good night, Milo. You probably won't have much to do on this one."

"Your mouth to some deity's ears."

She left. The techs began boxing their equipment and dismantling the lights.

The scene suddenly quiet. That made it worse.

I went home.

CHAPTER 15

Robin woke up when I slipped into bed. I kissed her forehead and made sure not to move too much. Next morning I told her about Zelda and she listened and asked if there was anything I needed. When I'd convinced her there wasn't, she went to her studio and I resolved to concentrate on people I could actually help.

That faltered when my service phoned a little after two p.m.

"Stevenson Beal returned your call," said the operator. "He used to be an actor on a show, I forget its name but I remember his."

"SubUrban."

"That's the one. He said he's in real estate now."

"Sounds like you two had a nice chat."

"Um...Doctor, I don't want you to think I get too friendly with your patients. He's kind of talkative, I figured I shouldn't cut him off."

"You figured right. Were you a fan of the show?"

"Not really. I watched it at the beginning but then it got stupid. That's what always happens, right? They run out of stories."

"Steve Beal, how can I help you?"

Booming baritone. No hint of the effeminate stereotype he'd played for two and a half years.

I told him about Zelda's death.

He said, "Shit. Poor Zelda...shit. I was thinking you were interested in one of my listings but this is way way more important. Did she kill herself?"

"When you knew her, was she suicidal?"

"Not like openly trying to hurt herself, but if she did do it, I wouldn't be shocked. Your service said you're a shrink. Weren't her issues obvious?"

His voice lowered. "In fact, why're you calling me?"

"I was her son's therapist and I'm trying

to locate him, to make sure he's okay. I haven't found any relatives so I'm trying people she worked with."

"You figured we'd know because we were her surrogate family?" said Beal. "Yeah, that's always the official story, we bond. But let me take a wild guess: No one besides me called you back."

"Not so far."

"Don't hold your breath, Doctor."

"Any idea what Zelda did after the show was canceled?"

"I'm sure she brooded and got depressed like the rest of us. Though I guess for her it would've been a helluva lot worse. Because of her issues—listen, Doc, I've got a show-ing out in Tarzana, need to book. But if you want to get together later today and chat about Zelda, why not? It'll allow me to flash back to my **ahem** days of stardom."

We agreed to meet at four, at a café in Sherman Oaks named Le Fleur. I took a run, showered, logged onto a **SubUrban** video, filed Beal's face mentally, and joined the onset of the rush-hour crawl up the Glen.

On the show, Beal had been in his late

thirties, slim, with cropped dark hair and a pencil beard, prone to lisping, mincing, and bursting into show tunes.

The man waiting for me at a corner table was twenty pounds heavier, clean-shaven with longish graying hair, dressed in an oatmeal-colored suit, a chocolate T-shirt, tan Gucci loafers.

"Doctor? Hey, Steve Beal." Both his hands remained wrapped around a coffee mug. He called the waitress over and asked what I'd be drinking.

I said, "The same."

Beal said, "Also a couple of croissants, Tara—make mine with almonds."

"Sure, Steve."

"You're not what I expected, Doc."

"You figured Viennese with a cigar?"

He laughed. "Want me to be brutal? The shrinks I've known—and I've known a few—came across like people who didn't get a lot of play in high school. Yeah, it's pigeonholing, blame it on my former profession. Acting's all about shortcuts but often they're just as good as taking the long road."

"Actors learn to make quick judgments?"

"TV actors do, we're always under time pressure. Ever read a teleplay? Abbreviations, suggestions, the content is arranged around commercial breaks, it's so the network can sell ad time. Anyway, you're here to talk about Zelda. What you told me has totally bummed me out. What a messed-up waste."

"She was talented?"

"She was as good as most—better. I'm not saying she was a Streep but she did have that thing with the camera you have to be born with. Transforming herself in a snap. People who can do that sometimes make the transition to the big screen but after her arrest I figured Zelda wouldn't. Though being screwy hasn't stopped others from making it big. You do know about the arrest."

"I do."

The croissants and my coffee arrived. Steve Beal raised his cup. "To Zelda and every other tortured soul trashed by the industry. Do I sound bitter? I kind of do, Doc. Thinking about her has flashed me back to my own servitude. I was six months old when I got my first job—soap commercial—then proceeded to sacrifice my childhood and my adolescence and a whole lot more because Mommy suffered from metastatic stage-door-itis. I barely got any education, so when **Sub** got canned and my agent stopped taking my calls, I was as marketable as a crippled quarterback. But it turned out to be the best thing that ever happened to me."

He flicked a lapel. "Learned a real skill, now I get to actually accomplish something. Ever watch **Sub**?"

"A bit of video."

"You catch me doing my thing?"

I nodded.

"So you're probably surprised I'm not queer." He pounded his chest. "Acting! **Brrrilliance!**"

I laughed.

"I dig that spontaneous reaction, Doc, apparently Steve-o's still got it going on. So what do you want to know about Zelda?"

I said, "Tell me about her mental problems."

"Okay...well, obviously, she was moody, everyone in the industry's moody. But with Zelda it was more intense. She could sink

real low real **fast,** then spring out of it and get hyper so fast you wondered if she'd been putting you on when she was down."

"Did that cause problems on the set?"

"No, that's the thing. If she had a scene to shoot, she was ready. It's like she was... a machine."

"How'd you know she wasn't putting it on?"

He put his coffee down. "You're saying she was a faker?"

I shook my head. "Just trying to educate myself."

"How do I know? For one thing, I spotted her doing it when she thought no one was looking. More than once."

"Doing what?"

"Going ultra-down, then ultra-up. Down would be sobbing in her dressing room and rocking like an autistic kid. Skulking off the set, face like a zombie. Up would be racing back and forth through a hallway, bouncing like a yo-yo, tearing at her hair while she talked to herself like a tweaking monkey."

I said, "Could she have been tweaking?"

"Hmm, good question, Doc. I've known plenty of dopers in my day including tweakers, and I have to say this seemed different. But you're the expert. I sure didn't see any signs of her being a meth-head—her weight was stable, her skin was gorgeous—**she** was gorgeous. Honestly, I wouldn't have minded getting with her but there just wasn't that vibe between us, you know?"

I nodded. "Did anyone else notice her swings?"

Beal's eyes slitted. "You need backup for what I'm telling you?"

"Just wondering how obvious it was."

"It wasn't obvious at all. Everything I saw was in passing, it's not like I was stalking her, it was my work ethic. I was always the first to arrive and the last to leave. Ask anyone if I ever needed more than three takes."

"Got it," I said. "Did Zelda ever show signs of mental confusion—hallucinating, talking about unusual theories or ideas?"

"If she saw flying elephants I never heard about it. Who knows what goes on in people's heads, right, Doc? In terms of nutty ideas, hell, yeah. She'd wander in late to the set, claim her plane got held up. But she'd never left town, we'd been taping continually. Then there was the religious shit, lots of that."

"Born again?"

"More like reborn constantly," said Beal. "One week she's a Buddhist, the next she's into Sufism. Then it's kabbalah, she's running her hand over a book to soak up secrets. Then it's boom, back to Jesus, she's wearing a humongous crucifix. It became a joke on the set, who's Zelda's God for the day. Once I asked her about whatever she was into, I forget, and she said she was being guided by an unseen spirit. I said like a guardian angel and she smiled and kissed my cheek and walked away. Like **she'd** seen the light but I could never hope to understand."

He leaned forward. "I just remembered the weirdest thing she did. She told me she'd just learned she **was** God. We were sitting around between takes and she drops that on me. I figure she's kidding, so I made a crack like, 'How bout giving me some stock-market tips, Jehovah?' She just stared at me and turned away and started doing some kind of crazy humming chant.

But maybe all she meant was one of those new-agey things—God lives in all of us."

"Did she ever talk about delusions that weren't religious?"

Beal slapped his forehead. "You know, now that you've got me flashing back, stuff's coming to me. Maybe that wasn't the insanest thing she said, maybe another thing was."

Picking an almond sliver off a croissant, he chewed, swallowed. "I'm not sure I even want to tell you, you might think **I'm** nuts."

I smiled. "Promise: no diagnosis."

"All right, ready for this? She thought she was her own mother."

"That is a new one."

"Even for you, huh? Well, that's reassuring because it totally threw **me**."

"What exactly did she—"

"That her mother was a movie star who'd disappeared when she was a kid and she'd just **re**appeared by inserting herself **into** Zelda. After Zelda had **her** baby. What made it even bizarrer was how calm she was when she said it. Like ordering an omelet. Then she starts poking different parts of her stomach and telling me

'Mommy's hugging and warming me here, here and here and here.'"

"Did she ever mention her mother's name?"

"Nope, just 'Mommy' or maybe 'Mother,' can't remember. Oh, yeah, she also said something about blood and dirt, made these scooping motions with her hands. Like she was digging something up. Not gonna lie, Doc, it weirded me out. After that I kept my distance."

"Did other people on the set avoid her?"

"Hmm...Zelda was never a big socializer. Honestly, I don't know what was in anyone else's head. Like I said, we weren't a close-knit bunch."

"Did her behavior have anything to do with the cancellation?"

"Oh, no, she did a fine job once the tape was rolling. We got dumped because the show was crap and people stopped watching and the network had better prospects. You were her kid's shrink, I assume you knew she had her own shrink. Some older guy, every so often he'd show up on the set, just hang back, not doing much. Zelda never said who he was but everyone knew because that's the way it is on a show. No one thought anything of it, she wouldn't be the first person to bring her therapist to work. Anyway, you should be talking to him."

"Dr. Sherman," I said. "He's the one who referred Zelda's son to me. Unfortunately, he's deceased."

"Oh. Too bad. So I'm last resort, huh?"

"Sometimes peers know things therapists don't, Steve. Did Zelda ever bring her son to work?"

"No, never. Never tried to wangle a part for him, either, far as I know. That's my Mommy Dearest thing kicking in. My old lady never got closer to the industry than being a script girl on commercials, convinced herself I'd be her golden goose. And I was. Not that I ever saw a penny of it."

"The Coogan Act didn't help?"

"The Coogan Act says kids get a guaranteed percentage, but it's small and can also be spent for the kid's benefit, meaning any damn thing the guardian decides. My maternal figure decided a five-year-old needed trips to Hawaii where he'd be left alone in hotel rooms while she partied."

I shook my head.

Beal said, "Don't bother feeling sorry for me, Doc. My life's fantastic." He finished the croissant, pointed. "That one's yours."

"No, thanks."

"A man with willpower. Doesn't life get boring?"

"Any idea where Zelda lived when the show got cut?"

"Nope. Don't the cops know her current address? You might find the boy there, with some caretaker."

I said, "She was a street person."

"Oh," said Beal. "Shit, that's why you're worried about the kid—crazy woman, who knows what she'd be capable of. I'd like to be able to tell you no way, Zelda would never hurt anyone. But I can't, people can't be predicted anyway, let alone psychos."

"Did you know Zelda changed her name?"

"I didn't, but no big shock, everyone reinvents themselves." Teeth flashed. "I was born Stuart Henry Russmeisl."

He reached for his wallet. I got to mine first and put cash on the table. His nod said proper procedure had been followed.

We left the café together and when I headed to the Seville, he said, "Nice wheels, what year?"

" 'Seventy-nine."

"My mom had a '76, painted it pearlescent pink and dyed the vinyl top eggplant. Original engine?"

"Third."

"So you're a loyal guy." He grabbed my hand, shook it. "I hope you find the kid and he's okay."

Wide, sunny grin, spasmodically sudden. "And if you're looking for a nice place in Tarzana..."

CHAPTER 16

Beal's account matched what I already knew: Zelda had displayed symptoms of mood and thought disorder. But he had lent some clarity to her Mommy-talk.

A vanished actress, blood and dirt.

Like she was digging something up.

Had the search for a long-buried mother—a mother whose soul she believed lived inside of her—fueled her incursions into strangers' backyards?

Had she been driven to **excavate**?

There'd been no sign she'd disrupted Enid DePauw's immaculate garden, but sudden death could've gotten in the way.

Had she been clawing earth when discovered on Bel Azura Drive?

Then again, her initial arrest had resulted

from a far more mundane motive: stalking an ex.

And what was the point of applying logic to psychotic behavior? Even if I came up with a "reason" for Zelda's trespassing, what did it matter?

The only worthwhile goal was finding an eleven-year-old boy.

First step: backtrack to Jane Chase. Or whatever her real name had been.

I phoned one of Milo's sources, a clerk at County Records named Linus McCoy always happy to "facilitate data access" in return for a bottle of twenty-one-year-old single malt, a nice Cabernet, or a caviar sampler from Petrossian.

"My fellow gourmet," Milo calls McCoy, though his own bent is for quantity rather than quality.

McCoy answered his office phone sounding sleepy. "Oh, hey, Doc. How's Dirty Harry? Haven't heard from him in a while."

"Detecting as we speak." I gave him my request.

He said, "Sir, that information is public access."

Click.

A minute later, he called back. "Sorry 'bout that, I'm on my cell now."

"Your work phone's monitored?"

"Probably not, but the county's been sending in snotty little MBAs to audit a bunch of agencies and one was passing by my desk. Anyway, you don't need me to look for a name change, formal requests aren't necessary anymore, people can call themselves whatever they want."

"I know that, Linus, but this change would've happened a while back."

"Got it. New name and approximate date of petition."

"Zelda Chase, at least five years ago. I've been told her given name was Jane."

"Back when she was married to Tarzan? Okay, hold on...found it, she petitioned thirteen years ago. Age twenty-two. Zelda Chase née...uh-oh, Doc, you're not going to want to hear this. Original name Jane no middle initial Smith."

Robin and I went to a Vietnamese place for dinner. At eight-forty, fortified by spring rolls, pho, and beer, we were already in bed reading, Blanche curled between us, when Milo called.

"I'm over at the crypt, just watched Zelda's autopsy. Cause and manner of death remain undetermined. But it's interesting."

"Nasty word."

"The nastiest. If you have time, I'd like to come by, run a few things past you. I can be there by ten, no prob if that's too late, we'll connect tomorrow."

I asked Robin if she minded.

She said, "Do I really need to answer that?"

He showed up at ten-fifteen, wearing a soot-gray suit vanquished by smog and sweat. Robin hugged him before returning to the bedroom and her copy of **American Lutherie,** then Blanche assumed leadership of the greeting party, nuzzling his trouser cuffs.

"Hey, there, poochette." He rubbed her head, plopped down on the nearest sofa.

No beeline to the fridge.

I said, "Something to drink?"

He waved that off. "When I said

'interesting' I meant 'oh, shit.' As in I was hoping to clear it quickly but forget that. Not a trace of illegal dope or booze in her system, just remnants of Ativan and the pathologist said it wouldn't have risen to a 'remedial level' let alone killed her. He couldn't tell me if she'd be walking around actively crazy or still suppressed because it's not just a matter of chemistry, he'd need to know her behavioral patterns. So I'm asking you: Think she was raving her way from Santa Monica to Bel Air? Some manic thing that might've caused her heart to whack out? Pathologist says if she popped an arrhythmia, there could be no physical evidence."

He pressed his hands together, prayerfully. "Please don't go all academic on me and say anything's possible."

I said, "Lou Sherman's original guess was she was a mixture of bipolar and schizophrenia and nothing I've seen or heard contradicts that. When I saw her she was either asleep or lethargic, but something drove her to leave the shelter and trek ten miles, probably on foot. So if I had to bet, I'd say a manic state was more likely than depressed. I talked to one of her co-actors, a guy named Stevenson Beal, and he described extreme and rapid mood shifts back when she was working."

"The gay fireman."

"You watched the show?"

"God forbid. I remember Rick working himself up about the character, last thing we needed was another lavender Stepin Fetchit. Beal have anything else to say?"

I described Zelda's God and mother delusions, my wondering about psychotic archaeology.

He said, "Digging for Mommy in other people's gardens? Interesting—and now I mean that literally. What if, in the process of getting down and dirty, she ate something toxic?"

"The pathologist found evidence of poisoning?"

"More like question marks, Alex. Her liver and intestinal tract were a mess. Given her lifestyle, his first thought was advanced hepatitis. But that didn't pan out and her tox screen came back negative. No carbon monoxide, either. I asked him—Bill Bernstein, he's a senior guy—why look for that, she wasn't cherry red and she died outdoors. He said I hadn't established where she died, only where she'd been found. I said there were no drag marks. He said that didn't impress him and besides, there are cases of people on boats dying from CO when they get too close to the exhaust, he's thorough, do I have a problem with that? At that point I bowed and scraped and shut my mouth. Then he took a closer look at her guts and found no discrete lesions or obstruction and that bothered him, considering the ravaged state of the tissue. He sent out tissue samples for further analysis. Problem with the advanced panels is if you don't know what you're looking for and the culprit isn't on the list, you're screwed."

"Bernstein have any hunches?"

"He's guessing some sort of alkaloid but that's as far as he'll go. If the tests come back negative, the case will remain open and we may never know the truth."

I said, "If she was a digger, she might've ingested some sort of mold or spore—anything that could live in soil."

"You see any evidence she mucked

around in Mrs. DePauw's flower beds? I didn't, that place was **Home and Garden** on steroids."

"If she plucked a random toadstool, there wouldn't be any mucking. And now I'm wondering if we could be dealing with pica—eating nonnutritive material like glass, plaster, and dirt. Psychotics exhibit a high rate of it. Did she dig at the house on Bel Azura?"

He pinched his nose. "Don't know, never read the file. If she did chomp the shrubs up there, it didn't hurt her."

"Maybe that was the problem," I said. "She'd gotten away with it before. Then she didn't. Also, pica isn't inconsistent with her former profession. Body image and food issues go with that territory."

"Actress with an eating disorder, big shock." He got up and paced, returned to the sofa but stayed on his feet. "Thanks for the hospitality and sorry for putting a damper on your evening." To Blanche: "That means you, too."

She followed him to the door.

I told him about my call to Linus McCoy.

He said, "Good old Linus. Jane Smith,

huh? It's like a bad joke."

"Any new thoughts on finding Ovid?"

"Sorry, insight deficit. Let me sleep on it."

"Could you help me locate other people from the show? Conventional methods haven't worked."

"I'm being asked to engage in extra-legal intrusion into the personal data of law-abiding citizens? Tsk." He opened the door. "Sure, why not tomorrow? My eyes are crossing."

He peered toward the kitchen.

"You wouldn't happen to have any edible scraps lying around? All the talk of poison has gotten me famished."

CHAPTER 17

True to his word, Milo phoned at ten a.m.

"Snagged you some info on the **SubUrban** folk. Got a pen handy?"

"I never gave you the cast list."

"Golly gosh, I discovered something new called the Internet. Ready? The producers you already know. By the way, they're married to each other. The guy who played the dad died last year, lung disease. The two Nigerians haven't paid taxes in the U.S. since the show got canceled and turns out they're not Nigerians, they're from Ghana. One of them, Robert Adjaho, runs The New Ashanti Theatre of Drama and Dance in London, here are his factoids."

I copied.

"The Nigerian wife, Diana Humado, I

couldn't locate. Justin Lemarque, the kid who played the son, is a freshman at Brown. His real name is Justin Levine, only address I've got is the school. The sister, Shay McNamara, is actually named Shay McNamara. She lives in Asheville, North Carolina, and does P.R. for that humongous estate they've got there, Biltmore. No news on the dog or the fish, here's McNamara's office number."

I thanked him.

He said, "This level of achievement, I'm sending Doritos to myself."

Six-twenty p.m. in London gave me a shot at reaching Robert Adjaho. But all I got at the New Ashanti Theatre was voicemail instruction on how to buy tickets. Next performance: **Revisiting Othello,** opening in three months.

Shay McNamara's number at Biltmore's corporate office was answered by a woman named Andrea. "She's away from her desk, sir. Can I be of assistance?"

"I'm calling about someone Ms. McNamara used to work with named Zelda Chase."

"Could you spell that, please, sir?"

Ah, fame. "She was an actress, like Shay."

"I'll let Shay know, sir. Have a nice day!"

I gave the producers, Hinson and/or Strickland, a second try. This time, I barely got past my name when the woman on the other end said, "I'm so glad I caught you."

"Pardon?"

"Doctor, this is Karen Anne Jackson, you knew me as Karen Gallardo."

"Ovid's babysitter. Hi."

"More like a P.A. grunt, back then. My secretary told me you'd called about Zelda and I was going to get back to you but it got pretty hectic. Is it a health insurance matter? Because her policy's long-lapsed. I wish we didn't have to be so corporate but after all this time, it's impossible to give her coverage."

"This has nothing to do with insurance, Karen. Zelda died two days ago."

"No! Oh, my God, that's terrible. Was she ill?"

"Quite."

"Did she...was it suicide?"

Same thing Steve Beal had asked. "Cause of death hasn't been established yet."

"Oh, wow. How's Ovid taking it?"

"It's Ovid I'm calling about. Zelda's been living on the streets but no one's seen Ovid for a while."

"And you thought Joel and Greer might know? I'm sure they don't, Dr. Delaware, they're my bosses and almost everything gets filtered through me and there's been no contact between the company and Zelda since **Sub** stopped taping. You're really worried something's happened to Ovie?"

"I'd feel better if I knew where he was."

"Now I feel horrible about not getting back to you sooner. I just didn't want to be the one to deliver bad news about the coverage. But this is so much worse."

"Would you have time today to talk in person?"

"I don't know what I could tell you."

"Your impressions of Zelda—that question you asked about suicide, for example."

"All I meant was, it was pretty obvious Zelda had issues. I really don't see that I can help, but sure, the idea of Ovie out there upsets me. He was a good kid, now that I have one of my own I appreciate how smart he was. His attention span, those fantastic things he built. I've got a meeting in a few minutes, should last until noon. And then two more from three p.m. on—I guess I could squeeze lunch in, say one-thirty? If we stay close to the office."

"You name it."

"There's a place on Washington near Motor, Brasserie Mosca."

"See you at one-thirty."

"It's the least I can do," said Karen Jackson. "God, I hope he's okay."

The years that had been so cruel to Zelda Chase had smiled kindly on Karen Gallardo Jackson.

The pallid, anxious minion I'd encountered in the rented house above the Chateau Marmont strode into the restaurant with the bounce of a woman who'd earned her self-confidence.

Thinner but far from thin, she wore a tailored brown suede jacket, a peacock-blue silk shirt, and tweed slacks that made the most of her figure. Burnt-orange lizard-skin boots gave her some height. A brown handbag swayed rhythmically as she walked.

Hair once abused to bristly flat black had grown out to a soft, rusty brown, styled in a layered, jaw-length cut that managed to project competence and softness. Her ring finger bore a platinum band set with a sizable ruby. Matching studs twinkled in each ear. No evidence, not even a pin-hole, of the steel array that had once crowded the lobes.

We shook hands and she sat down and ordered a chopped salad and iced tea. I asked for the Italian steak sandwich, medium rare, and water.

She said, "You haven't changed much."

I risked saying, "You have." Her smile said Good Bet.

"That was the plan, Dr. Delaware. I sure needed help."

"What do you do for Hyson and Strickland?"

Out of the bag came a brown leather card case. She slid the top card to me.

Vice President for Management.

"Basically, I gatekeep. Joel and Greer are constantly being hit on. Unsolicited scripts, requests for meetings, investment schemes. You develop a sense of who to let through, try not to offend those you block."

"How'd you go from P.A.'ing to that?"

"I sensed the show would be canceled and literally begged for them to keep me on. I told them I'd do anything and they took me up on it. Had me cleaning the offices at night. That freed up my days so I went back and finished my B.A., then I added postbac courses in management. I guess that impressed them because they started giving me more responsibility."

She smiled. "Greer also gave me some grooming tips. One thing led to another, and here I am."

"How'd you know the show would be canceled? What I read said it was a surprise."

"Where'd you read it? On some website? All that's nonsense, Doctor. Everyone knew. It was clear our numbers weren't good enough and the network was bored with us."

The food came. She picked. "I'm still unclear about how Zelda died."

"So am I. She was found on a stranger's

property with no obvious external wounds."

"A stranger? That sounds like her arrest— breaking into her boyfriend's."

"Apparently it became a pattern, Karen. She was arrested for trespassing a few days before she died."

"Out on the street," she said. "I guess anything can happen out there. How long's she been that way?"

"I was hoping you could tell me. Starting with what happened to her after the cancellation."

"Sorry, I can't."

"What about the problems you mentioned? What you thought could lead to suicide."

"Nothing specific regarding suicide," said Karen Jackson. "I just remember being told she was odd. By everyone on the set. When she came home to live with Ovie again, she didn't say a word to me. No thanks, no questions about how he was doing. She just unpacked her bags as if she clearly expected me to leave. So I did."

"We haven't been able to locate any family members. Are you aware of any?"

"Sorry, no. Have you spoken to anyone

from the show?"

"Steve Beal. He recalls her having strong mood swings."

"Steve," she said. "How's he doing?"

"Selling real estate."

"Yes, that would fit—he considered himself quite the salesman, especially when it came to selling himself. After **Sub** died, he kept hectoring Joel and Greer about casting him in another series."

She shook her head. "Worst approach, the hungrier you are, the faster people run from you. I'm glad Steve found another outlet."

"When you were watching Ovid, did he mention family?"

"Never. Let me ask you something: Zelda's mental illness, **is** there a serious chance she could've hurt him?"

"There's no evidence of that."

"But it's possible."

"Anything's possible, Karen."

"Well, I'm going to help you. First thing when I get back, I'll talk to Joel and Greer."

"Appreciate it. What about the other actors? Did any of them have a relationship with Zelda?"

"You mean romantic?"

"Romantic, platonic. I'm looking for anyone she'd confide in."

"There was no one I saw. She was a loner and the show was run pretty business-like, not much socializing. Dr. Delaware, is there a chance Ovie got sick, too? Mentally, I mean. Genetics being what it is?"

"Again, anything's possible," I said. "But like you said, he was a pretty together five-year-old."

Giving her a pat answer. But genetics **could** be a factor. And while some schizophrenics showed early signs of being odd, others didn't.

Reassurance was what Karen Jackson had been after. "I bet he's doing great. Wherever he is."

"Karen, I can use your help finding the rest of the cast." I told her about my calls to London and North Carolina, asked if talking to Justin Levine would be useful.

She said, "Justin was a kid himself. Mostly he tried to skateboard everywhere. He made it to Brown? Never knew he had the smarts. Robert was a nice guy,

soft-spoken, he and Diana stuck together—
they were an item off camera, too. Shay
was well behaved, just like her character,
and I never saw her hang with Zelda, but
you could try. If she knew something, I'm
sure she'd tell you."

"What about other people on the set?
Writers, camera staff?"

"That would be a huge list, Doctor, you
have no idea how many people it takes to
churn—" World-weary smile. "To create.
But, again, I'd doubt any of them would
know much. On some shows there's a lot
of interaction between the writers and the
actors, constant rewriting. **SNL**'s like that.
Joel and Greer don't work that way. You
get the script with ample time to get familiar
with it, study your lines, and deliver them."

I said, "Keeping the herd under control."

"Pardon?"

"Alfred Hitchcock's approach. He said,
'Actors should be treated like cattle.'"

"Did he?" said Karen Jackson. "Well, he
created some pretty great stuff."

I quizzed her a bit more, paid for lunch
despite what sounded like sincere

objections, and walked her to her Lexus SUV.

She said, "First thing when they're available, I'll talk to the bosses."

I believed her. Nice to have something to believe in.

CHAPTER 18

As I walked in my front door, my mobile chirped. True to her word, Karen Jackson.

I said, "That was quick."

"But unfortunately not too helpful, Dr. Delaware. Joel and Greer have no inkling about Zelda's personal life. Greer did say that Zelda being 'different' was the reason she cast her as Corinna."

"Corinna was an especially eccentric character?"

"Considering the type of show it was? No, not really. Corinna was basically a slut with a low I.Q. Greer's point was that Zelda had a talent for getting weird on demand, probably because she was odd in the first place. So they decided to capitalize on that. I know it sounds exploitative, but that's the way it is, Dr. Delaware. Like you said, cattle."

"Appreciate your trying, Karen."

"One more thing, I couldn't find Zelda's contract but I did come across her health insurance application and on it she listed her agent as Stan Guest. I've never heard of him and he doesn't come up in any of our records, so he may no longer be in the industry. Greer didn't remember him at all and Joel has a vague memory of his being 'a minor-league old guy.' But maybe you can locate him and he'll be able to tell you something."

"Again, Karen, thanks."

"One **more** thing, talk about a warning sign," she said. "The form asks for family members and Zelda listed 'father of my only son.' She put down his name as Joseph Bethlehem, living at her address. I searched, just in case, but of course it wasn't real. Guess she saw herself as the Virgin Mary."

And eventually, God.

"She was so ill, Doctor. Nobody noticed."

Twenty-three **Stan** or **Stanley Guest**s

floating in cyberspace. Of the three in California, Stanley Z., seventy-one, at a Northridge address kicked out by a real estate site, seemed the most likely. Number listed in the directory; maybe he was still trolling for business.

The man who picked up said, "Guest residence, Jamal."

"Mr. Guest, please."

"What about?"

"This is Dr. Alex Delaware. I'm looking for a Stan Guest who represented a patient. Was Mr. Guest once a TV agent?"

A beat. "Yeah, so?"

"The patient just passed away and—"

"**Sir.** Stan can't tell you anything, he's got Alzheimer's end stage."

"Sorry to hear that. Are there family members I could talk to?"

"The guy who was his partner bailed after the first six months."

"And you—"

"I'm a home-hospice worker."

"So Mr. Guest is nonverbal."

"**Sir.** He's non-**everything**."

Joseph Bethlehem.

Lou Sherman had missed the extent of Zelda's disease and I'd returned a five-year-old to her custody.

Don Quixote whispered in my ear: "Give it up, fool. You're only going to feel worse."

I called in for messages. Two from lawyers, whose questions I took care of quickly. Saving the best for last: Milo, a few minutes ago.

He said, "There's someone you'll want to meet. Can you be in Culver City in, say, thirty?"

"I was just there." I started to summarize the talk with Karen Jackson.

He said, "This might be worth a return trip."

Dr. William Bernstein, senior pathologist at the crypt, was midfifties, built strong and blocky, with a wide pug-nosed face crowned by kinky gray-blond hair. Square steel-rimmed bifocals were a bad cosmetic choice but they did the job, magnifying pale-blue eyes that remained skeptical when at rest.

He sat at a sidewalk table in front of a gourmet sandwich shop named Lauren's.

Four blocks east of where I'd met Karen Jackson.

Lauren was Bernstein's wife, a pretty brunette twenty years his junior. She owned the place and worked the counter with a young Latin guy. Bernstein was here because her car was in the shop and he'd quit work early to drive her home.

"Wild Bill beckons, you obey," Milo had explained. "He's got no patience for bull-shit or anything else."

Bernstein acknowledged both of us with what would've been a minimal nod if he were in the mood to burn calories. A tall beer and a pressed sandwich sat in front of him. Impressive creation, the sandwich, a twelve-inch roll teeming with meat and cheese, pickles and peppers. Half eaten, but Bernstein hadn't unfolded his napkin. His black suit, white shirt, and red tie were spotless.

He looked at me and said, "The psychologist," turned to Milo and said, "You."

Milo eyed the sandwich. "Cuban?"

"Cuban expatriate, it started as a Florida thing, feeding the cigar rollers.

She's taken it to a new level, this is her upgrade of **mixto,** veal instead of ham, sliced sweetbreads instead of tongue. Fifteen bucks. Buy one, it's worth it."

Milo said, "Sure," and went to comply.

Bernstein cocked an eyebrow at me.

I said, "Just had lunch."

"Your loss." He got up, told the counter-boy something, returned, took two surgical bites, and said, "She's a genius."

Seconds after Milo's return, the counter-boy hurried over with his sandwich, glancing nervously at Bernstein. Bernstein ignored him, Milo said, "Thanks," and the kid scurried off.

"New hire," said the pathologist. "We'll see." To Milo: "Eat."

Wild Bill commands, you ingest.

As Milo got to work chomping, Bernstein finished his food and his beer, flicked the napkin open the way a magician unfurls a silk handkerchief, and set about dabbing his mouth for no apparent purpose.

Milo put down his sandwich.

"Don't stop on my account," said Bernstein. "Knowing you, you'll probably want another." His smile was stingy, knowing, sour. "No discounts for bulk purchase. Heh."

Refolding the napkin into a square as equilateral as his glasses, he said, "Colchicine. Get your pad out, I'll spell it for you."

CHAPTER 19

As Milo copied, the counter-boy came over. "Is everything—"

Bill Bernstein waved him away. "Just as I thought, an alkali, plant-based, extracted from meadow saffron. It shows up in herbal medicines, can also be used for gout and other inflammation, but if my toes hurt, I'd sure as hell take something else. Victim Chase didn't look like a candidate for gout but you never know, so I checked. Negative. Do you have any knowledge of her self-administering herbals?"

Milo turned to me.

I said, "With her mental status, anything's possible."

Bernstein said, "Talk about a politician's

answer."

"I was wondering about pica. She had a history of trespassing in strangers' yards so she could've eaten something in the garden."

"You know her to have a history?"

"No, but if she ate dirt—"

"Irrelevant, colchicine's not in dirt, she'd have to eat the plant. It happens: Back-to-nature morons spot something that looks like a yummy onion, go home and stir-fry it with tofu or organic dandelions or whatever." He ran a finger across his throat. "You can landscape with the darn thing, it's also called autumn crocus, has a flower if you're into flowers. Like oleander—a killer. But they still use it for hedges. All sorts of nasty stuff looks nice."

Milo said, "There were flower beds but I have no idea if saffron was included."

"Not saffron, that's an edible spice, from a different type of crocus. Meadow saffron. Col-chi-cine, write it down."

"I already have."

"Then go ask the owner if she's growing it and if she doesn't know, look up a picture of the darn thing and go see for yourself."

"Will do," said Milo. "Though there was no sign of disturbance in the garden."

"My C.I. told me it's a huge backyard."

"More like an estate."

"My point," said Bernstein. "You're telling me you covered every inch?"

Silence.

"That's what I thought," said Bernstein. "Well, my job's done. Cause of death is colchicine poisoning, whether manner is suicide or an accident is likely to remain undetermined unless you do your job and produce evidence."

The door to the restaurant opened and Lauren Bernstein danced out, lively, light-footed, smiling. "Hi, guys." She kissed the top of her husband's head and rested a hand on his shoulder.

He said, "Lieutenant Sturgis is going to have another sandwich."

Her eyes widened.

So did Milo's. He said, "First one was great, I'll doggie-bag and have something for later."

"Everyone blames gluttony on their dogs," said Bernstein. "Easy targets, they're stupid and can't talk back."

"Oh, honey," said Lauren. "Sure, Lieutenant, coming up."

Bernstein watched her walk away, muttering "Love her," as if pressured to admit it. Removing his glasses, he said, "Here's something else to chew on, pun intended: Victim Chase's time of death is between two and six hours before the body was discovered. If she ingested a heavy dose, death could've been relatively quick, as in within that time frame. But it can also be a drawn-out process. Nausea, vomiting, diarrhea that can go on for days and then your organ systems fail. Basically, you fall apart, it's an unpleasant death, that's why she had that rictus on her face. In her case, the process could've sped up because apart from the candy bar, which was incompletely digested, her stomach was empty. But, still, a homeless psychotic thrashing around in your backyard, you'd think the homeowner would notice."

"The homeowner was away, in the desert."

"Working on a melanoma?" said Bernstein. "Okay, so much for that. Anyway, this wasn't easy for Victim Chase but she probably did it to herself, wittingly or otherwise. FDA can't get it together to regulate herbals, all kinds of garbage finds its way in. I had a poisoned DB turn up near the court building on Hill and Washington. You know the one, spillover from downtown, not a decent restaurant in sight."

Milo said, "Mostly warehouses."

Bernstein said, "Whoever put a court there is a moron. One time I thought of taking a walk, waiting to be called to testify. Idiot gang types lolling around, so much for exercise. Anyone, someone thought it would be a great idea to dump a body there after hours. COD turned out to be a toxic alkaloid, which is what got me thinking about Victim Chase."

Milo said, "The same poi—"

"Did I say that? Totally different poison. Last one before that, couple years ago, I had a fourteen-year-old girl, stupid parents pay a fortune for private school tuition and go buy her a headache remedy from a moron on Venice Beach. Turns out that particular shipment contained arsenic way above what was needed to kill their kid."

He shook his head. "Maybe they have a dog to blame it on."

We left Bernstein standing next to his wife, looking awestruck as she whispered in his ear.

Milo said, "One of a kind."

I said, "Patients who don't talk back, he can get away with it."

He chuckled, turned serious. "What he said about her suffering. That was hard to hear."

Fools write books about madness being an elevated mental state or an alternative form of creativity. It's not, it's anguish.

I said nothing and we walked to our cars.

Milo placed the second sandwich on the passenger seat. "Guess there's nothing much more to do but concentrate on the kid. Should you choose."

"I choose."

"Big surprise."

Back home I was surprised to learn that Shay McNamara had returned my call from Asheville and Robert Adjaho had phoned from London. Late, across the pond. I tried Adjaho first.

This time a man answered at the Ashanti Theatre, a voice recalling Olivier on a particularly good day.

"Doctor, this is Robert. I'm sorry to hear about Zelda, though I don't see how I can help you. Was it suicide?"

Same question, over and over. Everyone had known.

I said, "Most likely she died accidentally."

"From what?"

"Poison."

"Not self-administered?"

"It looks as if she ate the wrong plant."

"I see. Actually, I don't."

"She'd been mentally ill for a while, Mr. Adhajo. Ended up swallowing something she shouldn't have."

"Yes...the reason I mentioned suicide was back when we worked together she seemed extremely troubled. My father's a psychologist. Don't want to presume, but perhaps I picked up some knowledge."

"What troubles did you observe in Zelda?"

"For starts, her fluctuating activity levels. What seemed to be hyperactivity alternating with fatigue. I'd heard my father talk about bipolar disorder—he called it manic depression—and to my layman's eyes that seemed to fit Zelda. There were also instances where she appeared confused—in a daze. My wife and I—she was also on the show—wondered about drugs. We never saw Zelda indulge but something was clearly amiss."

"Were people on the show talking about it?"

"If they were, Diana and I never heard it. We kept to ourselves—young love and all that. Looking back, we were pretty obnoxious about it."

"So no rumors."

"None that I heard. Zelda may have been odd but she never failed to do her job and that's all that matters when you're taping under pressure. Now I have to ask: Why would a psychologist be phoning from halfway across the globe to discuss a deceased person?"

"I'm looking for Ovid."

"Who's that?"

"Zelda's son." I gave him background.

"I understand your concern but I'm afraid

I can't help you, Doctor. I was aware Zelda had a child, though I can't pinpoint how I knew. I never actually saw the boy."

"She didn't bring him to work?"

"She may have. But not that I observed."

"Are you aware of other family members?"

"I did notice an older man who came with Zelda a few times. Old enough to be her father but with no obvious resemblance to Zelda, he looked somewhat Asian."

"Smallish, white hair?"

"That's the one."

"That was her psychiatrist."

"I see. So someone **was** aware of her problems. But to no avail, ay? Father always said when it came to severe mental illness one couldn't rely on happy endings. He came to find his profession dreary, ended up switching to an administrative position with the National Health. Have you reached anyone else from the show? Perhaps someone knows more than I do."

"I've talked to Steve Beal and Karen Jackson. His description of Zelda's behavior is similar to yours."

"Don't know her," said Adjaho. "But Steve, I certainly recall. How's he doing?"

"He works in real estate."

"Selling or developing?"

"Selling."

"I can see that. Good for Steve. And good luck to you."

Shay McNamara said, "Omigod, Zelda? That's horrible, what happened?"

I replowed old ground, anticipated her next question and told her I was looking for Ovid.

She said, "Sure I remember him. She didn't bring him often but he was a cutie. You don't think Zelda would hurt him or anything? Because of her...situation? I mean I never saw anything like that, she seemed like a good mom."

"When I evaluated Ovid, she was. What do you recall about him?"

"Not much, he was a quiet little kid, stayed by himself building with blocks. Zelda would come over and smile at him or give him a little kiss. She really seemed loving, Dr. Delaware."

"What you said about her 'situation' . . . "

"Well, obviously from what happened she had psychological issues," said Shay

McNamara.

"What about when you worked with her?"

"She could get a little hyper—no, I take that back. **Real** hyper. I was a minor myself and my mom would come on the set—she homeschooled me—and she'd watch Zelda and shake her head and say stuff like, 'That girl is all over the place.' I didn't think much of it, not messing up my lines was all I cared about. I don't miss it. Way too much pressure."

Justin Levine's life was a short story on Facebook. The usual friends, party photos, detailed lists of favorite music and movies. He'd grown to be a nice-looking young man who favored baseball hats worn backward. The photos featured him with like-minded males and pretty females, the dominant mood glaze-eyed intoxication. Physics major, interests in rugby, lacrosse, skiing, skateboarding. No mention of his acting days.

I posted a message, asking him to get in contact about Zelda Chase.

Sometimes clearing a path for discovery

means eliminating the detours. But my only remaining route to finding Ovid seemed likely to dead-end because it was based on crazy-talk: Zelda's tale of a disappearing "movie star" mother.

Who happened also to be a deity, burrowed deeply inside her daughter's viscera.

Tempting to dismiss but I wasn't ready.

Maybe I was denying but my training had taught me that madmen and madwomen weren't the cage-rattling ravers depicted in low-rent movies and books. That the transition to psychosis could be subtle, more segue than quick flick of the on/off sanity switch.

I'd also discovered that truth could be embedded in the jumble of skewed perception, illogic, and decimated judgment that plagues a disintegrating mind.

More than that: Truth and logic could serve as **springboards** for psychosis.

On any back ward, you could encounter an apparently rational human being in a cell-like room and wonder what the hell they were doing there. Sit down with that person, begin chatting about a topic—say geography—and your skepticism grows. This is a perfectly **normal** human being clearly oppressed by the system!

But as you sit there, outraged, the cerebral short-circuits kick in and the conversation edges off kilter and finally veers into fantasies that grow progressively more florid and bizarre and now you're hearing about a planet grown flat and overrun with godlings who transmit evil messages straight to the sensors implanted in your co-conversationalist's head.

Does that matter clinically? Often not, but sometimes yes. Because crazy people are still individuals and learning what's on their troubled minds can occasionally elevate treatment beyond dosage-calibration.

What if Zelda's mother really had disappeared and tracing family ties could somehow lead me to Ovid? Because the few facts I had did fit early abandonment: a young woman with no known relatives.

On the other hand...

Only one way to find out.

Vanished actress pulled up a host of fan sites and blogs about women who no longer worked in movies or TV. The reasons for "vanishing" ranged from a series of flops to marriage and motherhood to motives unknown.

Not a promising start but scrolling through pages finally led me to two actresses who actually had disappeared. Both in L.A.

The first, a woman named Jean Spangler, had played small roles in big pictures, dated several organized crime figures, and been embroiled in a custody dispute with an ex-husband.

Provocative, but the time frame was off: She'd gone missing in 1949.

Zina Rutherford, on the other hand, had walked out of her West Hollywood apartment and slipped into the ether twenty-nine years ago, shortly after her thirtieth birthday.

Zelda would've been five. Old enough to remember.

Zina/Zelda.

I'd wondered if Jane Smith's name change had stemmed from identification with another tormented young woman, the unfortunate Mrs. Fitzgerald. But what if it had been an attempt to get phonetically closer to her mother?

She'd listed her given name as Jane **Smith,** not Jane **Rutherford.** But that could be explained by adoption. Or a five-year-old girl taken in by a relative.

I looked for everything I could find about Zina Rutherford, which turned out to be nothing but the same sketchy summary on four sites listing unsolved disappearances. No leads, no theories, description of Rutherford as an "aspiring actress."

I clicked every **contact us** icon, was rewarded with an instant quartet of out-of-service error messages.

Searching movie databases produced no credits for Rutherford, so aspiring was as far as she'd gotten. Galaxies from the "star" Zelda had claimed. Yet more delusion or pathetic wishful thinking? Or she'd made up the whole thing and had no connection to another actress, alive or dead?

One more try: Hollywood might've ignored Zina Rutherford but LAPD could've paid attention.

Milo picked up after one ring. "Just about to call you on a couple of things, guess you're my psychic friend, here's my credit card number."

"What's up?"

"No nasty flora in Enid DePauw's garden. She wasn't sure but she referred me to her landscape architect. Apparently, the estate's one of the landscaper's crowning accomplishments, 'classical but updated emphasis' on roses, azaleas, local sustainable fruit trees and ornamentals, blah blah blah. So herbal medicine is the probable culprit, like Bernstein figured, Zelda got her hands on the wrong batch of whatever. A couple of days and ten miles passed between her leaving the shelter and dying, plenty of opportunity to dumpster-dive for the wrong veggie."

I said, "I suppose she could've scored herbal meds at the shelter."

"That, too."

"I'll let Andover know. No sense someone else keeling over."

He said, "Good deed for the day? Why not, we can all use cosmic brownie points. The other thing I wanted to tell you is I heard from a Central patrolman, older guy works the desk, used to be on the streets. He remembers Zelda, confirms she was a street person. I checked the time period. Around half a year after her show got canceled, so she slid down pretty fast. He was the arresting officer on the second bust, said there were plenty of other times he could've hauled her in but he felt sorry for her, being so young and so messed up. He had no idea she'd been an actress, was pretty sure she was hooking to make ends meet, though he never caught her at it. She didn't have a particular turf, hung out in that patch of Skid Row near Little Tokyo, flops, shelters, freeway underpasses. The main thing from your perspective is he never saw a kid with her and I'm going to take that as a good sign: She knew she was falling apart and made provisions. Because some **psychology** savant once told me positive thinking's good for my health. Now why'd you call **me**?"

My mind reeled. I focused and told him.

He said, "Zina Rutherford, never heard about that one. If it was filed as a missing person twenty-five years ago, good luck. During the transfer from paper to computer a lot of stuff got tossed."

"Could you look into it anyway? Positive thinking and all?"

He laughed. "Sure, now go get positive yourself."

"Meaning?"

"Talk about role reversal," he said. "Meaning kiss your gal. Poochie, too. Who I thought of while enjoying that second Cuban sandwich from my doggie bag. Because Mademoiselle Flatface likes veal, right? I have a distinct memory of some scaloppine noshed on the sly."

"Save her any?"

"Hell, no. There's nostalgia and there's reality."

CHAPTER 20

Just as I was leaving my office, my phone pinged an incoming text.

justincabbalerial@brown.edu
inquiring: what about zelda

Unfortunately, she passed away.

no way! u her friend?

Psychologist. Can we talk?
I can call you.

here's the number.

Seconds later, I was giving the details to a soft-spoken young man.

He said, "That's unbelievably tragic. Zelda was a beautiful person."

"You knew her well?"

"Not really but she was one of the few people on the set who treated me like a human being. Which I didn't deserve, I was an utter pain in the ass, never wanted to act in the first place. My parents were kid actors, neither made it beyond commercials so they tried to live through me. When the show ended I stood up for myself and began taking my studies seriously."

"Interesting rebellion."

He laughed. "They still have their fantasy that I'm going to be Leonardo and buy them a mansion. Unfortunately for them, I'm a theoretical physics major. Anyway, Zelda was a cool person, said nice things when I came roaring through pulling ollies—flipping my board no-hands. Basically being a show-off dick. It drove everyone else up the wall but she seemed to enjoy it. She went psychotic, huh? I suppose I can see that."

"You noticed signs."

"I mean she had problems. Though I

never observed anything extreme. Sometimes she'd get really hyper and go off on crazy shit about God or Jesus. But that's actors, they're always vulnerable to nonintellectual stuff. I grew up with that, learned to tune it out and tuned Zelda out. To me, she was a hot older chick who didn't ignore me. That's kind of perfect when you're fifteen."

"Did you ever meet Ovid, her son?"

"She brought him once in a while, he'd just sit and play by himself, I really wasn't paying attention. Why?"

"We can't locate him."

"Maybe he's with his dad."

"Who's that?"

"The only man I ever saw her with was an older dude, he'd come onto the set, have discussions with her, seemed pretty intense."

"Short, white-haired, kind of Asian-looking?"

"That's him."

"Her psychiatrist."

"Oh really," said Justin Levine. "I heard she had a shrink. That would explain intense discussions."

At eight p.m. Milo called. "I keep amassing good deeds, got something for you on Zina Rutherford. Not LAPD, Sheriff's, she lived in West Hollywood. One of the old-timers remembered the detective who worked it, guy named Otis Ott the Second, they call him Double O. I left a message for him, asking if he'd talk to you. Just got his email: 'Yeah, why not.' Here's his info."

"Big Guy, I really appreciate it."

"That's why I did it."

CHAPTER 21

I called Detective Otis Ott II (ret.).

"This is Dub. You the psychologist?"

"Alex Delaware."

"Zina Rutherford, blast from the past," said Ott. "Never heard of any daughter so there's probably nothing I can do for you."

"Could we talk anyway?"

"You want to take me out to lunch tomorrow?"

Third case-related meal I'd had in as many days. I said, "Where?"

"How about Spago?" He laughed. "Nah, there's a deli, Pico near Robertson. Say, eleven-thirty? That way I'll be ready for an early dinner."

Otis Ott got there before me, had taken a

booth that gave him a full view of the deli's front door. Classic detective move.

A trim, light-skinned black man in his sixties, he had alert hazel eyes and a wide mouth that didn't budge much when he greeted me and said, "I'm Dub."

Like a well-trained ventriloquist. Perfect for intimidating suspects. He wore a charcoal cashmere sweater over a white polo shirt. Coffee in front of him. The deli was half full, mostly older people drinking soup and young mothers trying to eat anything while tending to toddlers.

He said, "I don't need a menu but you do."

"Pastrami sounds fine."

"Twenty years ago it sounded fine for me, too. Now it's turkey breast. At least here it doesn't taste like cardboard."

A Latina waitress came over, smiling warmly. Dub Ott said, "Hola, Elizabeth, usual for me, pastrami for the young guy."

"Oh, you're young, Dub."

"Compared to King Tut. What're you drinking, Doctor?"

"Cream soda."

"There you go, keeping to a theme," said

Ott. "We're doing the ensemble dining thing, Elizabeth."

She laughed and left.

Ott pushed his coffee mug to the side and favored me with a sharp-eyed scrutiny. "Doctor, explain why you care about Zina Rutherford."

My recap took a while. Ott listened without interruption—another virtue for an investigator. When I finished, he said, "Mental illness, huh? That's interesting, from what I was told, Zina also had some problems. But like I said, no daughter came to light. No kin in L.A., period. The one who reported her missing was a brother from Cleveland."

"Do you recall his name?"

"Something Smith—John, Jim, Joe. Maybe Bob, something common, sorry, it's been a while and I only had phone conversations with the guy." He reached down, produced a soft leather case, and drew out a fuzzy photo.

Faded photocopy of an enlarged driver's license. Zina Rutherford had been a pretty woman. But even accounting for the insult inflicted by DMV cameras, nothing like the beauty Zelda had once been. The license had been issued the day after Rutherford's twenty-eighth birthday, which was two years prior to her disappearance. Thirty isn't old, but in Hollywood, it's way past "aspiring."

I said, "Can I keep this?"

"It's your copy," said Ott. "The original's all I held on to—for the flyer I put out. Any resemblance to your Zelda?"

"Nothing striking."

"Too bad, I was hoping for a eureka moment. Not that it would matter, Zina's never going to be closed. The case was a bastard. For all I know she's living in Pakistan or Poland or Belgium. On the other hand, she could be buried in some landfill."

He pinged his coffee cup. "Missing person's different from other investigations because you don't even know if a crime's been committed. So you start way behind. On the other hand, unlike your pal Sturgis, I got to deliver good news to families more often than you might think. My wife's a nurse, she says I was doing the obstetrics of police work."

The food arrived. Ott grimaced and said, "Healthy," and lifted half a turkey sandwich. He nibbled a corner, put it down.

I said, "What kind of emotional problems did Zina have?"

"Her landlady thought she was weird. The brother never spelled it out but I got the feeling she'd always been the problem child. She was the youngest of a bunch of sibs. He sounded pretty conservative."

"The family didn't approve of her acting?"

"More like they didn't approve of her wanting to. Only evidence I found of acting was a couple commercials she did years before, just background, no lines. I suppose if she'd made it, the family might've changed their tune. Fame trumps everything. I contacted the Screen Actors Guild and they had nothing on her. Only reason she got called an 'actress' in the paper was because that's what I said to get the story run. The alternative wasn't suitable for family reading."

I said, "She hooked?"

"Maybe…the info came via her landlady."

"The same one convinced Zina was weird."

"Nasty old crone," said Ott. "But maybe she was on to something. She said she'd try to say something to Zina and get a blank look, like Zina was off in another world. She also suspected drugs but none showed up when I searched Zina's apartment. There **were** a lot of liquor bottles, which supports the landlady's claim that Zina would bring home guys when she was stone-drunk."

"That's the evidence of prostitution?"

Ott nodded. His expression was pained, as if reluctant to admit the possibility. Identifying with his victim. The good ones always did.

"She said Zina had no job—and I never found one—would sleep all day and go out 'all tarted up.' If Zina was a pro, it does make her a higher-risk victim. But neither West Hollywood or L.A. Vice ever arrested her and when I found a couple of local bars she frequented, all I got was that she sometimes tended to overdo, no solicitations of customers. No one remembers her getting picked up, period. More like they felt sorry for her."

He shook his head. "Bottom line, Doctor,

'actress' didn't demean her and it got her case in the paper."

"All those complaints from the landlady," I said. "Were there plans to evict her?"

"Nope. For all old biddy's bitching, Zina paid her rent on time, was quiet, and, except when she brought guys home, stuck to herself. That was my big obstacle, her being a loner. No friends I could locate, no local family, just that tight-ass brother in Cleveland. Maybe that **was** a symptom of a psychological problem, you tell me."

I said, "How'd the brother come to report her missing?"

"He tried to call her for Thanksgiving and couldn't get through. But he waited a full month after Thanksgiving to report, got squirrelly when I asked him why. So we're not talking dedication. Worst thing in MP is a time lag. It was like fishing without bait."

"What was the landlady's name?"

"Frances Bynum, but forget talking to her. She was old back then—eighties—and breathing with an oxygen tank. Bitter about everything."

"Anything from Zina's neighbors?"

"No backup on the lifestyle issues but a

couple of people did say she could look spaced out. But overall she hadn't made much of an impression."

Ott took a bite, dabbed his mouth. "I didn't like Mrs. Bynum but she may have been right about Zina being a pro. I never found any employment records and her checking account showed frequent but irregular cash deposits—hundred here, two hundred there. Also, I found some sex toys in her nightstand along with condoms of various styles and sizes. A john-book would've been great but no such luck. Nothing of a personal nature, period. The apartment looked more like a temporary setup, even though she'd been there for a while. My assumption was if someone killed her, they took anything incriminating."

"Do you see murder as likely?"

"More likely than any other possibility but I really don't know, Doc. If it happened in her apartment, someone cleaned up really well, not a trace of nasty. Maybe she did outcall and went to the wrong guy's crib and he covered his tracks. If the john-book, her license, and her house-key were in a purse, easy as pie. More to the point for you, no one ever saw her with a child. I can see why you'd want to know your victim's kid is okay, but do you really think some crazy woman talking about a movie-star mama can lead you to him?"

"Probably not."

He studied me some more, ate some sandwich. "I get you, Doctor. You're going to do what you can until you're convinced there's nothing more to do. That was my approach. Sometimes it worked."

I said, "Zelda's given name was Jane Smith."

He put his sandwich down. "That so? Her and the guy from Cleveland being named Humperdinck would be more impressive, but let's go with that, say your Zelda was my Zina's daughter. You still end up with two women decades apart. Even if I could connect you with the family and I can't, you'd be unlikely to learn anything. We're not talking a close-knit bunch—only that brother ever bothered to call me and he did it once. And when he talked about Zina, it was kind of...clinical. That's the reason I felt she'd been an outcast."

He smiled. "This brings back memories.

Guess that's what you get, talking to a psychologist."

Despite framing lunch as my treat, Ott tried to pay. "Forget it, Doctor, what I gave you wasn't worth the water."

I had Elizabeth wrap my sandwich and threw down enough cash to make her beam. Ott said, "Fine, you win," and I walked him to a little blue Mazda RX.

We shook hands again, a bit less energetically.

"Good luck, Doctor."

"Thanks. Do you recall Zina's address?"

"Man, you don't let go. Wetherly Drive between Beverly and Third, round the corner from the Four Seasons, but you won't find it. Couple of years ago, someone put up a huge condo development."

Couple of years ago.

He'd taken the time to drive by.

Back in my office, I phoned Sherry Andover and told her about the colchicine.

She said, "Herbals? Okay, thanks for the tip. Only thing we ever find around here is dope, not yuppie stuff, but I'll check.

Did Judy reach you?"

"Judy who?"

"Judy Meers, at the men's place. She told me she had something to pass along."

"Any idea what?"

"Not a clue," said Andover. "I'm not one for prying."

Judith Meers said, "Sorry, I lost your number, Sherry gave it to me, I was just about to call."

"Appreciate it. What's up?"

"After you were here I asked around. No one remembered Zelda until this morning when one of our alumni stopped by to donate clothing and said they'd done some drinking together. More important for you, he claims to have met her son."

"When did that happen?"

"I tried to pin him down time-wise but the best he could say was when he lived here, which was around three years ago."

Shortly after the show's cancellation. Shortly before the Central cop had seen her living on the street.

She slid down fast.

"What's this man's name and how can I

reach him?"

"We know him as Chet Brett but I doubt that's genuine. He claims he's Norwegian and he does speak with a little bit of accent. Reaching him is going to be tricky because he lives out of his car. I asked him how I could get in touch but he ignored me and left."

"Donating clothing," I said.

"He does it once in a while, I suspect he dives Goodwill bins. But, still, altruism's a good sign, right?"

"It's a step," I said. "What kind of car does he drive?"

"An old green one. Sorry, I'm not into makes."

"Any idea where he parks?"

"I saw him once, not far from us, east on Sunset. A few blocks west of downtown. There's a couple of vacant lots near a building supply place. I was driving from campus and he was sitting on the hood of his car and drinking."

"Thanks, Judith."

"There is one thing that might help you find him. He's not exactly...typical."

How many five-foot-tall, homeless Norwegian immigrants claiming to be ex-merchant-marines could there be out there?

When I called Milo and gave him the details, he said, "Chet Brett. About as Nordic as tostadas."

"You're not into lutefisk with a side of refried?"

"Yum...let's see." Click click click. "Got a Chester Ernest Brett in Saugus, six one, two sixty, Caucasian...a Chetley Armando Brett, Compton, eighteen years old, black, five nine, one forty...Chester NMI Brett-Lopez, Malibu, Hispanic, six foot, one seventy, twenty-five. Your guy into clever disguises? Maybe walks on his knees?"

I said, "The way things are going, I'm ready to join the circus to find out."

"That bad, huh? You hear from Dub Ott?"

"Just talked to him." I summarized the meeting.

He said, "Pastrami? You could gain weight on this one—no, scratch that, you probably sat there exercising iron control and took the damn thing to go, right?"

"Blanche digs nitrites as much as you

do."

"I find that doubtful...so, no obvious link between Zelda and Zina except for the Smith thing."

"It's thin but it's something."

"I do find myself intrigued."

"Really?"

"Call it empathy, Alex. Known otherwise as when you're up a creek at least be nice to your pals. I'll do some checking, maybe Dub missed something."

I hung up thinking: dead mother, dead daughter.

The worst kind of family tradition.

CHAPTER 22

Doing nothing chews at me and can lead me to bad places. I sat in my office, flooded with ugly outcomes. When that grew unbearable, I left Robin a note and drove to Echo Park, looking for a five-foot Norwegian living in a pea-green jalopy.

The vacant lot Judith Meers had described was fenced, with a construction notice hanging from the chain link. No sign of man or car up and down Sunset.

I didn't make another try but for the next three days I switched futility channels, shifting my daily run to lower Bel Air. Ending up on St. Denis Lane and passing Enid DePauw's spread before circling back.

Tree-cooled streets and gentle slopes provided a nice workout and allowed me to rationalize. I met up with squirrels, rabbits, feral cats grown chubby on gourmet trash. On the third day, I locked eyes with a stray dog that turned out to be a runty coyote hybrid. Mangy and feisty, he stood his ground for a few seconds before slipping into a thicket of pines, the only remnant of his presence a faint thrum of foliage.

Easy to disappear, here. I wondered if Zelda had hidden herself before scaling Enid DePauw's wall.

Living rough, with only a candy bar for sustenance, had she grown hungry and reached for an onion-like bulb sprouting in the greenery?

The pain would've blossomed slowly but steadily. How long had it taken her muddled mind to figure out something had gone terribly wrong? To lead her to seek refuge in a stranger's backyard.

How long had it taken her to die?

For all that zoology, the only humans I came across were motorists at the wheels of German and British cars and uniformed maids walking fluffy dogs and chatting with one another.

On the fourth day, I stayed home, stretched, and tried to recall some long-unused karate moves. Watch out, Chuck Norris.

After feeding the fish, showering and changing, I got in the Seville and drove back to St. Denis Lane.

This time I continued past the DePauw estate. A hundred yards up, the road slimmed and picked up grade. As I continued north, homesites shifted from flat acreage to wildly optimistic hillside perches. Less than three miles later, I was within walking distance from the ranch house on Bel Azura Drive.

The two properties Zelda had trespassed were closer to each other than I'd have expected. Had she focused on this area, specifically?

Given her mental state, no reason to think intent was a relevant concept.

I made the turn, anyway.

Bel Azura radiated the same treeless sterility and eye-bleaching glare. I retraced Milo's cruise up the street, reached the cul-de-sac and turned around just as he had, glided past the trespass house just as a young woman stepped out the front door.

She was ready for her own run, in leopard-spot leggings, a black jersey top, a pink sun visor, and pink-trimmed Nikes. Long dark hair was tied in a ponytail. A pedometer was strapped to one ankle.

She saw me and tensed and looked back at her front door, as if considering escape.

Edgy. Understandable.

I lowered my driver's window and smiled and showed her my long-expired, utterly irrelevant LAPD consultant badge. Doing that probably doesn't rise to the level of impersonating an officer but it's sketchy at best. Especially when I position my hand so it covers my name and title and leads the viewer's eye to the official-looking departmental seal.

The woman looked where she was supposed to but didn't comment. Early thirties, delicately built, pretty in a waifish way. She glanced back, again.

I said, "Sorry to alarm you but we're here to follow up on your trespass case." Nothing like the plural to beef up one's status.

Her hand flew to her mouth. "She's out

again? You think she might come back?"

Tight, hoarse voice. I said, "Absolutely not, you have nothing to worry about." I got out of the car, pocketed the badge.

She folded her arms across her chest. "How can you be sure?"

"She's deceased."

"Oh. How?"

"Accident."

"That's terrible. She freaked me out but I'd never wish that upon anyone. You came to let me know, Officer?"

"Actually, I'm not a detective, I'm a psychologist."

Her nose wrinkled. Her arms remained in place. "I don't understand."

"In certain cases, we do psychological autopsies. Trying to gather as much information about a death, so we can compile a database and hopefully help other people with similar problems."

Technically true; I'd advised the crypt on several postmortems. But never at Bill Bernstein's behest; he had the psychological sensitivity of a bull-moose during rutting season.

"Oh," she said. "Okay, sure, that's a good

thing. When I was in college I volunteered at a mental health center. I felt so bad for those people, it was really a downer."

One arm dropped.

I said, "Severe mental illness can be really tough but that doesn't make what happened to you any easier, Ms." I smiled again. "Sorry, the file's in the car."

"Tina Anastasio." Down went the second arm. "She's dead. Sad but predictable I guess. Someone that...I've been thinking of her as a threat but I guess she was pretty pathetic. Still, you're right, it was scary. We just moved here from New York, I still don't know what I'm—anyway, sorry to hear it turned out so bad for her. What happened?"

"She was committed for a couple of days then released to an outpatient residential facility. Unfortunately, she left there."

"Figures," she said. "I saw people in the Bronx, helpless, coming and going and never getting help." She adjusted her pedometer. "I'd better get moving. If I wait too long the will to exercise will pass."

"Tina, is there anything you want to add to what you told the police?"

"Like what?"

"Anything that would shed light on Ms. Chase's mental status—for example, you described her as screaming and digging up dirt. Did she say anything?"

"That's not in the report?" she said. "What she said?"

"No."

"Wow. I gave the information to the cops. Figures, I never felt they were really listening to me. You bet, she said something. One word, louder and louder until she was shrieking it. **'Mother.'**"

Another guess confirmed. Another so-what.

This time I really did put it to rest, but for occasional gnawing thoughts about Ovid Chase. A few days later—ten days after the death of Zelda Chase—Milo phoned and said, "Got something, not earthshaking but if you're not busy, how about lunch?"

It was just past ten a.m. I'd finished breakfast at eight-thirty.

Not earthshaking but he wanted a face-to-face.

I said, "Sure, name the place."

"Yours."

CHAPTER 23

He walked in toting his battered green not-even-close-to-leather attaché case and dressed for a day off in a gray golf shirt, brown poly slacks worn low to give his gut breathing room, and the eternal desert boots, this pair tan eroded to gray. A loose bit of sole flapped at one toe-end.

He saw me looking at it. "Hey, Rick says they're a fashion statement, now."

"Sole-ful, huh?"

He grumbled and loped to the kitchen and began the mandatory fridge-grope.

I said, "Off duty?"

"On duty but a slow day, no need to meet the public. Too damn many slow days recently."

"Bored?"

"Near-comatose. The citizens of West L.A. are failing to fulfill their homicidal obligations." He straightened, brushed hair off his forehead, turned toward me. "Rumors are circulating. Not enough crime, too many detectives, time to streamline."

"You're protected."

"Only up to a point. They can't dump me outright but they can bug me about early retirement. Or try to break down my already fragile psyche by shoving trivial stuff at me."

"Assaults, robberies, burglaries."

"If I wanted to fill out reports all day, I'd be working for the government."

"As opposed to…"

"Continuing to serve a paramilitary organization that makes use of my exceptional people skills, heroic nature, and inductive talents to bring bad guys to justice."

He bent and searched a lower shelf. "You guys are kinda sparse in the nourishment department…okay, here's a start."

Scrambling five eggs with slices of leftover steak and hastily shredded fried chicken, he tossed in onions, mushrooms, bell pepper, celery, and zucchini, topped it all off with spirited dashes of cayenne, garlic salt, and whipping cream.

Moments later he'd plated a shimmering yellow mound the size of a cat, tucked a paper towel under his chin, and sat down. "Where's the pooch? I'm Pavlov'd to where I need to feed her first."

"On an errand with Robin."

"So I caught you at a lonely-guy time."

"What's not earthshaking?"

"I owe a favor to a Rampart D." He shoveled in omelet, chewed, swallowed, repeated. "Damn, forgot fluids."

I poured him a glass of water and brewed a pot of coffee.

He said, "Sterling service. And you're not even an actor." He looked up. "Did that evoke Zelda? Sorry."

"Nothing to be sorry for. We live in L.A., everything's about performance. And I'm resolved about Zelda."

"Choosing to be optimistic about the kid? Good." His eyes drifted leftward as he took another forkful.

Hiding something?

I said, "Earth-not-shaking?"

"Okay, the favor is looking into a Rampart missing. Fifty-eight-year-old woman named Imelda Soriano, lives with her son's family in Pico-Union. She's always worked as a housekeeper, has been freelancing for agencies in order to spend more time with her grandkids. Eight days ago she headed to her current job, didn't return home, hasn't been heard from since. D II Lorrie Mendez took it as a favor to the family, there's some sort of connection. Lorrie and I have worked together, she's a peach of a gal—pardon the gender specificity. She hasn't made any headway past Imelda maybe being on the first bus of two she takes to work, driver thought so but couldn't be sure. Driver of the second bus had no idea."

He wiped his mouth. "Why am I telling you all this? Because Imelda's job is on my turf, Lorrie hadn't been able to make contact with the estate manager, and the agency's attitude was 'our labor pool is transient, she's already been replaced.'"

I said, "Living with her son's family is transient?"

"It's a euphemism, Alex."

"Immigration issues."

He nodded. "Lorrie thought maybe I could pull some Westside clout."

I said, "The part of your turf where estates are managed. How close to where Zelda died?"

A cherry-sized lump formed along his sagging jawline. His eyes drifted upward, then down. "Walkable. From here, drivable."

He gulped two cups of coffee and we left, taking an unmarked Chevy Impala I hadn't seen before, paint the color of an old scab, the interior smelling of ten thousand pine trees.

As he rolled south on Beverly Glen, I opened the attaché case. Inside were a page of handwritten notes and an enlarged color photo of Imelda Soriano.

The missing woman was white-haired, round-faced, bespectacled, and devoid of criminal record or any other complicating factors. For ten weeks, she'd worked as a four-day-a-week cleaner at a property deeded to a limited liability corporation registered to a family named Aziz. The manager was Jason Clegg, a thirty-eight-year-old white male with several traffic violations and one DUI to his credit.

Milo had written the address in bold block capitals: **1 ST. DENIS WAY.**

Narrow, hilly strip branching west off St. Denis Lane. I'd run past three days in a row.

I said, "That's closer than walkable. A baby could crawl there."

He rubbed his face. "Yeah, it's weird and so is the time frame—two days after Zelda. But I can't see any connection and if I didn't owe Lorrie it never woulda come to my attention."

"What did she do for you?"

"Last year I picked up an idiot gang shooting, I.D.'d the bad guy immediately, had an address in Echo Park but couldn't find him. Neither could the marshals, which tells you it was a serious rabbit. Lorrie doesn't only work in Rampart, she was born there. Turns out she knew the asshole from high school. Located him at a second cousin's and helped set up an arrest with, as they say, 'no incident.'"

"Cooperative policing. It's so nice when the kids get along."

"Hey," he said. "We're one city. Or pretend to be."

St. Denis Way (the sign said **Not a Through Street**) intersected St. Denis Lane a hundred yards above Enid DePauw's property. Low-hanging trees arched over the anorexic strip of roadway. Steeper than it appeared—pitched at twenty percent grade—and hosting only two properties.

On the south side, an old Tudor, topped by a collection of hand-carved stone chimneys, luxuriated atop a mossy-green, flower-bordered hillock. Set far back from the road but rendered visible by open iron fencing and gate; throwback to an era when bragging trumped anxiety.

The Aziz estate filled the north side of the road as well as its spoon-shaped termination. Nothing visible here; dense fifteen-foot ficus abutted the curb and a gate of the same height was recessed two car lengths in, exposing a broad drive paved in black, hexagonal stone. The gate and the posts flanking it were black, as well. Shiny as patent leather, probably some sort of high-tech plastic.

Black camera on the left-hand post. Black call box on a black post, the only spot of color a red button. Atop the box, a carved falcon perched. What looked to be black onyx.

Milo murmured "Warm and welcoming" and jabbed the call button three times. The phone rang eight times before a male voice said, "Yes?"

"Police."

Silence.

Milo repeated himself.

The voice said, "Seriously?"

"Couldn't be more serious."

"Right. There's no soliciting, my friend."

"Only thing I'm selling is justice for all. Open up."

"Seriously?"

Extending his arm, Milo flashed his badge at the lens. "Use your camera."

A moment passed. The voice said, "No worries."

The gate slid open.

We drove up a black stone drive bisected by a strip of flawless grass and ended a quarter mile later at a motor court. Parking for thirty vehicles but only two in sight, a black Range Rover and a battered brown four-door pickup with gardening gear in the bed.

Behind the court was a vast assemblage of white, flat-topped cubes. The kind of architecture that makes the covers of L.A. magazines.

This house dwarfed the manor across the street. Place it downtown and you'd have the latest concert venue.

Milo parked next to the gardeners' truck and we got out. Lawnmower buzz filtered from somewhere behind all the stucco. Before us was already mowed rolling green, acres of it. Four-story trees formed the borders, not a blossom in sight.

He said, "What's that say, psychologically?"

"Maybe 'We don't like flowers.'"

He cracked up. "Please remind me why I brought you."

We headed for the front door. It opened before we arrived.

A man in his thirties stood illuminated by a skylight. His hair was a cap of pale stubble, his beard downy and a shade lighter. Beneath him was white marble. Floor-to-ceiling glass formed a rear wall. Every other surface was white, as were the furniture, the abstract sculpture on pedestals, the huge unframed paintings. The theme continued with the man's white shirt, skinny jeans, and loafers. Ditto the band and face of his Rolex.

His hair and bronze face broke it up, as did gray eyes.

Small guy but toned. "Guess you really are the police."

Milo said, "We are, Mr. Clegg—"

"Man."

"Pardon—"

"I'm not Mr. Clegg, I'm Mr. Stoeller. Manfred, they call me Man." Smiling at what had to be an oft-used line.

"You work with Mr. Clegg."

"I'm Jason's assistant. I'd ask you to come inside but I'm under strict orders. What's your interest?"

"A woman who worked here has gone missing."

"Oh, dear," said Stoeller. "Who would that be?"

"Imelda Soriano. She was employed for

nearly three months, came to you from the Madeleine Agency."

"I'm sure she did," said Stoeller. "We've used them for years. But that's the thing with agencies: They vet the staff and we don't have to get up close and personal."

"No fraternizing with the help."

"I know that sounds snobby, guys, but given the complexity..."

"Would Jason Clegg be more familiar with the staff?"

Stoeller stepped outside. Sunlight dimmed him; he'd been livened by some sort of gizmo in the skylight. "Technically, Jason manages this property, but in reality, he's all over the place and I'm the one who handles day-to-day."

"All over the place meaning..."

"He travels to and from the family's other residences. There's an assistant at each but Jason oversees everyone."

"How many residences are we talking about?"

"Seven."

"Where?"

Stoeller ticked a finger. "Besides here, we've got Aspen, Kona, Manhattan,

London, Lake Como, and Singapore."

He smiled. Not sheepish, smug. "I know it sounds insane, guys, but we're talking a different world. Three G5s—private planes—hangared on three continents and a pair of Oceanco yachts, one for the Northern Hemisphere, one for the Southern."

"Time for a third boat," said Milo. "Keeping it synchronous."

Manfred Stoeller said, "I wouldn't be surprised if that has been discussed."

"The Azizes have edged past middle-class."

Stoeller laughed. "You could say that. Don't ask me how, I'm not at liberty to get into details. Let's just say they've invested wisely."

I said, "Everything on a need-to-know basis."

"And what I need to know is how to keep this place humming in case the family wants to use it on short notice."

"When's the last time that happened?"

"Six, seven months ago. Lately, they've been preferring Europe."

Movement coursed on the other side of

the glass wall. Three men in khaki driving mowers across an area that looked larger than the front acreage. Pool, tennis court, the same austere layout of lawn and trees.

Milo said, "How much notice does the family give before showing up?"

"Usually none," said Stoeller. "Sometimes they let Jason know so he can stock the fridge and he texts me. Six months ago they wanted McDonald's."

"So they're basically absentee."

"But maintenance needs to be maintained constantly. The biggest chunk of my time is spent here, letting people in and out, handling service calls. I also look into the family's commercial and industrial properties. Not the business end. Cleaning, repairs."

"Got your hands full."

"It's like the Golden Gate Bridge. The moment they finish painting it, they need to start again. But no worries, I like my job, no two days are the same."

I said, "A place this size needs a sizable crew. Who did Imelda Soriano work with?"

"Actually," said Stoeller, "we only employ one cleaner at a time."

Milo said, "How big is the house?"

"Thirty-two-thousand square feet, give or take, but our experience has been that one person's enough. I know that sounds skimpy but the family prides itself on thrift." He rolled his eyes. "Actually it works out okay. There's an automatic vacuum system, HEPA filters and other advancements attached to the HVAC system, and most of the rooms are unused."

"So no one we can talk to about Ms. Soriano?"

"Sorry, no."

"Except you," said Milo. "You'd see her regularly."

Even white teeth bounced atop Stoeller's lower lip. "I feel like I'm being tested. I'm cooperating, guys. But I can't help you."

"See it from our perspective, Man. A mother and a grandmother's been gone for over a week and her family's going through hell. She worked here, you still work here."

"I remember an older woman who stopped showing up, guys. Apart from possibly 'hello,' we had no contact. I can tell you she was a good worker. If she hadn't been, we'd have had contact, all right."

Milo showed Stoeller the photo.

Stoeller nodded. "So she's missing? How worrisome. When she didn't show up on schedule, I assumed she'd flaked and complained to the agency."

"How soon after she didn't show up?"

"When she was two hours late."

"A Detective Mendez spoke to Mr. Clegg and informed him Ms. Soriano was missing."

"That may be true, but Jason never informed me," said Stoeller. "Now, if there's nothing else—"

"Bear with us a bit longer," said Milo. "How do people get admitted to the property?"

"The same way you did. I check them out and if they qualify, I push a button."

"What about exiting?"

"There's a button inside the gate that can be used. But policy is not to inform everyone so generally I'm in charge of egress." From his pocket, he pulled a tiny white remote studded with red buttons.

"What about the gardeners?"

"Same process for everyone. And when operations are disrupted, as with Ms. Soriano's discontinuation, I change the gate code."

"Meticulous."

"Better safe than sorry."

"So Ms. Soriano was able to leave at will but would have to beep in."

Same setup as BrightMornings.

"Well, yes," said Stoeller. "Unless I place the gate on hold-open. Which I do when trash bins are wheeled to the street or there's a prolonged delivery."

"I assume your cameras feed to a computer."

"More than one computer."

"Including your laptop."

"No. To the house's central system."

"What about gate openings and closings? Are they coded separately?"

Head shake. "The movement of the gate isn't programmed per se. Obviously when someone leaves, the camera will capture that image. Though I have to say the camera on the gate doesn't pan widely, it just covers the drive."

"Well, we appreciate your getting things moving for us."

"Meaning?"

"It'll be good to see your video feed so

we get a handle on Ms. Soriano's comings and goings."

"There wouldn't be much coming and going, guys. She was here to work."

"She wasn't allowed any breaks?"

"Of course she was. Two for coffee and half an hour for lunch." Stoeller stroked his beard and took another look at the photo. "Did she leave the premises occasionally? I'm sure she did but she always returned promptly. I know all this sounds impersonal and elitist but you need to understand what it's like for me here. I don't sit around enjoying the ambience, I'm constantly dealing with issues—mostly with the rental properties—so when something goes smoothly, I ignore it. In terms of how often she left on break or where she went, all I can say is we're not talking huge blocks of time and she didn't have a car, none of them do, we've never had a single maid park here. So my guess is she took brief walks. You're not thinking someone hurt her out **there**?"

Gazing at the gate. As if the notion of violence in the vicinity was ludicrous.

Milo said, "We need to cover all bases,

Man. Now if you could retrieve the last month of feed from the gate camera, that would be great."

Stoeller clicked his tongue. "Wish I could help you but I can't set that in motion without authorization."

"From?"

"Jason. And he'll probably need to ask someone above him."

"Sounds complicated."

"You have no idea."

"How long will it take?"

"Hopefully, not too long—I'm sorry, guys, it's not my call. How about you give me your email and as soon as I've downloaded the file I'll send it to you."

"Thanks, Man."

That sounded hipsterish. Stoeller probably liked it. He said, "My pleasure, guys."

"Who'd the agency send to replace Imelda?"

Stoeller brightened. "That I can tell you right away—she's here now, hold on."

Darting behind the door, he closed it.

Milo said, "You find him hinky in any way?"

"Not really," I said. "More like job anxiety."

"My take, too. He doesn't follow through on the security feed, I'll change my mind."

The door opened and Stoeller emerged with a woman around twenty wearing a pale-blue uniform and carrying a dust-cloth.

"This is Rosa Benitez," he said, sounding as if he'd just learned a new fact.

Milo and I smiled at the young woman. Her eyes were huge, brown, terrified.

"Just a few questions, Rosa."

No reaction.

Manfred Stoeller said, "She doesn't speak much English but I do Spanish. Want me to translate?"

"Appreciate it." He showed the photo to Rosa. "Ask her if she knows this woman."

No need to translate. Rosa flinched and said, "Imelda."

"Ask her how she knows Imelda."

Stoeller rattled off rapid Spanish. Rosa replied haltingly. Stoeller said, "From the agency. They talked in the office a few times."

"Why did looking at the photo make her upset?"

Same routine. Stoeller said, "She heard Imelda disappeared."

"From who?"

"Other women at the agency."

"Anyone have theories about what happened to Imelda?"

Rosa's reply was rapid but quiet and Stoeller had to cant his ear closer. "No one has been told anything. That's what makes it frightening. The unknown."

Milo looked at me.

I said, "Ask her if she has any ideas about what might've happened to Imelda?"

Five hard head shakes. Saucer eyes.

I said, "Is there anything she can tell us about Imelda? What kind of person she was?"

Stoeller translated.

Rosa smoothed a strand of hair and looked off in the distance. Her eyes had moistened.

She said, **"Muy amigable."**

Stoeller said, "Very friendly."

Rosa talked some more. Stoeller turned to us, any trace of insouciance gone.

"She says it's wrong. Someone so nice to have bad luck."

CHAPTER 24

Manfred Stoeller clicked the black gate open and we drove out of the Aziz estate. Milo coasted to the end of the block and pulled over.

He said, "Eight days missing. Anyone taking bets she's okay? So the question is where did it happen? What's more likely, a Bel Air lurker nabbing her during a lunch-time stroll or she encountered a lowlife during her commute through a bunch of high-crime neighborhoods?"

I said, "Probability-wise, no contest."

"What's the 'but'?"

"There's logic and there's intuition."

"You've got a feeling."

"Two dead women within yards of each other, days apart? You don't?"

"I'm not seeing anything in common between them and Zelda was most likely an accident."

"Bernstein came to that conclusion by process of elimination. What if someone deliberately fed her the colchicine?"

"Pretty resourceful Bel Air lurker."

"This is the perfect environment for a lurker." I told him about the coyote. "It was there one second, gone the next, no big deal for a human predator to slip out of sight. Ironically, the fact that it's a high-end neighborhood full of security features makes it hospitable to squatting: huge properties, a lot of them rarely occupied. Scale a wall or slip through a security glitch and you could live undetected for a long time. If we're talking a bad guy with survival skills, he could know something about foraging plants for all kinds of purposes."

"Or he's a bum with gout—scratch that, it's a rich person's thing, right?"

"Nope," I said. "It used to be called the disease of kings because eating too much meat and shellfish can bring on attacks and the peasants didn't have much of either. But anyone with a tendency can develop it. And now that I think about it, there's nothing like chronic pain to make someone hostile."

"A sore-toed, angry lunatic taking it out on the world, just what I need." He drummed the dashboard. "You spotted this coyote because you were…"

"Running."

"Ah," he said. "A random exercise spot."

"Fine," I said. "You want a confession, here it is: I came back trying to get Zelda's death and Ovid's disappearance out of my system. That didn't work very well and on the fourth day, I drove up to Bel Azura. The woman whose house Zelda trespassed happened to be outside. We talked and she told me something not on the police report: While Zelda was pawing the dirt, she cried out for her mother."

"So your theory was right."

"Right but useless. At that point, I resolved to really get past it."

"Then I call you about Imelda and bring you back here. Hey, what are friends for? Okay, let's get out of here."

"Two women days apart," I said. "Imelda worked here for months, making her an

easily spotted target. And now I'm
wondering if Zelda put herself in the
crosshairs by wandering around for a
couple of days. I checked the distance
between here and Bel Azura on my
odometer and it's shorter than I'd figured,
less than three miles. Meaning she could've
easily covered it on foot. What do they sell
a few blocks down on Sunset? Maps to the
stars' homes. She could've fixated on Bel
Air because she'd convinced herself
Mommy had been a Hollywood luminary,
not a washout working as a call girl.
Unfortunately, she attracted a predator."

"Bad guy emerges from the bushes and
offers her nasty herb tea? I can see someone in Zelda's state falling for that but
how does Imelda figure in?"

"Nothing says she did. He discovered
he liked killing people and decided to
repeat a couple of days later using a blitz
attack."

"Pulling her **into** the bushes."

"It would explain her body not being
found."

"Moldering on one of these properties,"
he said. "If **he** exists."

"Maybe we're on the wrong track," I said. "Not a survivalist squatter, someone who'd blend right in."

"Twisted rich guy living behind high walls. Now all I have to do is go mansion to mansion asking residents if they grow poisonous plants...I'm gonna call Lorrie Mendez and let her know I've got squat."

"Confession without the benefit of pastoral guidance."

"Take your atonement where you can, lad."

The following afternoon, he phoned to let me know Manfred Stoeller had come through with the camera feed.

"Three months of Imelda's employment but I got through it. Not that hard—nothing much happens there and she was a creature of habit. Coffee breaks were usually taken on the property, same for most of her brown-bag lunches. But eighteen times she did take the bag offsite, was always back within twenty-five minutes. The camera catches her heading down the drive and turning right, which makes sense, left is the dead end. Unfortunately, Stoeller was right about the restricted range. No way to know how far she went."

"She couldn't have gone too far and returned in twenty-five."

"True, but it still leads nowhere. Literally and metaphorically. Lorrie agrees. She feels bad for the family but is moving on. Not a bad idea for all concerned, no?"

"Not bad at all."

The moment he hung up, I ran to St. Denis Lane and clocked the walk from the Aziz estate to Enid DePauw's front gate. Even slowing my pace to that of a strolling fifty-eight-year-old woman, just short of four minutes.

Leaving plenty of time to linger at the bottom of the road, noshing, or chatting with someone.

Ample opportunity to be spotted by a stalker.

To return to work, unawares.

Until the day you didn't.

Jogging back home, I showered and changed into respectable clothes. Pocketing my consultant badge and a photo of Imelda Soriano, I drove back.

Parking near the big Tudor on the south side of the street, I rang the call button. A male voice said, "Yes?"

"Sorry to bother you, sir, but the police are investigating a missing person and I wonder if I could show you a photo. We can talk at your gate."

"Who's missing?"

"A woman who worked as a maid across the street."

"Those people," he said. "Hold on."

Moments later, the mansion's front door opened and a white-haired figure began a slow, tottering descent down the flower-lined driveway, aided by a pair of elbow-grip aluminum canes.

It took a while for details to come into focus. Sparse gray hair, leprechaun face, eyes buried in a network of creases. Warm day but he wore a tweed suit, a checked shirt, a green wool tie knotted huge, and high, bubble-toed hiking boots, one heel noticeably higher than the other. My guess was childhood polio compounded by age. By the time he reached me, he was breathing hard.

I said, "Sorry for the imposition, sir."

"No problem, they say I should exercise. That place, eh? You manage to get in? I never have."

"Yesterday, briefly."

"Power of the constabulary. What's it like?"

"Think of the Pentagon on growth hormones."

He laughed. "Contemporary fortress, eh? What's next? Radioactive moat, computerized bow-holes, and nuclear-powered crocodiles. Doesn't surprise me, back when they were building the monstrosity they were insanely secretive. Put the walls and the gate up first, then the house. Trucks would roll in and out but the gate was never left open long enough to see what was happening other than a growing pile of ice cubes. Which unfortunately don't melt. I suppose that type of furtiveness is necessary when you're raping the earth."

He shifted his weight from one cane to the other. "I can't see tearing down a perfectly good—but you don't care about that." Corn niblet smile. "I'd shake your hand, but I need both of mine for balance.

Charles McCorkle. How can I help you?"

"How long have you lived here, Mr. McCorkle?"

"Forty-two years, going on forty-three. Had only two neighbors before those people. The first was Sidney Lanscomb, the director. He sold it to Earl Muggeridge, the Cadillac dealer. Both were all-about-the-money types but they had decent enough families, I believe Lanscomb had a son who went to Yale...the children played with each other, we even had lemonade stands. Not that anyone but our households bought or sold the stuff. The point is, sir, this was a neighborhood. Furthermore, the house **they** destroyed was a classic Paul Williams Georgian Revival. Gorgeous thing, very well balanced, with a normal wrought-iron fence with quite acceptable finials, the air moved through freely, the environment was fresh. Then **they** came and sealed everything up. For what purpose, God only knows. Maybe Allah knows— am I allowed to say that? Or is there a new amendment to the Constitution that has eluded me since I retired from the practice of law?"

I slipped Imelda's picture through a gate slat.

"Certainly I recognize her, one of their domestics. In the odd event our paths crossed, she'd always smile and say hello. I say odd because I don't get out much. Give me my books and my Amati—that's a violin—and I'm content. She's the one missing? For how long?"

"Nine days. She left for work, didn't show up here, never returned home."

"Oh, dear," said McCorkle. "That doesn't sound promising does it? And you think **they** did something?"

"Not at all," I said. "We're just trying to retrace her steps."

"Where was the home she never returned to?"

"Pico-Union."

"Ooh," said Charles McCorkle. "Did she drive a car?"

"She took the bus."

"Exactly what I assumed. Now, think about it, young man: A bus from there to here would pass through slums, ghettos, whatever you choose to call them. Why would you think something happened here?"

"We're being thorough, Mr. McCorkle."

He passed the photo back. "Can't help you, sorry. Darn shame, she seemed like a nice girl."

"Did you ever notice her talking to anyone?"

"Never," said McCorkle. "Except for other domestics."

As if that didn't count.

I said, "Any domestics in particular?"

"What do you mean?"

"Are you aware who they worked for?"

"Why would I be? They're all the same to me. Walking dogs, shooting the breeze with other domestics walking dogs...I don't believe I ever saw this girl with a dog." He glanced across the street. "Does **that** culture allow dogs?" He winked. "Or do they eat them?"

I said, "Any other problem neighbors?"

"Besides **them**? I've had no personal run-ins, but one does hear more and more of beautiful classic homes destroyed only to be replaced by grotesqueries."

His eyes sailed past me. "Look at that gate. Hermetic. **Plastic.** When you were inside, did you spot anything aesthetically redeemable?"

"I'm no expert, Mr. McCorkle. Thanks for your time."

"I should thank **you**. Now I can tell my meddling children that I got my daily exercise."

As he began the tortured climb back to his house, I returned to the Seville. Just as I shifted into drive I realized what had been missing from the conversation.

He'd been eager to gossip, but had made no mention of Zelda's death.

Too trivial an event to merit neighborhood murmurings? Not that this was really a neighborhood, because isolation is the ultimate luxury, and despite McCorkle's reminiscence I doubted it had ever been much different.

But still, it felt sad.

A brief, tortured life. Its termination not even a blip.

CHAPTER 25

Over the next few days, with no illusions of success, I continued running on St. Denis Lane.

With two women dead, what could it hurt to look around?

Of course, I knew the real reason: my chronic issues with unfinished business.

When helping patients assess their problems, I often use life-disruption as a yardstick. If symptoms don't disrupt your life, don't worry about them.

I convinced myself I was doing a fine job maintaining a healthy balance: making time for Robin, doting a bit more on Blanche because our morning walks had lost out to aerobic reconnaissance.

I organized my files, cleaned the garage,

spent half a day on an overdue pond water change, picked up a new referral from family court.

No disruption but for the questions I kept to myself.

On the morning of my eighth consecutive run—eighteen days since the death of Zelda Chase—I noticed a white van paused at the front gate of the DePauw estate. A female arm reached out from the driver's side and punched a code on the call box.

Nothing mysterious about the vehicle, its purpose proclaimed in metal-flake turquoise lettering topped by a cartoon of a pretty, smiling woman meant to evoke the fifties: blouse tucked tightly into pedal pushers, knotted bandanna atop coiffed blond hair, broom in one hand, dustpan in the other.

WHITE GLOVE CLEANING
Your Wish, Our Command

A toll-free number.

The gate clunked open and the van drove through, offering a view of the pathway I'd climbed the night I'd seen Zelda's corpse. As it rattled shut, a mental burr lodged in my brain.

Worth telling Milo about? Or just another symptom of neurotic tenacity?

During the run back home I tossed the question back and forth. Showered and shaved and dressed and drank coffee and ate some toast, before heading back to Robin's studio and making small talk with her and petting the dog, then settling in my office and going through email.

Taking plenty of time to see if the burr fell free.

I picked up the phone.

Milo said, "A cleaning service. That's significant because…?"

"When we spoke to Enid DePauw she said she had a maid. A woman who'd been with her at the desert. Who she gave the night off to when they got back to L.A. Why would she need a service?"

"It's a big place. She wants additional help."

"That's probably it."

"Alex," he said, "what the hell is this about? And why the hell are you still going back there?"

"Forget I called—"

"Whoa, whoa. What's bugging you?"

"We know Imelda was sociable and that she left the Aziz property occasionally for lunch breaks. The only people I routinely see when I'm running are domestics talking to each other. The neighbor across the street from the Azizes—yes, I talked to him—confirmed it. He rarely saw Imelda because he's housebound. But when she was talking to someone, it was another housekeeper. DePauw lives moments away so there's a good chance—"

"The DePauw maid schmoozed with Imelda. So?"

"What if DePauw hired a service because now her maid has failed to show up? What if there really is a stalker picking off women in uniforms?"

He sighed. "Back to the lurking loony... are you saying his tastes extend to homeless psychotic women? Because I spoke to Bernstein and he says he'd need strong evidence to be convinced Zelda's death wasn't an accident."

"Like I said, forget it, sorry for wasting your time."

"You never waste my time," he said. "That's what bugs the hell out of me. You keep life interesting and I'm phobic about ignoring you."

He laughed. "All this because you happened to see a van. Your mind's a **scary** place, Dr. Delaware."

"A call to DePauw could clarify easily. Extra help versus no-show."

"Last thing I need is freaking out the locals. These people have clout and their complaints get heard. Besides, how am I supposed to explain my sudden interest in her personnel issues? Transfer from Homicide to Labor Relations?"

"Good question," I said. "I'll give it some thought."

"You always do."

An hour later, I'd come up with a feasible approach to Enid DePauw: Milo following up, post-Zelda, just to ask how she was doing, had she or anyone on her staff noticed anything in the neighborhood they wanted to discuss.

All in the name of diligent public service.

But instead of telling Milo, I made an

uneducated guess about when White Glove Cleaning would be finishing their St. Denis Lane chores, drove back to lower Bel Air at three forty-five p.m., and parked south of the DePauw estate.

Uneducated because I had no idea how many cleaners were in the van or the details of the assignment.

I endured thirty-five minutes without spotting another human being and began to wonder if I'd missed a brief drop-in to polish furniture or something along those lines. I decided to leave at five p.m., was about to start up the Seville when the gates to the DePauw estate opened and the van's blocky white nose edged toward the street.

I jumped out and went over, smiling and waving and making myself conspicuous.

The van stopped. The driver's window was down. Young Latina at the wheel, an even younger Latina in the passenger seat, both drinking bottled water. They wore pink button-down shirts with **White Glove** and a broom logo sewn in black on the breast pocket. The driver had wrapped a bandanna around long black hair.

Pretty girl. Both of them were. A tattoo on the driver's neck read **Tonio.**

She said, "Hi!"

"Hi. I live around here and I'm looking for someone to clean."

"That's what we do." Wink. "We're **good.**"

"How long have you been working here?"

"Two weeks?" She turned to her companion.

The other girl thought. "Yeah, around."

I said, "It's a big house."

"We're used to that," said the driver.

"Will Mrs. DePauw give you a reference?"

Puzzled looks.

"Who?" said the passenger.

"The woman who owns the place."

"I dunno her."

The driver reached behind, lifted a purse, searched, handed me a stiff white business card.

J. Yarmuth Loach, Esq.

Revelle, Winters, Loach, Russo, LLP.

The address, a Seventh Street penthouse, downtown.

I said, "This man owns the house?"

"He let us in, gave the key."

"Mrs. DePauw's not home?"

"No one's home. We're bonded, that's why we get trusted." Sunny smile. "**You** can trust us."

A senior partner at a white-shoe firm gofering for an important client.

I said, "Okay, I'll talk to him."

"Take our card—here."

Cheap stock, beige. White Glove's West L.A. office on Pico near Centinela. As I took it, her fingers brushed mine and her neck stretched, elongating Tonio's imprimatur.

Lashes fluttered. "Call, we'll help you real good."

As the van drove away, I got on my cell phone.

Milo said, "I can only imagine."

"I'm back on St. Denis, please hold off commenting until I finish. I just spoke to the cleaners from White Glove. They've been working here around two weeks, meaning no more than two days after Imelda went missing. And Enid's not here. Her lawyer's managing the place."

He said, "May I comment now?"

"Go."

"Maybe the maid didn't want to work at a place where a body showed up. Or she'd been thinking about quitting for a while and the body was the last straw. Or she's on vacation. Or, since we're being comprehensive, perhaps Enid decided she needed some R and R and took the maid with her. Like to the desert, again. Those types don't carry their own suitcases."

"The lawyer could confirm that."

A beat. "What's this barrister's name?"

"J. Yarmuth Loach."

"Sounds like a buddy of T. S. Eliot, do I dare eat a peach...hold on...yeah, here he is. Well-groomed fellow, very CEO...big downtown firm, he...specializes in...estates and trusts. Which could mean being a rich woman's errand boy. Now the same question I raised about ol' Enid: What's my reason for calling?"

"I came up with an entrée to Mrs. D. but dealing with her surrogate would be even simpler," I told him.

"Empathic follow-up because I'm such a caring cop?"

"You're looking after the gentry. Rich people are accustomed to being catered to."

"I'll probably find out the maid's sweeping sand out of Mrs. D.'s condo, but sure. Then I can move on to more profitable ventures."

"There's profit in law enforcement?"

"I was thinking spiritually."

Two hours later, he called me.

"Mr. Loach was unavailable but I reached a rather talkative assistant. She had no idea who Mrs. D. was but when I told her I was looking for Mrs. D.'s maid on police business she was duly impressed, went into Mrs. D.'s file and pulled up the maid's name along with an address. Alicia Santos was terminated after two years of employment the day after Zelda's death, no reason listed. No driver's license but I got a phone number. Another woman answered, Spanish only, so I got one of my sergeants, Jack Comfortes, to talk to her. Name's Maria Garcia, she's Alicia Santos's roommate, and she hasn't seen Santos since she left for work the day she was fired. She claimed she'd reported it to the police but couldn't say which station. The home address is near Alvarado, Rampart, again, so I called Lorrie Mendez and there's no record of any report. Did the roommate do something bad to Alicia and is trying cover up? Maybe, but Lorrie and Jack think an immigration issue is just as likely. I'm hoping she's still around when Lorrie and I drop in."

"When, not if."

"Three women gone in less than three weeks? Yeah, the grammar says it all."

CHAPTER 26

Detective II Lorena Macias Mendez had cinnamon skin, honey-blond hair, black eyes, and a face that brought to mind Aztec carvings. We met up with her on Sixth Street, near MacArthur Park. A few grizzled men lolled hear the border of the park. Our presence cleared the area quickly.

Milo said, "Urban renewal."

Mendez said, "New strategy for the city council. So fill me in."

As Milo and I talked, she gazed at the lake, focusing on one spot for several seconds, then shifting suddenly and zeroing in on a new target.

Purposeful as a remote-operated camera. But she never lost the conversational thread.

Finally, Milo said, "Something in the park, Lorrie?"

"Pardon—oh, sorry, guys. Looking for junkies, used to patrol here." She shook her head. "It could be so beautiful but it's just a total dump."

"Spot anything iffy?"

"Plenty of iffy, but not our problem right now." Midthirties, five three, firm and stocky, Mendez wore a gray tweed jacket over black slacks and red flats and carried a black leather handbag. Nice tailoring on the jacket but you could still spot the gun. Maybe that was the idea.

Milo finished up and Mendez said, "Who knew a missing would turn out this way? I don't normally do 'em but Imelda's cousin knows a friend of a cousin of my great-aunt, et cetera. Moment I heard about it, I got a bad feeling. We're talking a lady who rarely left home when she wasn't working, had no vices or boyfriends. Obviously, I took a first look at the son and the daughter-in-law, interviewed them and picked up on grapevine stuff. If they're faking grief they deserve Oscars, and no one ever saw anything but affection between them and

Imelda. So I'd love to give them some sort of answer. But Mama being part of a twisted thing in Bel Air? You really think so?"

Milo said, "Too early to know, but Alicia Santos disappearing kicks it up a notch."

"Two ladies gone from the same neighborhood," said Mendez.

"The houses are literally minutes away from each other."

She whistled softly and scanned the park some more. "Dope deals, right in the open, shameful…something happening to Imelda near her home I could understand. But the poor lady travels to the safest part of town and gets taken by some psycho? That's evil. Are you seeing a link between two housekeepers and that patient of yours, Doctor?"

I said, "Haven't come up with anything yet."

Mendez said, "But who knows what motivates maniacs. Okay, so let's start by trying to eliminate Santos's roommate."

The three of us got into Milo's unmarked. As he started up the engine, Lorrie Mendez phoned Rampart Patrol and told them what to look for in the park.

Alicia Santos and Maria Garcia shared a one-hundred-square-foot room outfitted with an illegal kitchenette in a graffiti-abused, four-story dump on Hartford Avenue near Fourth Street.

We had no legal authority to enter anyone's lodgings. But the building had been cited repeatedly by the health department and when Milo asked to get in, the plastic-caged clerk, a smudge-bearded kid with light-brown dreads and a name tag that read **H. Galloway,** shrugged and handed over a master key.

Not even pausing to lower the volume of the gangsta rap filling his compartment.

We climbed two flights of stairs and walked a quarter of the way up a linoleum-floored hallway that smelled of stale semen and chili powder. A flimsy door opened on another olfactory war: must, tobacco, and bug-killer vying with fruity cologne and talc. The winning aroma depended on where you stood.

Not much of a home but the space had been kept up nicely, scarred wooden floor swept clean, double bed made up with a pearlescent spread tucked tight and decorated with a heart-shaped crazy-quilt pillow. A pair of rickety nightstands had been polished with the Lemon Pledge that sat atop a listing dresser. Toiletries and feminine hygiene products on the same surface were divided into twin allotments. Off to the left was a quartet of photos in cheap standing frames.

Two of the shots featured a slim, plain, youngish woman standing between an older couple. The man wore a ten-gallon hat and a broad white mustache, the woman a shapeless smock. The backdrop was a tiny adobe house on flat dirt. Chickens pecked in the foreground. A swaybacked burro idled several feet back.

The third photo was that of a broadly built, heavy-jawed, crew-cut woman in her forties holding a can of Dos Equis and leaning against a peacock-blue stucco wall. The final image, larger than the others, featured both women smiling and hefting margaritas near the same wall. Taken from a greater distance, that one revealed a neon **Cerveza** sign above a rough plank door.

Mendez photographed each picture with her phone, checked the final products, and looked at the dresser, then at Milo.

He nodded. "Might as well, we'll be gentle."

I stood back as the two of them searched through drawers. Nothing but clothing and not much of that. Same for the two-foot-wide closet crowding the left side of the bed.

"The simple life," said Lorrie Mendez. "Rich folk claim they want it. Boy, are they full of doo-doo."

Downstairs, the clerk looked at the photos on Mendez's phone while playing with his locks. The plain woman was Alicia Santos, "the fat one," Maria Garcia.

Mendez said, "Where does Ms. Garcia hang out?"

"I dunno."

Milo said, "What does 'H.' stand for?"

"Hartley."

"What do you think, Hartley? That her real name?"

"Far as I know."

"You have her Social Security on file."

"Yeah, right."

"You don't?"

Hartley Galloway said, "If someone has it, it ain't me. But no one does. We don't got to."

"Where are tenant records kept?"

"The main office."

"Where's that?"

"Huntington Park."

Milo took out his pad. "Name of the company."

"Progress Properties and Development," said Galloway. **"Inc."**

"Relatives of yours?"

"They was, I wouldn't be working here."

"Where would you be?"

"Vegas."

"So no idea where Maria Garcia hangs out?"

"Nope. She's a dyke. They both are."

Lorrie Mendez said, "Maria Garcia and Alicia Santos are lovers."

"Prolly," said Galloway.

"Probably or definitely?"

"They're all the time holding hands."

"They get along pretty well."

"Never complained to me."

I said, "And no one complained about them?"

"Everyone here is minding their own business."

As if punctuating that claim, a man entered the building, eyed us, and hurried up the stairs. Lorrie Mendez's jaw got tight as she watched him.

Milo studied her before turning back to Galloway. "Maria say anything to you about Alicia being gone?"

"Nah."

"Not a word?"

"When I dint see the skinny one, I assed the fat one and she said the skinny one was gone, she didn't know where. I assed because they both pay the rent and when I dint see the skinny one I need to know who's gonna take care of it. You get two or three in a apartment and one bails, they think they just gotta take care of their part not the whole thing. So I assed the fat one and she gets like…you know."

"We don't know," said Mendez.

"You know," Hartley Galloway insisted. "The eyes. Like…weak? Like she was crying before? Even her."

"Even?"

"You know. Trying to be like a dude."

I said, "Tough chick but she'd been crying."

"Yeah. I still assed her about the rent."

"What'd she say?"

"She'd take care of it."

"Has she taken care of it?"

"So far."

Milo said, "Any idea where she works?"

"The taqueria."

"Which taqueria?"

"Alvarado and Fourth." Pointing languidly at nothing in particular.

Mendez said, "Armando's?"

"I buy food sometimes there. She don't gimme no discount."

Mendez stepped closer to the plastic. "You told us you didn't know where she hangs out."

"She doesn't hang out there, she works."

"Anything else you're not telling us, Hartley?"

"Like what?"

"How about something that would help us locate Alicia Santos?"

"She done something I should know about?"

"Nothing other than disappearing."

"Happens," said Galloway.

Milo said, "People disappear a lot around here?"

"This ain't the Wilshire Corridor, they go in and come out, pay by the week."

"A hub of activity."

Galloway blinked. "Right."

Lorrie Mendez said, "You do rooms by the day?"

"No way, this ain't no ho-house. By the week."

"So Alicia and Maria rent by the week."

"No," said Galloway. "You can do monthly also, they did monthly."

"Maria has paid one month by herself."

"It was due a coupla days ago, so far she done it. She misses, she's out."

"Cash," said Milo.

"Is king," said Hartley Galloway.

"How long have Maria and Alicia been living here?"

"Long as I been here."

"Which is..."

"Year and a half. About. Basically."

"No problems in all that time?"

"Why?" said Galloway. "The skinny one did something bad? No troublemakers here. Whatever they did before, they can't do it here."

I said, "You run a tight ship."

Galloway's brow furrowed. "This ain't no ship. You see water?"

A thick-armed, white-haired man with a too-black mustache worked the counter at Armando's. Off-hour, only one customer, an orange-vested city worker toting a hard hat and texting as he waited for a take-out order.

The place wasn't much more than a kiosk, maybe a former pushcart deprived of wheels. Scant free space was filled with hand-lettered signage—breakfast, lunch, and dinner menus on wooden plaques hanging from chains. All that added up to iterations of the same basic food groups: meat, tortillas, beans, cheese—plus an impressive list of soft drinks from Mexico, Central America, a few from the U.S.

Terrific aroma wafting from the rear. One person working the grill and the oven.

When the hard hat left with a sack of massive burritos, Lorrie Mendez stepped up and took his place and spoke in Spanish to the front-man. He waved the cook over.

Maria Garcia stepped outside, wiping her hands on her apron. Her hair had grown out from the photo on the dresser, capping her full face with tight gray curls. She looked older than the photo had suggested, eyes and mouth struggling with gravity, meaty face weathered.

Under the apron, she wore a red-and-blue-plaid shirt and baggy jeans rolled into broad cuffs at the bottom. On her feet were wide, red-soled chukka boots.

Mendez said, "Hi, Maria. We're the police about Alicia. What can you tell us?"

Maria Garcia's narrow mouth quivered. She said, **"Solamente Español?"** in a high, plaintive voice.

Mendez stepped closer to her, forcing eye contact as she spoke.

Maria Garcia seemed to sink lower with each sentence. "Imelda Soriano" evoked a blank look but each mention of "Alicia" elicited a low moan. By the end of the detective's delivery, she was sniffling and crying silently.

Mendez began asking questions. Garcia dabbed her eyes with her apron and answered without apparent guile. Haltingly at first, then picking up speed and passion and volume. But the tears never stopped trickling and when I retrieved paper napkins from the taqueria and handed them to her, she said, "Tenkyou."

Milo and I know enough Spanish to get the gist but it's often the nuances that matter and when Lorrie Mendez finally gave her card to Garcia and the woman trudged back to her station, we were ready to listen.

We walked back to the car but remained on the sidewalk.

Mendez took out her phone. "Sorry, can I do one thing, guys? That loser who came into the building was one of the s-bags I saw dealing in the park, might as well tell someone where he bunks out."

Milo said, "Go for it."

She made the call, hung up, said, "To me she seems totally torn up, what do you guys think?"

Milo said, "No tells that I spotted. Alex?"

"Same here."

Mendez said, "We can all be fooled but for the time being I'm going to believe her.

Her story is she loves Alicia and Alicia loves her, she's never met anyone like Alicia, never will, they're inseparable. She's staying in the room and taking on all the rent by herself even though she can barely get by, because she's hoping Alicia will show up. Said she even started praying again."

Milo said, "As you were talking, she didn't seem too optimistic."

"She went up and down emotionally," said Mendez. "One minute she's in despair, the next Alicia's bound to be on her way back from some unexplained 'absence' though Maria has no clue where or why. She says they've never been away from each other. I asked if Alicia could've visited her parents. Maria says no way, they're intolerant rustic types—tenant farmers somewhere in central Mexico, Alicia never said exactly where."

"They're lovers and Alicia doesn't tell her that? Why so secretive?" said Milo.

"According to Maria, Alicia's estranged from her entire family because she moved away, supposedly to take a job, and also because they wanted her married off at sixteen. The real reason she left was she knew she was gay. So no way she'd go back there, let alone on the spur of the moment. No reason to, she was happy."

I said, "Estranged from her family but she still keeps a picture of them. Maybe that's denial on Maria's part. Alicia going home could mean she was ending their relationship."

"Good point, Doctor. Problem is, I've got no way to find them."

Milo said, "Is Maria also a country girl?"

"She's from a town south of Tecate. The two of them met in Tecate, cleaning rooms at a fancy spa. They fell in love and decided to take off together because they were hoping for more tolerance in the States. With all the machismo in Mexico, they were always getting hassled by local men."

Milo said, "Both of them are illegal."

"Yup. But I do believe Maria's using her real name. Frankly, she doesn't seem smart enough to weave a big-time web. She's probably also righteous about phoning the station the day after Alicia didn't come home. She admits that she spoke only in Spanish, got spooked and hung up without waiting for an answer. Happens all the time, no matter how often we tell them we don't report to La Migra, they get nervous. But she spoke freely to me, so at this point, Alicia's disappearance is overriding everything else."

I said, "Sticking around and hoping for the best."

"More like clinging to hope, Doctor. Down deep she's got to know it's not good. That's certainly how I feel. Because like Imelda, Alicia was a homebody. Once she was in her room, she rarely went out, Maria even did all the shopping."

Milo said, "So no reason for her to rabbit without explanation. Unless she and Maria had a big fight."

"Maria denies it, just the opposite, claims they were getting along great. So now we've got two ladies working near each other who've slipped off the face of the earth around the same time."

Milo said, "Right after Zelda Chase was found dead at one of their workplaces."

"And the morning before Alicia disappeared, she told Maria she didn't like her job anymore but wouldn't say why. Maria didn't push it, that was typical for

Alicia. She didn't like to talk. When Alicia was late coming home, Maria didn't connect it to a job issue. Still doesn't, she keeps talking about bad men all over the city."

"Anyone in particular?"

"No, just a general feeling," said Mendez. "I wouldn't be surprised if she's a rape survivor."

I said, "When did she start worrying about Alicia not coming home?"

"Not right away because Alicia typically arrived late. Nine, even ten p.m., the commute could stretch out due to traffic, buses breaking down. Around eleven, Maria started to get concerned and tried to phone Alicia. Even then, when she couldn't get through to Alicia's phone, she figured Alicia was still on the bus, that's why reception was bad. But by midnight, Maria's freaking out because Alicia's phone is turned off and that hadn't happened before. Unfortunately, it's one of those prepaids. Both women use them because they don't have paperwork for normal accounts and that fleabag has no landlines. Around twelve-thirty, Maria went looking for Alicia on the street, starting with the area around the bus stop. She describes that night as 'hell.' The following morning she called the cops. She still walks around asking people if they've seen Alicia. I think if she admitted the truth to herself, she'd have a breakdown."

I said, "Did she search in Bel Air?"

"Nope," said Mendez. "She wanted to, but she has no idea where Alicia worked other than it's near Beverly Hills. Her take on the city is pretty poor, I'm not sure she's ever been west of Vermont. So what now?"

Milo said, "Good question."

I said, "Something just hit me. Maria says she and Alicia never spent a night away from each other. She describes Alicia's position as a day job. But Mrs. DePauw told us Alicia was with her in Palm Springs, had earned time off—as she usually did— because of the time it took to drive back to L.A. That sounds like a live-in position."

Milo frowned. "So it does."

Mendez said, "Hold on." Jogging back to the taco stand and heading for the back, she returned a few moments later. "Maria says definitely not, never happened. She and Alicia made a pact when they crossed the border. No more live-in work like they'd done at the spa. And she's adamant about never sleeping apart. If she's righteous, and I think she is, your rich lady lied."

Milo's jaw tightened. "Ol' Enid playing fast and loose. Why?"

I said, "I can think of two reasons. It places her out of town when Zelda likely died. And it gets Alicia out of the picture so she can't contradict her."

Lorrie Mendez said, "She saw something that contradicted the boss's story? You're saying this dowager had something to do with Zelda's death?"

"Not necessarily homicide," I said. "Suppose Zelda found the colchicine in DePauw's garden, ate it, and grew incapacitated. Bernstein told us dying could've taken a while. DePauw arrived earlier than she said and discovered Zelda still alive, in agony. She shunted Alicia away, while she figured out what to do."

"What's to figure, Doctor? You call 911."

"In an ideal world," I said. "But DePauw's a woman of considerable assets, could've been worried about liability. She panicked, waited too long, and Zelda died. The fact that she's left home and put her lawyer in charge suggests she's still trying to dissociate herself."

"She got antsy about being sued so she let someone die? Still, what would be her liability? Zelda didn't belong there."

"Having a toxic plant on her premises might've seemed problematic. People can sue for anything and deep pockets are a huge incentive. For all we know, DePauw's been in lawsuits before and got burned."

Milo said, "DePauw's landscaper said there was no colchicine on the property and I had Moe and Sean go back with a photo and they didn't find any matches."

I said, "It's an ornamental. DePauw could've been growing it in a pot on the patio. Or it sprouted in some obscure corner of the estate and she got rid of it before finally making the call."

Lorrie Mendez said, "She stands by and watches another human being die. That's cold."

Milo said, "Not a pretty death, Lorrie. Ice cold." He turned to me. "Any panic DePauw might've felt was long gone when we spoke to her, Alex. Just the opposite, she was damn composed."

"Maybe she gave herself time to gain composure."

"Lying to cover up shameful behavior?" said Mendez. "But then what's happened to Alicia?"

I said, "There's where it could get evil."

"Alicia can blow the boss's alibi to smithereens and so she got offed? With all due respect, Doctor, that's pretty darn... imaginative."

Milo said, "He's got a terrific imagination. I've learned to pay attention."

"Oh, man," said Mendez. "This is getting nuts."

I said, "I could be way off, but the facts are there. DePauw lied about Alicia and the same day Alicia told Maria she didn't like her job she disappears."

She shifted her bag to the other shoulder. "An old lady without a record and we're actually considering a witness elimination homicide?"

Milo said, "Maybe a double witness elimination, Lorrie."

"Imelda," she said. "Oh, God, no."

"We need to consider it, Lorrie. Imelda was a friendly person, old enough to be Alicia's mother. What if Alicia confided in her and DePauw found out? Or just spotted them talking and got worried?"

"Maria just told us Alicia's not talkative."

I said, "Trauma can alter behavior. If Alicia saw Zelda die and realized Enid had acted cruelly, it could've troubled her enough to say something to Imelda. She went back to work but might have intended to quit—that's why she told Maria she wasn't happy. She didn't give Maria the details because that was their pattern. They didn't discuss much. Or she just wanted to protect Maria."

"There's another possibility," said Milo. "She went back to work and tried to exploit the situation."

"Blackmail?" said Lorrie Mendez.

"Rich woman, poor woman. A solid reason for DePauw to get rid of her."

"And Imelda died because she was in the wrong place, wrong time? I hope you're wrong. I hope I never have to tell the family that." She exhaled. "You pick up anything bad from DePauw? Apart from her lying."

Milo said, "She said the right things about

Zelda. 'Poor thing,' but there wasn't much emotion there. Just the opposite, calm, maybe even snooty. Didn't take her long to ask how long we needed to be there."

"Fine," said Mendez. "But just to play devil's advocate, that could be nothing more than having big bucks and feeling entitled. Which, granted, is the kind of attitude that fits with covering her affluent ass rather than trying to help Zelda. But morally iffy behavior's a long way from double homicide."

"True, but Alicia and Imelda going missing around the same time can't be ignored, Lorrie."

"Sure, but that could be due to your first theory—some psycho predator roaming around Bel Air—God, I'm starting to sound like my annoying sister the defense attorney, always with the what-ifs. But the truth is, this is moving too fast for me, guys. The entire scenario depends on Maria being righteous and like I said, anyone can be fooled. What if Maria is utterly **un**righteous, she's the one who killed Alicia and Imelda has nothing to do with it—**she** got waylaid somewhere between her two buses. If

Maria's guilty and we hassle some zillionaire based on no evidence, we could end up severely career challenged. Or at least I could, you've got seniority, Milo. And **you've** got a degree and a private practice. Am I totally being self-serving—God, I feel a migraine coming on. And I don't even get them."

Milo said, "No reason to rush into anything but we do need to educate ourselves. You have time for any follow-up on Maria? See if her story starts to crack?"

"I can ask patrol to do a loose watch on her, but sorry, no. My own El Tee's breathing down my neck on a bunch of cold robberies."

"Would it help if I talked to him?"

"Uh-uh, just the opposite. He doesn't like suggestions and he's a whole lot less benevolent than you."

Milo hitched his trousers. "If you only knew, kid. Okay, what I do ask is that you and I continue to share info."

"I get any, you'll be the first to know."

We got back into the car and headed to the park. As Milo pulled up to Lorrie Mendez's unmarked, she switched her purse to the other shoulder and opened the passenger door.

"From a **missing** to all this potential **weirdness**," she said. "At least your rich lady will have plenty of documentation."

CHAPTER 27

By three-thirty p.m., we were back in Milo's office, not talking much as he prepared to learn about Enid Lauretta DePauw.

"Got to tell you," he said, logging on, "I've got the same bad feeling you do but I hope to hell this ends up a big-time wrong turn because Lorrie's right. A rich, respectable suspect and no evidence ain't a formula for joy."

Nothing in the criminal databases contradicted "respectable." DePauw's first California driver's license had been issued thirty-two years ago when she was thirty-eight. The most recent renewal was three months ago, on her seventieth birthday.

Two vehicles currently registered, a one-year-old black Porsche Panamera GTS and a brown-over-tan 1956 Silver Cloud I Rolls-Royce sedan. The older car's registration had lapsed eleven years ago, renewed fourteen months later. No wants, warrants, moving violations, or parking tickets.

The trust deed to the house on St. Denis Lane was dated the same year Enid had been certified legal to drive. The property had been purchased from Metro-Goldwyn-Mayer Studios, Inc., and titled to the Averell D. and Enid L. DePauw Family Trust. Eleven years ago a new trust had been established in Enid's name only. A death certificate for Averell Dunham DePauw five months earlier provided the explanation. It also clarified lapsed papers on the Rolls.

The deceased had been seventy-one, twelve years older than his widow, when he'd succumbed to "atherosclerotic coronary artery disease."

Milo kept probing, limited to city and county data in the public domain because he lacked grounds for a peek at Social Security or income tax records.

The DePauws' wedding license was dated thirty-seven years ago, five years prior to purchase of the estate. Their address at the time, a rental in the Malibu Colony.

No record of children born to the couple, no co-beneficiaries, charitable foundation, or obvious source of income for Enid. When Milo logged onto a directory of old business listings, he found several dating back to the sixties for Averell DePauw and Associates, Ltd., first on South Beverly Drive in Beverly Hills and later on North Canon Drive in that same city. Stockbrokers, asset managers, financial advisors.

He said, "Guy bought the house from a studio. Maybe moneyman to the stars?"

I said, "Some kind of inside track. Enid told us 'interesting people' had lived there, including Jean Harlow. Back then the studios kept luxury properties as crash pads for A-list actors. The kind of asset that got kicked loose when money was tight. If MGM was having cash-flow issues, they might not want it publicized. A private sale to an insider would benefit all concerned."

"You follow that world?"

"I've had patients in the business."

"Ah." He searched for foreclosures and forfeitures, found none. "Looks like ol' Av managed his own money well. Let's see if he got sued for anything."

Moments later, he was shaking his head. "Not a single day in court for Mr. D. so that didn't turn Enid gun-shy. Next stop: Palm Springs. We get lucky and someone verifies her time line at the condo, we'll put her fib down to being flustered and get back to conjuring up an ignoble savage slavering in the shrubbery."

He typed, made several calls, pushed away from the desk.

No listing of any property deeded to Enid DePauw or her trust in Palm Springs. Same for the neighboring desert communities—Palm Desert, Rancho Mirage, La Quinta, Indian Wells.

"Too bad. I was hoping to forget about her."

I said, "She might rent. Or keep a unit in a development or a time share in a hotel where the deed's registered to a corporation."

"Gated paradise with a Greg Norman

course? She said, 'My condo.' That doesn't sound like renting."

"Pay enough monthlies and you start feeling like an owner."

"If that's the case, I'm screwed."

I said, "On the positive side, a resort or hotel might have detailed documentation of comings and goings."

"Optimism at this time of day is unseemly, lad."

"Late afternoon should be gloomy?"

"Anytime's the right time for gloomy. I've got my homework assignment, leave me to it and enjoy a normal life. I come across something, I'll let you know."

"How about I stay and we divide it up. You take developments, I try hotels. My end shouldn't take long, I don't see her bunking in a Motel 6. Or you could call that assistant at the law firm and see if she's still talkative."

"That would be nice...nah, don't wanna push it with her. Just in case ol' Enid **has** been bad and her lawyer finds out I'm snooping and battens the hatches tighter."

He turned back to his keyboard.

I sat there.

"Fine," he said, "you twisted my arm."

We went downstairs and he asked to borrow a civilian laptop from a clerk named Kanesha.

"The doctor here won't screw it up, I promise. I'll repay you with a humongous lunch, you choose the place."

She said, "You like vegetarian?"

"I could pretend."

"Secret of a happy life, Lieutenant. Like when we tell guys they're perfect." To me: "You'll be careful? I'm out of here in two hours, need to take it with me. And no downloads of monkeys who look like Hitler, please. Got enough of that with my kids."

Milo worked at his desk and I sat on a chair in the hallway outside his door, typing away and calling on his personal cell.

Lots of luxury lodging in the desert communities. An hour later, both of us had come up empty.

He said, "Never worked so hard trying to **verify** an alibi. Maybe I will try that assistant but I want to sleep on it, see if there's some other way to go. You up for a drink? Or two or three? Either way, I'm indulging. Or as you guys call it, self-reinforcing."

I phoned Robin. Her voice competed with background machine noise. "Oh, hi, hon, just started working, had to fix some jigs and got held up. I could use an hour or two, if you don't mind."

"Perfect timing. I'll be hanging out with you-know-who."

Milo said, "That's the best I get?"

Robin said, "I hear him back there. Hanging out as in distilled spirits? I was hoping we could share a bottle of wine out by the pond."

"I'll have a beer."

"There you go, a guy thing."

During the last case we worked together, Milo took me to a bar a few blocks from the station, a place I'd never been. He was greeted by name. I thought I knew all his haunts. Live and learn.

I figured we'd head to the same place but he pocketed his car keys and said, "Separate vehicles, save you some time," and scrawled an address on south Westwood Boulevard. "Right on your way home. Call me responsible."

I arrived first; a restaurant named Bosco's just north of Pico. The tricolor neon sign above the door roughly approximated a map of Italy. One of the few pre-mall holdovers on Westwood. Happy Hour lasted until three.

I was checking out the posted menu when Milo drove up and said, "**Buena sera,** Alessandro."

We entered a world based on nitrogen, oxygen, and marinara. Snug, dim, too warm, an oppressively low ceiling. A warped lattice partition divided the space into red Naugahyde booths for eating and red Naugahyde stools lined up at a scarred wooden bar. Every stool was occupied, mostly by older men who looked as if they were waiting for a casting call on the next mob movie. No one in the booths until we took one at the back.

An ancient waitress wearing a too-short dress and intense red hair ambled over. Her mouth moved as if she were chewing gum but she wasn't. If you called her a "server" she'd probably slap you.

"Hiya, Lieutenant."

"Hey, Mary." Milo ordered a double shot of whiskey, iced tea, and a large pizza with everything on it.

Mary said, "The usual. And you?"

My Grolsch order elicited a wink and a shimmy. "I figured you weren't a Bud guy. We might even have that." To Milo: "Class act, your friend."

"Doing my best to improve the neighborhood."

"Taxpayers deserve it from you."

When she left, I said, "How many of your hidey-holes don't I know about?"

"What—oh, this? A stopover."

"To where?"

"Like I said, right on the way to your place."

"You need to fuel up before you visit?"

"Don't get touchy. On certain days it helps to settle my system a bit so I can be civil to Robin and the pooch. You, I don't care."

The drinks came. My beer tasted like Bud.

I sat there as Milo drank and loosened his tie and plucked at an X of duct tape patching the arm of the booth.

He put his whiskey down, traced a line in the frost coating the iced-tea glass. "Let's say Enid is a rich lady who had the misfortune of being invaded by Zelda. Maybe or maybe not she had the colchicine on her property. Maybe or maybe not she watched Zelda die instead of calling for help and is covering her own ass by making up a cockamamie story. What bothers me is that next big step: offing two innocent bystanders. You see her able to transport corpses? Trucking them away in her Porsche or her Rolls and putting the bodies where they haven't been found? The alternative is a classic domestic: Maria Garcia **did** kill Alicia. But the problem with that is Imelda. I know Lorrie suggested her case could be unrelated to Alicia. But two women, same job, go missing at the same time?"

I thought about that. "There is another way to turn the prism. Imelda and Alicia aren't dead. They went off together."

"Imelda's gay and just came out?"

"What if they met while schmoozing during lunch hour and something clicked? Most affairs begin at work."

"Imelda would just bail on her family and leave them with all that anxiety?"

"Telling them could seem worse," I said. "Maybe she's still figuring out how to do it."

"Hey kids, guess what, Mom's got a see-cret...yeah, that could be messy."

He picked up his whiskey and finished it. "Alicia and Imelda being an item could lead somewhere else: Maria found out and dispatched both of them. She might've even surprised them at work. All we have is her word that she didn't know where Alicia worked."

"She's got no driver's license."

"So she borrowed wheels. Or hired a lowlife from the park to do a contract killing. Seeing as we're fact deprived, anything's possible. Hell, we sit here long enough, we could create a mini-series."

He called for a refill. Mary looked at me. I said, "I'm fine."

"Maybe you'll get thirsty when the pizza comes. We put too much salt in it."

A few minutes later she returned with

Milo's drink and the pie, a massive disk laden high with a few things I could identify, many I couldn't.

"Clams," said Milo, picking up an amorphous pink chunk. "Excellent."

"Even more salt to help your blood pressure," said Mary. To me: "Try it, see if I'm right."

I peeled off a slice and tasted. One of the unidentifiables might've been eggplant. Or another species of ocean invertebrate.

"Well?" said Mary.

"You're right."

"The magic words. Now teach my boyfriend how to pronounce them."

When she left again, I said, "Even if Enid's renting, she probably pays for some utilities under her own name."

He groaned. "So damn obvious—too late to call the power companies, I'll try in the morning." Pizza vanished down his gullet, washed down with the second whiskey and iced tea. "Any other wisdom you'd care to share? Pick your topic—including my horoscope."

"You feeling out of cosmic alignment?"

"The oracle in the paper says it's my

month to be charming and sociable but I ain't feeling it."

I smiled, though I wasn't feeling it, either. Plagued by the intrusive thought I couldn't shake.

No matter what had happened to three women, an eleven-year-old boy was out there somewhere.

One way or the other.

I finished the lousy beer, augmented with water because I'd be drinking wine with Robin. Lots of it.

CHAPTER 28

My head still throbbed and my eyes were gritty when my private line rang at eleven twenty-five the following morning.

Milo said, "No dice. She pays for gas, electric, and water in Bel Air, but nowhere in the desert. On the off chance she goes through Loach, I did call the assistant. Guess what: Britnee's not working there anymore and her replacement's a temp who came across brain-dead."

I said, "Too chatty and the boss found out?"

"I'm definitely going to connect with her. I also talked to Lorrie about an Alicia–Imelda romance thing. She says no way, Imelda was religious and conservative. But you never know. Bottom line: Enid made up a story and it's bothering me more than it did yesterday. She wasn't a suspect. Why lie?"

"People overreach when they're nervous."

"Exactly and I'm also liking your idea about liability. Her level of money could cause someone to do all sorts of things."

"Covering her assets."

He laughed. "In terms of a loony lurker, before I got to the office, I did a drive-by on St. Denis and neighboring streets, talked to a few residents and maids walking froufrou dogs. Everyone's happy in 90077. One guy even thanked me for doing my job. Just to make sure, I combed through a year's worth of incident reports in the entire old Bel Air area. A few burglaries but nothing psycho and the only prowler complaint was a bogus call from a spurned wife when her husband showed up to get his golf clubs."

"Busy morning." I popped my third Advil.

"The best kind," he said. "I also located Britnee. Axed, disgruntled, and saying so on Facebook. I sent her a like on her rant, asked if she'd talk to me. She answered right away with a whole bunch of happy emoticons. She lives in the Fairfax area, likes modern dance and Thai food. Can't do anything about the former but I found a place on Melrose. Couple of hours. That work for you?"

Britnee Leah Fauve was twenty-five, tall, leggy, blond with pink streaks, alluring in body-hugging black.

"Asshole," she said, chopsticking a nugget of shrimp into a perfectly glossed mouth. "I didn't deserve that."

Milo said, "Mr. Loach."

"Mr. **Roach**. He **is** a damn bug. Kept looking at my butt when he thought I couldn't see but barely spoke to me. It's like I was...decoration. I never got why he even needed an assistant, he's in the office like once a week and doesn't do much when he is there. I figured it would happen soon."

"Getting fired?"

"Getting hit on. Didn't have to deal with that on the job I had before. Then she died. My first boss."

"Also a law firm?"

"No way, dental office. Dr. Regina Korovnick, DDS, old Russian lady, never smiled but all business. I started working for her right out of the U., was there for two years. Not exactly what I wanted for a career, I was a theater arts major. But if you don't have a trust fund...Dr. Korovnick gave me responsibility. I ran her entire front office and if I worked late one day, she'd give me time off for an audition when I needed it."

"Nice setup."

"Then she had a stroke and the office closed down and I had nothing for four straight months, then I got stuck with **him**. His HR assholes put me on sixty days probation at sixty percent pay, no health plan. On day fifty-nine—three days ago—they ditched me. It's a scam. You get peons to work cheap then ditch 'em. My boyfriend's pre-law, he says I should sue."

She looked at us for confirmation.

I said, "Did Loach give a reason for letting you go?"

"Loach never said anything, it came through the damn HR. Email. At night when they knew I wouldn't see it until morning. Don't come in tomorrow, we'll be sending you a severance check for one week.

Which so far they **haven't**."

"Not nice," said Milo.

"You think?" She sipped water. "Looking back maybe I should've expected it. Something happened the week before. I didn't think it would come back and bite me but obviously it did."

She picked at her food.

Milo said, "What happened, Britnee?"

Putting her chopsticks down, she gave a theatrical sigh and aimed deep-blue eyes at us. "It was kind of gross. Not that they shouldn't be able to do it, I don't discriminate against anyone. But be discreet, okay?"

"They being..."

"Old people. As a group, I've got no problem with them. I respected Dr. Korovnick. I respected and **loved** my nana, she was awesome. I'm just saying...you want me to go into it? Maybe it'd help with a lawsuit?"

Milo said, "We kinda need to know what you're referring to."

"Okay. Here's the deal. Last week, I got a call from downstairs to pick up a whole bunch of papers Loach had requested,

Xerox and collate and staple and bring them back. Tons of paper, boring stuff—real estate laws, I think. As usual, he wasn't in the office, I'd been doing my typical sit around and wait. So why would I assume? It took a while, the first copy machine had a jam, but I finally finished and brought the stuff back up and knocked on his office door and went in. Expecting no one, a formality, you know?"

Her smile was sudden, sly. "Unfortunately...oh, man, that was some scene."

"Loach was there..."

"Him **and** a woman," said Britnee Fauve. "An old woman, maybe even older than him. And they—you really want to hear this? Hey, why not?" She licked her lips. "What I see when I go in is him standing in front of his desk and she's down on her knees in front of him. His face turns red and he makes this little squawky noise and she gets up real quick. I dropped the papers on the floor and bailed."

Milo said, "Caught in the act. Talk about awkward."

"It's crazy, right? You're in the mood for

some head, why wouldn't you lock the door? Sean—my boyfriend—says that's contributory negligence, I have a solid case."

I said, "Loach sure put you in a tough situation."

"It's always that way, right? You catch someone at something and they end up blaming you because **they** feel crappy about it. That's how it was with my boyfriend before Sean." She pondered. "Sean's different."

Milo said, "Catching someone being naughty and getting blamed for it. Kinda sounds like police work, Britnee."

"Yeah, I guess so...I was grossed out and went to Starbucks and didn't come back the rest of the day. They're probably using that against me. Can you blame me for not wanting to be around when he finally came out of the office? Hi, boss, enjoy getting your knob polished by some GILF in Chanel? I mean, yuck, gross."

"Had you seen the woman before?"

"Once or twice, she'd show up, they'd go out. So she's probably his girlfriend or whatever. But don't blame me if you're not careful. **Asshole.**"

Milo said, "Can you describe the woman?"

"Old, white hair—why, is she some kind of suspect?"

"Just collecting background on Mr. Loach."

"I meant to ask you about that," she said. "What exactly's going on with him? Please please tell me he's in serious trouble, some sleazy lawyer thing."

Milo smiled. "I wish we could get into that, Britnee. But too early in the game."

She smiled back. Perfect teeth. "At least there's a game. Okay, great. But can you promise me one thing? If whatever he did helps me with my lawsuit, you'll let me know?"

"Absolutely."

"Thanks, guys," she said. "I mean, if he's an ax murderer or something, that would help, right?" She laughed. "Sean says I could sue him, the firm, maybe even the agency that got me the job. Luck out, I can score some serious F-U money, finally get a vacation."

I said, "Haven't had one in a while?"

"Like in never. School and work and

nothing else since my sophomore year in high school, which is when my dad died."

Milo said, "You really do deserve a break, Britnee. Good luck—can you describe the woman a bit more?"

"Old," she reiterated. "Tall, skinny. Not a bad figure, I guess. Not bad, she might've been cute a long time ago. Rich-looking. That Chanel was real. So were her Louboutins, when she was going down on him I saw those red soles. I'd say she could be his wife but he's not married. Which he told me after I'd been there for a week. After shamelessly letch-leering my butt."

She ran a hand down one smooth flank. Flipped her hair.

I said, "Rich older lady."

"What else...I said white hair but it was really white-blond, probably cost a fortune...oh, yeah, GILF lipstick, coral red." She grinned. "All smeared up on the side of her face. She did move fast, kind of graceful, I'll give her that. Like maybe she danced when she was younger? Or she takes yoga, whatever."

Milo showed her Enid DePauw's DMV photo, careful to cover the name with his hand.

"Oh, wow. Yup, that's her. She doesn't look so great here." Shaking her head. "Itchy lips, lock the **door,** bitch. Guess I'm lucky to get out of there, it was only a matter of time before he'd be trying to get **me** to do it."

She ate another piece of shrimp. "Tell you one thing: I feel sorry for the next person they exploit."

I said, "There's a temp working there now. Not too bright."

"Figures. Not that the job involves brainwork. Taking messages from his Audi mechanic? His tailor? Sean says that's what senior partners do. Loaf around and exploit everyone below them. He calls it modern-day feudalism. Says the rest of us are the new serfs. Maybe I'm lucky. Maybe working for Loach is bad karma. The assistant before me had it a whole lot worse."

"Who's that?"

"I don't know her name," said Britnee Fauve. "Don't even know if it was even a her or a him. But soon after I started working there, some dude downstairs in the mailroom made the crack about a voodoo hex up in Suite 1100. Like 'Good luck, hope you do better than the last one.' I said what are you talking about and he told me. Pretty tasteless, joking about it."

We waited.

Britnee said, "Death isn't funny. I was fifteen when my dad died."

Milo said, "Loach's previous assistant died?"

"That's what the dude said. I didn't ask anyone to confirm it, there was no one to talk to anyway, I was basically in solitary confinement up there. And when I came downstairs I couldn't wait to get out of there because of all the chemical smells— toners and whatnot."

"Do you remember the dude's name?"

"Antoine," she said. "He's black, some kind of French-like accent. Maybe he was just messing with my head. But if he wasn't, you think it could be important? For my lawsuit?" She ate another piece of shrimp, said, "This is delicious, going to bring Sean here. Thanks, I mean it."

Milo said, "Our pleasure. Take the rest to go. And get some dessert—get two, for you and Sean."

"That is really sweet, sir, but I'm really not much of a dessert person."

"Given what you've been through, maybe you should be. Go ahead, on us."

"Naw—you really think so?"

"We know so, Britnee."

"Well…I do try to stay away from white sugar. But maybe they use something else."

Milo called for a menu. She scanned. "Coconut custard…I do like coconut… custard's eggs, that's protein—okay, custard. Thanks."

"How about Sean?"

"I'm not sure if he'd eat anything, he's like Mr. Workout…hmm…okay, mango and coconut rice. He **loves** mango. Puts them in the blender for smoothies."

Milo put in the order, asked the waiter to pack it up along with her barely touched lunch, and handed over cash.

The waiter smiled. Britnee Fauve smiled.

Milo and I worked at keeping our faces neutral.

When the take-out bag arrived, she stood up and briefly touched Milo's shoulder. "Bye. You really know how to take care of people."

Her breath caught. "My dad was like that."

We ordered more tea. The still-happy waiter brought a pitcher and a plate of cookies.

Milo said, "Lawyer and client extending the relationship. That remind you of anything?"

Last year we'd worked on the murder of Ursula Corey, a wealthy importer of Asian goods, gunned down in the parking lot of her divorce lawyer's office building. The attorney, Grant Fellinger, was also her sometimes lover and became the prime suspect.

I said, "These two are both alive."

"But people around them are trending dead. Let's chat with Antoine from the mailroom. Black guy with a French accent, can't be too many employees who fit that bill."

Keywording the name and that of the firm, he googled. Held up a Facebook page, said, "Thank God for the social network," and began scrolling.

"Antoine Philippe Bonhomme. Xeroxes but bills himself as an administrative legal assistant...originally from Port Au Prince, Haiti...came to Florida as a kid in a boat... bunch of sad pictures...likes Mexican food and, get this—light opera...graduated four years ago from Columbia U., majoring in anthropology, did research on...some biological thing on alleles."

"Genetics," I said. "Welcome to the age of lowered expectations."

"Him and Britnee, both. Tough being a kid, nowadays. Old age, on the other hand, seems to present erotic opportunities. Enid being naughty in Chanel. Who'da thunk?"

"The pleasure principle is an equal-opportunity employer."

"Nothing surprises you?" he said. "That could get boring."

"It's the reason I take your calls."

"Let's hope Monsieur Bonhomme is just as amiable."

It took a while to connect to someone in the law firm's mailroom. "Tony" Bonhomme was out sick. A DMV search produced an address on Fuller Avenue in Hollywood and a photo. The reverse directory supplied a landline that went unanswered.

Milo said, "Let's chance a drive-by, I can leave him my card."

The house was a hulking, dark-green Craftsman. Tony Bonhomme was visible from the curb, sitting in a lounge chair at the rear of the driveway, reading. As we got closer, I saw the charge cord from a lap-top on the ground snaking through the open doorway of a smaller, rear structure. Inside was a kitchenette, dishes stacked neatly on a counter. Work space or guesthouse.

The book Bonhomme grasped with both hands was a large-format paperback with a bright yellow cover. Riveting; he didn't notice our approach.

Slight and bespectacled with thinning hair, he wore a white T-shirt and jeans. Earbuds trailing to an iPod in his lap made me reassess the book's page-turning qualities. So did the title: **Prep for the LSAT Exam.** As Bonhomme underlined in yellow, he chewed his lip.

It took the shadow cast by Milo's looming

form to make him look up. He removed the buds, took in Milo's badge, and relaxed. Not the usual reaction.

"The form was sent in. I faxed it myself. They're not here to verify."

Milo said, "Where are they?"

"Venice," said Bonhomme. "Italy, not California. Don't tell me you didn't get it."

"Get what?"

"Oh, man—the request. Fine, I'll send another."

"Who's in Venice?"

"You're kidding—who? The owners. Chad and Darren. They go every year, buying trip. C'mon, gentlemen, let's not start from scratch. Every time a new one of you comes on, it's inventing the wheel."

Milo said, "Mr. Bonhomme—"

"Fine, I'll go over it. **Again.** The burglary you know about. What you obviously haven't been informed about is that the insurance company keeps being obstructionist by insisting on a detailed list of stolen items with an official police sign-off **before** Chad and Darren can ask for an outside appraisal. Even though they're certified antiques appraisers. I keep sending you guys an official request, it keeps getting lost, no one admits anything."

Milo said, "The burglary was here?"

"No, the shop—" He sat up. "Hold on, who are you?"

"LAPD. It's you we're here to see."

"About what?" Bonhomme held up his book. "Studying without a license?"

"You're not in trouble—"

"Well, I should **hope** not! What now?"

"Sorry for the intrusion," said Milo. "We called but no one—"

"I turn off my phone when I'm studying. You have any idea what this is?"

"For law school."

"I take it next week, that's why I need to concentrate."

"This won't take long, Mr. Bonhomme—"

"**Bone-ome.** It means 'good man.' I'd like to think that's accurate. So you've probably confused me with some random black male who—"

Milo said, "We're here about a death at Revelle, Winters, Loach, and Russo."

"And I'm supposed to know about that because..."

"You told someone about it."

"What? No way."

"You made a joke about a hex at the firm."

Bonhomme removed his glasses, squinted up at us, grimaced. "Oh, shit, Blondie. You're kidding. She took that seriously?"

"She took the fact that someone died seriously. She took your comment as tasteless levity."

"Levity...well, that's exactly what it was. Tasteless? Ear of the beholder."

"So it never happened? No one died?"

"It happened," said Bonhomme. "But the hex thing was...just silly stuff. It was an accident, anyway. Least that's what I heard. I was just giving her a hard time because she invited it."

"What kind of accident?"

"That's all I know, an accident." He shifted higher. "Are you telling me that's not true?"

"What's the name of this accident victim?"

Tony Bonhomme shot us a knowing smile. "You're just poking around because Blondie freaked out. That was like months ago. A joke, gentlemen. Which, as I said, her manner invited."

"What manner was that?"

"Being so uptight and superior about everything. As if she was too good to be there. As if anyone's too good for anything. She made sure I knew she was going to be an actress. You can always tell the dramatis personae. They're utterly incapable of regulating their emotions. So I messed with her. A hex? That's kid stuff, she should've known better."

Milo pointed to the book. "Looks like you're planning on leaving the firm."

"Soon as I can," said Bonhomme. "But not because I think it's below me. I moved to L.A. to get a Ph.D. in physical anthropology and found anthropology's been taken over by politically correct nitwits. I also realized I hadn't evolved to the point where I no longer need to eat or drink and so far, I'm not happy with my practice test results. So may I study in peace and try to aim for the affluent class?"

Milo laughed.

Bonhomme said, "See, Officer? Levity. It's my thing. Now, please. Allow me to resume Fifty Shades of Dull."

"One more thing, sir. How'd you find out

about the accident?"

"Talk around the dungeon—that's what we call the mailroom and everything else on the lower floor. I can't remember who said what, it was more 'poor guy, stuff happens.'"

"Poor guy," said Milo. "The person was male."

"Hmm," said Bonhomme. "I believe I did hear the word 'guy,' so probably. But don't hold me to it. It was months ago."

"How many months?"

"You're really taking it seriously."

"Pays to be careful," said Milo. "We were working your burglary, stuff wouldn't get lost."

"Touché," said Bonhomme. "How long ago...two months, give or take."

Perfect sync with the onset of Britnee Fauve's probation.

"Again, don't hold me to it," said Bonhomme. Already thinking like a lawyer.

Milo was thinking like a detective. "You met Britnee but not the assistant who died."

Bonhomme thought. "Yes, that is interesting. Assistants of senior partners rarely descend to the dungeon. They tend to make their requests by text or phone. Perhaps Blondie didn't know the drill. Or she was hired at a lower pay grade. They're doing a lot of that. Belt-tightening." He flexed the book. "Another reason to keep my options open."

Milo said, "Good luck with that."

"Good luck to all of us," said Tony Bonhomme.

CHAPTER 29

As we returned to the car, I said, "Britnee went down there because Loach planned on fun with Enid and gave her a make-work assignment mission. Unfortunately for him, she got back early."

"Yeah...an accident. If it wasn't classified as a crime, we won't have it. I'll check with the crypt."

"One way to find out."

"Soon as we get back."

I had other ideas. No sense arguing.

He drove and I played with my phone.

L.A. murders are cataloged in several places. There's the LAPD roster, the list kept by the coroner, and supplemental files, mostly for statistical purposes, maintained by a host of state and federal agencies.

All of which require a password or other evidence of official approval.

Anyone with Internet access can log onto the **Los Angeles Times** Homicide Report, a regularly updated cache that promises to provide "a story for every victim," and does a fine job of fulfilling that pledge.

I had the name in less than a minute. Told him and read him the summary, verbatim.

" 'Roderick Salton, thirty-four, a white man, was found dead in a warehouse district near the courthouse on 1945 South Hill Street in Historic South Central. Though Salton worked as a legal assistant at a downtown law firm, his employers said his job wouldn't have included court business. His family had no ready explanation for what Salton, a Utah transplant slated to enter law school this fall, would be doing in a warehouse district at night. Anyone with information is requested to contact Detective Roger Enow, LAPD Southwest Division.' "

An attached color photo showed a full-faced young man with short dark hair and an open smile. Date of death: sixty-eight days ago.

Milo said, "Enow. Good luck."

"Not an ace?"

"You'd never mistake him for someone who cares. I gave testimony in that court, what a dump."

"I've been on the stand there, too."

"Custody cases get heard there?"

"They do when the main court's overloaded."

"So you know the neighborhood, like they said—industrial and storage. Supposedly respectable citizen ends up dead like that, it's usually sex, dope, or both. But everything around there closes up at night. Never heard of hookers or dealers congregating."

I said, "Which would make it the perfect dump spot. So would being relatively close to Salton's work downtown. And a lawyer would be familiar with the area."

"Back to that damn firm. Something bad starts there and finishes a few miles south? Did I miss cause of death?"

I re-read. "None listed." My chest got tight. "Do me a favor and call Bernstein

now."
    "Why?"
    I told him.
    He went bone-white.

The pathologist's voice boomed through the hands-off speaker. "Correct, Victim Salton is the only other adult poisoning of uncertain manner in the county other than Victim Chase. I already told you it wasn't the same toxin so don't get all heated up."
    "You have any feelings about manner?"
    "I don't deal in feelings, I deal in data. If I was a betting man, I'd go for suicide as most likely, then homicide. But until I get some evidence, it will remain undetermined."
    "Enow's on the case, you're unlikely to get anything close to evidence."
    "I'm aware of that, not my problem," said Bernstein. "How'd you come across it?"
    Milo explained, leaving out Alicia and Imelda and concentrating on the link to J. Yarmuth Loach.
    "DePauw's lawyer?" said Bernstein. "You've got a connection between him and Victim Chase?"

"He's got business and personal relationships with DePauw. Is managing the property in her absence."

"That's a connection?" said Bernstein. "What, you're thinking she's absent because he wants her to be? Be careful, too much creativity erodes the soul."

Milo and I looked at each other. That possibility hadn't entered our minds.

He said, "Anything's possible, Bill."

"Hopefully not," said Bernstein. "A universe of possibilities is the definition of hell. Well, this isn't probative but I suppose it's provocative. You've complicated my life."

"Complicated my own. Could you please fax Salton's file?"

"I don't fax, my assistant does and she's gone home. I should be gone, too—all right, I'll bring it to your office, you're on the way. I'm talking the original, you're responsible for copying and getting it back to me."

"Great. When?"

"Confirmation: You're at your office."

"On the way."

"I beat you there, I'm not waiting around."

Milo raced back to the station, we ran up the stairs to his office, and he pulled up the file on Roderick Salton.

"Typical Enow," he said, reading. "The bare minimum. He even spelled the guy's name wrong, here. R-O-D-R-I-C-K, in one place, an E in the next paragraph."

His desk phone rang.

Bill Bernstein said, "Come down immediately."

The coroner idled a car in the entrance lane of the staff lot, wearing a white baseball cap over the same brown tweed suit and a bright-orange tie patterned with silver scalpels. The car was a sixties Corvette Stingray convertible, electric blue, the white canvas top lowered, chromed tailpipes growling.

Bernstein said, "Finally." He revved the car. Smoke unfurled around him.

It had taken us all of a minute to reach him.

Milo held out his hand.

Bernstein said, "We're going to discuss this. Get me in the lot."

Milo used his card to open the gate and Bernstein sped into a slot marked

Reserved Deputy Chief. He stepped out hatless, carrying a larger version of a black leather doctor's bag, continued past us, and crossed the street without apparent caution.

Milo said, "Thanks for taking the time, Bill."

"You need to work on your parking situation. I shouldn't have to make a special request. No way am I leaving my other girl on the street."

"Nice wheels. You actually drive it to East L.A.?"

"Why not? I've got a designated space there in full view of the camera." Bernstein hefted his bag hard. Something thumped. "I've also got a Glock nicer than the ones you get and a carry permit, let some scum try to jack me."

Milo grinned at me. "We should start calling you Wild Bill."

"My fraternity brothers beat you to it."

Bernstein threw open the station door, bounded up the stairs, stopped at the mouth of the corridor. "Which one's your office?"

Milo led him there.

"This?" said Bernstein. "Who'd you offend? Find somewhere appropriate for human habitation."

Milo already had; an interview room several doors down. He said, "Good idea, Bill—okay, that one will work."

"It better," said Bernstein. "You've put me in a foul mood."

Once inside, he said, "Three chairs, good." His pug nose wrinkled. "Stinks, you need better maintenance."

My nose picked up a faint trace of perspiration. I'd been at the crypt when the stench of decay permeated the entire building.

Bernstein placed his black bag on the floor, sat and unclasped, placed papers on the table and squared the pile. "Victim Salton."

Off came his glasses. He tugged his tie knot. Scalpels flashed. "Being assigned to Enow is tantamount to drifting in the miasma."

Milo said, "Roger being Roger."

"He's a goldbrick, you need to do something about your internal standards. On top of his usual incompetence, he was annoying. Trying to pressure me to rule it as suicide so he could file it as a close and go off fishing somewhere. Fat chance, as if I'd help him clean his plate." Wry smile. "So to speak. Seeing as we're talking about oral ingestion."

"Oral ingestion of what, Bill?"

"I'm getting to that." Bernstein spread pages, selected one. "Aconite. From the plant aconitum. Also known as monkshood, devil's helmet, wolfsbane, women's bane." He laughed. "Choose your poison."

Selecting a sheet, he slid it across the table.

Color photo of a long-stalked plant with striking purplish-blue flowers.

"You're going to say it's pretty," said Bernstein. "Don't think of sticking it in your garden if you've got a dog or a small child or a squirrel you care about. It's got a noble history as an implement of extremely unpleasant death. E.g. Shakespeare— **Henry the Fourth,** Medea trying to polish off Theseus. As well as various witchcraft loonies, cretins who believe in werewolves, that kind of crap. Even that kiddie book— Harry whatever."

Milo said, "It's legal to grow."

"Why wouldn't it be? You'd be amazed at how much death potential there is in a random garden. Aconite's a particularly efficient assassin, a couple of hours and poof, maybe a bit longer if the dose is smaller. The mechanism is the opening of tetrodotoxin-sensitive neural cells—why am I bothering getting technical with you—it screws up the nervous system, okay? You get nauseous and vomit, your internal organs basically explode and bleed out, you shut down, end of story."

"Sounds like colchicine."

"It's far more precise than colchicine. Your victim Salton had minute specks of vomitus on his clothes but he was pretty clean overall so I suspected he'd died elsewhere. I told Enow. Per usual, he didn't care."

Milo said, "Any external marks on the body?"

"Not a pinprick. When I see something like that, the first option isn't going to be poison, it'll be disease, even young people keel over from strokes, aneurysms, occluded arteries. But even before I opened him I noticed cyanotic fingernail beds, which was intriguing, we're talking acute oxygen deprivation. Of course, anything cardiac could theoretically cut off—never mind, bottom line, carbon monoxide had to be considered, just as with Victim Chase. Negative. And when I did get inside, I found a total mess that was definitely **not** CO. I took lots of samples for biopsy and ordered a tox screen immediately. The third extension pulled in aconite. I listed it in my report."

"Enow didn't. He just said 'Poison.'"

"Again, not my problem."

I said, "Colchicine can be used as gout medicine. Any legit uses for this?"

"Some British homeopaths like it for a diuretic, which I think is insane. Even at the dilutions they use, why take a chance? I want to lose water, I'll eat asparagus, better my pee should smell than my entire body implodes. It's been used in China and India for herbal concoctions, but those people also grind rhinoceros horn to help geezers get hard-ons, which is about as useful as prayer, so big surprise. To answer your next predictable question,

has it been used for murder recently? Not
in the U.S., but a few years ago an Indian
woman in England cooked up a tasty
curry that killed her boyfriend because
he'd gone back to his wife. Women's bane.
Hell hath no fury."

He produced a spotless linen handkerchief, wiped his glasses, put them back on.
"Enough neurobiology for dummies. Am I
to understand that you're hypothesizing a
connection between Victim Chase and
Victim Salton solely because of this lawyer?
What's your theory? A white-glove type
buys two poisons from an herbal quack
and laces high tea? If so, good luck
confirming. There are crap peddlers
everywhere from Venice to Chinatown,
even worse, the **Internet.** And none of
those idiots register with their fellow idiots
at the FDA."

Milo said, "Actually, we're wondering
about a link to Enid DePauw's garden."

Bernstein said nothing.

"Women's bane, Bill?"

"I **get** it. What's her connection to
Salton?"

Silence.

"You don't have one but you're ready to complicate matters."

"Bill—"

"I suggest you keep a clear head. The only common link is the lawyer and in the case of Victim Chase, it's indirect at best. We know the colchicine didn't originate on DePauw's property. We looked, you looked." His finger jabbed the photo. "Did you observe **this** growing there?"

"I wouldn't have been looking, Bill."

I said, "We could be talking potted plants. Or something that got dug up."

"Coulda woulda. Either way, you're not going to find the evidence this late in the game. The larger question is why this lawyer—or that woman—would kill a homeless psychotic and a legal assistant. What's the connection between your victims?"

Milo shook his head.

Bernstein said, "Precisely."

I said, "Maybe the motive was fun."

Milo swiveled toward me. Bernstein stared. "Are you basing that on psychological data or fishing?"

I said, "Everything needs to be

considered."

"Ridiculous. If that was true, the world would be chaos," said Bernstein. "So Lucretia Borgia is alive and well in Bel Air? What's next, eye of newt, tongue of toad? Be logical, narrow your focus to a point where there are concrete steps you can take."

Milo said, "Such as?"

Bernstein flushed. "I'm on the stand now? The answer is I don't know. Happy?" Clasping his suitcase, he got up. "You learn something that clarifies manner, let me know."

I said, "Did Salton's family try to contact you?"

"You've got the answers **and** the questions."

Milo said, "It's a good question, Bill, seeing as manner is still undetermined and Roger didn't give them squat."

"And **you'll** do better by them? Not from what I've heard so far."

He turned to leave.

Milo said, "Sorry if doing my job annoys you, Bill, but I need to make sense—"

The coroner stopped short, rotated

slowly. His color remained high.

"I'm grievously overworked because the county is a tight-fisted bastard and refuses to staff adequately. Last night I was there until two a.m. and ate crap takeout instead of the gourmet dinner my bride had prepared. Yet again. Yes, there was contact with Salton's widow but it was minimal and not relevant to you. She phoned around a month after the death, wanting information. One of my assistants handled the call, we had little to give her, she wasn't pleased. She certainly didn't like the idea of suicide."

"Any theories on her part?"

"Not that I'm aware of." Bernstein groped in his pocket, produced a flip-phone, punched. "Enrique, do you remember talking to a decedent's wife, two months ago, give or take, surname Salton? . . . you do? Excellent, Enrique, low risk of Alzheimer's in **your** family. Tell me, did she have any theories about what killed her husband? . . . I see. Did you inquire about that...I understand, no reason to, we don't have all day to jaw with families...no, probably not. No, you're fine. Keep that cerebrum healthy, Enrique. Get the hell out of there and have a couple of margaritas. Back to your roots, margies originated in El Paso...you did? Good for you. You should go on **Jeopardy!**"

He clicked off. Color faded, but more fatigue than relaxation. "Apparently she said something about it having to do with work. Even if we **had** passed that along to Enow, what's the chance he'd have done anything about it?"

"Zero," said Milo.

"Less than zero," said Bernstein.

"One good thing about Enow not giving a shit is no toes to step on when I contact the wife myself."

Bernstein stooped, unclasped his black bag, sifted through paper. "Here's her number."

Milo and I remained in the interview room.

He said, "Bill makes me look light and airy. But even for him, that was intense."

I said, "Rigid personality coming up against new possibilities."

"Not a good trait for a coroner."

"Usually it's no problem, you know the typical homicide."

"Shot to the head, knife to the gut, write the report."

"Zelda he pegged as accidental, Salton as undetermined, even though he thought the body had been moved. Now he's got to consider both as possible murders and wonder if he missed something. He didn't, but he has high standards for everyone, including himself."

"Zelda, Salton, the maids," he said. "You really think this could be a fun thing? God, I hope not." His eyes lowered to the phone number Bernstein had given him. "Let's see if the widow has any suggestions."

Roderick and Andrea-Leah Salton's listed address was an apartment in North Hollywood. At this hour, a trip to the Valley would be a hydrocarbon crawl.

Milo switched his phone to speaker and called. A woman answered. He hadn't gotten far explaining when she said, "Something came up about Roddy?"

"We'd like to go over the case in person, Mrs. Salton."

"You've still got nothing."

"We're taking a fresh look. If you could

spare some time—"

"Fresh," she said. "**He** was certainly stale—your predecessor. Why not, come over."

"Traffic's gonna slow us down, ma'am. If we set out later, say seven, seven-thirty, will you still be around?"

"I'm around. I don't go anywhere."

CHAPTER 30

Before setting out for North Hollywood, Milo did a surface background check on Andrea-Leah Salton. Full-faced like her husband, sandy hair cut in a Dutch boy that ended at earlobe level. At forty, six years older than her husband. Safe driver, no criminal record. Solid citizens abounded but four people were dead.

Next step, the mandatory call to Southwest Division. D II Roger Enow was gone for the day but Milo cadged his private cell from the desk sergeant.

A low, languid voice drawled, "Ye-llow." Music in the background. Something overwrought from the eighties.

"Hey, Rog, it's Milo. I need to talk to you about a case."

"Workday's over."

"Gimme a sec, Rog. Roderick Salton, legal assistant, found near the court—"

"That one," said Enow. "Suicide. Why the hell would West L.A. be pawing it up?"

"It might be related to one of mine."

"Another suicide?" Enow laughed. "There's an epidemic, call Public Health."

"Mine's not a suicide, Rog."

"Yeah, well, mine was. But, hey, you want to carry the ball in a game that's over, be my friggin' guest."

"What can you tell me about Salton—"

"It was suicide, the guy was Mormon."

"Mormons are likely to commit suicide?"

"All religious types," said Enow. "They expect life to be good, all of a sudden it sucks and they fall apart like a sack of moist shit."

"What sucked in Salton's life—"

"It was suicide, Milo. I got a feeling right away and it stuck. I trust my feelings."

Dial tone.

Milo put the phone down. "Poor woman dealing with **that.** She's gonna love us."

I thought, **Poisoning the well.** Something Bill Bernstein would say. Better left unsaid.

Andrea-Leah Salton lived in the best part of North Hollywood, near Toluca Lake where Bob Hope, William Holden, and other Hollywood types had homesteaded in order to avoid their colleagues on the Westside.

Her building was a three-story traditional on a block of high-rent multiple dwellings. External cameras were mounted in the right places. Warning signs made sure you knew that. The front door was double-locked, accessed courtesy occupants' consent. Milo's button-push was answered by an immediate buzz.

He said, "Safe and sound."

I said, "Good reason to pick him off at work."

We climbed plush-muted stairs to the second floor. A and B units, one door on each side. Andrea-Leah Salton was waiting on the left side, her wide-open door casting a rhombus of light onto the carpet.

Five six, buxom, softly sculpted, she wore white jeans, a black linen top, and black moccasins. A wedding band frosted with pavé diamonds circled her ring finger.

She said, "Good start. You're not **him**."

Her apartment was spacious, set up with fifties furniture that looked expensive and original, including a black leather Eames chair. A pitcher of ice water garnished with lemon sat atop a glass-and-brass table, along with matching goblets, linen napkins, and a plate of chocolate cookies that looked home-baked.

She stood in front of the Eames and waited for us to sit before settling and crossing her ankles. Directly behind her hung western art: cowboys, horses, buttes, and mesas. Off to the left were three framed photographs: a wedding picture with the happy couple gazing into each other's eyes, two others crowded with faces, white, black, brown, Asian.

Andrea-Leah Salton said, "That's all family, both Rod's and mine, we could barely fit everyone in. And yes we're LDS— Mormons—and no, that has nothing to do with Rod's death. We are **not** weird people, despite what **he** thinks."

Milo said, "Detective Enow—"

"A prejudiced nincompoop."

"He suggested your religion had something to do with it?"

"He didn't have to. Every time he said 'Mormon,' he rolled his eyes. Then he smiled, to let me know he was a good guy. We're used to that. A Broadway show ridiculing us made a fortune. Try that with Muslims." She recrossed her ankles. "Are you reopening Rod's case?"

"It was never really closed, ma'am."

"Cause undetermined and no serious detection? It was functionally closed. Has that changed, Lieutenant Sturgis? Has a similar murder come up to get you in gear?"

Milo sat back and studied her.

She said, "Good guess, huh? I'm used to figuring things out. Worked as a stock analyst and then in investment banking until I quit to get a Ph.D. in philosophy at the U. Next year, I defend my dissertation. Qualitative and quantitative analyses of uncertainty. So how about some details?"

"I wish I could get into details, ma'am."

"But you did find a similar case—don't bother to deny. Just let me know how I can help you."

Milo looked at me.

I said, "Tell us about your husband— what kind of person he was—"

"He was an honest, dependable, devoted, hardworking person. If he had a flaw, and I don't think he did, it was that he could be stubborn. But even that sprang from a strong moral core. He was bright, an honor student, planned to be an attorney but chose to work as an assistant for a couple of years to save up money, so he wouldn't have to borrow."

I said, "Avoiding student loans."

Andrea-Leah Salton looked to the side, then back to me. "You'll note, I said '**he** wouldn't have to borrow' not '**we** wouldn't.'" My family has money, his doesn't. Some men would've jumped at the opportunity to take advantage. To Rod, my family's affluence was an obstacle to overcome. I respected that, though I wasn't going to live like a pauper. That's why we got this place and not some student dive. That's why I got a new BMW even though he insisted on buying a junky used Dodge Neon rather than have my brother give him **his** BMW when he bought a new Jaguar. Speaking of which, what do you think of the way the Neon was found? To me it makes no sense."

Milo said, "Actually, Andrea…"

"You don't know about that." Her smile was sour. "Okay, I'll assume nothing. Regarding the car, I didn't hear about it from Enow, I got a call from some auto-theft detective instructing me to pick it up at the tow yard. He, of course, had no idea about Rod. I told him to call Enow. Just in case there was no follow-through, I called Enow myself a few days later and wouldn't you know, they still hadn't talked. I'm not sure they ever did. Enow said the car didn't matter. I doubt anything matters to him."

"Where was the car found?"

"Three blocks from where Rod was found. And not until three weeks later. Someone had left it in a huge industrial parking lot behind a warehouse, it took a while to realize it didn't belong there. Enow said the time lapse made it meaningless as evidence and even if it had been put there shortly after, all it proved was that Rod had driven there, then taken a walk and…" A tear fell from one eye. She wiped it quickly.

"I don't care what he says—what anyone says. The notion of suicide is absurd and **hideous.** Rod swallowing poison? That completely abases Rod spiritually and flies in the face of who he was. Which is what you were asking…okay…no more ranting. Rod was happy, well balanced, optimistic, there's no possible way he'd ever destroy himself. Enow asked me if we'd dabbled in herbal medicines, worshiped crystals, got involved in 'counterculture.' I said of course not and he said okay, he had to ask. I could tell he was patronizing me. He's got that manner—starts off casual and friendly but turns snide. Like everyone's got a nasty secret and it's his job to pass judgment. I know you guys encounter the worst side of humanity all the time but that **wasn't** Rod. It **wasn't.** If anything, he could be naive."

I said, "How so?"

"Overly trusting, idealistic."

"You called the coroner—"

"I was desperate, Enow had stopped answering my calls. I wanted to talk to an expert because the poison thing made no sense, there's no way Rod would know anything about that, let alone use it on himself. The person I spoke to wasn't a doctor, just a lab person. Nice enough but he couldn't tell me much. I left a message for the coroner, passing along the same thing I told Enow, maybe they should look at Rod's work. I requested a call-back, never received one."

Milo said, "Let's talk about the work situation."

"Let's," she said. "First of all, Rod was hired under false pretenses. He was promised at least some training in trusts and estates. His interest was in estate work, he felt it was less confrontational than most other aspects of law. Also, I encouraged it. Thought it would be helpful to have someone in the family with those skills."

She sighed. "Rod always called me the heiress. Kidded me about his being a hired hand."

She got to her feet, ran out of the living room and up a short hallway. A door closed sharply, just short of a slam. She remained away long enough for Milo to eat three cookies, before returning with straighter posture and her hair released, a mop of blond cascading over her shoulders. I noticed her eyes for the first time. Gray, sharp, active.

"Sorry," she said. "It hasn't gotten easier. What makes it worse is I feel I'll never **know**."

After she'd settled and drunk some water, I said, "Hired under false pretenses."

"Oh, yes, that. It was supposed to be a standard legal assistant's job—doing scut in return for being able to shadow a senior attorney. And at first, Loach made Rod feel welcome. Took Rod out to lunch at the Water Garden, couldn't have been nicer. But the next day, he was out of the office. Same for the following three days. When he finally showed up on Friday, he stayed an hour and gave Rod nothing to do. Rod was going out of his mind with boredom but Loach didn't seem to be aware. Or care. He'd just walk by Rod's desk, clap Rod's back and leave. Another person might've loved getting paid to sit around. For Rod it was torture. He was like one of those dog breeds that needs to work. The second week, he tried to talk to Loach and Loach said there'd been a temporary lull, things would pick up. But it didn't, Loach continued to be absent with no explanation. After a month of that, Rod tried to raise the issue with another lawyer in the firm and was informed since he was Loach's assistant, all decisions were made by Loach."

"Did Loach see any clients at all?"

"Only one," said Andrea Salton.

"Who's that?"

"All Rod told me was one, he wouldn't give me details because of confidentiality."

Milo said, "Assistants are bound by confidentiality?"

"That's what I said to Rod. He said it wasn't a matter of the law, it was the law's intent, as far as he was concerned anything conducted under the 'rubric' of the firm was bound. I must admit I got a little contentious and challenged him. Did that include parking lot attendants? A plumber who came in to fix a toilet? He laughed it off and told me to put it in my dissertation."

"He did communicate that Loach had only one client."

"He blurted it out once when he was totally frustrated. 'Can you believe it, Andrea? He gets a huge corner office, a massive salary and bonus, all for one client.' Then he made me promise I'd never repeat it. He could be a little overly...I know this is going to sound bad to you guys but I used to tell him he was overly law-abiding. We're talking about someone who if he came out to his parking meter and saw that he'd overextended his stay and gotten away with it, would reimburse the machine."

Milo said, "Too many like him, I'd be collecting unemployment."

Andrea Salton laughed. "Thank you, Lieutenant. That's the first time I've come close to levity in a long, long time."

I said, "Rules meant a lot to Rod. The worst person to put into such an unstructured situation."

"Perfectly put."

"Why didn't he quit?"

"He felt if he left too soon, it would look bad on his résumé. He and I discussed the minimum time he could stay without appearing flaky. I felt three, four months was enough, he felt it needed to be longer. We agreed on six months, worked out a way to cope. He'd use the time to study his first-year law books in advance, get a head start, maybe be able to free himself up to do research with a professor."

She smoothed her hair and shook her head. "Six measly months. He never made it."

I said, "You told the coroner's assistant you thought his death was work related."

"I didn't say that, I was trying to tell him suicide was out of the question, our home life was ideal, the only stress in Rod's life was work. He was getting lots of studying done but he didn't feel right about it. I told him Loach had to be a rainmaker. Someone with connections who brings business in and doesn't have to do much else. My dad plays golf with a guy like that."

"Anything else we should know?"

"I wish there was. If my remark about work was taken out of context, I'm sorry."

"Nothing to be sorry for," said Milo. "I can't promise you we'll solve it but we'll treat you differently than Enow."

"I know you will—have some cookies. If you don't take them, I'll eat them and that's the last thing I need."

She filled a bag and gave it to us. We thanked her and headed for the door.

"You think of anything that might've

bothered your husband," said Milo, "you call. Anything at all, for that matter."

Andrea Salton stood there.

"Ma'am?"

"There is one thing that happened but I can't see any possible way it's related."

"Try us, anyway," said Milo.

"A few days before he...before it happened, he came home looking even grimmer than usual and I asked him why, expecting him to tell me everything was okay, as he usually did. But instead he said it had been an interesting day but not in a good way. A homeless woman had wandered into the outer office where Rod sat and demanded to see Loach. When Rod told her Loach wasn't in, she started screaming, making a scene. Rod had to call security and they escorted her out. At the end of the day, when he was leaving the building and walking to his car, the same woman appeared out of nowhere and began haranguing him, right there on the street. As if she'd been waiting for Rod. He tried to calm her down but she got aggressive, grabbed his arm and insisted he needed to bring her to Loach, her mother was a movie star and Loach had killed her, she demanded justice, if Rod didn't give it to her, he was just as guilty. The area's full of mentally disturbed people, Rod had been panhandled aggressively several times, but never anything like that."

She smiled. "Of course, he gave money to anyone who asked. Sometimes he'd take the time to talk to them. Which is what he tried to do with this one. He asked her if she wanted to sit down and tell him her story. She said he was wasting her time, she'd told him everything he needed to know. Then she turned her back on him and left. It bothered him. How deteriorated she was. His inability to help her. Rod cared when other people didn't and that night I found him on the computer reading up on mental illness. I tried to get him to come to bed and he said he needed to understand what led people to be like that. That's the way he was. Engaged. And God-fearing and principled."

She trembled. Hugged herself. "Like I said, it's not relevant. I guess I'm just telling you to show you what Rod was like.

When that nincompoop suggested he'd ended his own life, it was beyond ridiculous. He even had the gall to ask if it was a sin in our religion. Implying I was in denial because I didn't want to see Rod as a sinner. Yes, LDS believe suicide falls under 'Thou shalt not kill.' But it's also something to be treated with sensitivity. We don't judge the person who self-destructs nor do we assume intention and rationality on their part. That said, Rod **was** rational and God-fearing and most important, he believed in the sanctity of life. We were talking about starting a family. We got a late start because I did the career thing rather than settle down. Maybe we wouldn't produce a huge clan but we'd do our best to make up for lost time. Does that sound depressed to you? No way would he destroy himself."

CHAPTER 31

Milo drove west on Riverside Drive, both hands clenching the wheel. "Poor woman, she has no idea what she just accomplished and we couldn't tell her."

I said, "We go fishing and snag a link between Zelda, Salton, and Loach."

"A movie-star mother. Who the hell expected **that**? Not that Rutherford was a movie star. A delusion, like you said. Or could there be truth to Zelda's story?"

"I'm not sure it matters. Zelda believed it and it drove her actions. Five years ago, when she was working and managing to be functional, she told her cast-mates about it. When she dug up the yard at Bel Azura she was screaming about it. And during her final days, when she was just about mute, one of the few words she uttered to me was 'Mother.' Now we know she believed Loach was behind it."

"So she gets into Loach's girlfriend's place and ends up dead. How would she connect the two of them?"

"Enid is Loach's only client, she visits him in the office. Zelda was stalking the building. She could've seen them together."

"And found out where Enid lived? How?"

"No idea, but she did and switched her surveillance to the estate. Meanwhile, she's breaking down mentally. But still clinging to her goal."

"Justice," he said. "Aka revenge."

"As her Ativan wore off, she got crazier but less lethargic. Had enough energy to leave BrightMornings and walk ten miles to Bel Air. What if she spotted Loach driving in and went after him—she wouldn't even have had to scale the wall, just squeeze in before the gates closed. As you guys say, a confrontation ensued and Zelda ended up the loser."

"Lunatic home invader attacks society lawyer and he defends himself. We're talking no charges filed, Alex. Why the need for them to cover up with two calculated murders?"

"Because we're not talking about an errant backhand or gunfire. Zelda was poisoned, as premeditated as it gets."

"Two old sadists deciding to have some fun along the way? Toss in a couple of housekeepers as collateral damage? It's way beyond sickening. Add Rod Salton and it's something I don't have a word for. Speaking of Salton, why'd he have to go? Weeks **before** the others."

"We just heard him described as someone who'd feed his own overdue parking meter. That's admirable but it can also lead to zealotry. Salton was bothered by his encounter with Zelda. What if he mentioned it to Loach expecting Loach to laugh it off. But Loach didn't, he reacted. Maybe subtly but enough to make Salton wonder. He had access to Loach's papers, poked around, and found something. Loach found out and took care of him."

"Poison," he said. "Strange choice and when you do see it, it's often women. And we know a woman with a world-class garden."

"They're in it together," I said.

"Zelda died in Enid's place, Alicia was Enid's maid."

We drove awhile.

I said, "That makes me wonder about a primary link between Zina and **Enid,** with Loach just the trusty assistant. Averell DePauw managed serious money and had industry connections. Hollywood folk like to be entertained and what better venue for a high-end party than a gated estate in Bel Air where Jean Harlow used to crash? Parties require entertainment. And certain types of parties employ sketchy entertainment."

"Failed actresses doing one-nighters," he said. "How your mind tracks."

"Dub Ott told me Zina had an income stream but no job, her landlady was convinced she was hooking. He never found a john-book or evidence that she'd worked nearby bars. But no need for any of that if you're a freelance party favor. What if she got an outcall at Enid and Averell's love nest and something went really bad? If Loach goes that far back as a minion, he'd have been a young lawyer on the make."

"So they disappeared her," he said. "But would Zelda ever find out? Whether or not she really was Zina's daughter? She's wrestling with serious demons **and** managing to be an ace detective?" He laughed and pointed a finger at me. "Don't say it's been known to happen."

"Never crossed my mind."

"And here I thought you were open and honest."

We caught the red light at Mulholland and stopped. Milo said, "How old was Zelda when Zina disappeared?"

"Five," I said. "But Ott found no evidence of a child living with her during the two years she was in that apartment so if Zelda was given up, she was no older than three."

"What I'm getting at is kids that young don't have clear memories, right?"

"Not generally. You're thinking someone had to point her in that direction."

"It's the only thing that makes sense," he said. "However she found out, she decided she needed to take care of business and began living rough in Bel

Air…nah, it doesn't explain Bel Azura. If she'd fixated on St. Denis, even someone in her state wouldn't have confused it with a totally different house. I know you said the houses are close but we're still talking miles, not yards, and they're not remotely similar. I'm getting a headache, amigo."

The light turned green. We began descending the Glen.

I said, "Make a stop at my place."

"Your car's at the station."

"I know. I want to check something. Actually, I want you to."

"It can't wait an extra ten minutes?"

"This time of day, could be fifteen, twenty minutes," I said. "We're right here, humor me."

I explained.

He said, "That's theoretically interesting."

I fidgeted on the battered leather patients' couch in my office as Milo worked my desktop.

Soon we had it: complete ownership records for the house on Bel Azura Drive.

Original date of construction: forty-three years ago. Original purchasers, a couple named MacAndrews.

Eight years after that—just after Zelda's birth—ownership had passed to Zina Jane Smith, the down payment proffered by the G. S. Smith Family Trust of Shaker Heights, Ohio, mortgage payments to be handled by Miss Smith.

Eighteen months later: foreclosure on the grounds of non-payment, reversion to Ahmanson Savings and Loan.

In the ensuing years, the house had been bought and sold several times. Nothing that seemed tied to J. Yarmuth Loach, Esq., his firm, or Enid DePauw.

Milo's eyes were wide. "She was making a pilgrimage to her childhood home—or what she imagined was her childhood home." He grimaced. "Digging up the dirt."

I said, "Digging and crying out for her mother."

He wheeled my chair back a couple of feet and whirled so he faced me. "You think she believed Zina's buried there? Then why didn't she return to find out?"

"The arrest and commitment could've scared her off. Or her mental deterioration made it impossible to follow a sequential plan. I really don't know and I probably never will."

"I'm trying to imagine what it was like to be her," he said. "Groping her way around the city, hearing things, head buzzing like a nonstop acid trip. Nothing can be done for people like that?"

"Some people respond to treatment, some don't, some get worse. No one really understands the successes or the failures."

Milo re-read the foreclosure documents. "A family rich enough to have a trust and they let Zina lose the place."

I said, "Ott said it was the most disinterested family he'd ever come across. No one called or followed up except one brother who phoned once, a month after he couldn't reach her on Thanksgiving. He made it clear that Zina had always been a problem child."

"They got fed up carrying her financially."

"And/or her lifestyle issues repelled them. As in a child out of wedlock, if Zelda really was her daughter. She's never talked about a father."

"All that plus living the La La party life, yeah, I can see noses getting bent," he said. "We're both from the Midwest, it's a zillion parsecs from upper-crust Ohio to here."

He put the papers aside. "Would the family kiss her off if they knew she had a child?"

"If it was a child they didn't approve of? Who knows? The brother didn't express any concern to Ott."

"So maybe Zelda **was** delusional. Or she wasn't and Zina had problems that led her to lose the kid along with her house. Psychosis can run in families, right?"

"Genetics isn't destiny," I said, "but it can be a factor."

"So it's possible Zina had serious mental issues of her own. Unstable party girl is hired for a party, freaks out, poses a threat to someone who can't afford scandal, gets disappeared. I like it, we could sell it as a script. But I can't see any way to prove it."

I said, "Let's learn about the Smiths of Shaker Heights."

CHAPTER 32

The City of Shaker Heights website offered a laid-back summary of public records policy. Personal inspection available during business hours, written requests not required for copies though a detailed description would "facilitate" the process, information provided "within a reasonable period of time."

Those seeking data were instructed to contact the public records manager for the city department most likely to retain their particular record.

No phone numbers or email addresses listed.

Milo switched to the homepage of the Shaker Heights Police, called the Investigative Bureau, and talked to a sergeant named Anton Bach who said, "So we're not talking suspects."

"Just doing some background."

"If it's the Smiths I'm thinking about, never heard of any problems from them."

"The trust is under G. S. Smith."

"Hold on."

Moments later: "Yeah, a guy here says those are the Smiths I was thinking about. G. S. stands for George Seward, he started the company back around the Civil War. My grandfather worked for them during World War Two. Smith Machine Works, parts for cranes, suspension bridges, the big stuff. They closed down when the steel industry tanked. I'm not sure any of the family is still around."

"Would you have any specific names?"

"Hold on."

Moments later: "My guy says no, can't help you there. What kind of background are we talking about, Lieutenant?"

"One of their possible descendants is a homicide victim."

"Possible?"

"That's what I'm trying to clear up."

"Ah, got it," said Bach. "In terms of names,

I could see if we can locate that trust."

"That would be highly appreciated, Sergeant."

"Andy's fine. To be honest, I'm not sure where to go with it, never looked for a trust. Give me your number in case it takes time."

I motioned to Milo.

"Sure, one more question from my partner, Andy. Gimme a sec."

I said, "If the trust owned real estate, there'd be a record of that in the property tax rolls."

Milo relayed the message. Bach said, "Hmm, good idea. I'll put you on hold, if it goes fast, right back at you."

Dead air.

Milo drummed my desk, pulled a pencil out of a drawer and rolled it between his fingers.

I said, "That went smoothly. Talk about connections."

"Get me a private deal for an enormous party pad and I'll start to feel important."

Andy Bach clicked in. "You were right, real estate was the way to go. Trust owned a bunch of properties, sold 'em all a while back. But I found the same face page attached to some of the transactions and it's got names on it. City's been converting to PDF, give me your email."

"Thanks a heap. You come to L.A., I'll take you out for a big steak."

"Last I was in L.A. it was years ago, with the wife and kids. Disneyland, Space Mountain, junk food, those pickles at Disneyland look like they're made in outer space. God forbid I should have time for a quiet meal. But who knows?"

The information had arrived by the time Milo switched to his departmental email.

The sixteenth iteration of the G. S. Smith Family Trust had been set up sixty-four years ago for the benefit of the children of Oletta Elizabeth Smith and Weston Osmond Smith.

The minor children Weston Abel Smith, fourteen; James Finbar Smith, eleven; Sarah Oletta Smith, eight; Enid Lauretta Smith, six.

A separate page on the seventeenth iteration, four years after that, added another beneficiary: the newborn child of

Oletta and Martin Rutherford, Agatha Zina
Rutherford.

Milo said, "Enid and Zina. Finally, the
gods have had enough random."

He printed and we went into the kitchen
where I made coffee and he scrounged
himself a piece of cold roast beef and
couple of less-than-optimal bagels that
aerobicized his jaws. We'd just sat down
when Robin came in with Blanche.

Hugs, kisses, Milo's fake-grudging stoop
to pet Blanche and feed her shreds of
beef. She lingered near his trouser cuffs,
panted a couple of times, and burped
lustily before settling her head atop his
shoe.

Robin said, "Someone's in love."

"Can't help myself, kid. Animal magnetism
strikes again."

"I can feel the earth tilting on its axis.
What are you guys up to?"

I poured coffee for her, pulled out a chair.

"Thanks but I think I'll stand, hon. Been
at the bench all day."

I gave her a recap as she stood next to
me sipping, her free hand running through
my hair.

She said, "Blended family. That can get complicated."

I said, "A half sister tossed into the mix, ten years younger than the youngest of the full sibs."

"Baby of the family got displaced?"

"If Mr. Rutherford stole Mommy away from Mr. Smith, there'd be way more reason for hostility than that. It would also give Enid good reason for not wanting to deal with a usurper's offspring. If Zelda really was Zina's daughter. Or even claimed to be."

"Someone shows up out of the blue, declaring herself family," said Robin. "Not a pleasant surprise."

Milo said, "Psychology's fine but money talks. Membership in this family would mean being an heir. What sounds like serious dough, even divided four ways."

I said, "Even more so if some of the others have died."

Robin said, "Bigger slice of the pie, more motivation not to share."

"Easy enough to find out who the current beneficiaries are, now that we've got full names."

Milo looked down at Blanche, rubbed behind her ears. She purred. "You know how to work the Internet, mademoiselle?"

"Not yet," said Robin. "We're still on basic math."

Blanche cocked her head and smiled. When Milo and I returned to my office, she waddled after us and resumed her position near his feet.

Death certificates for Enid DePauw's three full siblings were confirmed, giving her the entire pie.

I said, "Can't stop being a psychologist," and tunneled into a massive for-pay newspaper archive, pulling up the Cleveland **Plain Dealer**'s society page coverage of the marriage of Miss Oletta Elizabeth Barnaby to Mr. Weston Osmond Smith. Fourteen months prior to the birth of Weston Jr., so everything was by the book in Marriage Number One.

Gala affair, the right orchestra, the right guests, ceremony in the Presbyterian church, reception in the "luxuriant, flower-rich" gardens of the Smith family estate.

Using Zina Rutherford's birthdate as an approximation, I searched for coverage of

the union between Oletta and Martin
Rutherford.

Nothing.

I said, "Time for the census rolls."

Several Martin Rutherfords in Ohio. But
narrowing it down to Shaker Heights and
estimating the time frame pulled up what I
was looking for.

Martin Phillip Rutherford had been
twenty-six years old when he switched his
residence from the city of Cleveland to
the affluent suburb. Occupation prior to
that: gas station attendant and automotive
mechanic. Afterward: automotive steward
and driver.

At the time of the trust revision, Rutherford
had been working for the Smiths for six
years.

His new wife was forty-five.

Milo said, "Taking up with the chauffeur.
In the market for a cliché? Stick with the
classics."

I said, "That explains no attention from
the paper. And it sure must've thrilled the
other kids. Not to mention Husband
Number One, if he got thrown over."

"Traded in for a stud who knew his axle

grease...okay, show yourself, Weston O."

Back to the census. No listing for Weston Osmond Smith during the period after his wife's second marriage. I scrolled back, finally found him five years prior to Zina Rutherford's birth.

A year after Martin Rutherford began driving for the family.

Milo said, "Even if he died prior to her conception, there are three hundred sixty-five days' worth of potential hanky-panky."

A switch back to the newspaper archives pulled up Weston's sizable obituary in **The Plain Dealer.** Manufacturer, sportsman, philanthropist. Aged fifty-four, natural causes.

Milo, "That makes him...fourteen years older than Oletta. Almost the same difference as between her and Martin. Establish your status and moolah by marrying a rich older guy, then go for youth and a masterful stick shift."

I said, "Toss in a twilight baby and you've got serious breeding ground for volatility."

"Oletta must've been some gal. I'm thinking heavy breathing in the backseat of the family Packard. For all we know, Martin and Oletta met before Martin became the chauffeur, when he was still pumping gas. She wheels in for a lube—stop me."

He swatted hair off his brow, stood and paced, sat back down. "Amazing what you can learn from a bunch of dates. Or are we getting too creative here?"

I said, "Whatever the specifics, it's easy to see why Zina wasn't embraced by the bosom of the Smith family. And as we said, her lifestyle choices would have only made matters worse."

"Problem child comes to Hollywood," he said. "Okay, shunning I can see. But how could she get foreclosed on and end up scrounging for a living? She was a beneficiary of the trust, had her own dough."

"That would've depended on how the trust was structured. If there was a cutoff clause—spendthrift, moral turpitude—she could've been left with nothing."

"Oletta has a late-in-life kid and allows that kind of vulnerability?"

"If the trustee was a third party—a banker, a lawyer, an old friend of Weston's who disapproved of Oletta's choices—the contingency could've been inserted without her knowledge. Or it was part of the trust all along. Those kinds of restrictions are pretty standard with irrevocable trusts and we're talking about a document that goes back generations. For Oletta to change things, she'd have needed to be paying attention to details. In those days, women were often shunted away from financial matters."

I took another look at the trust's face sheet. "What's interesting is that it adds Zina but doesn't include Martin. Maybe another fund was set up for him. Or he wasn't around long enough."

I checked the next census count. As far as the federal government was concerned, Martin Phillip Rutherford didn't exist.

Neither did Oletta.

Milo said, "Neither of them was around by then?"

Death records confirmed it: The couple had perished on the same day, within months of the trust's inclusion of baby Zina. No cause listed.

I said, "Could be an accident."

"Chauffeur cracks up the Packard?"

"Leaving behind five kids, ranging from

eighteen to infant."

"An infant the others resented. Yeah, Zina didn't have a charmed childhood."

Back to the newspaper records. No obits for Martin and Oletta Rutherford.

I said, "Same blackout as the wedding. Oletta inherited a fortune but her social status was gone."

"If it was an accident and local, Shaker Heights might still have a record of it, I'll try Bach. But first let's concentrate on what we know about Zina. Left as a baby to the good graces of people who hated her guts. Probably handed off to some servant. Later, maybe a boarding school. I can sure see her wanting to get the hell out of Ohio. So she comes out here and does the reinvention bit."

I said, "She was a good-looking woman, tried to break into the industry. Instead, she got pregnant and triggered a clause that made her poor."

"Bye-bye house in the hills," he said. "So she does what it takes to make a living— uh-oh, hold on. That totally monkey-wrenches the party-house scenario. You see Zina freelancing at Sister Enid's bash?

Who has **also** moved out west. Which is kind of interesting—maybe she also had Hollywood aspirations."

"Another tall blonde," I said. "She was ten years older than Zina but maybe still young enough. Or believed she was. Sure, why not?"

"Neither of them made it in pictures but Enid snagged herself a husband with connections. You think at some point the sisters could've had a decent relationship? If they did, Zina could've been an invited party guest."

"It's a thought," I said.

"Even if they didn't get along, Zina could have still been at Enid's party, as a crasher. And something happened. Or we're totally off base and she died some other way."

He got up again, paced longer, remained on his feet. Blanche watched him, then shuffled over. He didn't notice her until she began breathing hard. "Fine, fine, relax, you're appreciated...Alex, what I still can't figure out is how someone in Zelda's state managed to put any of this together."

"As I said, we may never know," I said. "But her mental status may have been less of a factor than I thought. Her breakdown was a process, not an event. When I saw her five years ago, she was acting odd but functioning well enough to do her job. Doing it well enough to be kept on a second season. Before that, she was likely more lucid."

"You're saying she mighta been sufficiently together to do the snooping."

"More likely paying someone to snoop."

"Fine. But she waited until she was homeless and full-blown crazy to go into action. Breaking into Enid's place and announcing she was a rightful heir."

"Maybe that wasn't her first attempt."

"She's been bugging Enid for a while? Look who's here, Auntie. Your worst nightmare?"

I said, "Expensive nightmare."

"If Zina **was** cut off, would Zelda have a claim on anything?"

"The mere threat of going to court might've been enough. Beyond the money, there was the issue of **Enid's** social standing. Rich aunt in Bel Air, helpless, impaired niece on the streets? Can you imagine if the **Times** got hold of it?"

He returned to the sofa. "You're making sense but is any of that a motive for multiple murder?"

"Get someone sufficiently threatened and there's no telling," I said. "You've seen enough chain reactions, one thing leading to another."

"True but there could also be something to your fun factor. You want to eliminate complications, there are quicker, neater ways than feeding someone poison and watching them die. That says hatred—oh, man, we still need to find out how Oletta and Martin died. Remember what the paper said about her first wedding? Big gardens, lots of flowers? If the two of them got bad stomachaches after drinking homemade consommé, it's gonna get **way** more interesting."

"Enid was nine at the time," I said.

"You don't believe in bad seeds? So to speak."

"A calculated dual poisoning? That would be very precocious."

"So one of the other sibs did it. Or all the kids conspired, family that slays together, stays together."

He phoned Andy Bach.

"That, Lieutenant, I can probably get right here in our records."

"You're a prince."

"Tell my wife, she's been looking at me like I'm a frog...we've got a real good record of automotive accidents, had a federal grant to organize it, so sit tight... yup, here it is, single-car collision, ice on the road, your basic skid-out...hit a mulberry tree. Two fatalities, driver and passenger, Mr. and Mrs. M. Rutherford."

"Was it a Packard?"

"Nope, a Lincoln."

"Shucks," said Milo. "Here I was thinking of becoming a think-tank cowboy!"

He thanked Bach again, hung up, returned to the computer. "Now it's time for a seminar on Counselor Loach."

Jarrell Yarmuth Loach was sixty-seven years old, with an occasional penchant for speeding in his Audi but no criminal record. The headshot on his firm's website showed a square-faced man with snow-white hair and rimless glasses. Squinty eyes behind the lenses, a crooked smile that had probably once been boyish.

Milo had called him Mr. CEO. My first thought was Cary Grant's plainer brother.

Berkeley undergrad, Hastings law, no problems with the state bar. The summary on the site featured an impressive list of civic organizations and a lectureship at the U.'s law school.

Milo said, "Get this: He's taught classes on business ethics in estate law."

"The halls of academe," I said. "Those who don't do, teach."

Loach paid property tax in the State of California for two addresses: a house on Thayer Avenue in Westwood and a condominium at Arroyo Blanco Estates, Palm Springs.

Milo began leafing through his notes. "Thought so. Damn. One of the places I called when I was looking into Enid." He phoned, used his Nice Guy voice and a mutual need for discretion to get what he wanted from the on-duty manager, hung up looking fulfilled.

"Loach pays for the place but he never uses it. But guess what, Enid has. Her name didn't come up because they were checking the owners book and guests are entered in the tenant log."

"Organized," I said.

"High-security and all that. Guests need to be preapproved by the management. They've also got a card-key system that feeds straight into their central computer, so they can tell if someone's there and exactly when they come and go. Last time Enid clocked in—last time anyone did— was three months ago. By herself, no maid, the place provides housekeeping services."

"Three months ago is around the time of Rod Salton's death."

He frowned, flipped more pages. "Interesting. She arrived two days before Salton's body was found, departed two days after. Think that's significant?"

"Gives her somewhat of an alibi," I said. "Maybe that was the point."

"Somewhat?"

"She cooks up a batch of aconite and gives it to Loach, her being elsewhere means nothing. Is it certain Loach wasn't at the condo with her?"

"According to the manager, a hundred

percent certain. Every person gets logged in and out at the gatehouse, no exceptions, the residents want it that way. And like I said, Loach is an absentee owner, the manager's been there two years, hasn't laid eyes on him."

"A condo in Palm Springs," I said. "Enid tweaked reality, Smooth Lying 101. So where are the two of them now?"

"For all we know, back at her place. Or, lacking that, his."

We drove to St. Denis, pulled up to Enid DePauw's gate, and pushed the button. No response to three attempts. Searching for a thin spot in the trees behind the stone wall, Milo walked a bit before finding a niche for a foothold. Hoisting himself up, he lost his footing, tried again, and hung on long enough for a brief peek.

"Lights off everywhere. Unless they're having a slumber party at eight, they ain't here."

We continued south, across Sunset, into the section of Westwood that flanks the U. on the east. J. Yarmuth Loach's house was an unassuming two-story traditional.

Audi coupe in the driveway, no mail piled up in front of the door, a smatter of lights on.

Milo eased to the curb. "No sign of Enid's Porsche or her Rolls and I don't have a plausible story for showing up at night. Can you think of one?"

I couldn't.

He said, "I'll bop by tomorrow morning, try to catch him before he leaves for work. Or the country club or wherever he hangs out, seeing as he doesn't work much. Let's collect your wheels and you can go home and kiss both the women in your life."

He showed up at my front door at eight-thirty the next morning. "Spoke to Loach's maid. **Señor no aqui,** left with two suitcases. She had no idea where he was headed but two pieces of luggage says more than an overnight. I called the manager at Arroyo Blanco, asked to be notified if they show up. Just in case they decided to go international, I've been trying to reach my contact at Homeland Security, let me give it another whirl."

Plopping down on a living room sofa, he

switched to hands-off and punched a preset number.

Dry croak: "Hello-o."

"Irene? Finally got you. Milo."

"You're calling me at home?"

"Tried the office."

"Hnh." She coughed. Cleared her throat. "Sick?"

"You must be a detective. Yeah, some kind of shitty flu. All last week I was in the arrival hall. Customs had word on maggots trying to smuggle in snakes and birds but it futzed out. Meanwhile, there's hordes of who-knows-who from who-knows-where bringing in who-knows-what diseases. Should've worn a mask but I can't stand the way they feel."

"Sorry, Irene. When you do have time—"

"You already interrupted my soup. What?"

He told her.

She said, "Any reason these two would set off our alarms?"

"On the contrary," said Milo. "Older, affluent, respectable. No problem from your end at all, Irene."

"So this is a one-way street." She sniffled. "You don't like them, huh?"

"Wouldn't want them on my buddy list."

"Old and rich," she said. "That gives me an idea. Give me some time to get the soup down and I'll see what I can do."

She coughed again. "That one was to make you feel guilty."

Ten minutes later, she was back. "Like I thought, they both registered with Global Entry, our Trusted Traveler Program."

"Paying to avoid long lines."

"People without jihad affections like it, sir. Sometimes we let them keep their shoes on. Anyway, it makes it easier to pinpoint their comings and goings. Three days ago, Ms. DePauw and Mr. Loach booked adjoining first-class seats on an Alitalia flight to Rome. Round-trip, they're due back in six days."

"Thanks a ton, Irene."

"That's **grazie** to you."

Milo put down the phone. "I'm gonna sort all this out in my mind and see if John Nguyen has any time to chat. He does, I'll beg and scrape for a warrant to search Enid's estate."

"Homeowner out of the country?" I said.

"Going to be tough."

"I'm not after the house at this point, just the grounds and nothing intrusive, a look-see. John's been known to be creative."

"You could moonlight with White Glove Cleaning and get in."

"There you go, me with a dust-mop, whistling while I work." Gathering his materials, he headed for the door.

I said, "By look-see you mean searching for vegetable and animal matter. As in deceased human animals?"

"Well," he said, "I don't see minerals being a problem."

CHAPTER 33

Alone in my office, I thought about Zina Rutherford, born to rejection and hostility, rendered helpless soon after. I could only imagine her childhood. But somehow, she'd survived.

Coming to L.A. to reinvent herself, floundering, failing. As her big sister made the scene in Malibu, Beverly Hills, Bel Air.

A sister who despised her enough to ruin her?

Now Zelda, dead at the same woman's hands.

Broken-down mother, broken-down daughter?

The next generation, a son I couldn't locate.

Knowing what had happened to Ovid felt

far out of reach, one of those moving
targets you chase endlessly in dreams
that don't end up well.

Then I thought of something. The Ursula
Corey case, again. Her husband's divorce
lawyer was a Beverly Hills octogenarian
named Earl Cohen who'd broken
confidentiality and helped break the case.
Explaining the ethical lapse as a terminally
ill old man doing what was right.

Skeletal, frail. **They give me months, not
years.**

A year had passed. Scratch that.

I sat there awhile longer, found Cohen's
number in my book and was ready to call
when my service rang with an urgent
message from Judith Meers.

I phoned BrightMornings, Hollywood.
She said, "Hi, Dr. Delaware. Chet Brett is
here right now, and he says he'll talk to
you about Zelda Chase. But you know
how it is, that could change any second.
Are you close?"

"Forty minutes away. I'm leaving now."

"Ooh," she said. "I'll try to keep him here—
he's always hungry, maybe snacks will
help."

I made it in thirty-four. Judy was behind the desk, working on her laptop. A couple of empty-eyed men sat in armchairs at the rear of the lobby, neither of them five-foot-tall Norwegians.

She said, "Sorry, he wouldn't stay inside, went back to his car. Five minutes ago, he was still there, parked up that way." Pointing east. "Approach him slowly and try not to alarm him. He may not remember your name."

I hurried outside. The car had been in full sight but I'd walked right by. Pea-green Plymouth Valiant as old as my Seville but far less pampered. The rear compartment was piled to the roof with folded clothing and slices of cardboard. A man sat in the driver's seat. I edged forward slowly. He was holding half of an Oreo in each hand and licking crème from the good side.

Warm day, but the windows were shut. I walked up to the front passenger window, waited to see if he'd turn. When he didn't, I rapped softly. He curled his tongue back in his mouth and gave another lick. I waved to get his attention. Rapped again before he turned and studied me.

Homeless-ageless, anywhere from fifties to eighties, with a tiny, withered face under hair that looked like cotton wool. Yellow perforated Lakers jersey far too large for him. Magenta sweatpants.

I'd been told he was a small man but he sat in the driver's seat as high as I did.

He kept staring at me while tonguing the cookie. I said, "Alex Delaware," just loud enough for him to hear.

He pointed to the passenger door and mouthed a word. **Open.**

The car was hot, humid, ripe as a dumpster full of old produce. As I settled, another wave of aromas hit me. Vintage laundry basket, Lysol, a touch of fermenting cantaloupe. His legs proportional to the rest of his body, everything in miniature. Two cushions under his butt propped him. The pedals near his sneakers had been mechanically extended, a surprising touch of high-tech.

In his lap were packets of cheese crackers, licorice sticks, another set of Oreos.

"Thanks for seeing me, Mr. Brett."

"The full name is Carlsson Mathiass

Brekken, two pairs of S's, one pair of K's. Double letters are good luck to the Chinese." High-pitched voice, suggesting prepubescence.

"Thanks, Mr. Brek—"

"Eh eh eh eh eh eh, don't get formal. To the world I'm the esteemed Chetley Bretley, aka Chet Brett aka me." Deeply puckered lips spread, revealing a tooth-less maw. "I'm telling you to educate you. Don't want to be Brekken anyone's heart."

My laugh was genuine.

He said, "That's me, still crazy after all these years. You're a doctor. You know Zelda."

No sense complicating things with past tense. "I do."

He began singing softly, in a surprisingly good alto. "If you knew Zelda, like I knew Zelda, oh, oh, oh, what a gal...so what's going on with her?"

I hesitated for an instant but that was enough.

"Something bad," he said. "No one comes to me with good news. Even the Chinese."

"The worst, I'm afraid."

"Really?" he said. "Really? That's not

good. When?"

"Couple of weeks ago."

"Really? How?"

"She ate something poisonous."

"That makes no sense," said Brett. "She was a slim girl, had no appetite for food, let alone poison."

He nibbled the frosted Oreo half, chipping off bits with his gums until it was gone.

"Actresses," he said. "Always watching their weight. I was a film director back in Oslo, made art movies. Made **Citizen Kane** but that didn't work out so I switched to documentary movies on symptoms of depression among the palace royalty. I needed serious money so I resoled shoes in Gottenborg, that's Sweden. After that, I worked in Copenhagen—you know that **Little Mermaid** sculpture by the harbor? I made it."

Not a trace of Nordic accent.

I said, "Wow."

"I've been known to wow." He studied the remaining half cookie. Rotated it and said, "This could be the sun on an alien planet. I used to be an astronomer. Then I switched to engineering." Tapping his right foot on the extended gas pedal. "Made these in Cal Tech, everyone wants one but I keep the formula to myself."

I sat there as he worked on the other cookie half. Focused, meticulous, not a single falling crumb.

When he finished, I said, "So you and Zelda were friends."

"Acquaintances," said Brett. "Two ships passing on the street. How's her boy? Judith said you knew the boy, your interest is the boy."

"I saw him five years ago, would love to know he's okay."

"She felt bad about giving him up but I told her it was the right thing to do. Why wouldn't he be okay?"

"With Zelda living on the street and now, deceased—"

"No problem," said Chet Brett. "She gave him up before she hit the street."

"Really."

"Really really really really really. I met her soon after she hit the street. He wasn't with her, I never saw him."

"Where was he?"

"All she said was she missed him, was

thinking of getting him so she could be with him. I told her not to, it wouldn't work out, kids need TV and she had nowhere to plug in."

"How long ago did this happen?"

"Time," he said. "That's also a magazine. It was…when she was out on the street. Near a flop on Fourth and L.A., I was eating beans out of a can, cut my finger opening it, blood was getting into the beans, everyone thought it was ketchup."

"Near a flop."

"Not inside," said Chet Brett. "You could get a room with bugs if you saved up. I did. Zelda never did but I was outside anyway, eating red red beans. She showed up looking like a slim actress and put a blanket down next to my sleeping bag. Wrong thing for her to do, she was too young and clean for the adventurous life. When I found out she was an actress, I told her to go on auditions. You never know. Maybe she did. She'd be gone for days, come back looking like she'd lost something."

"You have no idea when—"

"Let's estimate. That's how I built these." Tapping the pedal. "Sometime between the world wars. Up in Scandinavia, all those northern lights, we use a different system of calendar computing. Not Gregorian, not Julian, we use Olafian. It makes predictions more difficult but also more relaxed."

"Ah."

"Ah so," said Brett. "That's Chinese for 'there you go, Shogun. Give me a double letter.'"

He reached for a packet of cheese crackers, opened it carefully.

"So you never met Zelda's son."

"Never. But he's okay. I feel it right here." Patting the empty Oreo packet. "Way the cookie crumbles."

"Did Zelda ever talk about Ovid?"

"That was his name?" said Chet Brett. "She just called him 'my son.' What else does a mother need to know? Sometimes she'd cry. Then she'd cry some more. One time I told her she needed to tell me what was bothering her so she could relax. She said she'd given him up because she had no money to take care of him but she wanted him back. I told her she did the right thing, why make a child starve? It didn't make her feel better. But she listened."

He scratched his head for a long time, reached down and crinkled the snacks in his lap. "Usually I can make people feel better. Next year, I'm going to be a psychiatrist. Maybe that'll help."

He began work on a cracker.

"Did Zelda ever talk about her mother?"

"She had one? No."

"A sister?"

"Nope."

"Did she mention anyone in her family—"

"She wasn't into mentioning. Just lots of crying. Maybe she wore herself out. Emotionally. You can't lubricate for that."

"True. Anything else you want to tell me?"

"I like your shirt. Goes with your complexion."

"Thanks."

"That'll be twenty bucks."

I reached for my wallet.

Chet Brett said, "Just kidding, I can't take payment. Not until I pass my boards. Next year, it's going to cost you."

I drove away wanting to feel reassured but knowing what I'd just heard was as reliable as a campaign promise.

Time to try Earl Cohen.

"Crazy man, probable dead man. What's next."

I realized I'd thought out loud. Talking to myself. As long as you didn't move your lips—or held a cellphone to your mouth—you were fine.

At the next red light, I punched numbers.

"Earl Cohen's office."

"Dr. Alex Delaware calling for Mr. Cohen."

"He's in a meeting. Would you like his voicemail?"

"Please. So he's okay?"

"Pardon—oh, that." She laughed. "He's fine."

Cohen's recorded voice, stronger than a year ago, declared: "This is Earl. Speak."

I spoke.

CHAPTER 34

My private line rang moments after I stepped into the house.

Earl Cohen said, "Hopefully you're not in need of my services."

"Not married."

"Your gain is my loss."

"You sound good, Mr. Cohen."

"Meaning why am I not dead? What can I tell you? Nothing a few spare parts didn't take care of. What's on your mind?"

"I'm looking for information on some people who were around thirty years ago—"

"Thirty years ago? Gee whiz, we wrote on stone tablets back then. So you reach out to Methuselah? Who are these cave people?"

"Enid and Averell DePauw."

"I see." Cohen's tone had changed. Guarded. "Never represented any of them."

"But you know them."

"I'd like to know why you're interested."

"It's complicated," I said.

"I'm able to deal with complications."

"Could we meet? Drinks or dinner, on me."

"I don't drink, nor am I currently hungry. Are you conducting this inquiry for yourself or for that heavyset police fellow—Sturgis?"

"It's related to police work."

"Is anyone else involved?"

Strange question.

I said, "No."

"What I'm getting at, Doctor, is my own brand of complications. An official inquiry, I talk to you and suddenly I'm getting calls from civil servants."

"No, nothing like that. Sturgis doesn't even know I'm calling."

"And I'm not having this conversation with Sturgis because…"

"I'm doing my own research. No sense drawing him in if there's nothing to learn."

"You're seeing if I have anything to offer

first, in order to conserve his energy? From the looks of him, he conserves quite a lot of energy. All right, remember where I talked to the two of you, last year? I don't mean my office, our alfresco meeting."

I said, "The park at Doheny and Santa Monica. Walking distance to your house."

"You remember—and you're older than thirty! I can be there in an hour or so. I assume you look the same. I don't."

He appeared five minutes after I got to the park, walking from the west as he had the last time. True to his word, he'd changed. So much so that I might not have recognized him.

Meager white hair was dyed an uneasy meld of brunette and copper, accentuating the spots where it thinned to the scalp. He'd put on considerable weight, inflating from gaunt to average build, his skeletal face round and padded.

Last year, he'd worn an overcoat on a warm afternoon. Today was cool and he had on apricot-colored linen pants secured by a brown knit belt, a corn-yellow dress shirt, maroon slip-ons. Every plodding step exposed pale ankles.

At times he seemed to falter but when he reached me and proclaimed, "Doctor!" he shook my hand with vigor.

I said, "Spare parts seem to be working well."

"Medical science proclaims me a miracle man. A few bypassed arteries, a couple of tumors sent packing, a reconstituted disk in my neck, and thyroid hormone to keep me metabolizing. Been feeling so hale, I'm pondering Viagra. My wife's worried I'll go blind and grope another woman."

The only other people in the park were two gorgeous women in yoga clothes perched on the rim of a dry fountain, luxuriating in perfect posture as their dogs socialized. Cohen admired them for a moment, before veering to the northern periphery of the lawn and walking.

Bionic man on fuel-saving mode. I slowed down to keep pace.

He said, "So you're Sherlocking full-time? No more listening to people's problems?"

"No, I still do that."

"Mixing it up," he said. "Keeps life

interesting. Fine, tell me a complicated story."

I kept Alicia, Imelda, Rod Salton, and Loach out of the narrative, described Zelda, without naming her, as a homeless trespasser who'd died in Enid DePauw's garden, cause of death still "undetermined."

"But you'd like to determine." Unmoved, unimpressed. A guy who'd heard it all.

I thought of the odd question he'd posed. **Is anyone else involved?**

"Resolution's always better, Mr. Cohen."

"You're saying it could be foul play? On the part of Enid?"

Not shocked by the question. I shrugged.

The look Cohen gave me was one I knew well. Sitting on the stand as an expert witness, as a lawyer prepared to attack.

Then he shrugged, too. "Enid I was aware of because she was married to Av and Av I knew well. There was a time you'd term us chums. Bright boy, he had a law degree but never practiced, found it more profitable to move money around. We met forty-plus years ago when he sent business to the firm I worked for before I went out on my own. They assigned me to his company and we hit it off."

"Were you doing family law at the time?"

"That's all I've ever done, Doctor."

"The business he sent was rich people divorcing."

"As you know, rich people create difficult situations when they get emotional. Too much incentive for mischief. What I did for Av's clients was what today you'd call forensic accounting. My father was a bookkeeper, I knew how to add and subtract."

I said, "Finding hidden assets."

Cohen smiled. "You're not the only one who likes to detect."

"What kind of person was Av?"

"Friendly, outgoing. As I said, smart, though clever would be more accurate. Knowing what he had to know but not bothering to delve further."

"Surface intelligence."

"Mile wide, inch deep, like every politician I've met," said Cohen. "His talent was conversation. He could talk about anything and if you got too specific for him, he'd switch to listening. Or pretending to. I liked him, terrific company, always a positive attitude. We were around the same age, played tennis whenever we could at Roxbury Park. Not golf, golf was a country-club thing and he, being of the Gentile persuasion, played at Wilshire, I at Hillcrest. Good backhand, Averell. We'd also meet on business matters, usually over dinner and too many cocktails. Back then, young Beverly Hills bucks frequented the same locales."

He held up a finger. "I can tell you what he drank. Moscow Mules, those little copper cups. He liked his ginger beer sharp."

One of the beauties rose from the fountain rim, bent liquidly, and leashed her dog. Cohen watched her and sighed. "It goes by fast, my friend...where was I—the watering holes. The Polo Lounge, Chasen's, Scandia, they all closed down in the eighties and nineties. If we were feeling a little less buttoned down and didn't mind umbrellas in our drinks, Trader Vic's—still there, but different. Or the Luau on Rodeo—that one was owned by Lana Turner's husband, went under even earlier. Averell was a generous tipper, took the time to schmooze with waiters and busboys. When you were with him, you got great service...what else...good-looking fellow in that Bob Cummings way."

"What was his background?"

"Perfect for managing rich people's money. East Coast prep school, Amherst, law at Virginia. I'm Harvard all the way through, used to kid him about being bush league. He'd make a crack about laboring under the weight of a massive foreskin."

Cohen turned toward the remaining yoga princess. "Such perfection they achieve today. Anyway, that's Averell. Enid came later, he married her when he was well into his forties, she must have been midthirties at least."

"I've learned he had studio connections."

"You learned?"

"He bought his house from MGM in a private sale. Did he do a lot of industry work?"

"Anyone worth their salt in Beverly Hills wanted industry work," said Cohen. "Was Av a unique whiz with investments? Naw, just a competent stocks and bonds man, cautious strategies, conservation of wealth. If he had any corporate clients, I never heard about them. Don't read too much into a private sale, Doctor. People had their ears to the ground because the studios were always hustling to raise quick bucks by unloading real estate they'd picked up on the cheap. Not just in the Golden Triangle, we're talking huge acreage in Burbank they didn't need anymore for shooting westerns, Thousand Oaks, the Antelope Valley. Private sales worked out for everyone: A seller could discount up to the amount of the brokerage fee they avoided, and if the documents were fudged to reduce property tax and put some extra cash into someone's pocket, who'd know?"

"Still," I said, "that's an impressive place on St. Denis."

"You're showing your age, Doctor. Or rather the lack of. By today's standards, it's Xanadu. I'm not saying it was ever cheap but back then, if you had money—I don't mean Buffett–Gates money, a solid six-figure income—you could acquire some serious soil because real estate didn't take off until the midseventies. My daughter works with me so I know what she earns. She had to take a big mortgage to buy a nice but not fancy house on a south-of-Wilshire seven-thousand-foot lot. For three million dollars. I have a twenty-thousand-square-foot lot on Sierra and paid a hundred grand in 1968."

A wisp of breeze caused red-brown strands to flutter away from his skull. "Long-term capital gain is a benefit of being a dinosaur. One of the few."

I said, "So Averell bought the estate with his own money."

"Did I say or imply that? What I said was it didn't take that much for anyone with decent cash flow to get a place like that. I could've bought an even bigger property than he did, nine acres on Bellagio. Forget it, too much maintenance."

We continued walking.

Cohen said, "What I heard but can't confirm is that Enid chipped in big-time, or maybe paid for the whole caboodle. She came from big money in the Midwest. The family made tractors or something."

"Cleveland. Machine parts."

"So you know. So what do you expect to learn from me?"

"What do you think of Enid?"

"What do **you** think of her?"

"Only met her once," I said. "Despite a dead body in her garden, she seemed pretty cool and collected."

"You're seriously considering she had something to do with it."

"You consider that unlikely?"

Cohen's hair flew up again. He made no effort to suppress it. "What haven't you told me, Doctor? If that little précis you gave me is 'complicated,' **my** foreskin's going to grow back."

"This needs to stay between us."

"I am the soul of discretion." Cohen laughed. "You're thinking that's a hoot, last we spoke I spilled more beans than a drunken chuckwagon cook. I explained at the time: I wanted to die in a burst of altruism. Now that I realize I'm going to live forever, I'm back to keeping my mouth shut."

"The woman who died on Enid's property claimed she was the daughter of Zina Rutherford, Enid's half sister."

"Claimed?" he said. "You think she was raving?"

I'd said nothing about mental illness.

Rather than waiting for an answer, he went on. "You know better than me, Doctor. People **claim** they see little green men. Pink elephants." Going on too long, his voice losing conviction.

No sense challenging him. I said, "She was mentally ill but that doesn't mean there was no truth to her claim."

"Zina's daughter," he said. "Never met Zina, let alone her daughter."

"What was Enid like?"

"The first time I saw her was at Scandia, they had a lattice gazebo at the back of the main room, a bunch of us were dining there and Averell entered with a woman and everyone noticed her. Was she gorgeous? If you like Bette Davis. Tall, blond, nice shoulders, great haunches— she wore a blood-red dress, designed to show off what she had."

His hands formed an hourglass.

I said, "Making a statement."

"A classy statement, those days every woman of means projected class. So did the fellows, we wore suits and ties to the Rose Bowl."

"Bette Davis," I said. "A little hard around the edges?"

"More like strength of character—her, Joan Crawford, Barbara Stanwyck, Ida Lupino. Some fellows go for that, my taste runs to pillowy and emotionally vulnerable—Monroe. I met her, such a fragile gal."

He laughed. "Not that I ended up with vulnerable. My wife's Japanese, I thought I'd be getting a geisha and woke up with a samurai. Though she **has** remained gorgeous. What does Enid look like nowadays?"

"Keeps herself up, elegant. She has a boyfriend."

"Really. Who?"

"J. Yarmuth Loach."

"Him? He's younger than her."

I waited.

Cohen said, "Got to be what, ten years younger?"

"Three."

"I would've thought more. Back then, he seemed like a kid."

"How'd you know him?"

"He worked for Av. I thought of him as a kid but I guess he had to be late twenties. Yarmie and Enid, huh? Guess it makes sense, he imitated everything Av did—four-in-hand tie knot, same phraseology. If Av wore an ascot, a few days later you'd see one on Yarmie. Av used to joke about it, I'm Pete, he's Repeat. Not in a nasty way, I think he enjoyed being emulated. Being held up as the standard of Wasp savoir faire."

"Loach didn't share that background."

"With his name, you'd have thought so," said Cohen. "J. Yarmuth, don't recall what the J stood for…I know he didn't come from money because during the Pete and Repeat conversation Av said look how far a Bakersfield hick can go with good tailoring. I remember that because it made me wonder what Av really thought of me. My parents never owned a house, I went to Bronx High School of Science, got into Harvard on a scholarship and caught plenty of bigotry there. I resolved to keep my own name and not pretend I was someone else. That's why I moved here. L.A. was wide open for anyone with brains and drive. Where are you from?"

"Missouri."

"Come from money?"

"Not even close."

"And look at you, a man of sophistication, a healer of minds. **And** a self-styled Sherlock."

"What did Loach do for Av?"

"He was also a lawyer but didn't want to be. Instead of clerking or joining a firm, he took a low-paying apprenticeship at Av's company. What that entailed, I couldn't tell you."

He shook his head. "Young Yarmie consorting with Enid, go know."

"He's practicing law now."

"Where?"

"Revelle, Winters, Loach, Russo."

"He's a named partner? Bakersfield made it big," said Cohen. "Don't know the firm, never had dealings with them. Must be downtown, not the Westside."

"Seventh Street."

"As downtown as you can get. What's Yarmie's specialty?"

"Estates and trusts."

"For that, training with Av would be an

asset."

I said, "He doesn't seem to work much, could be a rainmaker."

Cohen looked at me. "You've been researching him, too? You suspect both of them are up to something? Are you saying this insane woman really **was** the sister's offspring and put the screws on Enid for serious moolah and Yarmie overstepped trying to defend his honey?"

I stared at him.

He said, "Been deducing for a long time." He looked away. Even old lawyers give up tells.

I said, "That's all it is, deduction?"

"What else would it be?"

"With all due respect, Mr. Cohen, that's a helluva lot of information to pull out of the air. I also find your remark about raving interesting since I never mentioned mental illness."

He took a second to answer. "I don't have a crystal ball, Doctor, deduction is all it is—logic. You said she was homeless and broke into Enid's place. To me that sounds crazy."

Plausible, but no conviction at all in his

voice.

Is anyone else involved?

"Mr. Cohen, I get the feeling I'm not the first person asking you these questions."

"Why would you think that?"

"You asked me if anyone else besides Lieutenant Sturgis was involved. And despite your explanation, that question about raving was a significant conceptual leap."

"Homeless? The majority of them aren't seriously disturbed?"

I smiled.

He faced me. "Who do you think I talked to?"

"All I can do is guess, Mr. Cohen. Someone also interested in 'psychological' issues. Maybe a psychiatrist named Lou Sherman?"

He stopped short, pitched forward scuffing dirt, held his hands out for balance.

I reached out to brace him; he shook me off. "I'm fine, I'm fine. So what is this, a game? You know the answers but you're testing me? The way cops do with suspects—what I do when I cross-examine? When I passed the bar, I said no more tests.

Got that?"

"Just trying to get to the truth, Mr. Cohen."

He puffed his lips. Above us, a cloud passed over the sun, leaving a glare that turned his dyed hair the hue of bloody cotton. For an instant, he looked like a battered man. Then another cloud arrived and restored him to mere cosmetic pretense.

I said, "Lou Sherman would want you to talk to me. We were friends and colleagues, he's the one who got me involved with Zelda. That's her name, by the way. Zelda Chase. But you already know that, don't you?"

"Then have Dr. Sherman release me from confidentiality."

"Unfortunately, he's passed on."

Cohen flinched.

I said, "Not everyone benefits from spare parts—"

"I get it," snapped Cohen. He resumed walking. "If you're playing on my survivor guilt, you're succeeding. When did he die?"

"A little over two years ago. When did he come to see you?"

Cohen sighed. "Good man, Dr. Sherman.

He impressed me as a shrink who actually cared about his patients, you don't see that often."

He paused again, pivoted sharply but managed to maintain his balance, eyes narrow and acute. "You really were colleagues?"

"If you'd like I can send you his chart on Zelda. My name's in there, that's how I reconnected with her."

"No, no, I believe you. He came to me around four years ago. What was your involvement?"

"Lou asked me to evaluate Zelda's son. To see how he was functioning and to find out if Zelda was competent to care for him. At the time, she was. The boy's eleven, Mr. Cohen. If he's alive. He hasn't been seen since Zelda began living on the streets. I'm trying to find out if he's okay."

"And if he's not?" said Earl Cohen. "That'll be tough to hear."

"Better than not knowing."

"So now you toss in guilt over a child's welfare, wonderful. You understand my reluctance. You've already seen me relax my ethical standards and I'm not sure I want to repeat it. For some reason I seem to care what you think of me."

"I wouldn't—"

"Yadda yadda yadda, as Lenny Bruce would say. Met him, too. All doped up, tragic kid. But people forget how funny he was...so Sherman's gone. Pity."

The remaining yoga beauty leashed her dog and left. Cohen said, "Let's take a load off," and made his way to the fountain. He sank down precisely where her posterior had rested and I settled next to him.

"All right," he said. "Since he's dead, I see an opening. Sherman came to me because he'd already begun his own research and like you, thought I could help him. Why? Because newspaper archives on Enid and Av also contained my name. Social stuff—tennis finals, fundraisers. Like I said, we were chums."

Wide grin. "Not that mine was the only name but everyone else Sherman looked up was dead. I told him I didn't know whether to feel flattered or worried. He laughed—he had a hearty laugh. He wasn't like other shrinks I've met, most of them come across like they didn't get laid much in college. Not you, I'll bet you had plenty of fun."

I smiled.

"Enigmatic?" said Cohen. "Monte Lisa?" He crossed a leg, examined a scrawny ankle. "Sherman enjoyed a good single malt. We drank together in the Four Seasons bar and he ponied up for a bottle of Oban. He told me he was looking into Enid and Av due to a personal matter that required professional confidentiality. He insisted on giving me a retainer, though I assured him none was necessary. The basic story was that he had a patient whose veracity couldn't be taken at face value due to mental health issues. She'd convinced herself she was the child of a movie star who'd disappeared and he wanted to know if there was truth to it, so he could treat her appropriately. I was impressed, Dr. Delaware. His going the extra mile."

He turned, placed a hand on my shoulder. "I can see why the two of you would get along."

"Thank you."

"It is a compliment. I don't give them out like Halloween candy."

His hand returned to his lap. "He asked me if I was aware of any vanishing movie stars and I said I wasn't. He said he hadn't come up with anything, either, the closest was a wannabe named Zina Rutherford and looking into her led him to the DePauws, apparently he found some out-of-town documents."

Taking the same steps Milo and I had. Great minds. Suddenly, I missed Lou. Could imagine what it felt like to be Cohen, last man on the mountain.

He said, "Unlike your situation, there was no suggestion of foul play, all Dr. Sherman was trying to verify was a family link between Zina and Enid, which I gave him. That was it. Whether or not he proved to his own satisfaction that his patient—the Zelda woman—was accurate or delusional, I haven't a clue."

"You knew Zina."

"I knew **of** her. Enid's much younger, even better-looking sister. In fact, it came up that first night when Enid walked into Scandia with that red dress. Someone gave a low whistle and said Av had snagged himself a looker. Someone else—

don't ask, I have no idea—said,
'You think **she's** something, you should
check out her baby sister, Av sure did.
Guess he likes them more mature now.'"

"Av dated both of them?"

"What I heard was that both girls came to
L.A. trying to break into the industry. Enid
thought she could buy herself in with her
money and did manage to get a few no-
dialogue walk-ons that were basically
vanity things—crowd scenes, that kind of
thing. The harsh truth was, being in her
thirties put her over the hill. And there
was already one Bette Davis."

He shook his head. "According to the
wags I was with, there was also the matter
of talent. Enid had none. Zina was younger,
prettier, and at least marginally competent.
She landed some small parts in cheapies.
But her career also went nowhere."

Zelda had topped both of them. Had she
thrown that in Enid's face? Probably not,
too broken down to muster up a complex
thought.

"Failed actresses, they should build a
monument to them," said Cohen. "Like the
poor girl who jumped off the Hollywood

sign. At least those two had dough to fall back on."

"They also had an interest in the same man. Who Enid ended up with."

Cohen nodded. "Spiteful. You're thinking spite stuck in her soul and was directed at Zelda."

"I think Zelda might have threatened her directly by declaring herself an heir."

Cohen smiled. "Look at us. I go psychological, you go financial."

"It's all related."

"Yes, it is, son. Do I believe Enid capable of murder? Can't say, I spoke to her at parties and such, that's the extent of it. I recall her as a frosty dame. You're the one with the license to analyze."

"Did your dinner companions at Scandia have anything more to say about Zina?"

"They did but it's...unchivalrous, Doctor. More than that. Rude."

I said, "Something about her sexual talents?"

Cohen cleared his throat. "The term I believe I heard was 'crazy sexy.' Then someone else said, 'Crazy **and** sexy is the perfect combination, you can do what you want with one of those.' And the rest of us laughed. What can I say? Times were different."

"Any idea what happened to Zina after Enid poached her boyfriend?"

"Dr. Sherman said she'd spiraled downward before disappearing."

"Did Dr. Sherman say anything about who raised her daughter?"

"He wasn't certain Zelda **was** her daughter. He did say Zelda was adopted, had embarked on one of those journeys to discover her roots only to be disappointed because she couldn't have a reunion with a woman who'd vanished."

"Who adopted her?"

"He didn't get into details, just told me they were also deceased and not...what's the word he used...'ideal.' The implication was the girl had it rough."

Cohen threw up his hands. "Nice man, paid for the entire bottle. Now he's gone. It keeps happening to me, son. I call someone to have lunch and learn they keeled over. Guess I'm the only one cursed with immortality."

CHAPTER 35

Refusing my offer of a ride, the old lawyer shuffled back home.

As I reached the Seville, a homeless couple wheeled his-and-her supermarket carts toward the dry fountain. Two humans camouflaged as shags of filthy cloth, bruised feet barely covered by tattered sneakers. The man's lips moved. The women's mouth hung open.

Outpatient mental health in the twenty-first century. The twentieth had been a combination of incarceration and occasional nurturance.

I pictured Zelda, her show canceled, her agent ill, trying to make her way in a city that prized looks and availability.

Crazy and sexy. You can do what you

want with one of those.

Learning about her mother's maltreatment at the hands of her sibs would've changed her quest. No more search for her roots, time for payback. As her own mind disintegrated, she'd have struggled to hold on, terrified by suggestions of damaged lineage.

She hadn't become an ace detective. She'd learned everything from her beyond-the-call-of-duty therapist.

Well-meaning, caring Lou had no idea where his compassion would lead.

I phoned Milo. "I found out how Zelda learned about her family."

"I found out there's no chance for a goddamn warrant."

"John wasn't impressed."

"Hell," he said, "as I was laying it out, I wasn't impressed. Bottom line: Without a solid reason to enter the premises, I couldn't even stroll in if the gates were open."

"What defines solid grounds?"

"A moldering corpse would work nicely, but 'obvious evidence of wrongdoing' is the operative criterion. Like I needed John to tell me that. I got too caught up, amigo. Too bad we didn't spot Enid growing cannabis that night."

"You could hire a bird to drop seeds."

"Crows R Us, there you go. So how'd Zelda become a detective?"

"Lou Sherman detected for her. He was trying to figure out if her story about her mother was real or not."

"Who told you this?"

"Earl Cohen."

"Him? He's still alive?"

"A medical miracle."

"Why'd you go to him?"

"He was around back in the day." I gave him Cohen's description of the DePauws. What the old man had heard about Zina.

"Coupla would-be actresses," he said. "On top of all the other family crap, sisterly competition."

"Neither of them made it but Zina failed a little less obviously."

"So Enid got back at her by stealing her boyfriend. That's pretty primal."

"Cohen called it spiteful, I like your description better."

"Getting the boyfriend and snagging her inheritance, too, if we're right about the shutoff clause. Sexy crazy, huh?"

"In those days, mental illness would've been an easy trigger. And that crack Cohen's buddies made was telling: She was seen as easy prey. Add booze to the mix, and taking everything from her, including her baby, would be easy. Sherman also told Cohen that Zelda's adoptive situation hadn't been ideal."

"Coup de grâce by Sister Enid," he said. "Stripping Zina down to nothing. Zina hangs on, doing what it takes to get by, then one day, poof. But you know what John's gonna tell me: A woman with that level of problems, there are all kinds of ways she could end up missing."

"Sure," I said. "But her daughter **was** most likely murdered. Along with—"

"Three innocents, I know. John was impressed by that. The blood potential. Assured me if it ever got to court, he had first dibs on prosecuting because a trial like that could be a career builder."

"But he's not holding his breath."

"Way he put it was 'My wife bugged me

to take her to Maui, we're leaving in two days and I'm not trading in my tickets.' "

Clear evidence of wrongdoing.

Rescue fantasies clogged my head.

I could call White Glove Cleaning, buy myself a tag-along with the cute girls.

I could find out when the gardeners arrived on St. Denis and wangle my way in with them.

Or just take the simple route: hitching myself over a wall and engaging in some freelance exploration.

All of which would screw up the case if I found anything incriminating. Officially, I was a private citizen, but even a bottom-feeder defense attorney would have no trouble convincing a judge I was an agent of the police.

Expired name tag notwithstanding.

Enid DePauw and J. Yarmuth Loach had the money to hire an ace.

Banish all thoughts.

That got me thinking about the prime suspects. Even with two of them doing the dirty work, a seventy-year-old woman and sixty-seven-year-old boy-toy transporting bodies and burying them seemed unlikely.

If Alicia and Imelda had fallen prey, they'd likely been driven somewhere and dumped in a remote location where burial wasn't necessary.

The desert.

Had Enid's story about Palm Springs been a nasty private joke?

If so, no sense pursuing it. East of the city stretched hundreds of miles of sand and sun-cracked gullies, an alternative universe where raptors, canids, and fire ants had evolved fierce and focused, striving to survive.

Flesh would be devoured greedily, bones picked clean in days and scattered.

When thinking about that proved too depressing, I returned to a more hopeful scenario: Why not somewhere on Enid's estate? No need to dig deep because it was private property, protected by the lack of clear evidence of wrongdoing.

I recalled the layout. Hedged and terraced formal gardens backed by forest-like growth at the back. Zelda had been found in the manicured section, no attempt to conceal.

You can do what you want with them.

If two other bodies were concealed anywhere on the property, it would have to be at the back.

Same problem: serious tote for a pair of senior citizens, even a duo who could've stepped out of a cruise-ship ad.

I supposed a wheelbarrow would help. But the interment itself would entail strenuous effort.

I got on Google Earth.

Wouldn't you know.

Learn something new every day.

CHAPTER 36

The wonders of technology.

In seconds I had full-color, one-year-old, 3-D satellite photos of the property at a variety of angles, the forest-like area at the rear of the property revealed in high definition.

Old-growth pines, sequoias, cedars, and cypresses rendered in...forest green. A central passage began several feet in, passing between stout trunks. Narrower lateral cuts provided additional access. Behind all that was a high stone wall, easily ten feet, with an offset wooden door to the right. From the ground, what appeared to be the estate's rear border.

An aerial view said it wasn't.

Behind the wall was a beige rectangle of

bare earth, around half the width of the property, flanked by columnar Canary Island pines. Backing that was a second wall, even higher, with no outlet.

Planted in front of the pines were clumps of shrubbery, some flowering. Unlike the manicured garden, these plantings had been left rough and natural.

I zoomed in, scanned, printed several times before drawing back and examining the overall layout.

The soil of the forest was dark and rich-looking, that of the pocket garden, pale and dry and littered with leaves and pine needles. But just off center, in line with the door, the ground was clear. A well-trod entrance.

At the end of the clear area, two oblong depressions in the ground.

I printed some more, saved and filed, looked up an email address and sent a message.

Dr. Elizabeth Wilkinson, assistant professor of (forensic) anthropology at the med school where I held a faculty position, answered immediately.

In addition to her academic qualifications,

Liz had served a coroner's fellowship at the crypt, still consulted to LAPD, and was the girlfriend of Detective Moses Reed.

Hi, Alex. I'm in San Francisco at a conference. Yes, theoretically even a covered grave could be visible as a slight darkening of the soil. But it's hard to differentiate from natural irregularities such as disruption caused by scavenging animals, or another perfectly innocent excavation. The time of day when the photo was taken would matter, as well. Early-morning sunlight is the least distorting because the angle is oblique.

Thanks for the quick reply, Liz. Would there be any way to find out, short of actually being there and digging?

Are we talking a recent burial?

Three or so weeks. Probably shallow.

Both work in your favor. Shallow for obvious reasons and recent because decomp would still be active, raising the surface temperature sufficiently for an aerial infrared camera to pick up. If you needed to go deeper, you could use ground penetrating radar and/or dogs.

How would I arrange infrared photography?

Are you talking about financing it yourself?

Yes.

It's pretty pricey. I'd go helicopter, not plane because helicopters are good at slow speeds. A jet-powered copter could run you a thousand dollars an hour. Smaller ones would probably cost in the hundreds but they're pretty cramped and have limited weight ceilings. So this isn't official business?

It could turn out to be.

I see. Well, just to let you know, LAPD has crackerjack helicopter pilots and many are adept with IR. Last year someone reported a mass grave out in Chatsworth and the department did an IR flyover. It was a grave, all right, but for horses. Nothing ominous, just an owner who couldn't bear to send her older animals to be processed so she and her sons shot them and buried them. They'd been doing it for years.

Sad.

I'll bet your story's even sadder.

Well into tragic. Do you have a referral?

The name that comes to mind is Clint Bostrum. He's retired LAPD, did mostly traffic. Now he does aerials for real estate transactions, not sure if that includes IR. Would you like me to talk to him for you?

That would be great. Thanks Liz.

If it does turn out bad, please let me know. Been going to way too many meetings and I'm itching to get out of the office to do some digging. I can get authorized easily, they call me in to supervise because the new postdoc is still getting his hands wet. So to speak.

Ten minutes later:

Hi, Alex. Clint does IR. Here's his number.

One ring before a clipped, smoker's voice said, "This is Clint."

"Alex Delaware. I was referred to you by Liz Wilkinson."

"I've heard of you vaguely. You sometimes work with Sturgis, right?"

"Right."

"He's not on this? Dead bodies are his thing."

"It's his case but my guess," I said. "I want to have something substantial before I get the department involved."

"And the department's too cheap to give up copter time without serious grounds for a warrant?"

"Haven't asked them."

Clint Bostrum said, "Even if Sturgis put in a request, it would be a hassle, so you're smart. I did twenty-five years in the air for the department. Movie star wants a shot of her kid's birthday party, it just might happen. Joe Average? Not so much. Give me the coordinates."

"I've got an address."

"Fine, I can get the coordinates with the address. Let's talk money. My usual is eleven hundred bucks an hour, two-hour minimum, two-hundred-buck upcharge for infrared. Liz said you're a stand-up guy and I figure anyone who'd pay out of his own pocket has to be crazy or supermoral. So I'll cut it to seven hundred bucks, total. If you don't ride along. I've got a mounted camera I can operate while flying, don't want the liability of a passenger."

"That's fine."

"Also, don't tell anyone what I'm charging."

"I really appreciate it, Clint."

"Get hold of the money as soon as we hang up, I'll give you my PayPal account. Should take a few days to clear but I'm already at the airport so I'll go out on a limb and fly tonight. Nothing to do, anyway, and my girlfriend's playing bridge at some nerd club I can't stand. Now, tell me exactly what you're looking for. Also, how late you stay up. I'm going to know one way or the other soon after I go up, you might as well, also."

Robin went to bed and I spent the next few hours examining the photos I'd taken, consulting the Internet, managing to get a friend on the phone who confirmed my suspicions.

I was putting it all together when Clint Bostrum called just before midnight.

"You've definitely got two hot spots, there, couple of nice little red blotches, I'll email you the images. Can't say it's human but I'd put money on something rotting."

"Thanks, Clint."

"Anytime, Dr. Alex, long as you pay. This is a lot more fun than shooting McMansions."

CHAPTER 37

Deputy D.A. John Nguyen said, "I'm still going to Hawaii."

Milo said, "You're not impressed?"

"I'm impressed. I also think it's going to take time to get all the details in place and while the state doesn't really carry out the death penalty, Shannon believes in it and she'll kill me if I cancel. Keep me posted as I sun and sip Mai Tais."

"You will issue the warrant."

Nguyen fingered a signed Dodger baseball he used for a paperweight. "Sure, why not, seeing as our civilian volunteer here found bodies and pretty pictures of plants." To me: "You actually paid out of pocket for a copter? Hope you don't expect reimbursement."

Milo said, "I'm working on that."

"Yeah, well," said Nguyen, "good luck. Alex, how certain is your botanist buddy that both..." He consulted his notes. ". . . meadow saffron and...monkshood are growing there?"

"A hundred percent," I said.

"From photos."

"He's a full professor of botany at the U."

"Fine...what about the other stuff...lily of the valley, foxglove, larkspur, and purple nightshade. All poisonous?"

"Every one," I said. "A little pocket poison garden."

Nguyen shuddered. "And this was missed. Twice."

"Easy to miss with that first wall."

"What's behind the second wall?"

Milo said, "Neighbor's property, hedge-fund whiz."

"He's actually closer to it than DePauw."

"It's a twelve-foot wall and all the bad stuff's on her land, John."

"Yeah, yeah," said Nguyen. "I'm just anticipating. Okay, I'll write up the warrant and get it to a good judge. But I'm still leaving today."

We were in his office in the giant down-town egg-crate known as the Clara Shortridge Foltz Criminal Justice Center. Nguyen had recently merited a promotion, meaning a bit more square footage and a sidelong view of smog. Lots of unpacked boxes on the floor, only a laptop and the baseball atop his city-issue desk.

Milo said, "We'll get out of here so you can do your thing."

"One more thing. In terms of executing the search, your suspects are still in Italy, right?"

"Rome," said Milo. "The Hassler Hotel."

"Probably a big suite," said Nguyen. "Damn them to hell. The problem I see is if you bring in the bone-crew and DePauw hears about it, she could stay overseas, end up somewhere extradition's a problem."

"Where's that?" I asked.

"Mostly places you don't want to go— Afghanistan, Somalia," said Milo. "But also some decent ones like Andorra, or an island in Micronesia. Or Montenegro, where they're building a big yacht harbor. That's not far from Italy."

"You've researched it," said John.

"We had a case last year, drug schmuck ended up in the Maldives, went on Instagram and flipped us off. But even without getting exotic, people with resources can burrow in mainstream Europe and get away with it. It's something we need to be proactive about."

I said, "A few factors weigh in our favor. It's a sparsely traveled neighborhood with lots of distance between the properties and no direct visual access from any of the neighbors."

"Including the hedge-fund whiz?"

"He's got six acres. I suppose if he decided to trek to the back and climb a ladder—"

Milo said, "He's in South Korea, cutting deals."

"Go Samsung," said Nguyen. "How do we keep it low-profile?"

I said, "Service vehicles to go in and out—cleaning service and gardeners. Easy to use that for cover."

Milo said, "We find out their schedules, make sure we avoid them, slap some fake signs on a coupla vans."

"Use the absolute minimum of people—

your basic skeleton crew," said Nguyen. "Yeah, yeah, I've got no sense of propriety...you really paid out of pocket, Alex?"

"No big deal," I said.

"Private practice going well, huh? Sorry, I've just been thinking about my college days, everyone else partying, I'm grinding. So now, I'm a glorious civil servant. Maybe it's time for a change."

"I'd miss you, John," said Milo. "Meanwhile, think pension after retirement."

"Are you?"

"Hell, no."

Nguyen tossed the ball up and caught it. "What about going in at night?"

"Service vehicles don't, John. It could attract more attention."

"True...be careful, we can't afford any screwups. Because the only real thing you have is something buried out there and if it does turn out to be human and is ruled inadmissible, I'm screwed."

"Two bodies ruled inadmissible?"

"Not likely," said Nguyen, "but anything's possible, like I said: anticipate. As is, we're vulnerable because the poison stuff was missed twice, I can see some defense ace claiming it was planted. Ha ha. It's lame but L.A. juries believe in screenplays. When are your suspects due back?"

"Five days."

"Little luxe jaunt to **Rrrroma**," said Nguyen. "Rat-bastards. They should choke on pasta."

CHAPTER 38

The warrant arrived shortly after eleven a.m. Two suspects named in the murders of three victims, Rod Salton excluded because Nguyen termed him "insufficiently related."

Permission granted to enter and search indoor premises as well as the entire 5.23-acre parcel. Milo said, "So what do you think? Day or night?"

I said, "Still day. Night's more likely to attract attention."

"I agree. Got the schedules for the cleaners and the gardeners and tomorrow's clear. Hopefully, a pool service won't show up. Let's see if Liz can."

The anthropologist would be back tonight

from San Francisco, would begin setting it up and be ready to work.

Milo told her about the plan to mislabel civilian vans. "How many vehicles will you need and what kind of staff are we talking about? Fewer the better."

"If I can poach the new postdoc for a day, two of us should be able to handle the digging. Equipment's nothing heavy. At this stage, we're talking stakes, rope, chisels, trowels, spades, cameras, brushes, distilled water, vials for samples. One good-sized van should be fine."

"I'll get two."

"This is all covert because you don't want it getting back to the suspects."

"Exactly."

"Well, that's fine for initial exploration but I can see a problem if we find something. The crypt won't allow transporting remains except in their vans and those are anything but inconspicuous."

Milo groaned. Picturing the vehicles like I was: official seals and blue stripes running across the sides topped by **Coroner** in the same color. Just in case you missed that, the same identification in larger lettering at the rear, along with multiple applications of the legend **Law and Science Serving the Community.**

"I'll talk to Bernstein, see if he's flexible."

"I can raise it with him, was figuring to ask him to borrow Gregor—the postdoc. Otherwise, I'll need to find a grad student on short notice and try keeping their mouth shut."

"Let me do it, Liz. Hope he doesn't screw us up."

"He probably won't. Not because he's a softie at heart but he's after the same thing you are. Pathologists hate undetermined."

Bernstein said, "Your geniuses missed an entire damn section? After my geniuses did the same damn thing?"

"There's a high wall that's easy to mistake for the property line, Bill."

"Bleh bleh bleh bleh. All right, spilled milk. What's the alleged plan?"

Milo filled him in.

Bernstein said, "Not terrible. Okay, take Gregor, I'm tired of hearing that accent of his and all he's been doing is rehydrating disarticulated fingers so he can learn how to print our more damaged guests with finesse."

"I'll need help with transport if we find something. Vehicles without official labeling."

"You need?" said Bernstein. "Didn't you ever study economics? There are no needs, only preferences."

"Okay, I strongly prefer—"

"All because you don't want to spook these fine citizens currently cavorting in Rome."

"They're rich and socially connected—"

"They're still thousands of miles away. I think you're worrying over nothing."

Milo didn't answer.

"Passive resistance?" said Bernstein. "Okay, maybe I can fix your problem. One of our vans is supposed to be repainted. It's stripped down to primer, looks like crap, but we've been keeping it in service because we can't afford to give it up, does that tell you about our workload and our budget? We send it to socially **un**connected neighborhoods and stick on a magnetic sign. Kind of—what do those idiots call themselves...Goth."

"Thanks, Bill."

"Hold on, I said maybe. For all I know they took it to the paint shop. Wait."

Moments later: "Your lucky day, it's still in service, currently doing a pickup in Willowbrook, should be back in a couple of hours. You need it, come pick it up. Hideous ugly heap of scrap, you don't think that's going to bend some Bel Air noses?"

"Better than going public, Bill."

"Your call," said Bernstein. "I don't want to hear any more about this until there's something to dissect."

Logging onto the White Glove Cleaning website, capturing an image of their sign, and having six copies made at a sign store in West L.A. took a while. I stood outside the sign store and watched as Milo, dressed in a T-shirt and jeans, paid cash, hoping the man behind the counter wouldn't ask questions.

The guy didn't even look up. Most people aren't overly afflicted with curiosity. It separates the creative and the tormented from the rest of the pack.

At noon the following day, a white Ford Econoline driven by Liz Wilkinson, and a blue Dodge Ram ProMaster with Milo at the wheel, made their way from the impound lot to Bel Air. Both were tagged with White Glove signs. If you didn't notice the three bullet holes in the rear bumper of the blue one, you'd never give it a second thought.

No one around to think. The only human walking on St. Denis was a uniformed maid accompanying a mastiff the size of a pony. The dog noticed us. She didn't.

Once we arrived at the DePauw estate, there was still the matter of getting onto the property without attracting attention or inflicting conspicuous damage.

Milo nosed his van to the gates first, got out and walked to Liz's window. "I'll climb over, there's gotta be a button on the other side. If not, we'll figure something out."

"I will do it," said the crypt postdoc, a crew-cut, muscle-bound M.D., Ph.D. from Warsaw named Gregor Poplawsky. Before Milo could argue, he'd bounded out and scaled the wall. Seconds later, the gates swung open.

Poplawsky beamed. "Correct hypothesis,

Lieutenant." Pointing to a red button atop the swing-arm of the right-hand gate motor.

"Good to hear, Gregor."

"Yes, I like that, too," said Poplawsky. "The world being sometimes rational."

The five-hundred-foot path I'd walked the night of Zelda's death was a brief motorized ascent. The vans parked in front of the house, the four of us got out and gloved up, and, just as before, we entered the garden on the north side. First step: inspect the house's rear loggia for potted plants. Seven large ones, in blue and white porcelain pots. Four palms, three ferns. Milo peered through French doors into the house and said, "Nice place. Onward."

In daylight, the terraced garden was glorious, hedges razor-edged and emerald, trees shaped to uniform height dripping with oranges, mandarins, and lemons. The air was tangy with citrus perfume and wealth.

Despite that, a rancid stink of evil squatted in the back of my sinuses but I doubted anyone else could smell it.

Nothing rational about it; the spot where Zelda had lain was clean. As if she'd never been there.

Liz, Gregor, Milo, and I descended slowly, inspecting flowers along the way. Tea roses, barbered and abloom, were bottomed by hexagonal, brick-edged beds of begonia and vinca. The latter could be used therapeutically—vincristine was an anti-cancer drug. Nothing here suggested the destruction of life.

We kept climbing down, passed the statuary—Greek warrior goddesses—and the pool, a bit tatty, up close. The menagerie of topiary animals was anything but martial: bunnies, squirrels, kittens, birds.

Liz Wilkinson said, "Am I the only one who finds this freaky?"

Gregor Poplawsky said, "A little Disneyland."

Milo said, "Creepyland."

We continued walking, arrived at the wall of forest where brick met up with the dirt floor. Parting branches led to the central opening I'd seen online. Maybe three feet wide. The side accesses were narrower,

JONATHAN KELLERMAN

impromptu gaps between the trees, not
actual pathways.

Milo cupped his hand over his eyes and
peered in. The earth beneath my feet was
paler, tan splotched with gray when
overhead branches cut off sunlight. Firm,
possibly laced with decomposed gravel.

Milo pointed. The rest of us collected
behind him and saw what had captured
his interest: a rut running through the
central walkway.

I said, "Wheelbarrow?"

"Dr. W.?"

Liz had a look. "Something with a single
wheel and enough weight to exert
pressure, that's for sure."

Gregor said, "Unless someone's a
unicyclist, like in a circus, I say yes,
wheelbarrow."

Liz kneeled, pointed to faint lozenges on
both sides of the wheel rut. "Those are
shoe prints but too indistinct to tell us
anything."

Milo took pictures with his phone,
scrawled in his pad. "You bring casting
material, Dr. W.?"

"In the van," said Liz. "I wanted to get an

overview first. If we don't get better than these, casting won't be worth it. Though I can do a few to look thorough. The wheel print is interesting. Ideally, it'll run all the way to the back and you'll have clear evidence of transport. If there are human remains back there. So let's stay off this stretch and try one of those side paths. Hopefully there's at least one that hasn't been used recently."

We inspected the gaps. Three irregular ribbons, none exhibiting signs of use. None wide enough to walk through without having to draw back branches.

Milo glanced back at the rutted path. "One-lane highway."

Liz said, "I love how the earth tells stories."

The forest was a couple of hundred feet deep, growing denser as we neared the wall that pretended to be a border. Freckles of blue sky sparked through the green-black of old growth. The temperature was ten degrees cooler in here, the acid-sweet of summer fruit replaced by a resinous bite of pines and firs, the yeasty smell of dry needles and pinecones crumbling to dust.

Just before the wall was a belt of dry dirt, six or so feet deep and equally wide. The wooden door was unusually tall, running nearly to the top of ten feet of fieldstone. Substantial thing, the door, with stout vertical oak slats crossed by three horizontal boards. Hints of green paint.

Heavy-duty slide bolt, as well. Bronze, handmade by a long-ago craftsman.

No lock.

I said, "No worry anyone would figure it out."

Milo said, "Let's hear it for overconfidence."

He took a closer look at the area directly facing the door. The wheel rut continued, hooked right for a foot, then resumed its trail. Gloving up, he stepped carefully to avoid marring the impression and freed the bolt. Easy slide. He bent and sniffed. "Been WD-40'd recently."

A soft push opened the door.

A new smell took over.

Gregor said, "Oh, boy. For sure we know this."

Liz said, "Go back to the van, please, and get the cases marked A and B. A's the small tools, B's the camera and the casting materials."

"Stakes and pins in there, too?" said Gregor.

Someone else might've been put off by the second-guessing, but Liz said, "Smart question. Yes, it's part of the casting kit."

"You got it, boss." Gregor turned and retraced the way we'd come, holding back branches and moving gracefully, not missing a step.

Liz said, "He wrestled in one of the Olympics." She turned back to the open doorway. "There could be prints on the bolt, I forgot to ask for the print kit, but we can glove up and do it later. I'm also going to get a lot of before shots, so no one can say we set anything up."

Milo pulled out his phone and began taking photos.

"That's okay for backup, Milo, but I'm going to use my Leica, get as high def as possible."

Milo said, "I really want to talk to the gardeners. And the damn landscape architect, she certified the place free of colchicine."

Liz said, "She could be telling the truth,

from her limited perspective."

"She never went back here?"

"There's no sign anyone tended to the property behind the formal area. The needles and leaves are piled high in there and the trees haven't been trimmed in a long time. That could work to your benefit, harder to claim a casual intruder."

Behind us, branches rustled. "Better than the gym," said Poplawsky, beaming. He toted a large black case in each hand, clamped a smaller box under his arm. "I also bring the fingerprint kit. For the door and what else could happen."

"Good thinking," said Liz.

"I need to prove myself."

Dozens of photos taken at various angles, the bitter-swill stench growing stronger.

One of the cases contained tightly folded white paper suits and booties that the four of us donned, along with latex gloves. The color contrasted nicely with Liz's chocolate skin. The rest of us looked like ghosts.

Gregor was eager to try out his fingerprinting skills, but Milo said, "Let me."

He's adept at lifting latents, sometimes takes over when techs are overburdened or moving too slowly. He pulled up several from the bolt but none from the wood or the bordering stone. "Ready, Dr. W?"

Liz said, "Couldn't be readier."

Experienced up close, the rectangle felt like a miniature walled graveyard. We began by examining the border shrubs, using color photos Dr. Ben Haroyushi had sent me, for comparison.

The graceful, crocus-like, lilac flowers of meadow saffron sat at the front of the beds, alongside the lovely, purplish-blue blossoms of wolfsbane. At either end, ephemeral white lily of the valley buds sprouted, at the rear stood the taller plants, both evoking hollyhocks: foxglove with its bright pink saucer-like blooms and a riotous mix of larkspur in white, blue, and mauve.

"Pretty," said Gregor. "Arranged nicely."

"Get ready for the garden show," said Milo. "Look but don't eat."

Liz, back at the center of the rectangle, pointed to impressions in the dirt. "This is going to go quickly."

A pair of lumpy, careless heaps, loose dirt scattered nearby, the rut from the forest running straight to the nearer one. Lots of shoe prints, deeper than those in the forest, mottled the immediate area.

Liz said, "Two sets, one larger than the other, both look like tennis shoes...a couple look clean enough to print. Great!"

She directed as Gregor poured and cast. Once he'd found his rhythm, she returned to the lumps. As she whisked away soil with a brush, the reek grew stronger and she wrinkled her nose and put on a face mask.

Milo said, "Good idea," and got three masks.

Gregor said, "I'm okay. I want to experience."

Liz began troweling surface soil, working slowly, meticulously.

Milo walked back to the poison garden, where he squatted and scrawled, Gregor continued casting shoe prints, and I stood around with nothing to do.

My wandering eye spotted a scrap of paper in a far corner and pointed it out. Liz got up and tweezered.

"Gum wrapper," she said, holding the scrap up to the light. "Oh, you're kidding—Louis Vuitton makes gum?"

"Fresh breath for the privileged," said Gregor.

"Something that unusual, let's bag it. I suppose it could've blown in by itself—from that hedge-fund neighbor. But there hasn't been much wind recently and nothing else has drifted over."

"Chewing while they worked," said Milo, taking the wrapper and bagging it.

Gregor said, "Like to them it was casual. Here, what do you think?"

Liz examined the printed shoe impressions. "These are nice. Okay, help me get to the bottom of the real stuff."

"Shallow grave" didn't begin to describe it. The bodies had been left less than a foot beneath the surface.

Two bodies, both female. Bloated skin, a pink-white mottle not unlike salami where it wasn't green. Slipping off the bones and settling in hideous pleats. Deeper discoloration—nearly black—at the tips of digits and the nose. The legs more leathery, particularly where they connected to the feet.

Dark hair for the nearer corpse, white for the other. Generous pelvises on both. Even with the rot, my inexpert eye tagged the bodies as female.

Milo said, "Don't see any maggots."

Liz said, "They do their thing early on— the first week or so. Blowflies can arrive within hours. This is early decomp, it could last for months given the dryness and the temperature."

"Don't see any lesions, either."

"Not so far, let's see." She got close to the dark-haired body, lifted the skull gently. Reverently. "I see one, now, in the occiput. Discrete, clean hole, my bet's on a small-caliber bullet."

Performing a similar inspection of the other body, she said, "Same thing."

"Execution," said Milo. "All that poison but they used a gun on these two."

I said, "Tickets to Rome, no time to spare."

"Or," he said, "they'd had enough fun with the others, it was personal. These poor women were vermin to be dealt with quickly."

Liz probed in the grave. "I'm feeling something down here—if it's what I think it is—Gregor, come here and give me a hand." Pointing down at the white-haired corpse.

A plastic sheet was worked under the body and the anthropologists lifted it out. Exposed to the light, the corpse looked smaller, pathetic.

I thought of Imelda Soriano's family. What they'd learn soon. What Liz pointed out drew me away from that.

Below Imelda was a third body, skeletonized, the bones bare and dry, not even a hint of mummified tissue. The merest fuzz of pale yellowish hair crowned the skull.

Liz Wilkinson said, "This one's been here for a while."

"Thirty years," I said.

"You know who she is?"

Milo said, "She's the crux of a crazy woman's reality. I'm calling Wild Bill."

CHAPTER 39

Two "high profile" suspects, due to return to the country in three days, qualified as "complicated" and complicated means everyone has an opinion.

Milo's captain weighed in. So did a deputy chief who claimed to be representing the chief. Though beckoned back from Hawaii by his boss, John Nguyen bargained for a few extra days with his wife ("to avoid a shallow grave for myself") and communicated by phone. ("No Skype, Milo, all I've got is aloha shirts.")

The result of all that discussion was a decision to "fast-track" the investigation but no details about what that meant were offered by anyone above Milo.

He did what he'd planned to do all along,

aided by the grudging cooperation of Dr. William Bernstein.

Imelda Soriano's body was identified quickly using dental records provided by her family, with DNA confirmation pending once a sample harvested from her bone marrow and a cheek-scrape taken from her grief-stricken son were analyzed at the Department of Justice lab.

Maria Garcia had moved from the room she'd shared with Alicia Santos. Lorrie Mendez finally located her at a flophouse in East L.A. and after doing her own crisis intervention, pried out the fact that Alicia hadn't seen a dentist since arriving from Mexico. But she had been seen at a walk-in **clinica** for a sprained wrist just prior to beginning work on St. Denis Lane.

An X-ray taken there revealed a healed hairline fracture in her radius, a defect that matched one found on the right arm of the dark-haired corpse.

Genetic material from the long-buried skeleton under Imelda was harder to obtain, but Dr. Gregor Poplawsky, working with an experienced crypt tech named Selena Merton, kept at it and managed to pull up specks of tissue from inside the left femur, yielding minute amounts of mitochondrial DNA. That and tissue taken from Zelda's body—still unclaimed and unburied—had also been sent to the DOJ.

"Results won't come back before the bad guys do but I'll take bets it's Zina," said Milo. "Unless they killed someone else and she's still down there."

I said, "You're wondering about other bodies?"

"Who the hell knows? Someone gets away with stuff for years, why stop at three? I went looking for details on the deaths of Enid's other sibs, finally got hold of them a few hours ago. Two are clearly natural: the oldest brother died of lung cancer, the sister, ovarian. But James Finbar, the one who bothered to call Ott, is listed as exsanguination from a bleeding ulcer with associated gastritis and that doesn't sound so different from what happened to Zelda. And Rod Salton. Speaking of which, John's adamant: only three names on the arrest warrant, insufficient evidence on Salton."

"Two poisonings with plant material found in Enid's garden doesn't impress him?"

"John knows the truth and so does his boss, but **you** know lawyers. At graduation they get a kit for sewing ass-covers along with their degrees. If colchicine had also been used on Salton, that might've been enough to squeak it through, but two different poisons means an opening for defense sharks. I'll be searching the house later today. I luck out and find Enid's written recipes for two flavors of witch's brew, it's a different story. Barring that, I'll settle for diaries, financial documents, explicit written confessions."

I said, "Four people and maybe her brother. The only sib remotely sympathetic to Zina, so he had to be taken care of."

"Or she just wanted his inheritance too. Poor Jimmy had no wife, no kids, seems to be what they used to call a confirmed bachelor."

"His will didn't make bequests to anyone else?"

"No will on record, so far. Rich guy living off a trust, not expecting to die, he could've put it off."

"Giving Enid the chance to finish him off before he filed papers."

"Or maybe he told Enid he **had** plans to write a will and she did some preventive pharmacology."

"When did he die?"

"A few months after he called Ott."

"He could've had suspicions about Zina's disappearance."

"Would I like to have Cleveland disinter him? You bet, at some point, but right now I'm concentrating on local bodies. Meanwhile, I'm hassling with Homeland Security."

"Over what?"

"Who gets to put the cuffs on the evil bitch."

We spoke the following morning. The house search hadn't uncovered any diaries or financial documents but he was smiling.

Milo said, "Papers could be in Loach's office, or her safe, still waiting for someone who can get in there. The main thing is, other goodies abound. I found a box of Vuitton chewing gum in her nightstand drawer and Gucci sneakers that match one of the casts in her closet. Along with about three hundred other pairs of shoes.

Ol' Averell had a nice firearms collection, mostly Italian and British shotguns that haven't been fired in a long time but also an old but recently oiled .22 Smith and Wesson revolver that I just sent to Ballistics. The finishing touch was a whole collections of books on poisons in the library, nonfiction as well as novels. They were easy to spot because everything else on the shelves was that leather-bound stuff decorators install by the yard."

"Speaking of decorators, anything from the landscaper?"

"She's in England at a big show, obviously I'm not going to leave a message. But the gardeners confirm they never went into the forest. White Glove is scheduled to clean today, I was careful to finish last night, kept it neat. Unless they count the guns, they'll never know I was there."

"Have you worked out the cuff thing with Homeland yet?"

"Still under review," he said. "You know the feds. They're all into process."

CHAPTER 40

The "process" was established after much interdepartmental head-scratching and formalized in a two-page, single-spaced Document of Intent.

Officers from U.S. Customs and Border Protection (CBP), working in concert with Los Angeles World Airport Authority (LAWA) at the Tom Bradley International Terminal's customs clearance area, would carry out a "strategic focused capture and custodial operation" with approved representatives from LAPD and the district attorney's office "in observance" along with a single approved prosecution consultant (APC) authorized by LAPD and the D.A. Once the security status of the arrestees had been ascertained to the satisfaction of CBP, formal custody would transfer from CBP to LAPD at an approved location, yet to be determined.

Alitalia Flight 62, nonstop from Rome to Los Angeles, scheduled to arrive at one twenty-eight p.m., was delayed an hour and a half. At two p.m., Milo, John Nguyen, and I—honored to be the APC—drove to LAX in Milo's unmarked trailed by three black-and-whites from the West L.A. station.

The cop cars drove into the parking lot across the street from Bradley and re-mained there. The three of us entered the terminal expecting to be met by an airport police sergeant named MacArthur Davis but encountering only harried-looking incoming and outgoing travelers.

Several calls finally produced an officer named Fred Barefoot who told us Davis had taken a sick day and led us downstairs to a suite of Homeland Security offices where a cadre of armed, blue-uniformed CBP agents waited.

In charge was a five-foot-tall sergeant named Mary Dobbs who outlined the plan on a whiteboard.

Milo said, "Sounds good."

Dobbs said, "I should hope so. We worked on it."

At two thirty-two p.m., a phone in the customs office rang informing the assembled that the plane had pulled up to the gate early.

At two thirty-eight p.m. the border uniforms and their privileged guests entered the vast customs clearance hall. A billion or so dollars had been spent renovating the building but that didn't extend to manpower. Fewer than half the stations were operating and the hall was clogged with coiling queues of the recently deplaned doing a collective impression of Wretched Refuse.

The exception were passengers who'd qualified for and paid to participate in the Global Entry Trusted Traveler Program (GETTP), allowing them to breeze past the lines to one of the Automated Passport Control (APC) kiosks at a special Federal Inspection Station developed in concert with the Tom Bradley International Equipment Company (TBITEC). There, they offered their passports and a thumbprint for machine-scanning and, once approved, were directed to the baggage carousel. Upon procurement of luggage, they'd continue to designated GETTP customs officers, usually to be waved through without inspection.

"Nice," said Milo.

Mary Dobbs said, "It is if people behave themselves. If they don't, they're off the bus forever."

"That happen a lot?"

"Last week we had a joker trying to sneak in a guitar with ivory all over it, clear CITES violation." She waved jazz hands. "Bye-bye, Music Boy."

At two fifty-three p.m., Enid DePauw, in a black vicuña shawl, black silk blouse, and gray herringbone slacks, was first off the plane, race-walking and carrying a small black clutch with a gold clasp. Right behind her, J. Yarmuth Loach in a double-breasted navy blazer, cream linen pants, and white silk shirt carried a crocodile-hide Louis Vuitton hard-case and wheeled a matching carry-on bag.

Loach was a tall man but his long legs had to strain to keep up with DePauw. She put all four limbs into it; get too close and he'd feel the impact of her elbows.

Milo said, "That's them."

Sergeant Dobbs said, "Last time **they'll** get to jump the line."

The six border cops moved ahead of the couple, now being processed at side-by-side kiosks. Milo, Nguyen, and I were ordered to stand to the right of the kiosks but that exposed us visually and when Milo pointed out that Suspect DePauw had met us and could recognize us, Dobbs said, "Shit," and hurried us forward.

"Over there, somewhere they can't see you."

We found a vantage point behind the carousel bordering the one serving the Rome flight. Loach, still trailing Enid DePauw, wheeled a luggage cart near the chute. She stood a few feet away, powdering her nose.

For the first few seconds, they were the only people at the carousel. Then a few other first-class passengers joined them.

The first piece dumped down the chute was an unobtrusive black bag that Loach hefted onto the cart. DePauw paid no notice until, seconds later, a large crocodile suitcase matching the hard-case and the wheelie tumbled forth and she said something sharp to Loach that caused him to spring for it. After he'd loaded it in the cart, she inspected it, turned her back on him, and headed for the customs desk.

Nguyen said, "Croc. That stuff costs a fortune."

Milo said, "Killer lizard giving up its life. There's a lesson there, somewhere."

The customs officer designated to participate in the production was a thickset, mustachioed man who'd have flunked Acting 101. His eyes kept darting around and he avoided looking at Loach and DePauw.

"Nervous Nellie," said Nguyen. "C'mon, dude, this is more than confiscating guitars."

Enid tapped a foot and smoothed her hair as Mustache took a long time reviewing the couple's documents. He pointed to the cart and said something that made her scowl.

J. Yarmuth Loach remained silent. The submissive one. That made him the preferable target for interrogation. I'd say something later.

Now he lifted the hard-case to the customs desk and the officer took it and shook it. Enid DePauw's foot tapped faster. She looked furious.

Not used to being kept waiting.

Finally, Mustache returned the case to Loach and she began to edge forward. Before Loach got the case back on the cart, Dobbs and her officers had swarmed the couple on all sides.

Sergeant Dobbs walked up to Enid and said something to her. Received a hard slap across the face for her troubles.

J. Yarmuth Loach's mouth had dropped open. He accepted the handcuffs passively. Not so, DePauw. She'd tightened her hand into a fist and took another swing at Dobbs, using her height to bear down and aim at the top of Dobbs's head.

Dobbs, with one hand still flat against her smarting cheek, used the other to haul off and deliver a gut-punch that lowered

DePauw to the floor.

Both suspects were propelled out of the hall.

As we left, I heard someone say, "Old people like that? Why don't they go after some real terrorists?"

CHAPTER 41

One cop car drove Loach to the Men's Central Jail in East L.A. The second transported Enid DePauw to the Women's Central Jail in Lynwood.

The third, driven by an officer who said, "Lucky me," took the luggage.

Within hours of booking, both suspects had high-powered lawyers stonewalling on their behalf.

"Big surprise, big deal," said John Nguyen. "We've got bodies."

The luggage revealed nothing. Milo's search of Loach's office was another story.

When he arrived at the law firm with a search warrant, two dollies, a departmental locksmith, and Detectives Lorrie Mendez,

Moses Reed, and Sean Binchy, he was confronted by an administrative partner, "one of those pompous twits" named Robert Malley.

Malley made a show of blocking Loach's door, first insisting entry was impossible, then taking a long time to read the warrant, only to sputter about egregious violation of client confidentiality.

Milo said, "His only client is my other suspect."

Malley said, "What if you don't know everything? How will you differentiate between relevant and not relevant?"

"I'm doing it right now, you're irrelevant. Now **move.**"

Nothing to differentiate; the only files in Loach's bench-made, English-import, mahogany Regency Revival cabinet pertained to Enid and Averell DePauw.

It took a while to comb through the eight boxes retrieved from the office, with Milo taking on the job in an empty conference room at the station, and I his volunteer assistant. Most of the documents were what you'd expect with big money being moved around: limited liability real estate syndications, prospectuses, investment reports, tax forms, invitations to participate in corporate proxy votes.

A few told the story.

Three months prior to foreclosure on the house on Bel Azura Drive, a petition to declare Zina Rutherford mentally incompetent, backed up by a psychiatrist named Roberta Waters, was approved by a Superior Court judge named Arthur Ernest.

The push to make commitments more difficult was well under way by then, but you could still pull it off if the patient was sufficiently impaired. Or you had the right connections.

A search of **doctor roberta waters** pulled up the fact that she'd lost her license several years later due to substance abuse issues.

A search of **judge arthur ernest** pulled up the fact that eight months after he'd disenfranchised Zina, he'd retired from the bench to take a position of counsel to Loach's law firm.

Waters had been dead for twenty-three years, Ernest for seventeen. Zina's court-appointed counsel at the time, a Legal Aid newbie named Donald Pkach, was in practice now in Tacoma, Washington. Milo reached his office and asked him.

He said, "You expect me to remember that?" and hung up.

As a result of Ernest's decision, Zina had been committed to a private facility in Denver, long shuttered. Nothing further on her until her brother reported her missing and Dub Ott tried to find her.

At the time of commitment, legal and physical custody of "minor child Jane Z. Rutherford" had passed to petitioners Enid and Averell DePauw.

Milo said, "Handed over to the evil aunt, what a nightmare."

I said, "Five years old. Going back to St. Denis wasn't psychotic, she'd lived there."

He passed me another sheet. "Not for long."

Within six months of being separated from her mother, minor child Jane Z. Rutherford's welfare had been entrusted to the county foster care system, with petitioners DePauw requesting termination of custody due to "incorrigible behavioral issues."

This time, an associate at the law firm had handled the couple's business affairs. J. Y. Loach, Esq.

Nothing in the file on any subsequent adoption by the non-ideal Chases. If they were still out there, good luck finding them.

I said, "Enid eliminates Zina, makes a show of parenting her daughter, then, after a token period, she cuts her off, too."

"And takes her inheritance," said Milo. "What a fucking monster."

The two of us spent a long time putting together numbers. Enid DePauw's cash, securities, and real estate holdings, including several absentee partnerships spread across five states, neared one hundred million dollars, forty percent of that the property on St. Denis.

Milo said, "Even a small part of that woulda made Zelda a rich woman."

My stomach lurched. I got up and left the office, walked up and down the hall, returned feeling clammy.

Milo said, "You okay?"

"There's an eleven-year-old boy who'd be rich if he's alive."

"Hey, the jury's not out yet—that little Swede said she didn't take the kid with her to Skid Row."

"That little Norwegian is psychotic. Any plans to dig up the poison patch?"

"Matter of fact, in a few hours," he said. "Your botanist buddy will be there. Why do you ask?"

"Before you go, see if you can pull up prints from any of these docs related to Zelda."

"Why?"

I told him.

He said, "Interesting. You usually are."

CHAPTER 42

No need for the big dig to go unnoticed by the neighbors. The stream of crypt and police vehicles brought them out, gawking and exchanging misinformation.

Milo said, "More foot traffic than this place has ever seen."

I said, "Let's have a block party."

The onlookers were a mixed bunch of residents in expensive leisure clothes, uniformed domestics, and a motley group of dogs. A couple of canines got into altercations with each other, with cross words exchanged by their humans.

I said, "Peace in the canyon."

As Milo and I prepared to walk through the gates, a hollow-cheeked woman wearing black velvet sweats and several pounds of gold and gems marched up to us. "I **need** to know what's going on, Officers."

Milo said, "We're doing police work," and walked away.

The woman said, "Well, **he's** got an attitude. What's his name?"

I said, "Masterson Earp," and caught up just in time to slip through the closing gates.

The digging crew was Liz Wilkinson and six graduate students. Ben Haroyushi, in a pith helmet and khakis, was off to the side, photographing plants, snipping, bagging, tagging.

When he finished, he walked up to me. "Thanks for the opportunity, Alex. This'll make for a great lecture."

"Lethal horticulture?"

"A lot of horticulture is lethal but I never get to talk about it," said Ben. "Seeing it all in one place, there's an...aura." He grinned. "Don't quote me on that, too new-agey. But it's hard to ignore, no?"

No use bringing in cadaver dogs. The scents from two graves in a limited area would satiate them in seconds.

Ground-penetrating radar brought up nothing. Neither did a visual inspection of the surface dirt.

Liz said, "If anything's down there, it's going to be deep. But we'll start with surface exploration and take it slowly."

Milo and I and a couple of uniforms stood around and worked our cellphones as the grad students began staking and gridding, then picked up their hand tools. Earning their stipends with sweat equity. But process doesn't matter, outcome does, and after a while the futility of the exercise was obvious.

The initial three feet of earth contained no remains other than the skeletons of small animals—moles, gophers, a desic- cated twig-like thing Liz I.D.'d as a shrew.

No bones at all in the next tier. Milo said, "That's six feet under. Going deeper?"

"Let's do another eighteen inches," said Liz. "Just to make sure."

As daylight began to dim and the students replenished with sports drinks, candy bars, and texting, she proclaimed the area "clean."

I didn't know what to feel about that.

Enid DePauw and J. Yarmuth Loach remained incommunicado in their jail cells, their lawyers reacting to denial of bail with pro forma outrage and making noises about suing for unlawful arrest. Neither attorney had been given anything but the basics on the arrest warrant. If they had been clued in, they might have sung another tune.

DOJ had confirmed a mother–daughter link between the skeleton buried beneath Imelda Soriano and Zelda Chase. The lab also firmly established the identities of Imelda Soriano and Alicia Santos, each fatally shot with bullets that matched the rifling marks of the .22 found in Enid DePauw's S&W. Only one set of finger-prints on the weapon: hers.

Milo said, "She didn't even bother to wipe it. Or to get rid of those documents on Zina and Zelda."

I said, "Why would she think she'd need to?"

"Living in her walled world and getting away with it for so long? Guess so—oh, yeah, I called the Cleveland D.A.'s office. They're not rushing to dig up Jim Smith but they're not saying no."

"Frosting on the cake for you, a hassle for them. Have you spoken to Ott?"

"Just before you got here. He said, Great, but he sounded bummed about not closing it years ago. Still, talking to him was one of the more pleasant conversations I've had recently. Had a second go with the families, along with Lorrie. The worst was Andrea Salton. You can imagine what she had to say about Rod being left off the indictment."

He wiped his face. "Meanwhile, I'm feeling like an ass because I can't come clean with her—God, I hate feeling like a bureaucrat."

His phone rang. "Hi, John...that so? You're kidding—well, yeah, that **was** an ad lib...fine, fine, glad it worked out. When?"

He hung up. "So much for keeping our cards close to the vest. Nguyen took it upon himself to give Loach's lawyer the basics of the case. An hour later, he gets a call: J. Yarmie wants to chat." He shrugged. "Ends, means, I guess."

Buttoning his collar button, he tugged his tie toward his gullet, collected his papers, checked his sidearm, and stood to slip on his sport coat.

"Presentable?"

"Downright authoritative," I said. "You're heading over to the jail, now?"

"John is apparently operating on his own schedule. You can come, too. Being the APC and all."

Milo stashed his gun in one of the lockers the men's jail provided for such, and we both submitted to cursory searches by a pair of bored-looking sheriff's deputies. Nguyen was waiting for us as we passed through the metal detector and the sally port, dapper in a midnight-blue suit with a stars-and-stripes pin on the lapel, a TV-blue shirt, a red power tie patterned with crossed muskets.

He bounced on his feet, punched air.

Milo said, "You're looking happy, John."

"Cracked the bastard, gentlemen. It was more than improv. It was deductive reasoning based on logic."

I said, "Loach is the submissive and since there's no hard evidence against him, you suggested a plea for accessory after the fact."

Nguyen looked as if I'd eaten his birthday cake.

"Actually," he said, drawing himself up, "I made no specific plea suggestions because that would be amateurish, Alex. What I **did** communicate was that my case was growing stronger by the moment due to unnamed biological evidence and that time was running out. His counsel began yammering about cooperation in return for a reduction to mistreating a corpse and violation of county burial rules."

He raised a middle finger. "Good luck with that."

His voice had risen with each sentence. Two deputies stationed on the other side of the port looked at each other.

Milo sidled closer to Nguyen and spoke softly. What he told Nguyen made the D.D.A. stiffen. "And you learned this when?"

"Couple of hours ago."

"And you were planning to tell me—"

"Just about to share, John. You've been busy."

"Well, yeah, that's...okay, obviously that changes things," said Nguyen. He played with his tie. "All right...good...though it really doesn't change the overall tenor of my attack...is that **everything** I need to know?"

"It is, John. How's Loach adjusting to jail?"

Nguyen pouted and ran a finger down his cheek. "Big boo-hoo story. Constant verbal assault and humiliation from the ruffians who are housed here, an upright senior citizen grows older by the minute. Which I can actually believe, he's not exactly Crips/Bloods material. That's why I put him in High-Power. Can you can imagine how long he'd last in general population? Though, according to my source at Lynwood, Madame DePauw seems to be adjusting quite well. She refused High-Power, insisted on joining the blue-scrubs gang, seems to be one of the popular girls."

I said, "Life-coaching the young 'uns."

"God help us," said Nguyen. "Okay, let's talk strategy on Mr. Wimp."

I watched through a one-way mirror as Milo and Nguyen entered the room and sat opposite Loach and his counsel of record, a Yale-educated, Beverly Hills–based trial lawyer named Fahriz ("call me Flip") Moftizadeh.

Milo had prepped by asking Earl Cohen about Moftizadeh and Enid Depauw's defender, a Columbia-educated, Beverly Hills–based trial lawyer whose sterling career had overcome being named Siobhan Malarkey.

Cohen asked around and reported back quickly. "She's smart but tends to go broad-stroke and miss details. He's good with details, sometimes gets overconfident. Overall: A-minus. Your suspects could do worse."

This morning, Moftizadeh was attired in a peak-lapel, charcoal-brown shadow-stripe bespoke suit with covered buttons, a stiff-collar shirt that made fresh snow look grimy, and a massively knotted gold jacquard necktie that drained some of the power out of Nguyen's strip of silk.

His client sat hunched in too-large orange scrubs, the designated color for inmates judged too violent or vulnerable for inclusion in general population.

Incarceration had turned Loach's

complexion gray and grainy, added weight to his eyelids, stripped the shine from his hair, and rounded his shoulders. He picked at his cuticles and pumped a leg.

Not a hint of Cary Grant. At best, a low-level character actor, the type relegated to playing boozers and hangers-on.

Flip Moftizadeh said, "Good morning. How about we establish some ground rules...is it John?"

Nguyen said, "The rule is that your client answers questions truthfully and I decide his fate."

Loach flinched. "If I might," said Moftizadeh, airily, "you'll file the charges but a jury will decide his fate, no? Now, you say there are biological factors that will—"

"I've got enough to indict Mr. Loach for first-degree homicide. I can go special circumstances given the cruelty factor."

Moftizadeh blinked himself, then recovered with a patronizing half smile. "My client is not a cruel man, John."

"We'll see how a jury feels about that."

"Well," said Moftizadeh, "we're here to exchange ideas. Let's see how things develop."

Loach gnawed his lip, tugged at his orange blouse, ran a finger behind one ear.

Nguyen looked at his watch. "If Mr. Loach has something to say, let's hear it."

"C'mon, John, no need for zero-sum. Folks can get along, even in this context."

"Folks," said Nguyen. "That sounds like a campaign speech."

Loach burped. Grimaced in shame. Covered his mouth.

"Cuisine around here takes getting used to," Nguyen told him. "You'll have plenty of time to adjust."

"John," said Moftizadeh.

"Have we met?"

"Now we have."

"I was just wondering, sounds like you knew me. Fah-reeeez."

"Flip is fine."

"Flippant **isn't,** Fahriz. Are we doing this or not?"

Moftizadeh turned to his client and patted his hand. "You ready?"

Loach's response was a low grunt.

Nguyen said, "Should I take that as a yes? I don't speak inmate."

"John," said Moftizadeh, "I'm here to

make your life easy. Mr. Loach has compiled a statement that I will read. You'll like it."

The statement, printed on Moftizadeh's stationery, took four minutes to read and once you got past the lawyer's metaphoric flourishes and overuse of adverbs, the essence was simple:

Enid DePauw had killed Zina Rutherford thirty years ago without J. Yarmuth Loach's prior knowledge, telling Loach, then an employee of her husband, that her half sister had trespassed her property in a state of mania and attempted to attack her. Believing the assertion of self-defense, Loach had buried the body at the rear of Enid's property.

Moftizadeh paused. "An error in judgment, not a real crime."

Milo and Nguyen remained stony. Moftizadeh resumed the narrative.

Flash forward. Enid, long accustomed to relying on Loach, now her estate attorney, had phoned him in a panic, reporting that Zina's daughter, "shockingly" mentally ill in a way that "eerily" evoked her mother, had trespassed in a "bizarrely, brazenly, and unprovokedly similar" manner and attempted to attack her without provocation. Loach had no trouble believing the assertions of mental illness because he recalled Zelda living with Enid and Averell as a child, the couple "doing its best to adequately and wisely parent" but giving up because "the child displayed rabidly unpredictable behavior—tantrums, bursts of anger, and disruptive defiance."

Zelda's death, Enid insisted, had been natural—a seizure, heart attack, or stroke, right in front of her. Probably as a result of "manically induced arousal."

This time, Loach had advised a different approach: Instead of hiding the body, he suggested Enid phone in the episode as a stranger home invasion. Imagine his shock when mere days later, Enid called yet again, explaining that she'd been examining a gun she kept for personal protection and had "accidentally and fatally" shot her housekeeper.

Making matters worse, the housekeeper's friend, another "Hispanic housecleaner," had been visiting at the time and, in an "unwisely carried-out panic move," Enid had shot her, too.

Milo said, "A single bullet in the back of each head is panic, let alone accidental?"

Moftizadeh was unfazed by the question. "My client only knows what he was told."

"He saw the wounds?"

"He saw two bodies, the shock was overwhelming. I'd like to continue, John."

Ignoring Milo, trying to put a wedge between cop and D.A., Nguyen got it and said, "Any questions Lieutenant Sturgis asks are important to me. And the two he just asked should be important to you, Fahriz." He sniffed the air. "No riding stables around here, why am I picking up horseshit?"

"John."

Nguyen said, "Anything else, Milo?"

"Nope, I'm ready for more entertainment."

"Hmm," said Moftizadeh. "Where was I...?"

He told the rest of the story. Yet again, Enid had turned to her trusted advisor and said advisor had made another "hastily concocted grievous error in judgment" burying "those women." A mistake for which he realized he now needed to be held accountable.

Moftizadeh put down the paper.

Milo and Nguyen studied Loach. Loach studied nicks and stains on the tabletop.

"Gentlemen," said Moftizadeh. "Do we have an understanding?"

Nguyen said, "You're serious."

"I couldn't be more serious about my faith in the truthfulness of Mr. Loach's accounts of his motives and actions. Particularly in view of the fact that the Chase woman died of natural—"

"She was poisoned, Fahriz."

"You know that to be—"

"Without a doubt, Fahriz."

"Well…I don't see how that's relevant—"

Nguyen took the typed statement, folded and placed it in a jacket pocket, and got up. "You brought us down here for this? Let's go, Lieutenant."

Milo stood. Moftizadeh said, "Whoa whoa whoa. Please allow me to explicate further, John."

"If anyone explains, your client does."

Moftizadeh said, "I am, essentially, my client. We're trying to work with you. If that's your additional evidence, an alleged poisoning that my client cannot have been expected to recognize as such, I have to say I've heard more compelling. Overconfidence can lead one astray, John."

The criticism Cohen had heard leveled against **him.**

Nguyen patted his pocket. "If you're confident about **this** load of crap, you're in big trouble."

Moftizadeh's face hardened. "Over the phone I told you we've recontextualized. Are you willing to listen or not?"

"If Mr. Loach has found his voice. I need to hear it from him."

"I don't see why that's—all right, I'll be flexible, John. And I'll trust you to recipro-cate at arraignment."

Nguyen remained on his feet.

Moftizadeh nodded at Loach.

Loach said, "I was a fool. Believing her. She uses me, always has. Given the issue, obviously she was at fault—"

"What issue is that?" said Nguyen.

"The...the chemical agent."

"Let's just call it poison," said Nguyen. "Colchicine. You've heard of it, right?"

"I'm not a horticulturist," said Loach. "Be that as it may, I realize in retrospect that the other two were deliberate."

"The other two what?" said Milo.

"The domestics."

"They have names," said Nguyen. "Alicia Santos, Imelda Soriano."

"I never knew their names," said Loach. "The disturbed woman I never saw. It's a terrible thing. That Enid did. When she told me, my heart sank."

He ran hands along his temple. "She must be a radically different person from the one I thought I knew. So disillusioning. At my age, to be such a gullible fool."

Moftizadeh patted his hand again. "We'll get through this." To Nguyen: "My client is prepared to testify fully against Mrs. DePauw in return for consideration—"

"Not with that story," said Nguyen.

"It's the story he was told, John. It formed his opinion set. Does it lose credibility when one steps back contextually? Of course. But we're talking a senior citizen. Things slow down. It takes a while to put things into place."

That sounded like the seeds of a

diminished capacity defense. No doubt there'd be a selection of experts willing to certify Loach was suffering from dementia.

Moftizadeh leaned forward. "Besides, the very ludicrousness of Mrs. DePauw's story can play to **both** our benefits."

"We're on the same team now?"

"Aren't we, John? You want to punish a calculatedly, egregiously cruel murderess— if there was ever a case for special circumstances it's her. So does Mr. Loach. He's shattered by the deception she put him through and wants to make things right."

"He's a victim."

"Isn't he, John? Which isn't to say he's not culpable. Or rueful."

"Rueful," said Nguyen. "Even by his account Imelda Soriano was cold-blooded murder. He put her in a shallow grave and hightailed it to Rome for a vacation."

"Not a vacation," said Loach. "We needed to decompress."

"We," said Milo.

Moftizadeh said, "There were two of them traveling. A collective pronoun is in order."

Nguyen said, "How lawyerly, Fahriz.

When are you running for Congress?"

Loach said, "What I meant was, I needed to keep an eye on her." Quick glance at his lawyer. "It's confusing, I've been feeling more and more confused...the memory."

Nguyen said, "We've got an EEG coming, Fahriz? Don't bother answering, I couldn't care less. You can dim cap to your heart's content. We're talking three murders, you think a jury's going to view your client as kindly Uncle Joe? At the absolute minimum, we're talking accessory after and I'm not convinced of even that. In fact, nothing I've heard changes my mind about Murder One."

Loach lowered his face.

Moftizadeh said, "I understand where you're coming from, John, but I sincerely believe that would be a misstep on your part. You know what happens with a pair of defendants—particularly defendants able to arouse sympathy. She'll blame him, we'll blame her, the jury will grow confused and you'll experience dilution of verdict across the board. If there was a poisoning, she did it. She pulled that trigger. Twice. Are you really willing to see her skate on manslaughter in order to crucify my client?"

Nguyen headed for the door, Milo following.

Moftizadeh said, "This isn't right, look at objective elements here, John. Given the lack of physical evidence against my client, Murder One is highly unlikely. He killed no one, he wielded a shovel. A man with no criminal past and unlikely to have a criminal future. A man whose charitable contributions to inner-city—"

Nguyen waved him silent. "Forget about abusing a corpse. The least I'm willing to consider is accessory **before** the fact."

"But that wouldn't be accurate, John. He really was informed after."

"That's his story."

"It's a true story."

Nguyen pulled the statement out of his pocket and scanned. "No way will he avoid a serious charge on Imelda Soriano. Even if I believe that he swallowed DePauw's ludicrous story and I don't, even by his account he was aware Soriano was cold-blooded homicide—and don't insult my intelligence with that panic crap. Santos was shot because she had incriminating information about the murder of Zelda Chase and Soriano was shot because she was seen speaking to Santos. This is witness elimination, pure and simple, and that's special circumstances."

J. Yarmuth Loach said, "I can tell you something."

Moftizadeh said, "Hold on—"

"I can tell you **why.** The first domestic was...what happened to her. She knew Zelda didn't fall over, outside. Enid had locked her in the house for two days. Kept her in the cellar. Fed her soup. The domestic wasn't supposed to see it but she disobeyed Enid and went downstairs to sweep the steps and heard something and got a key."

Milo said, "Soup."

Loach nodded. "Canned vegetable soup. She...fortified it."

"With?"

"Something from her garden," said Loach. "She likes doing it. Devising her own pesticides."

Nguyen and Milo sat back down. "If Mr. Loach is willing to write down what he just said, along with a statement specifying his awareness that Imelda Soriano was a premeditated homicide that he helped cover up, I'll go with after the fact. Even on her."

Moftizadeh said, "Appreciate that offer, John, but we really need more."

"Once he's convicted, if you petition for reduced sentence based on infirmity, I won't challenge you. He could be out in a short time."

Loach said, "I'll take it."

Moftizadeh said, "Yarmie—"

"I'll take it. I can't stay here." As if ready to check out of an inferior hotel.

Nguyen said, "You have more stationery in your briefcase?"

"I do, John."

"Get it out. Start composing, Mr. Loach."

The handwritten addendum was examined and agreed upon. Two pages in Loach's shaky hand, signed and dated.

Nguyen placed both sheets in his pocket.

Moftizadeh said, "In view of the reduced charges, let's revisit the issue of bail. Give me something reasonable."

"Reasonable being..."

"What Mr. Loach can actually pay. It's in

your best interests, John. He'll be of far greater utility to you once he's out of this terrible environment."

John Nguyen smiled. "I could go with that logic if it was only three victims, Fahriz."

"Pardon?" said Moftizadeh.

"Have I said something confusing? We've got your client's story on **three** murders but there's a fourth."

"I don't under—"

"Three plus one equals four, Fahriz."

Moftizadeh turned to Loach. Loach's eyes bugged.

"What the hell's going on, John?"

Nguyen said, "Fresh evidence. Out-of-the-**oven** evidence. Fill them in, Lieutenant."

Milo said, "A man named Roderick Salton—your client's assistant—was murdered by poisoning prior to the other three homicides. That crime took place nowhere near Mrs. DePauw's property and, in fact, Mrs. DePauw was out of town. Unlike Mr. Loach who, on the day in question, used his corporate credit card to pay for lunch at the Water Garden restaurant. Food for two, wine for one. Which makes sense because Mr. Salton was a Mormon."

"That's an assumption—"

"Restaurant staff identify Mr. Loach and Mr. Salton as dining together that day. One server describes the atmosphere as shifting from friendly at the beginning of the meal to tense by the end. Given Mrs. DePauw's proclivity for poison, we checked her whereabouts and she was at the Grand Hyatt in Lake Tahoe. She flew in privately the previous night, returned two days later to L.A. by commercial jet."

Loach blurted, "Of course she was gone. She went there for an alibi!"

Nguyen said, "That was the plan the two of you cooked up?"

"I—"

Moftizadeh barked, "Quiet, Yarmie!"

Loach buried his head in his arms and began mewling.

No sympathy from his lawyer, just morbid fascination.

Milo said, "I'm sure Mr. Loach is correct. Mrs. DePauw went to Tahoe to establish an alibi after she furnished Mr. Loach with a toxic substance from her garden called aconitum. Deadly stuff, Mr. Loach slipped it into Mr. Salton's food. By the end of the day, Mr. Salton was dead, his body dumped after dark near the courthouse on Hill and Washington."

Nguyen said, "A neighborhood and a facility that Mr. Loach knew well, as he'd filed papers there on behalf of Mrs. DePauw on various real estate disputes."

Moftizadeh's Adam's apple rose and fell. "Without admitting acceptance of this... tale, what possible motive would my client have to kill this Salting person? And what evidence do you have that remotely supports such a fanciful—"

"Sal-ton," said Milo, spelling it. "The motive was similar to Soriano and Santos. Mr. Salton knew too much. But unlike Soriano and Santos, he had the ability to do something about it."

"How in the world—"

"Hear me out, Counselor. We know for a fact that Zelda Chase entered Mr. Loach's office and made statements about Mr. Loach killing her mother years ago."

Nguyen said, "Which was taken for psychotic ranting but was obviously true."

"That," said Moftizadeh, "is categorically false. We just—"

"You spun a yarn," said Nguyen. "We've got it on paper."

"This is absolutely—"

Milo said, "What Zelda Chase told Roderick Salton sparked his curiosity enough for him to look into her claims. We have his fingerprints on documents obtained from Mr. Loach's files on Mrs. DePauw. Specifically, papers pertaining to Zelda Chase. Being a moral person, Mr. Salton raised the issue with Mr. Loach. Being an immoral person, Mr. Loach suggested they discuss it over lunch and contacted Mrs. DePauw. Who did her Bad Chef bit."

"The rest," said Nguyen, "was history for poor Mr. Salton. Nasty death, he suffered. So whatever happens on Chase, Soriano, and Santos, your client's going down on Salton. **With** special circumstances."

"Ridiculous," said Moftizadeh, regarding his mute, hunched client with horror. "Tell them, so, Yarm. This is a yarn, never happened."

J. Yarmuth Loach sat up slowly. Looked at each of us. Belched again.

Then he vomited all over the table.

CHAPTER 43

Enid DePauw and J. Yarmuth Loach remained in jail. He began refusing food and had to be intubated in the medical ward. Flip Moftizadeh persisted in filing requests for bail based on a variety of theories. All were refused.

Prisoner DePauw, the once-popular, self-described "mentor of disadvantaged girls," saw her social status slip when it was learned that two of her victims were Latina and that one, Imelda Soriano, had been distantly related to a neighbor of a member of the Chicas Locas gang. On the thirteenth day of her incarceration, she was ambushed and beaten and ended up in the infirmary. Once treated, she was sent to a one-prisoner isolation cell and compelled to wear orange scrubs.

Going to trial would take a while, but John Nguyen felt serene about his prospects. Milo said, "I'm on an optimism diet but I'll splurge."

I added my enthusiasm to the mix but my heart felt as if dry rocks had replaced tissue and blood. The likeliest reality was Ovid Chase had met a terrible end—despite what Chet Brett had told me, one of those living-rough horrors of the street.

Or, even worse, something cold and horrific at the hands of DePauw and Loach.

Either way, long buried where he'd never be found.

I needed to stop imagining.

I was working on that with little success when John Nguyen called and asked me to submit to an interview by an L.A. **Times** reporter. The four murders had captured the public's attention and the paper wanted a "human interest follow-up."

I said, "She the one Milo talked to?"

"Myrna Strickland. She talked to both of us."

"He said she was annoying."

"She's a journalist, Alex."

"What exactly does she want?"

"Your name came up in the court docs and she's curious about a psychologist's take, the whole mental health thing, oppression of the helpless. My advice is talk to her, otherwise she'll find someone else who tells her what she wants to hear. She asked for your private number, I said I'd talk to you first. Can I give it to her?"

"Okay. What **shouldn't** I tell her, John?"

"Anything beyond the basics of the case."

"Meaning?"

"Try not to get too emo, if you know what I mean. Newspaper hacks are zombie aliens who steal our thoughts and mutate them into something they can digest."

Myrna Strickland called me that day and said, "A phoner will be fine, Doctor."

She was clear about her goal: I was to expound on "entitled white perpetrators versus low-income victims of color and those from the disabled community."

I said, "What about Rod Salton?"

A beat. "The Mormon? Well, he's a

minority, too. At least, if you're not in Utah. But I'm going to concentrate on the others."

I stuck to the basics and she grew bored. "That's all, Doctor. Thanks."

"There's another victim no one's talking about."

"Like who?"

"The most vulnerable victim of all. A child."

"There's no child mentioned in anything I got from the D.A."

"Zelda Chase had a son who'd be eleven if he was alive."

A beat. "You're saying he's not?"

"He hasn't been seen for several years. He'd also be an heir to the DePauw estate. So there'd be a motive to kill him."

"Wow," she said. "I'm putting my tape recorder back on."

When I finished, she said, "Prince and Pauper, totally consistent with my theme."

The story ran two days later, with "the tragedy and mystery of a throwaway child repeatedly victimized by the system" its primary focus.

The following afternoon, my service phoned with a message to call a Maureen Bolt.

Unfamiliar name, no reason stated, a 310 number. I'd just finished a session with one of the kids in the latest custody dispute, was collecting my thoughts and trying to figure out what to write down and what to leave out. Another couple of hours was spent on my report. It was early evening before I returned the call.

A melodious female voice said, "Hello."

"This is Dr. Delaware returning Ms. Bolt's call."

"Hello, Alex. If I might. You don't know me but I know **about** you. You worked with my husband, Lou Sherman."

"I actually tried to reach you. The med school had you listed as Maureen Sherman."

"I was working as a clinical social worker under my maiden name when I met Lou, by the time I retired, changing it didn't make sense. Now here I am, contacting **you.** I suspect for the same reason you looked for me. Can we meet? I'm pretty much open time-wise and I'm not far from you, Studio City, just over the hill, half a mile east of Beverly Glen."

"That is close."

"Lou told me about your house in the Glen, said you'd described a great view. He always wanted a place with a view. We never got around to that. Would you be able to come over tomorrow?"

"I could drop by tonight."

"No," she said, "tomorrow would be better. Say four p.m.?"

"I'll be there."

"I figured you would," she said. "Lou said you were one of the most thorough people he'd ever met."

CHAPTER 44

Ten-minute drive, a side street I'd passed thousands of times.

Miss one shred of information and you might as well be on another planet.

The neighborhood began with unobtrusive houses on pleasant, gently winding streets. The address Maureen Bolt had provided took me another mile east, into a section of older, larger structures.

My destination was a two-story whiteboard colonial with a brick motor court and green-shuttered windows. A silver Porsche 911 and a copper-colored Volvo station wagon shared the court. Behind the house rose a fifty-foot crown of Aleppo pines, evoking Enid DePauw's forest-shrouded poison patch.

It didn't take much to make me think of that.

The woman who stood in the doorway wore a white silk tunic patterned with pink flowers, black leggings, and silver sandals. Sixtyish, amply hipped, she had a pink-cheeked pixie face capped by steel-gray hair. Average height; in heels she'd have towered over Lou.

She had a hand out well before I got out of the Seville. Soft skin, just enough firmness to her grip.

"Thanks for coming, Alex. Nice to have a face to go with the name."

She ushered me into a two-story foyer topped by a bronze chandelier. Down three steps was a living room set up with overstuffed furniture and cane-backed chairs, everything directed toward a fireplace with a book-topped mantel. Art consisted of a few rainy Paris street scenes, the kind of stuff relegated to the final lots of obscure auctions. Crimson-and-olive-striped drapes were drawn across the rear wall, blocking the only windows and dimming the entire house.

Funereal; that seemed an odd choice for

a cheerful woman and I wondered about it as Maureen Bolt guided me up a short hallway. A couple more paintings—flowers in vases. I found myself surprised by the capital-T traditional décor.

What had I expected? Acoma pottery and a Hanukkah lamp?

She stopped at the first open door. "Here we are."

Stepping aside, she waved me into a birch-paneled study lined with books. Another fireplace, the surround green marble, hosted a collection of Japanese vases. A writing desk sat atop a worn Persian rug, its weathered leather surface hosting a blotter and a pipe rack. Shutters were drawn. Soft light came from two floor lamps. A tufted red leather chesterfield faced a brown leather couch not unlike mine. Lou had seen patients here.

A man sat in the center of the couch and for one absurd moment I wondered if I'd been beckoned to treat someone.

He stood, looked straight at me, and tried to smile.

Maureen Bolt said, "Alex, this is Derek Sherman, Lou's nephew. Derek, Dr.

Delaware. I'll leave you to it."

Once she'd left and closed the door, the office felt smaller.

Derek Sherman said, "Nice to meet you, Doctor." Brief handshake; his palm was damp.

I said, "Same here," and studied him. His appearance had already triggered a storm of possibilities.

Forty or so, small and spare like Lou, with an unlined bronze face under dense, black, side-parted hair. Round-lens pewter eyeglasses framed wide black eyes. A stubble goatee, compulsively shaped and flecked with gray, emphasized a firm chin. His cheekbones were set high and cleanly defined. He wore a black polo shirt, tapered seersucker pants, brown deck shoes with fresh white soles. The gold watch on his right wrist looked expensive. So did the diamond wedding band on his left hand.

A well-put-together man, the kind who'd look neat and composed without much effort. Today, beads of sweat had collected alongside his nose and his lips ticced.

He said, "I guess you should take the

chair. That's where Uncle sat."

I said, "When he saw patients."

"That and just being Uncle. When I was younger and came here for family things, he'd joke about it. 'Got a problem, kid? Take a load off and get some free therapy.' He had a great sense of humor."

"He did."

Derek Sherman winced. "He's my only uncle. Was. My dad was his younger brother. Not a doctor, a truck driver. He's gone, too. So is my mom."

His shoulders dropped, as if recalled loss suddenly weighed on him. He sat back down, in the precise spot he'd occupied when I arrived. I took the tufted chair.

"I'm sure it was a surprise, Auntie Mo calling you. That article in the paper made me realize I needed to do something."

He exhaled. "I'm Ovid's dad. He's fine. I wanted you to know."

I was seated but felt as if I were falling. Taking time to order my thoughts, failing and talking through the buzz, I said, "That's great to hear. Thank you."

"He seems to be doing okay. With his mother's death, I mean. Maybe I'm missing something. Maybe you can tell me what I should look for. I knew about you, should've contacted you sooner, but there didn't seem to be a reason...it's complicated."

Pressing his palms together, he sat up straighter. "Uncle was a dedicated psychiatrist but now you understand that his interest in Zelda and Ovid went beyond that. That's the reason he consulted you all those years ago—I guess I should backtrack. If you want to know the whole story."

"I do if you're comfortable talking about it."

"Normally," said Derek Sherman, "I wouldn't be, I'm a private person but Uncle **made** me comfortable talking about it. Insisted I deal with it properly. And he was right. So sure, I'll tell you. This must've been rough for you. I'm sorry. You deserve to understand."

He got up, walked to the desk, removed a briar from the pipe rack, sat back down and began rubbing the burnished wooden bowl.

"I used to come in here and he'd let me do this, I loved the feel of these things. The smell of the place, back when Uncle smoked. One time, I was probably eight, everyone was out back and I snuck in and loaded up with tobacco and tried to light up. When Uncle found me I was sick to my stomach from sucking in fumes...all right, the short version: I'm Ovid's dad but Zelda and I never had a relationship."

He looked away, passed the pipe from hand to hand, began waving it in tiny concentric circles. "There's no way to make it sound better than it was. It was a one-night stand."

His eyes swung back to me.

I said, "It happens."

"I appreciate you being a professional. Like Uncle, trained to suspend judgment."

He inhaled slowly, let his breath out quickly. "I'm an architect, used to work at a firm in the Bay Area, got assigned to a project down here. Tasting room in Malibu for a big Napa winery. I was commuting back and forth but when it got too late, I'd stay at a single in Santa Monica my bosses rented for me. Not near the beach, the basics, pretty depressing. I was lonely, unattached, had never been much of a bar person but I began trying various lounges. Fantasizing about meeting women, even just for company. I wasn't too successful, socializing isn't my strong point. The night I met Zelda I was pretty low. Overworked, dealing with egos and an unrealistic budget. I decided to kick it up and went to the lounge at the Loews Hotel, which was close to my apartment but a little intimidating, size-wise and cost-wise. Zelda was at the next table, also alone. I know it sounds trite but our eyes met and there was some kind of chemistry. She was gorgeous, way above my pay grade, but something about her smile relaxed me. A gentleness. And she wasn't dressed like a party girl. Simple blouse and skirt, I figured her for an office worker. Anyway, our eyes kept meeting and finally I built up the courage to ask her to join me and she did. She was easy to talk to—actually, that's not accurate. She didn't talk much and didn't make me feel I had to, which was even better. Sweet and quiet, a little spacey—I'd say something and she didn't seem to hear. But the main thing was no attitude. I tended to get intimidated back then. My dad wasn't like Uncle Lou. He was a rough character."

He placed the pipe on a seat cushion. "I'm getting off topic. Zelda and I had a couple of drinks, she told me she was an actress looking for work but didn't know if she had what it took. I said I was sure she did and that really seemed to matter to her, suddenly she's hugging me and kissing my cheek. Not sexual, more like gratitude. But then we were holding hands and I asked her if she wanted to go back to my place and to my amazement, she did. We... no need to get into details. When I woke up, she was gone and I felt let down but then I figured that was L.A., actresses were flighty. She was gorgeous, I thought about her for a while but eventually put her out of my mind."

He picked up the pipe, rotated it. A speck of something fell out. He retrieved it from the seat cushion, got up and dropped it in a leather wastebasket.

"Five years later," he said, "she called me out of the blue. At my office—by then I was living down here, running my own firm in Encino, two people working for me. I'd told her my name and it wasn't hard to find me in the phone book."

"That must have been some surprise."

"I nearly fell out of my chair. My situation was different. I'd been married for two years to a woman I totally loved and still do. Anne's also an architect, we met bidding on a job, began as friends and eventually it became more."

He inhaled and exhaled again. "When Zelda called, Anne was six months' pregnant. Our daughter will be four next month. Dorothy, after Anne's mom, we call her Dolly...what I'm trying to get across, Dr. Delaware, is my life was on an even keel when I got the call from Zelda. Even though it started off casual, I figured for some reason she wanted to hook up again. I listened and she told me she'd made it as an actress, was on a TV show. I said, Great. But then she told me I was a father. From the one night we were together. A boy, five, she named him Ovid after a romantic poet. She never got in touch because she felt she should take total responsibility. But now she wasn't feeling so well and was worried about Ovid and since I'm his dad..."

He looked away. "Then she apologized. Then she cried for a long time. I was floored. How do you deal with something like that? I said nothing, too stunned, and it made her upset and she said forget it, she'd figure something out and all of a sudden I was telling her I needed to take respon-sibility, too. Meanwhile, I'm thinking she's probably wrong, a woman that beautiful she'd have tons of guys, I'll get a DNA test, that'll be the end of it. I took her number and told her I'd be in touch. Then I had to figure out how to explain it to Anne. I didn't, right away, why burden her, the whole thing would fizzle out. But acting normal when I got home was a challenge, Doctor, let me tell you. I waited until she went to sleep and went online to see if what Zelda said about being on a show was truthful. I guess I wanted her to be a liar. But there she was on video, doing a pretty good job, I thought. The next morning I phoned Uncle Lou and we met in his office. Not this one, the one he kept in a medical building, also Encino."

"I've been there."

"I know you have. Uncle's always been the one I turned to and he helped me sort it out. First step **was** a paternity test and I was to pay for it. Ovid shouldn't be involved directly, Uncle would make sure to get a cheek swab. But he wanted Zelda to be there, so he could evaluate her. Also, he said, it was more respectful to her, she was a person no matter what the result was. Especially because she'd said she was ill."

He paused. "That's the kind of man he was."

I said, "I know."

"A few days later, Uncle arranged for Ovid to be swabbed at his pediatrician—they made up some kind of story—and he picked up the sample and delivered it to the lab when Zelda and I were there. She was more beautiful than ever and extremely nice—but nervous. We both were but we managed to talk pleasantly. Uncle Lou also spoke to her and they seemed to like each other. He asked if she had a photo of Ovid and she had several on her phone. The moment I saw Ovid's face, I knew the test was unnecessary."

"The resemblance was strong." My

thought, the moment I'd met him.

"Unbelievable," he said. "It was strange, seeing someone who looked exactly like I had when I was his age. Anyway, the results were to be expected and now Zelda and I and Uncle Lou had to figure out what to do."

He put his glasses back on. "And now I **did** need to tell Anne."

I said, "That had to be tough."

"Actually, what turned out to be tough was worrying about it, she was great. She said just what you did: It happens. Still, I worried. Here she was, about to have her own child, would it not be as special? As it turned out, there was no issue. Because of Zelda's illness. Anne and I ended up being Ovid's parents and it brought more love out of Anne, she adored having two."

"When did you find out about the nature of Zelda's illness?"

"After the test results came in, Zelda did a total about-face and said she didn't want me in the picture. I was confused and upset, had started thinking about being a dad to Ovid. Uncle Lou told me he'd handle it. I told him it was my problem, at some point I needed to step up and take care of my own affairs. That's when he told me about Zelda's illness. She'd reached out to him and he'd had several sessions with her and knew what was going on. Nothing physical, she knew she was breaking down mentally. Uncle agreed and told me I needed to face the possibility that she'd grow worse and that I would have to eventually take care of Ovid no matter what she said now. Meanwhile, she was fragile so challenging her was a real bad idea."

"He wasn't hopeful."

"He said he'd do his best to treat her, she might get better, there was no way to know. The point was, at that stage, between her job and taking care of Ovid, she had enough to deal with, a custody battle would be cruel and inhuman. So I talked to Anne and we decided to concentrate on our own lives. It bothered me, first I have a son, then I'm being kept away from him. But then Dolly came and we had our hands full— she was colicky."

He gripped the pipe with both hands. His knuckles whitened. The stem snapped in two.

"Oh, no, this was his favorite!"

His eyes were wet. I took the pieces of the pipe, placed them on the desk, scooted my chair closer. "What an ordeal to go through, Derek. Did Lou keep you posted on Zelda's mental health?"

"I asked him but he refused, confidentiality issues. That made me upset but I knew he was right."

He licked his lips. "I still thought of Ovid but I kept it that way. I thought. Then Uncle called me and said the time might be growing near."

"When was that?"

"A couple of months before he died, so a little over two years ago. But then he got too sick to deal with it and I didn't hear from Zelda or see her until the funeral. Which she wasn't invited to, it was just a small family affair, a cremation. But somehow she found out. And she looked flat-out crazy, standing off to the side, dressed weird, muttering to herself. I tried to talk to her, she started ranting. Something about her mother, evil people had been conspiring against her since she was born. What I assumed was paranoia, it made me worry about Ovid's safety so I told Anne I needed to deal with her and got Zelda to drive with me to the other side of the cemetery, a quiet spot, where we talked. I thought she'd freak out when I told her my concerns. Just the opposite, she thanked me and tried to hug and kiss me. She didn't smell good. She didn't look good. It was awkward but I knew I couldn't reject her. So I let her kiss me. Not on the lips, just on the cheek, she really smelled sour. We arranged for her to bring Ovid with her, along with his things. To my office, the next day. I wanted to do it right then but she refused. Wouldn't let me see where she lived, so I had no choice."

He swiped at his eyes.

"I was messed up, Doctor. Certain she'd never follow through, should I hire a private detective, get into a struggle? Uncle was no longer there to guide me. I waited for her at my office and amazingly, she showed up. It was the first time I'd seen Ovid in the flesh. His worldly belongings were in two big black garbage bags. She looked homeless but she'd dressed him in clean clothes. His hair was untrimmed and he looked stunned and refused to talk and later we found out his teeth had been neglected, he needed vaccinations, he had ringworm. He asked to go to the bathroom and I showed him where it was. When I got back, Zelda was gone. Poor little guy, he just stood there, so small, so afraid. But he let me take him home. And he's been there ever since."

"My God," I said.

"It was a challenge, Dr. Delaware. But Ovid, God **bless** him, made it easy. No tears, no tantrums and when he saw Dolly, he smiled and she ran right up to him— she's a gregarious girl, more like her mom— and that's the way it's been. Anne was obviously shocked, but she rebounded, she always does. So now we're a family and Ovid goes to the local public school and gets fantastic grades, he's really smart. But I don't delude myself he's unscathed. The only time he smiles is when he's with Dolly. Never when he's with me or Anne. He's obedient but probably too obedient. And he doesn't have much in the way of friends, just likes to be by himself and build and draw. Then again, I was like that."

"What have you told him about Zelda's death?"

"Anne and I both sat down with him. We didn't tell him she'd been murdered, only that she'd gotten sick and passed. He listened and said she'd been sick for a long time. As if he'd been expecting it. An eleven-year-old shouldn't expect that, should they, Dr. Delaware? And one day, he will learn the truth about what happened to her. I'm not sure when that should be and neither is Anne. And with Uncle gone...we could use some help, Dr. Delaware. Uncle had confidence in you, I wish I would've talked to you sooner. I mentioned your name to Ovid. He remembers you. Said you didn't bother him. From him, that's high praise."

I said, "Happy to help."

"That's incredibly gracious of you, Doctor. He's our son—both of ours—and we love him."

"Let's set it up."

"It's kind of...potentially set up, Dr. Delaware. If you don't mind."

"Mind what?"

He stood. "Please follow me."

CHAPTER 45

Maureen Bolt sat in her dark living room, a cigarette in one hand, an amber-colored drink in the other.

"A little early," she said, "but you know." No more ebullience; her smile was tentative, anxious.

Derek Sherman said, "All's well, Auntie."

She put her cocktail down, walked to the drapes blocking the rear wall, and pulled a cord, exposing French doors. Sunlight bathed the room. My eyes ached.

The yard on the other side of the glass was a quarter acre flat; cement patio, safety-fenced pool, a patch of grass. A single tree, an apricot, looked ancient. The pines I'd seen towering above the house belonged to the neighboring property.

Open space, nothing to hide.

Ovid sat at a patio table, sketching in a pad.

His father opened a door and said, "Hey, look who's here."

The boy looked up. Still small for his age at eleven, but his features had solidified, suggesting the man he'd turn into. At five, he'd worn his hair long. Now it was short and side-parted like Derek's. He dressed like Derek, in a black polo shirt, pressed jeans, deck shoes with fresh white soles. Kids don't go for timepieces anymore, preferring to live their entire lives on their phones. This kid wore a wristwatch.

I said, "Hi, Ovid."

Fleeting smile. "Hi."

The drawing in his sketch pad was an expertly drawn and shaded pencil rendition of an automobile. Not a vehicle I'd ever seen; a testosterone fantasy with a retro feel: swooping fenders, boat-tail rear, flames running along the flank, smoke pouring out of cannon-like exhaust pipes.

Typical boy fantasy but talent elevated it way above typical.

"That's amazing," I said.

Derek Sherman said, "He's into cars now. Draws my Porsche with his eyes closed. We're going to visit the automotive studio at Cal Arts. They train the best designers."

The boy's eyes widened. A corner of his mouth tugged upward.

I said, "Can I sit down?"

"Sure." A beat. "Can I keep drawing?"

"You bet. If I was this good, I wouldn't want to stop."

He studied his creation, began filling in spaces. Flipped a page and began another drawing, this one huge and ponderous—a perfect rendition of a new Rolls-Royce Phantom.

For the next hour, he drew and I just sat and watched and I didn't mind one bit. When I got up to leave, he nodded as if my exit had been pre-scheduled. Putting down his pencil, he shook my hand, then turned back to his art.

I left feeling better than I had in a long time.

I got home wanting to talk to Robin. Nothing in particular, just talk. She'd left a note: "Grocery shopping, back soon."

I made coffee and checked my messages. A couple of new custody referrals; families kept falling apart and I was getting busier than I had been in a while.

One message was different, a call from Dr. Sally Abramson, an area code I didn't recognize. Sally and I had interned together at Langley Porter. She'd also known Lou Sherman. Another revelation? Some tie to the case yet to be learned?

I called her back.

She said, "Alex, thanks for getting back so quickly. How've you been doing?"

"Really well. And you?"

"Can't complain, four kids, full-time faculty Washington U., Dick and I both got tenure a while back."

"Sounds great. What's up?"

"I do some consulting for the government. NIMH and NIH, mostly visiting grant sites. I've been asked to take a look at a project over there in your neck of the woods, just finished reviewing their renewal summary and they list you as both a 'clinical partner' and someone who'll have nice things to say about them. Which I found a bit...

scratch that, I need to keep an open mind."

I said, "Kristin Doyle-Maslow, the Los Angeles County Behavioral and Affective Re-Integration and Services Project."

"So you do know it. What do you think?"

I laughed. Kept laughing.

When I finally stopped, Sally said, "I was hoping you'd say that."

ABOUT THE AUTHOR

Jonathan Kellerman is the #1 **New York Times** bestselling author of more than three dozen bestselling crime novels, including the Alex Delaware series, **The Butcher's Theater, Billy Straight, The Conspiracy Club, Twisted,** and **True Detectives.** With his wife, bestselling novelist Faye Kellerman, he co-authored **Double Homicide** and **Capital Crimes.** With his son, bestselling novelist Jesse Kellerman, he co-authored **The Golem of Hollywood** and **The Golem of Paris.** He is also the author of two children's books and numerous nonfiction works, including **Savage Spawn: Reflections on Violent Children** and **With Strings Attached: The Art and Beauty of Vintage Guitars.**

He has won the Goldwyn, Edgar, and Anthony awards and has been nominated for a Shamus Award. Jonathan and Faye Kellerman live in California, New Mexico, and New York.

jonathankellerman.com

Facebook.com/JonathanKellerman